Dread Coast - SoCal Horror Tales

Dennis K. Crosby

KC Grifant

"Introduction" copyright © 2025 by Dennis K. Crosby * "Beachcomber's Ear" copyright © 2025 by Luke Dumas * "The View From Here" copyright © 2025 by Elle Jauffret * "The Box Born Wraith" copyright © 2025 by Kevin David Anderson * "Skin in the Game" copyright © 2025 by Brian Asman * "The Suitcase" copyright © 2025 by C. D. Oakes "The Gold Must Go" copyright © 2025 by S. Faxon * "Rainy Day" copyright © 2025 by Scott Sigler * "Acheron Gas & Go" copyright © 2025 by Dennis K. Crosby * "The Sandman" copyright © 2025 by TJ Kang * "H is for Hell" copyright © 2025 by Jon Cohn * "Birds of Prey" copyright © 2025 by KC Grifant * "Flesh Trade" copyright © 2025 by Peter Clines * "Growing Darkness" copyright © 2025 by Greg Mollin * "Swipe Right for the Afterlife" copyright © 2025 by Theresa Halvorsen * "In the Banned" copyright © 2025 by Henry Herz * "Slay, Wolfma'am Jackie, Slay!" copyright © 2025 by Chad Stroup * "To Speak in Silver Linings" copyright © 2025 by David Agranoff * "Checked Out" copyright © 2025 by J.A. Jensen * "Sun Kissed" copyright © 2025 by Benjamin Spada * "What Lurks in Dreams" copyright © 2025 by Rose Winter * "Hollywood's Land" copyright © 2025 by Lisa Diane Kastner A.K.A. Kali Metis * "Death Phone" copyright © 2025 by Ronald Coleman * "The Demons on Bunker Hill" copyright © 2025 by Indigo Halverson * "Rust" copyright © 2025 by Jonathan Maberry Productions

All rights reserved.

No part of this book may be reproduced in any form or by any electronic or mechanical means, including information storage and retrieval systems, without written permission from the author, except for the use of brief quotations in a book review.

To those individuals and families impacted by the devastation of the 2025 wildfires. Please know that we see you, and our hearts are with you.

Contents

Foreword	7
BEACHCOMBER'S EAR By Luke Dumas	11
THE VIEW FROM HERE By Elle Jauffret	23
THE BOX BORN WRAITH By Kevin David Anderson	37
SKIN IN THE GAME By Brian Asman	47
THE SUITCASE By C. D. Oakes	73
THE GOLD MUST GO By S. Faxon	89
SWIPE RIGHT FOR THE AFTERLIFE By Theresa Halvorsen	95
ACHERON GAS & GO By Dennis K. Crosby	107
THE SANDMAN By TJ Kang	125
H IS FOR HELL By Jon Cohn	135
BIRDS OF PREY By KC Grifant	147
FLESH TRADE By Peter Clines	159
GROWING DARKNESS By Greg Mollin	179
RAINY DAY By Scott Sigler	193

IN THE BANNED By Henry Herz	201
SLAY, WOLFMA'AM JACKIE, SLAY! By Chad Stroup	215
TO SPEAK IN SILVER LININGS By David Agranoff	229
CHECKED OUT By J.A. Jensen	241
SUN KISSED By Benjamin Spada	259
WHAT LURKS IN DREAMS By Rose Winters	275
HOLLYWOOD'S LAND By Lisa Diane Kastner	285
DEATH PHONE By Ronald Coleman	297
THE DEMONS ON BUNKER HILL By Indigo Halverson	313
RUST By Jonathan Maberry	335
Acknowledgements	355
Authors of Dread Coast	357

Foreword

Friend, colleague, mentor, and contributor to this collection, Jonathan Maberry, shared a helpful tool for writers when talking about their books. He suggests making two lists. The first list is what your book is *not* about. The second list, naturally, is what your book *is* about. When it comes to *Dread Coast: SoCal Horror Tales*, this collection of horror stories is unlike most projects we've been a part of in recent years. So much so, that we're better off focusing on a couple of things that this book is absolutely about.

First, this anthology is about camaraderie and fellowship. Earlier this year, chaos reigned in Los Angeles County. For weeks, wildfires cut a swath of destruction through the area, and lives were forever changed. Those directly impacted not only lost their homes—symbols of family, friendship, and security, but they also lost a sense of belonging and community. Displacement is not an easy thing. Imagine being displaced *and* losing everything you own. Whether you knew someone directly impacted or not, it was terrifying and heartbreaking to witness. Almost immediately, Californians stood up and sought ways to help. Everywhere they looked they saw their brothers and sisters in pain, and they rallied.

It was that desire to help that brought together the twenty-four authors in this collection.

From the publisher to the copyeditor, from the bestselling veteran authors to the writers who have their very first published stories in this book, there was not one person that declined the invitation to be a part of this project. That is the very definition of fellowship. Twenty-four authors saw people in pain and did not hesitate to use their talents to help. That is the definition of camaraderie. Life is a long and winding road that's full of detours. Not all those detours are for the better. But they are made better, made *bearable*, when you walk that path with people rooted in the goal of a better tomorrow for all. The contributors to this collection are ready to do just that with you.

This book is also about the art and beauty of horror, which can entertain, teach, and impact the lives around us. When this world gets heavy, we often escape into another one. We might watch a movie, listen to music, catch a play, or read a book. Those performances, publications, and productions take us away from the everyday challenges we face and transport us to a place where we can insert ourselves for a brief time and experience a life vastly different to our own. More than just cheap thrills (though those are fun too), horror stories can provide a sense of catharsis (*you* survived, even if the main character didn't) and as a safe way to process fears, traumas, and dark thoughts. Horror is also incredibly bonding, as friends walking out of a horror movie or telling stories around a campfire can attest. Through the art of horror, we let our guard down and get swept away. During that time, we learn and, if we're open to it, we grow—as individuals, as a community, and as a society.

It may sound strange to say that you can learn something about yourself or the world through horror. But remember, horror is not just about terror or monsters. It's about *people* and how they navigate those terrors and fight those monsters–whether visible or invisible, external or internal. To quote John Carpenter, "Horror is a universal language; we're all afraid. We're born afraid." In horror, we can learn

Foreword

so much. While these stories feature creative monsters of all types, squeamish body modifications, and characters making bad choices, these masterful tales also speak to the universal experiences of isolation, loneliness, heartache, and desolation. These authors opened a portal for readers to take a walk on the dark side and learn more about themselves in the process.

Lastly, this book is about hope. It can be hard to see hope in horror. But that's exactly where you *must* see it. When things are at their darkest, when that last bit of patience is wearing thin, when it seems like the light at the end of the tunnel is dimming, we must hold onto hope. There is hope in the stories you're about to read. Hope that we don't make mistakes that take us down the wrong path. Hope that we can walk away from anger, from vice, or from the so-called deadly sins. Hope that if we endure just one more day, we'll get on the other side of the horror and walk toward brighter, more fruitful days. When you feel that hope is lost, remember the hundreds of thousands of people who banded together during a crisis in Southern California to offer their assistance—even if it was only to be present so people felt less alone. Remember that people and communities continue to band together in the face of seemingly relentless attacks and dangers. And remember these twenty-four authors who leaned into their art to entertain, guide, teach, and walk with you from dusk to dawn.

Dennis K. Crosby
KC Grifant
Co-Editors

Beachcomber's Ear
By Luke Dumas

It was Devon's first real beach day in years, and he couldn't even enjoy it because of all the homeless. They had spread their filth all over the place: their tents and stolen shopping carts and the shit piles left by their toothless yapping dogs. They sullied the grass along the boardwalk with their weedlike presence, snoozing curled up with their butt cracks showing, reaching out to passing pedestrians with grabby crab-claw hands.

He tried not to let it ruin his day. He had earned it after how hard he'd been working. His first real morning off in weeks. Unlike these derelicts, the hustle never slept.

He trudged across the beach in search of his friends. The sand was soft and spiteful, pulling the flip-flops off his feet to scald his soles. It swallowed him up to the ankle, making each step an effort.

"D, over here!" shouted his boy Jason in his $15 sunglasses, waving from a patch of sand past the lifeguard tower, on the side of Ocean Beach designated for swimming.

Devon slogged over, dropped his stuff, and clapped his friend's hand. "What's up, bro? Long time, no see," Jason said, darkly tanned from so many weekends spent right here. They'd been friends since high school, but fifteen years out from graduation, it was clear that their priorities had diverged.

"Nothing much, just working. You know."

"Holding it down."

"Yup."

Jason turned to introduce him to the rest of the group—his new girlfriend, Brit; her friend, Maisie; and another chick and guy he'd never met before. Devon forgot their names by the time he pulled up his shirt, then, hearing the guy's effeminate lilt, yanked it back down. *You fucking can't enjoy anything anymore*, he thought.

The others headed off to throw a Frisbee around, but Devon stayed, needing space. He was already second-guessing having come.

He laid down a towel, sprayed sunscreen over his limbs and face, cursed as it stung his eyes. A Toyota Tundra, fire-engine red with the word LIFEGUARD in white, tossed a wave of sand as it motored by.

With a sigh, he finally lay back with his hands behind his head.

The stress of his week washed away in the scudding of a wispy cloud across azure skies and the distant crash of waves against the shore. He wiggled his toes under the sand, into the cool underneath.

He felt something there. Round, ridged. Maybe a shell. It tickled—

"Fuck!" he shouted, shooting up to a sit.

"What happened," said a voice from under an umbrella a few feet away. Not a question so much as an amused observation. It was the chick whose name he couldn't remember; Devon hadn't realized she'd stayed back too.

"Something bit me." He pulled his foot toward him and inspected the spot where he'd felt the jolt of pain, his big toe red and pulsing, cartoonlike. "Or pinched me."

Face tightening into a scowl, he crawled forward and scooped sand out of the divot where his foot had been.

A glimmer of brown-flecked shell appeared, then burrowed deeper.

Devon dug more furiously, sand flying into the air behind him and burying his towel. The sediment became darker, moister, more compacted as he dug. He uncovered the shell again, and this time it wouldn't get away: With hard, probing digits, he fished out the shell and raised it into the light.

He expected spiny legs, maybe a claw, to flail out of the opening. But to his consternation, the shell was empty.

"You know they shed them," said the nameless chick. The umbrella cast a shadow over her face; Devon could barely make her out, only her straggly black mane and leathery, rawboned arms. A tattoo of a peacock drooped out of her bikini top, its vibrance sapped after years in the sun.

"What?" he said.

"Crabs. Hermits. The shells get tighter as they grow, start to crush them. Eventually they can't take it anymore. They ditch them to find something more . . ." A vape glowed in the dark as she puffed, illuminating a busted smirk. ". . . *spacious* to live in. Saw it on a nature documentary. David Attenborough."

Devon's eyes slid back to the shell and narrowed. Had the thing that pinched him crawled out at the last second? He gave it a shake, held it up to his ear, and heard the sea.

Convinced there was nothing in it, he crushed it in his hand and chucked the broken detritus out toward the water.

It fell short, but what mattered was that it was gone.

He reclined again, the sand forming a pillow under his head.

Slowly he drifted toward sleep. Rest was what he needed—what he deserved.

He startled once, briefly, having thought he heard something shuffling by his ear. Then, deciding he had only imagined it, he lay back and let it in.

DRIVING HOME in his Lexus SUV a few hours later, Devon couldn't keep his finger out of his ear. He must've gotten water in it when that big wave flipped him over. His punishment for spending ten minutes in the ocean he paid so much to live near. His hearing was slightly muffled. His pinky tip couldn't reach the itch. If he didn't get this water out, he'd regret it. It had happened to him all the time as a kid growing up a few steps from Kellogg Beach, one of San Diego's hidden gems. Swimmer's ear, the doctors called it. A bacterial infection of the outer ear canal, caused when water is left to fester. Hurt like a bitch.

He drove with his head tilted to the side, letting the seawater drain out.

Somehow the itch only moved higher.

When he got back to the house he went into the bathroom and attacked it with a Q-tip. Dismayed to find, when he pulled it out, the cotton swab dry and dusted with sand.

A QUICK SHOWER, and then he ran out to a showing in Pacific Beach, work crowding out all thought of his janky ear.

The property was a turnkey Spanish-style three-bed, 740 square feet, decent-sized backyard for entertaining. On the market for $1,849,000. About the same size as his own place but nearly twice the price. He'd been smart. Bought when the market was down, did a lot of the work himself. Fuck privilege: savvy investments, good timing, a bit of elbow grease—that's what separated the haves from the have-nots.

"I spoke with the selling agent this morning and they've already got a couple of offers," he told his clients, Lana and Ralph, as he locked the house up after. "If you want it, you're gonna need to move quickly—"

He cursed, stopped, and dug his pinky back in his ear. A low scratching sound erupted through the right side of his head, like the shuffling of tiny legs magnified one thousand times.

"You okay?" asked Lana. They were an attractive couple, mid-thirties, pregnant. Work friends of Devon's ex. Fortunately he'd locked them in before the split.

"Yeah. Sorry," he said through gritted teeth. "Just got something—"

They grimaced at him digging for gold.

He pulled his finger out. "Anyway. Let me know about that offer."

"DON'T SEEE ANYTHIIIIING," the doctor said a few days later, peering into the magnified tunnel of Devon's ear. The cold penetration of the speculum's lighted tip sent a chill up his neck, but it was some ways off from the source of the discomfort—the scratching, the blockage. The *thing*, as he had come to think of it, in an attempt to disassociate the periodic cacophony of booms and scritches from the idea of something alive inside him.

"Trust me, there's something in there. I can—"

As if sensing it was being talked about, the thing moved around, drowning out his thoughts with its awful ruckus. Devon pulled his head away from the instrument, massaging his ear.

In the time it had taken him to get an appointment, his condition had worsened. His ear had begun to ooze and ached with an uncomfortable tightness, as if his ear canal was shrinking around the thing. Or—another thought he preferred not to entertain—the thing was growing.

"Could try a few drops of warm vegetable oil," said the doctor. Older guy, Midwestern—not from here. Hardly anyone was these days. "See if you can float it out—"

"I already tried that. Can't you just go in with tweezers?"

"Don't like to do that if I can't see what's in there. Wouldn't want to risk damaging your eardrum."

"Jesus Christ." Devon slid off the exam table with a crinkle of wax paper. "This is ridiculous. Something's *living in my head*, dude."

"Right—I mean, that must be a real pain."

Was Devon overthinking it, or was there something unspoken in the old man's eyes? Concerned, even. *There's something wrong with your head, all right.*

BACK AT HOME, Devon stared into the bathroom mirror. Jaw clenched, hands gripping the Carrera marble countertops. The thing had moved deeper, so large now he could feel its spiny exoskeleton needling the soft flesh of his inner ear, rubbing it raw, bleeding him out.

He touched a finger to his earhole, and when he pulled it away, his fingertip was coated in greenish-yellow pus. It had a dark swirl of red through it, like a beachside ice cream cone. Lime with a strawberry ribbon.

A hot zing of anger ran through him. Instinctively his hand wrenched open a drawer and fumbled for a Q-tip. Within seconds, both sides of the swab were saturated with bloody discharge.

He tossed it in the trash, reached for another, dug deeper—deeper than he'd normally go, especially with his ear as squishy and tender as it was, but he could feel the thing back there.

He nosed the swab up to it, prodded it once, and felt a tiny inward tug.

He withdrew the swab at once. *What the fuck?*

The thing had tried to pull the Q-tip out of his hands. Like it was defending its territory.

Standing its ground.

Gassed up with pure animal rage, Devon fumbled again through the open drawer, pulled out a pair of old tweezers.

He went in deep, stabbing at the thing, trying to get a grip on it. Judging from the pain and the blood that dribbled from his ear, he was probably doing more damage to himself, but it seemed to put the fear of God into the thing: His ear exploded with the sound of its nervous scuttling.

Finally the tweezers latched onto something. Devon squeezed and pulled. A snapping tear reverberated through his eardrum.

His grin of satisfaction curdled to nauseating disbelief before the spiny, grayish-brown claw hanging limply between the rusted tongs.

A sick, horrified urgency flooded him. *Get it out, get it out NOW*, was all he could think. He shoved the tweezers back in, too fast, too far—

A punch of excruciating pain.

He screamed, clamping his hands over the side of his head. The tweezers hit the sink with a tinkle of metal, a cartilaginous shred of eardrum stuck to the tongs like a bloody booger.

"*Fuck*," Devon roared, stomping around. "*Fuck, FUCK!*"

The pain came in waves, like the succession of ice-cold realization breaking over him.

One, he'd fucked his ear, maybe permanently. He could barely hear out of it.

Two, somehow his tweezers had missed the thing. It was *still inside him*.

Three, not only had Devon failed to root it out, but he'd opened a new door to it.

Like a gracious host, he had welcomed it in.

DEVON USUALLY SLEPT LIKE A LOG, but that night he was driftwood, dragged out to the sea of unconsciousness only to be tossed back to shore. His mind roiled with memories, dark and cloudy with silt: Lana and Ralph's judgmental faces. The doctor's confusion. His ex-girlfriend, during one of their last fights, calling him an empty shell, a hollow echo chamber of ego and entitlement.

He drifted through a vision of that morning on the beach—the sun and the sand and the shuffling at his ear—somehow experiencing it both outside and inside his body.

He could see the crab, naked and horrible, climbing his lobe, poking around the dark cave of its new potential home.

Could feel it shoving itself inside him: the laborious drag of its pincers, the ticklish tread of its feet.

Could hear it trampling the tatters of his punctured eardrum, pushing deeper.

Could taste it working its way through the channels of his sinuses, up into his head—

HE JERKED UPRIGHT IN BED. Huffed out with relief. It had just been a dream.

But had it? That last part had felt so real. He could still feel the clickety itch of it crawling upside down on his skull.

The squeaky friction of it wriggling between the slippery coils of his brain—

Fuck off. Of course it was a dream.

He flopped back on the pillow and lay there. Allowed relief to lap against him and soak him through.

He rolled over and reached for his phone.

But as he started to scroll, he sensed something was off. His eyes remained bleary even after several minutes; he couldn't make out the words on the screen. When he tossed the device aside and took in the dark room, fine detail had abandoned it, leaving only dark shapes, bold shadows. Like someone had lowered the sharpness on his vision and cranked the contrast way up.

It should've concerned him.

It didn't.

His thinking had changed in more or less the same way: his thoughts distilled into fuzzy black and white.

He should get up. Answer emails. He had a showing at ten.

He pulled the covers over his head and breathed in the sweet claustrophobia.

Here was where he belonged. Here in his shell.

Devon didn't leave the house. He lost count of the days, couldn't keep hold of the arithmetic of the week. Mostly he lay coiled in bed, not sleeping, barely moving. Surviving off deliveries of sushi and salt. Numb to the incessant ringing and pinging of his phone—clients angry he'd missed appointments or ghosted them mid-deal, friends and family concerned he hadn't posted.

He couldn't see why any of it mattered. Couldn't remember why he'd ever cared. A little dark to hole up in—that's all he needed. A place to call his own.

Then one day, a knock at the door.

He wasn't expecting a delivery. He ignored it.

But unlike the times before, that didn't make it stop.

"Devon, are you in there?" something called from the front of the house. Wild, threatening. "Quit fucking around. I know you're in there!"

A female.

He knew that call.

"I'm coming in," she said.

He heard the front door unlock and swing open. A shriek of surprise. "*What the fuck?*"

Footsteps on trash. The female burst into the room, silhouetted in a shaft of light from the open front door. He recognized her shape as the one he used to mate with.

"Devon?" she said, her fear steeling over into anger as she saw him. "What the *fuck*! This place is disgusting!"

She stomped over, ripped the greasy twist of covers off his carapace.

"What's wrong with you? Where have you been? Ralph and

Lana said they haven't heard from you in weeks. Your mom and sister—"

She hid her face behind her claw, blocking the smell.

"You fucking reek! What's wrong with you, are you okay?"

Devon reached out and clenched her wrist.

"Devon, let go of me. What are you—"

She raised her voice above the sound of his call, a short, frayed chirp. "Why are you making that sound? Let go of me!"

He stood before her and wrenched her wrist back and forth, rubbing his free claw up her stomach and over her breast. He had never wanted to stop mating with her. His heart ached behind the armor of his chest.

"Devon, stop— *Devon!*"

She drew back and punched, her fist landing in the soft underbelly of his throat. He staggered and crumpled on the floor, coughing. The sharp edge of a crushed clamshell dug into his side.

She scurried from the room. A moment later the front door slammed shut—once again extinguishing the light she had brought briefly into his life.

EVER SINCE HIS failed mating attempt, Devon had felt on edge, uneasy in the darkness that had once been home. It closed in around him, squeezing, itchy. At first, he feared he was outgrowing his shell. Then he realized: It was his skin that didn't fit.

The instinct to molt called him back to the sands where he'd been conceived. The white before the biggest dark on Earth, where even the most monstrous souls were welcome.

In the dead of night he slumped out of bed. It had been days since he'd gone farther than the edge of the mattress, even to make waste. His joints popped and cracked as he crawled toward the door, his chitinized feet clattering against the premium laminate.

He scaled the side of his Lexus, poked holes in the leather bucket seat. With a glance into the rearview mirror, he froze. He didn't recognize the creature looking back at him, the bloodshot eyes not raised on stalks.

There were no cars on the street that time of night. He was there in minutes, had no trouble finding a spot.

The moon glazed his exoskeleton in silver shine as he skittered across the boardwalk, clambered over the poor shell-less hermits slumbering in the shadow of the sea wall, clinging to any scraps of dark they could find.

At last, sand.

It crunched under his feet, restorative as a tonic, or the first breath of water after too long away.

He couldn't help it. Immediately he sank down, his claws burrowing madly underneath him, digging out a cave in which to shed his hard outer layer.

He was out of practice, and his new body required a bigger hole. He was at it for hours. By the time he'd dug a pit deep enough to stand in, a golden light had crept over the horizon. He was exhausted. His claws must have begun to molt already, tender and raw at the tips.

He needed to hurry. Crouched in the hole, he dug sideways, hollowing a cave out of the wall of moist compacted sand. Soon it was big enough that he could get his head and most of his torso inside, fling sand behind him as he continued to burrow.

A strange rumbling drew his attention. Something was happening above. It was too soft to be thunder. Terrestrial but not animal. He could feel its vibrations through the earth: They grew stronger as it approached.

Then a fissure opened in the wall of his cave.

Panicking, Devon plastered the crack with wet sand. But another split the opposite wall, and another above his head.

The cave shook as the rumble became a roar, and now he recognized the sound, like something out of a dream: the engine of the lifeguards' pickup making its morning rounds.

Instinctively he clambered back from the cave but only managed a few inches before the world collapsed into sudden, crushing darkness, the mound of excavated sand sliding in to fill the hole.

All was black and silent and still.

As the weight of the world above bore down on him, Devon returned to himself with a terrible relief.

His hard exoskeleton melted into soft epidermis.

His claws morphed back into fists, hammering the roof of his earthy coffin, which might have been miles underground instead of feet for how little he was able to move it.

His throat, airless and choked with sediment, seized around his desperate cries for help, which he already knew would not be heard —not over the crash of the waves, and the squawks of seagulls, and the complaints of the hardworking everyday people who just wanted to enjoy this place they called America's Finest.

Not up there.

And at last, the thing crawled down off its throne, forced its way back through the scarred pinhole of his ear canal, and thrust itself free from the side of his head, restoring Devon's hearing just in time to register the loudness of his city's apathy.

The View from Here
By Elle Jauffret

The sharp scent of decomposing flesh hit Tessa Sorel before she even stepped out of the elevator: a metallic tang that wormed its way through her police-issued mask. But underneath that familiar crime-scene copper was something else—a subtle sweetness that made her think of her mother's hospital room, of the day the doctors had pulled her aside to discuss "cognitive decline."

With a hand wave, she rejected her colleague's offer of the peppermint oil they usually used when checking scenes like this: a victim dead for over twenty-four hours in a south-facing Los Angeles apartment. The gesture would prove her strength. Her mint-free nose would detect odors that might lead to priceless evidence. If she managed to solve this case, she would be guaranteed a place on the LAPD detective squad. And she needed that promotion. Needed it with the kind of desperation that made people do things they would rather not think about.

"Must be the dead wife," Tessa said, taking the lead. She was the one who had discovered the first body. Male, white, 45, half-eaten by what the report claimed were coyotes. But she had seen coyote kills before, and something about the precision of these wounds had seemed . . . deliberate. The unidentified corpse had the phrase "my wife wants to die" written in the palm of his hand and a bright yellow key fob that led her to the thirtieth-floor luxury penthouse.

The moment Tessa crossed the threshold, her instincts screamed at her to turn back. Growing up on Skid Row, she trusted those gut feelings, but this was different. This wasn't danger she was sensing. It was like walking into a familiar room and finding all the furniture shifted two inches to the left. She froze and held her breath, afraid a scream would escape with her exhale. She grasped onto the entry table to stabilize herself, trying to ignore her wildly beating heart and the line of sweat erupting along her hairline.

Beyond the foyer, the floor-to-ceiling walls offered a precipitous 360-degree view of the cityscape, threatening to send her spiraling into the abyss below.

"Million-dollar-view, am I right?" Reed's voice came from behind her, followed by his elbow driving into her back.

"Reed! What are you doing here? Captain put me on the case, not you," she groaned, stumbling, her voice steadier than she felt. In her peripheral vision, the glass walls rippled with each throb of her racing heart.

"Chill. No need to get aggro. Thought you'd need my help." He stared down at her from his six-foot frame and sneered. Tessa studied his face, trying to pinpoint what seemed off about him that day. The way he held himself, perhaps, or something in his eyes that hadn't been there before. Oh, did she regret spilling her guts about her fear of heights the drunken night they had celebrated their police academy graduation together.

"I don't. You can leave now," she said, battling through what she told herself was just an anxiety attack.

Her colleague ignored her request and walked to the window where a lifeless form lay. Tessa followed, keeping her eyes fixed on the corpse, refusing to acknowledge how the city below seemed to writhe and shift like a living thing.

A woman was sprawled on a white couch, her right hand rigidly wrapped around a knife handle whose blade disappeared in her chest, right where her heart would be. Her left arm was outstretched as if reaching for help. The blood from her pastel pink blouse had pooled on the white marble floor in patterns that looked almost deliberate, like writing.

"No need to panic. This is just your brain playing tricks on you," she mumbled to herself, the words feeling hollow in her mouth, coercing her limbs into motion despite their reluctance.

"Something's bothering you?" Captain Holt's sharp gaze assessed Tessa's movements, his wrinkled brow questioning her hesitation.

"No, sir. It's the panorama . . . Left me speechless." She walked sideways, avoiding the vertiginous view, pretending the Vitrocsa glass walls were merely ultra-large TV screens. But with each step, she could feel the weight of the city pressing against the glass, waiting.

"As I mentioned to Sergeant Faust, if you solve this or find a major lead, the detective position is yours. He'll supervise you and Reed," the captain said. "I've asked the M.E. to send you the autopsy findings ASAP. For now, why don't you stay here and post guard for the next forty-eight hours?"

Tessa's stomach dropped. "Post guard here?" The idea of spending more time in this acrophobic nightmare seemed unimaginable.

"You're not afraid of ghosts, are you?" the captain asked, his smile not reaching his eyes.

"Maybe it's her arachnophobia, right, Tessa?" Reed's laugh echoed strangely in the space, as if the room itself was laughing with him.

It's acrophobia, not arachnophobia, you moron, Tessa thought. Though lately, she wasn't sure what she was afraid of anymore. The heights, yes, but there was something else now, something she couldn't quite name.

The captain studied her, ears perked, waiting for her answer. Waiting for the reason she shouldn't be promoted. If he learned about her phobia, she could say goodbye to her promotion. She wasn't going to let that happen.

"Nope. Not afraid of anything, Sir. That's why I joined the force." She forced a smile. As long as she avoided looking directly at the window, she would be fine. "I assumed my skills would be better used in the investigation itself, interrogating witnesses and such, as part of my detective training."

The captain nodded. "This is part of your training. Detectives may work long hours and irregular schedules, overnight, or through weekends when necessary. That'll help you decide if detective work's really for you."

"What about the Commissioner's Ball tomorrow night?"

"Why? You have a date?" Reed asked, and for a moment, Tessa could have sworn his teeth looked sharper than they should.

Tessa shook her head. "No, but I don't see how that's relevant."

Reed grinned. "We've all got family obligations and dates for the dance, while you won't be missed by anyone. Think of yourself as lucky: you'll have the entire crime scene to yourself. You might solve the case before everyone else."

Captain Holt quieted Reed with a glance and stared at Tessa. "We need a tight police presence in the penthouse to make sure no one gets in. No housekeeping, no neighbors, or friends who might have the keys. I can't force you to spend the night here, outside work hours, unless you volunteer," he said. "It's up to you. So, are you volunteering for this assignment or not?"

Volunteer, voluntold. Potato potahto. It's not like she had a choice. The promotion dangled before her like bait in a trap, but she was already caught. She needed that promotion badly. The pay increase alone would cover the cost of her mother's Alzheimer's medications—a small financial boost that would loosen the tight noose of filial responsibility and student loans strangling her.

"I do, sir. I volunteer." The words felt like a door closing behind her, like the final click of a lock.

THE VIEW FROM HERE

THE PRELIMINARY AUTOPSY results arrived in Tessa's inbox just as the sun began to set, casting long shadows across the penthouse floor. She watched them creep across the marble like reaching fingers while the forensic unit finished their sweep. Post-mortem examinations were completed astonishingly fast, and searches were unusually thorough when the victims happened to be obscenely wealthy.

Tessa settled at the kitchen counter, her back to the window so she wouldn't catch sight of the void outside. A short glimpse toward the green-tinged windows showed her a distorted reflection of herself caught between shadow and light. She took a deep breath and swiped through the reports, studying the findings and first crime scene photos.

First, the female victim, Mrs. Barker, had died of cardiac arrest and exsanguination. The angles of the victim's arm, elbow, and wrist indicated self-stabbing. The cut through the sternum and cardiac puncture supported that theory. However, the victim could have been forcefully guided by someone holding her arm from behind. Or something else entirely. Tessa's mind flashed to the way the blood had pooled on the floor, those strange patterns she'd thought she had seen.

Second, the male victim, Mr. Barker, died of blunt force trauma and head/brain injury resulting in loss of consciousness and cessation of vital functions. The report didn't mention the warped expression on his face—that look of rapture Tessa couldn't forget.

Third, the victims' brains showed signs of widespread neuronal damage consistent with heavy drug use.

Lastly, both victims' bodies presented with green dust on their hands—lab results pending. Tessa glanced at her own fingers, wondering if the apartment was truly free of it or if traces of the dust still lingered, unseen, in the corners and on the surfaces around her. She didn't need to test positive for a new drug and risk her promotion—she had too much to lose.

Attached to the digital case file, in the section left blank for investigative notes, Reed had already commented: "Looks like we've got a couple of professional junkies who snorted themselves to delirium and death. Husband got high, stabbed his consenting wife, got a rideshare to Griffith Park, and committed remorse-suicide by jumping from the Hollywood sign."

Tessa scoffed. The husband's time of death was estimated seven hours earlier than his wife's. In addition, the toxicology report hadn't detected any drugs in either victim. A new, undetectable drug must have hit the market. Or someone else was involved.

There was also no credit card transaction showing the husband took a rideshare to Griffith Park. She doubted he had walked eight miles up the steep Mount Lee to end his days when he could have simply jumped off his thirtieth-floor penthouse. While the trek to the Hollywood Sign wasn't technically challenging, it was still a hike that required some physical exertion and preparation. Something or someone must have driven him to that location. Or maybe . . . She imagined a man floating through the night air, arms spread wide, smiling that terrible smile on his way to his death. She shook her head, pushing away the ridiculous thought.

Tessa picked up a shiny brown pen from the counter and jotted down her thoughts in her police notebook until the scratchy sound of lock picking disturbed her concentration. A glance through the judas told her a skinny twenty-something was trying to get in. His jeans and tattered t-shirt hugged his body closely, revealing no hint of any concealed weapon, so Tessa whipped open the door.

"What are you doing?"

The lockpicker jumped back and recoiled. "I didn't know people were still here . . .""

"That doesn't explain why you were picking the lock. I could arrest you on the spot. Who are you and what do you want?"

"I'm Gideon . . . Gideon Pryce. I'm a downstairs neighbor . . . I was trying to get my pen back."

"You were committing a crime to retrieve a pen?" she sneered.

"Not an ordinary pen. One worth a hundred thousand dollars." His eyes fixed on her hand, where she had been holding that same pen just moments ago, and something hungry flickered across his face.

Tessa jerked back. "A hundred-thousand-dollar pen? What is it made of, pure gold?"

"Petrified wood from Antarctica, actually. I left it behind at the party two days ago, before . . . you know . . . The night before they died."

Tessa wanted to believe him, but something about him was off. His paleness, frailty, and worn-out clothes made him stand out amid the building's luxury atmosphere. A normal man his age, living here, would be oozing with style and cockiness if not confidence.

"Can you describe it?" she asked, blocking the entrance of the penthouse with her body as he tried to get in. Beyond the one she had used to take notes, she hadn't seen any pens in the house.

"It looks like brown marble."

The one Tessa used to take notes. "Why do you need it?" she asked.

Pryce's fingers twitched against his thigh. "It's not really mine. I borrowed it from the lab where I worked and need to return it STAT."

"So you aren't just a lockpicker, you're also a thief. I can't give it back to you; it's evidence."

"Can you at least place it in the fridge in a Ziploc bag for preservation and call me when I can get it back? It's fragile and one of a kind," he pleaded, his words coming faster, tumbling over each other.

"Sure. But why bring it to the party and why leave it behind if it wasn't yours?"

The man shifted his weight back and forth between his feet. "To show off, I guess. It's hard to compete with the rich. They always have better stories to tell and have seen everything." A tinge of shame filled his sideways gaze.

Tessa grimaced, confused. "Doesn't living here mean you're also rich?"

"I'm only house-sitting and watering the plants while the owner is away. I'm a starving student living off the building's free morning bagels and ramen."

"I see."

"I bet a cop's salary isn't much better. From one struggler to another," he said, leaning closer, his breath carrying that same sweet-rot smell from the crime scene, "is there any chance I can get the pen back now?"

"No, but maybe tomorrow. I'll let you know." Tessa shut the door quickly, but not before she saw something dark and desperate in his eyes.

According to the building concierge, Gideon Pryce was an arthropodology student much disliked by the residents for having brought terrariums full of hissing cockroaches and peyote beetles on the premises.

"Can you believe it? What was he thinking? If we don't allow pets, how did he expect we would welcome pests?" the night concierge said. He had invited Tessa to share a cup of coffee at the lobby counter behind which he stood at the ready for residents' requests.

Tessa stared into her cup, watching the black liquid ripple and swirl, as if it were a threatening vortex—like the dizzying drop of an endless void she feared to fall into, but this size she could handle. She nodded in agreement, processing the information. Besides a love for bugs, there was only one reason to cultivate peyote beetles: for mescaline, their psychoactive compounds.

"So, what happened?" she asked, her voice bouncing off the marble walls of the empty entryway. The echo came back wrong, distorted, like someone else's voice answering.

"The exterminator took care of them all. Didn't matter if the kid was studying them for his PhD; this is a cockroach and bug-free building. The rules are the rules."

"Do you have any reason to believe Pryce had something against the Barkers?"

"Not about the bugs, no, but about the noise. He filed several noise complaints against them, saying he couldn't focus on his studies. Since the Barkers moved in, two months ago, they had parties almost every night. They were so loud, you could hear them from the elevator shaft. Though some residents swore it wasn't music they heard, but screaming."

Tessa raised an eyebrow. On Skid Row, you learned really fast: noise means nothing unless it's silence. You get used to the screaming. Hell, you can get killed for a noise complaint if you're not careful. "What did the board do?"

"Nada. The board doesn't listen to house-sitters, but they told the Barkers to send Pryce a courtesy invite next time they had a party."

"Which they did," Tessa mumbled to herself. And that's when Pryce brought the pen to their party.

THE LAST PHOTOS taken on Mrs. Barker's phone were happy ones. Too happy. The kind of happiness that looks like madness when you stare at it long enough. One of them featured her husband flashing Pryce's pen in one hand and a wad of cash in the other. A transaction gone bad?

Tessa grabbed the pen and settled on her makeshift bed to ponder the question. She had set it up in the windowless closet. The extra thick carpet, which was softer than her futon, and her balled-up police jacket would be fine for the next two nights. There was also an outlet to charge her phone. The perfect place for an acrophobe to post guard, hide from the city's hungry gaze, without losing her mind.

She studied the petrified wood pen, twirling it between her fingers. It was difficult to believe that a pretty but otherwise unremarkable pen was worth twenty times her car. Rich people tossed money at ridiculous things like this, while people were starving on the streets—she wished they could redirect a little of that waste.

Her internet research had confirmed Pryce's statement: petrified wood from Antarctica was the rarest of all and could go for millions depending on the size. However, fossilized wood did not require refrigeration for preservation. So why had Pryce insisted on keeping it cold? You'd only freeze something to keep it dormant or to prevent it from growing. What was he trying to stop from growing?

A background check on the student led nowhere. He wasn't in the system, which came as no surprise. Young nerds rarely had records; they were less prone to violence and better at covering their crimes. But Pryce's absence from any type of social media besides a bare LinkedIn profile left Tessa nonplussed. She didn't know any Gen Z who wasn't at least on Instagram. The only information she found was a scientific article about newly discovered mites called *Viridipulvis Antartico*, but it was blocked by a paywall.

"Two hundred dollars to access an article! No way I'm paying that," she said, yawning.

She googled *Viridipulvis Antartico* but came up empty. Damn scientists and their elaborate bug names! The only part of the word she could figure out was *pulvis*, from her catholic school days. *Quia pulvis es, et in pulverem reverteris*; for you are dust, and to dust you shall return.

"Dust mites." Tessa shrugged and turned off the light, concluding it wasn't important. Then she drifted to sleep, hoping the night would bring her clarity if not advice. But in her dreams, she saw the city spread below her like a web of green light and heard voices whispering about transcendence and flight.

The View from Here

THE NEXT DAY, Tessa walked through the penthouse without fear of heights—a first in her life of basement living and sewer searches. It wasn't just the absence of fear. The height called to her, sang to her. The glass walls no longer seemed like barriers but like windows to freedom. She had awakened past twelve with green dust on her hands, like the one found on both victims. "Dust" as in *pulvis* and "green" as in *viridis*. *Viridipulvis Antartico* meant green dust from Antarctica in Latin. The victims' damaged brains and Pryce's petrified wood might be linked. The inconspicuous pen could be the stash of a new drug!

It wouldn't be the first time individuals inhaled or smoked insects to get high. From what she had learned during training, the psychoactive effects of ingesting insects, if any, were likely to be unpredictable and potentially harmful; they could lead to death.

But was it a bad drug? The way it made her feel—lighter, clearer, braver—seemed more like awakening than intoxication. Like she was becoming something new. Something better. Something that could finally break free from the cage of gravity and human limitation. But she couldn't shake the nagging thought—wasn't this how it always started? The high, the illusion of freedom, before it twisted into something darker, something that ravaged you from the inside out, too addictive to escape its grip?

Tessa thoroughly washed her hands, hoping her skin hadn't absorbed the drug. She thought about sending the pen to the lab right then, but decided to wait. She needed to gather more information and close the case first, before Captain Holt took away the case from her because of her contact with the drug, or Reed would find a way to steal this victory from her.

She settled at the kitchen counter, facing the window to enjoy the midday sun, and sealed the pen in an evidence bag. Los Angeles sprawled in front of her like an offering with Griffith Observatory, the Hollywood sign, and the Disney Music Hall all viewable from where she sat. Her mom had been right: her fear of heights was only a mental block caused by her lack of confidence. Or maybe it had been something else holding her back all this time—something human and small and afraid. Something she was finally ready to leave behind.

She returned to the password protected website of last night, entered her credit card number, and clicked PAY AMOUNT TO ACCESS ARTICLE. Catering a whole new drug to the wealthy had to be Pryce's get-rich-quick scheme until yesterday when his Antarctica mites killed two of his clients.

"Please, please, be the proof Pryce is a drug dealer and a murderer," she mumbled as the website buffered.

But what appeared on the screen wasn't an article. It was a warning pulsing with urgency: "New mite species discovered in Antarctic ice core samples. Venomous, potentially lethal. If found, limit exposure, seal immediately, and place at a temperature below ten degrees Celsius." There was no further explanation, but for the list of researchers, including Gideon Pryce, and the name and email address of a contact person.

Tessa sent an email without waiting. She explained who she was and how the green dust was found on two suspicious deaths in California. She ended her letter with: "How dangerous are those mites? Please call me ASAP. Any time of day or night. It's important." She left her phone number. Her hands trembled as she typed, not noticing the green dust falling from her fingertips onto the keyboard.

OUTSIDE, the sun was setting, painting the city in shades of green and gold that shouldn't have been possible. Tessa had ordered sushi delivery for dinner to celebrate her upcoming promotion. She felt confident she would solve this case by midnight. Her contact with the dust or manufactured drug couldn't be that potent, or she would already be dead. Antarctica being only four hours behind Los Angeles time, the scientist would contact her any minute now. They would explain everything, tie Gideon Pryce to the murders, provide his motives, and help her close the case.

In her notebook, she meticulously described the investigative trail she followed and wrote "from Tessa to Reed with love" on the pen's evidence bag. The green dust fell from her pen like snow, spelling out messages in an ancient language. Then she stepped on the balcony in the Californian summer heat. Her vertigo hadn't just vanished; it had transformed into something else, something beautiful. The height didn't frighten her anymore. It called to her, sang to her, promised her things she had never dared to dream.

"Goodbye, self-sabotaging acrophobic anxiety! I'm ready to conquer new heights!" she shouted at the cityscape. Los Angeles glittered golden in the sunset light. The ocean breeze brought the intoxicating scent of jasmine to her nostrils and carried whispers of a new life.

Her phone rang in the background, but she let it go to voicemail. The voice was frantic, urgent: "The mites are parasites with advanced neural engineering capabilities . . . They don't just damage the brain, they remake it . . . Make you want to spread them . . . like spores . . . like seeds . . . Tessa, if you're exposed, get somewhere cold immediately. They're not just parasites, they're something else, something that's been waiting in the ice for millions of years, something that wants to—"

But Tessa wasn't listening anymore. She was laughing as she straddled the railing. Her fear had been ridiculous. She was no longer the acrophobe, cowering at the edge of her own potential; she was a force to be reckoned with, a true, formidable detective. Reed wouldn't bully her anymore or steal her promotion; nobody could. She could do anything, even fly if she wanted.

She leaped.

The Box Born Wraith

By Kevin David Anderson

"Not like this, Frank," Benny pleaded. "Just shoot me. Please."

Frank shook his head. "You know I can't, Ben. The Boss was very specific. He wants to make an example. Now get in the damn box."

Benny gazed at the six-foot-long wooden crate at the bottom of the shallow grave. It looked to be hurried work, all imperfect corners and protruding nails. Frank's men weren't carpenters. They were killers. This box, with all its imperfections, buried in the middle of an unkempt, nearly forgotten graveyard, would be Benny's coffin.

He knew it was pointless to beg but didn't know what else to do. "Please, Frank, not alive. Don't bury me alive."

"Jump down there, you skimming prick, or I'm gonna blow your kneecaps off." Frank aimed his gun at Benny's legs. "If you don't panic, you got maybe four or five hours of air in there. You want to spend that time in agony?"

Benny considered for a second, but before he decided, one of Frank's men pushed him in. He landed on all fours, then slowly stood, the top of the grave coming to his chest. Benny's heart pounded, and even in the cool October night, sweat matted his black hair.

Frank knelt. "Ya' know, the Boss owns this old bone-yard. Bought it back when Lake Elsinore was half the size it is now. When the last hole was filled, the city opened that big industrial-sized cemetery off the freeway where the dead can spend eternity surrounded by a Home Depot and a Sam's Club."

"I think it's a Costco, Frank," one of his men said.

"Who the fuck cares?" Frank snapped, glancing back at his man.

The henchman cowered, a scolded dog.

Frank peered into Benny's glassy eyes. "Point is, you won't have that problem here, not in this neighborhood. Real peaceful. Mostly empty nesters now, but back in the fifties, genuine movie stars came out here to unwind, get away from Hollywood for a while." Frank suddenly points north. "Bela Lugosi used to own a house right over there. You know who that was?"

Benny nodded, looking out at the sea of gravestones jutting up from a thin layer of fog. Orange moonlight shimmered off the forgotten epitaphs, and the only terrestrial source of light came from the porches outside the cemetery—Jack-o-lanterns burning brightly.

"The Boss's goomar said she saw Lugosi once. Well, his ghost," Frank said. "Hanging out at a 7-Eleven at two in the morning, black cape, slicked back hair, the whole shebang." Frank chuckled. "She'd been drinking but swore up and down she was sober. Swears it was him." Frank waves a dismissive hand. "But I digress." He knelt on the edge of the hole and looked at Benny with cold, unfeeling eyes. "The Boss always had the idea this could be the perfect place to bury the trash. Make an example for those who might consider taking what is not theirs."

Frank leaned forward, and Benny felt his gaze like a noose. "You'll be the first."

Benny was about to start begging again when he caught a glint of movement. Frank saw it too, and with lightning speed, moved the revolver. Benny felt the muzzle pressed up to his jaw. "Go ahead, Ben, call out."

Benny gazed at the trick-or-treaters skipping along the sidewalk outside the cemetery, a small group with their elderly grandparents struggling to keep up.

"Make one sound and I'll blow your mouth clean off, then I'll have to go kill some kids. You don't want to go down like that, Ben, and I ain't in no mood to kill kids."

Benny opened his mouth, and Frank leaned closer. "Then, when that is done, maybe I go pay a visit to your house, Benny-boy. Say hi to that nice wife and kid of yours. Is he out trick-or-treating tonight?"

Benny grabbed Frank's collar. "Stay away from my family you son of a bitch."

Frank pointed the gun at Benny's grave. "Get in the box and they'll be fine."

Benny knew far too well that Frank didn't make threats. He made promises. The sadistic pig would have no problem abusing his family while Benny slowly suffocated. Sighing, he let his hands fall to his side and gazed down at the place where he was meant to die. It was cold, hard, and dark.

"Attaboy. Now, lie down like a man and let's get this done."

Benny lowered himself into the box, and the darkness swept over him like a blanket. "Frank, let me have a light."

Frank kicked some dirt into the grave, landing on Benny's chest. "Won't change nothing."

"I don't want to die in the dark."

Frank pulled a flashlight from his back pocket and tossed it down. "We all die in the dark, Benny."

Fumbling with the flashlight, Benny pulled it to his chest as Frank's men threw down the lid. One of them jumped into the hole with a hammer and nails. Benny placed his hands on the lid as it was slid into place, then he lifted his head and peered through the cracks.

Frank stood, holstered his gun, and turned to go. "Hey, Frank," Benny called.

"Yeah?"

Benny clenched his teeth. "If I ever see you again . . ."

Frank smiled. "You won't."

Benny closed his eyes as the first nail was put in place. He managed to make it through the hammering, staying calm, retreating into thoughts of his wife and son. But when the dirt fell in loud clumps, Benny started to lose control. His body shook, and he started pounding, then clawing, at the lid. Wooded shards broke loose and stabbed the tender skin under his nails.

Blood ran down his fingers as the sound of falling dirt became distant, replaced by the creaking of the wooden coffin. He placed his hands flat on the lid, realizing it was bowing inward from the weight of the dirt. He started to laugh, thinking that the lid might implode and crush him. But after a few silent moments, Benny realized he wasn't going to be that lucky.

The smell of earth, sweat, and freshly cut wood filled his nostrils as he tried to take slow breaths. The sounds of his breathing bounced around the box like a trapped bat, amplifying his panic, feeding his dread.

Benny tried to occupy his mind and not think about his itching neck or his aching legs. He desperately wanted to bend his knees, just for a few seconds, and the fact that he couldn't was maddening. He pounded the lid with his fists and screamed. Then he heard the faint sounds of someone sobbing. As he pressed his forehead to the top of the box, he realized it was him. His echoing cries continued for twenty minutes, then, energy spent, he passed out.

He awoke with a jolt and smacked his head on unforgiving wood, an instant reminder that the nightmare about being buried alive hadn't been a nightmare.

He moved the light to check his watch. Just past midnight. He'd been buried for almost three hours. Maybe one more hour to go before it became hard to breathe. Maybe less. He hoped it would feel like going to sleep, but his rational side knew that wasn't true. When the brain is starved of oxygen, the body begins to panic, and the heart races, trying to pump the dwindling oxygen supply to vital organs, sending waves of horror throughout the system. The only mercy would be the loss of consciousness before the painful and life-ending cardiac arrest.

A distant sound seized his attention. Benny held his breath, straining to hear. He pressed his ear to the lid and there it was again —a faint digging.

"I'm in . . ." He tried to call out, but his previous screams had strained his voice.

It had to be Frank digging him up, Benny thought. Maybe the Boss just wanted to teach him a lesson. Seemed a bit extreme, but . . .

The digging got closer.

Or maybe it was teenagers on a dare, digging up a fresh grave. Yeah, that might be it. It's the kind of Halloween stunt he'd have pulled as a kid. Benny pounded on the lid again. "Here! I'm in here!"

But even before the echo of his voice had faded, he noticed something wrong with the sounds of dirt being moved. It was getting closer, more hurried, and seemed only a few feet away. But the closer it got, the more wrong it seemed.

It wasn't until Benny turned his head and pressed an ear to the bottom of the box that he realized what it was. The digging wasn't coming from above. It was coming from below.

"Oh, Jesus," Benny cried, gripping the flashlight, shining its beam around the box. He could feel dirt fall away beneath him, the bottom of the box sagging downward, but somehow hanging over a black hole in the earth.

Something scraped on the bottom, and Benny flinched. He squirmed, trying to roll on his side, but before he did, something clawed its way down the length of his coffin. Benny froze. Holding his breath, he turned his head to the side, aiming the light into the widest seam in the bottom of the box. The beam bounced off the wet earth, revealing deep claw marks.

Suddenly, he heard movement beneath him. He tried to chase it down with the flashlight, but each sweep of the beam caught nothing, intensifying his dread. Then, like earworms caressing his skin, he felt warm air on the back of his neck as something very close exhaled through cracks in the box. Pulse pounding, he turned his head around, only to be met by the chilling sight of something peering in from the outside.

Large white eyes with thick eyelids of pale skin blinked and then narrowed curiously. Benny kicked the box. "Get away!"

He reared for another kick, but a dozen clawed hands burst through the box, seized his limbs, and pulled him, screaming, downward. His head slammed hard onto the dirt as bits of wood rained down. He blinked a few times to focus, instantly wishing he hadn't.

A dozen golf ball-sized eyes, set inside hideous faces—grotesque parodies of apes with pale, hairless skin stretched taut over thick, ridged skulls—surrounded him. Before Benny took a breath, he felt clawed hands grab his shirt. The creature pulled Benny's face in close, sniffing him through a pair of slits below its wide eyes. It howled angrily and pushed him away. Some of the other creatures moved away in revulsion, some looked angry, and one just stared, astonished.

Sitting up, Benny studied his captors. Their long arms allowed them simian-like movements, reaching forward on worn knuckles and swinging their legs underneath. If it wasn't for their noseless faces and the bald skin that hung off their bodies like a Shar-Pei, Benny would have thought them hairless chimpanzees.

A few of the creatures wore clothes, not for function, but more as decoration. He cringed in horror, recognizing several popular tattoo patterns on their garments, realizing their clothes were fashioned from human skin.

Benny was shoved toward a torch-lit corridor, and as the small group started to move, he had to stay crouched in the four-foot-high passage, which was the perfect size for its inhabitants.

Stumbling along the descending tunnel, Benny was prodded

from behind with a blow every few minutes. They spoke in a language he'd never heard, but the tone was unquestionably angry.

Suddenly, he emerged into an enormous gymnasium-sized chamber. Coffins, stacked like bleachers, lined the walls. The seats were filled with what looked like females of the species and hordes of their brood. As he walked past, the smaller eyes of the young ones, glazed over with hunger, stared at him, disappointment flashing over their gaunt faces. The scene reminded Benny of pictures of starving children, bloated stomachs ripe with malnutrition.

A tall, thin female, wearing human teeth around her neck like a pearl necklace, emerged from behind a pile of discarded jewelry, watches, and gold fillings. She walked toward Benny, holding a staff constructed of interlocking bones like an enormous spine. The others cleared a path, and Benny tried to stand up straight.

She tapped his chest with the staff and then placed a hand over his heart. Benny felt it beat faster at her touch. She shook her head, then turned to her people and spoke in their strange language.

They didn't like what she had to say. Commotion exploded around the room. Some yelled with rage, some sobbed. The one that had grabbed him earlier pushed to the front and started yelling. He held a broken femur like a dagger and thrust it up and down.

The female jabbed her staff into the dirt defiantly. The larger male took a step back with a slight bow, but then roared savagely and lunged at Benny. Benny brought his hands up as the creature landed on his chest. Swinging a fist, Benny connected with the side of its bald head. It fell back, howling like an enraged ape, then came at him again, this time with teeth.

Benny heard a crunch and screamed as the creature bit into his wrist. Feeling teeth touching bone, he knew he had only seconds before he lost his hand. He pulled with all his strength, wildly thrashing and kicking at his attacker. But the creature suddenly let go. It stumbled back, gagging, Benny's blood splattered on its face. It gasped for air, grabbed its throat, and fell to the dirt floor. Its tiny legs twitched, and then it lay still, dead.

Before Benny could check his wound, the female pulled him up, dragged him to the rear of the chamber, and through an opening. Crouching, Benny whirled around and saw her wave the bone staff at the doorway. In an instant, the opening to the room vanished, replaced by a wall of dirt.

Thinking it safe for the moment, Benny examined his wrist. To his astonishment, he wasn't even bleeding. The cuts were deep, but there was no pain. It's like he was looking at a wound on someone else's body.

The female moved past him, and Benny gazed around the enormous communal room. Benny hadn't frequented many, but he knew a place of worship when he saw one. It had a cathedral ceiling molded of earth, spotted with imprints of the creature's hands. Rows of pews fashioned from coffin wood were laid out on the smooth soil floor, facing a podium of clay and skulls. Beyond lay an altar, decorated with elaborate hieroglyphs. The creatures were depicted carrying coffins, worshipping them, and feasting on the contents.

"Life," the female said in a primal, guttural tone. "The boxes are life."

Benny was shocked to hear words he could understand. Her voice was neither male nor female but more like one of Dr. Moreau's experiments—a creature teaching itself a language it was not meant to speak.

"His head was spinning. Benny contemplated her words, mixing them in with the images he had seen. After a few moments, he thought he understood. A word floated around in his mind, seemingly searching for a sane place to land. When sanity seemed unavailable, he finally just said it. "Ghouls."

"Boxes empty for so long," she said, her speech labored as if struggling for every syllable. "Then you. But you not food. You not dead. Why?"

"It's a long story . . ." Benny shook his head. "But you and your kind . . . you eat the dead, to live," he said, more to himself than to his savior. Remembering what happened to the one that had just bitten him, it seemed they could not consume him alive. Living blood was poisonous.

"But why not just kill me, and eat me after?" he said. "I mean, you're . . . ghouls."

She thrust the staff past the altar, toward a mud statue of a female, arms spread wide, reaching for the surface. "The Mother forbids. Must not make dead."

"Mother forbids," Benny repeated. "Well, don't that beat all. The ghouls got religion." Looking into her wide, hungry eyes, he was seized by a sudden inspiration. "I think you and I can work this out." He pointed up. "You send me back up there, and I'll fill your boxes. Man, oh man, will I fill your boxes." Benny saw the female smile, a yellowed jagged-tooth grin, and he knew that she understood.

BENNY CLAWED his way out of the ground through a narrow hole in the earth the female ghoul had created with a thrust of her staff. Flopping down on the cemetery grass, he took air deep into his lungs, the cold night invigorating every muscle in his body.

He rolled over and looked at his wound. It still didn't hurt, and he'd almost forgotten about it. The wounds in the flesh seemed only scratches, and beneath, he could feel the muscle pulse with energy he'd never felt before. His scalp tingled, and he ran his fingers through his hair. Thick black strands fell away. He looked at the clumps in his hands, sighing. "Small price to pay," he said, with a grin. Benny took a deep breath and then jumped to his feet with a simian's grace.

He felt strong, hungry, and ready to make good on a promise. He didn't know what he was becoming, but he did know that Frank would be the first to find out.

Skin in the Game
By Brian Asman

People call me the Horror Detective.

The nickname wasn't my idea, and maybe it's kind of cheesy, but I can't argue that it fits. After all, I've experienced real-life horror. Been saved by make-believe horror. My great-aunt Lana starred as Amunet in *The Mummy Queen* and its sequels. I followed in her footsteps, playing Gregor Mundy in the first two *Campgrind* films.

So, yeah. I guess you could say horror is my life. And in between the infidelity and insurance fraud cases that are my bread and butter as a PI, you could even say it's my business, too.

Certain cases have a way of finding me. The weird ones. The occult ones. The kind of shit that sounds unbelievable, but by the time I'm done flipping over whatever rocks the client wants flipped?

Sometimes, there's something dirty and squirmy with way too many fucking legs.

This is one of those cases.

Most of the time, I meet clients in a booth at *The 4th Horseman,* an apocalypse-themed pizza joint a few floors beneath my downtown Long Beach loft. But if that's too public for a client's taste, I'll link up with them down the street at an art gallery owned by the same guys, both named Jeremy. They're both slasher fans, so they don't mind if I use their businesses to run mine.

My current client is the shy type, so we're in the back room at Dark Art Emporium. I expected the stuffed raccoons and bird skulls in the front to make an impression on the guy—a dentist, real upstanding citizen—but he wasn't fazed in the slightest. I practically had to drag him away from a Cthulhu sculpture made with real, taxidermied octopus tentacles.

Which would usually make me think I've got a kindred spirit on my hands, but this guy gives me the willies. He's got a certain oiliness about him.

"I can't believe I've never been in here before," the dentist gushes. "This place is awesome!"

"Definitely unique," I reply. "So, Mr. Froman—"

"Call me Dr. Steve. That's what all my patients call me."

I have zero desire to call this guy doctor anything, but he's paying the bills. "What can I do for you, Dr. Steve?"

"There's an . . . item that was stolen from me. I want you to recover it."

"You were robbed? You should call the police."

Dr. Steve looks away at a cardboard box that's probably full of taxidermied butterflies. "That's the thing."

I stand, pushing back the folding chair I'd been sitting in. "I'm a PI, not hired muscle. If you've got a *thing* about going to the police, I can't take the case."

Now Dr. Steve stands too, hands up. He's a few inches shorter than me. "Look, Mr. Craven—"

Ordinarily, this is the part where I'd say *call me Dex,* but Dr. Steve is seconds away from not being a client, so *Mr. Craven* is just fine.

"I'm not asking you to do anything illegal. It's not like that."

"So what's it like?"

"Can you sit down again? Please?"

I sink back into my chair, now a few inches further away. "Make it fast."

Dr. Steve leans forward, voice semi-hushed, even though we're alone. "Look, nothing's illegal, but I'd rather not risk anything getting out."

"Something untoward, then? Something your high-dollar patients might frown upon?" I checked out Dr. Steve beforehand, since I'd be one shitty PI if I didn't. He's slapped veneers on half of Hollywood.

"No, it's not that either. I collect items of a specific . . . nature. Items that certain kinds of people would do anything to get their hands on. So I'd rather not risk my interest in such items becoming public, especially since now one has been stolen from my home. Do you understand?"

I nod.

"It's why I came to you. Your reputation–"

"I'm aware of my reputation. What's the item?"

Dr. Steve pulls out his phone and shoves it my way.

On the screen is a photo of a framed object hanging on the wall. Weird design in the middle, some kind of squiggly geometric thing printed on parchment, maybe, or–

"Is that *skin*?"

"It's a tattoo."

"So, yes."

"I have documentation confirming its provenance." Dr. Steve slips his phone back in his pocket. "That tattoo once adorned the back of a mystic named Brother Enochious. He started out as a director, then left the business to start a cult up near Big Sur. Claimed to be able to see into other dimensions. Also claimed the tattoo was a portal. I think they mostly smoked grass and had orgies. One of his followers eventually killed him over a woman. His will explicitly stated the tattoo be preserved. I bought it from his next of kin."

"You ever think about collecting something less morbid? Like stamps?"

"Your buddies out front have real human skeletons for sale."

"Touche. So you want me to find whoever stole the embalmed back piece of a psycho cult leader?"

"And get it back."

I sigh heavily. Haven't acted in years, but I guess I still lean dramatic. "I can do some checking, but when it comes to recovering the *item*—" saying "psycho cult leader's back tattoo" is a mouthful, "I'll need to coordinate with the police."

Dr. Steve leans forward and grabs my wrist.

I was right. He *is* kinda oily.

"It's incredibly important you recover the item as soon as possible," he says in a hushed voice. "Something like this should never fall into the wrong hands."

I shrug off his grip and wipe the back of my wrist on my jeans. "And yours are the right ones?"

"I'll give you fifty thousand dollars."

Well, *that* changes things.

"This is really important to me," Dr. Steve continues.

"All right, I'll take the job. But like I told you, once I find your *item*, I'm calling the police. I've got friends on the force." I don't. "And they'll keep quiet." They won't.

Dr. Steve considers this for a moment. "Okay."

"Good," I say, standing up. "Let me show you out."

We don't shake hands.

DR. STEVE LIVES in a tony Victorian mansion in Los Cerritos, not far from the Virginia Country Club. I poked around there earlier today, searching for nonexistent clues, and now I'm back in my loft, watching the only lead Dr. Steve has: a video.

I'm looking at his home from the comfort of my loft, two thousand square feet of high ceilings and exposed brick, located in a former warehouse on 4th and Pine. It's south-facing, so I've got a good view of the harbor, the Queen Mary, the endless rows of cranes lined up at Terminal Island. The interior's decorated with Thai movie posters for all of my favorite flicks. *Creepshow, Tombs of the Blind Dead, Return of the Living Dead 3,* countless others. I got into collecting Thai posters years ago because they're cool. Hand-drawn art that's often based on a cursory knowledge of the film itself. It's like seeing into an alternate reality.

The video picks up just after eleven p.m. when the dentist's Hollywood Bowl concert ended—which meant Dr. Steve still had a forty-five-minute drive ahead of him–two men dressed in black with balaclavas over their faces entered the yard.

I watch them cross the yard—one's lagging behind and scratches his leg mid-stride–and go around the side of the house, where they jimmied a window. Dr. Steve, for all his paranoia about his *collection*, only has a Ring camera on his door, so there's no other footage. I watch them walk at regular speed. Then I watch them again in slow motion. I study their gaits, try to estimate their sizes based on the shadows they cast next to the shrubs.

They're wearing motorcycle boots. That's something. The only other mildly interesting thing in the whole video is the leg scratch.

I go back and watch frame by frame. When the second guy scratches his leg, his pants ride up slightly. Enough for me to see a flash of metal.

Dude's got a prosthetic leg.

I push away from my desk and say, "you've gotta be fucking kidding me" to the framed Romero zombie behind me.

Because I happen to know a biker who's missing a leg.

Only problem is, he's got friends.

You don't want to mess with Los Pedros MC. They're one of the baddest biker gangs in the South Bay and easily the most confusingly-named. Being based in San Pedro, you might think that's where the name comes from. But no, the gang was founded by Eastern Orthodox Balkan immigrants and, like the city, is actually named after Saint Peter.

Could've called themselves the Los Piotrs and saved us all some time, but here we are.

Here being a shithole bar near the port, nestled in an industrial area next to a junkyard. The bar's so shitty it doesn't even have a name, although it does have the gang's logo in the window: a cartoon Saint Peter, leather-vested and astride a Harley. There are more bikes in the gravel parking lot, lined up and gleaming next to some old trucks that should probably be parked at the junkyard next door instead.

I'm across the street, watching the entrance and wondering why every fence on the block is topped with razor wire. Just in case anybody tries to Flinstone-foot a rusted '78 Honda with no engine, I guess. The guy I'm looking for is named Jovan Stovanovic. Jovan's a forty-three-year-old two-time loser who lost a leg in a boating accident.

Ironic, given he's a gearhead. Maybe Eastern Orthodox Jesus has a better sense of humor than the Roman Catholic one.

Jovan wasn't home, so the next logical place to look for him is Los Pedro Central. Paid off immediately. I clock his bike out front. Of course, I'm not going to go looking for him *in* the bar. I can handle myself just fine, but it's like Mr. Miyagi said, the best way to win a fight is "no be there."

So the plan is to watch the door, wait for Jovan to leave, then tail him. In the meantime, I'm listening to episodes of my favorite horror podcast, *Who Goes There,* and eating Sun Chips.

Crunch. Crunch. Crunch.

I'm getting to the point where I'm going to have to decide whether to piss in the empty Gatorade bottle on the floor or the junkyard fence when the door opens and Jovan comes out, one arm around a blonde biker chick. They hop on Jovan's bike and pull out of the parking lot, the Harley's rumble shaking my windows when they pass me. I give it a beat and then follow.

Jovan winds through the industrial streets, headed north, away from the port. I try to hang back a bit, if he spots me, his bike'll easily outrace my work car, a sensible and nondescript Toyota Camry. But I've got nothing to worry about. He's clearly drunk, the bike's weaving, and he and the girl are yukking it up about something.

I hope the lovebirds make it wherever they're going without crashing into a semi.

Turns out, they aren't going far. Jovan pulls into the Pedro Tides motel. It's a rancid-looking two-story motor court, the kind of place where the bedbugs have herpes.

Should've brought a Hazmat suit.

I park roadside and grab my crowbar out of the back. It's a family heirloom, my great-aunt Lana used it to pry open a stage door and save the cast and crew of *Scream of the Mummy Queen* from burning to death thanks to a special effects mishap way back in 1957. Mucho sentimental value, but it's also useful in my line of work. Great for opening a stuck door or a stuck mouth.

To be clear, I'm not muscle for hire. Sometimes people try to hire me for that shit—there's plenty of folks who seem to think PIs moonlight as killers for hire—and I always say no, because I'm not a fan of orange jumpsuits and invariably the person trying to hire me to beat someone up is the one who deserves a beating themselves. But sometimes jobs get rough, and it helps to have a 10-pound iron bar at hand.

Guys like Jovan Stovanovic only speak one language and this crowbar's my motherfucking Rosetta Stone.

The other thing I grab is my mask. After my parents died, I started making masks. Cutting up bedsheets, stuff like that. This is the last one I made, stitched together from my mom's studded leather jacket and one of my dad's flannels. It's patchwork, hella ugly, and weathered from years of use. It's not a disguise, per se. More of a calling card.

Like that masked killer I played in two *Campgrind* movies. What's Gregor Mundy without his sackcloth mask?

By the time I cross the parking lot, Jovan and his old lady are off the bike and drunkenly stumbling up the stairs. They don't see me approach, don't have the slightest inkling anything's off until I snake my crowbar around the biker's ankle—the fake one—and give it a good yank.

He pitches forward, cracks his chin on the step so hard it makes *me* wince.

His lady turns, slowly, more confused than panicked—she's probably seen him eat shit plenty of times.

Then she sees me, her eyes go wide, I can sense a scream building.

I put a finger to my lips. Or where my lips would be if I weren't wearing the mask.

That stops her.

Other reason I wear the mask—it kills fight or flight impulses dead.

Jovan rolls over, moaning and spitting up blood.

I watch him, crowbar ready, in case he's going for a gun or a knife, and say, "Sorry about your chin, Jovan, just needed to get your attention."

Jovan moans again, eyes fluttering. I hope he's not concussed.

"Leave him alone," his lady finally says. She's shaking and holding her purse in front of her like a gift.

"I'm not going to hurt him. Uh, any more. And I'm not going to hurt you. Jovan took something that didn't belong to him. I need to know where it is."

The woman scowls. "You dipshit! I told you that was a bad idea."

Jovan pushes himself to a seat, holding his face in both hands. "I didn't do nothing," he slurs.

I take a step forward. "I've got you on video. Now—"

"I told him not to take that job," the woman says, talking to me but glaring daggers at Jovan. "Fuck around with rich people like that dentist and bad shit'll follow, mark my words."

I nod at Jovan's bloody mouth. "Tell me where the tattoo is and maybe Dr. Steve'll give you a discount."

"Fug you." He spits a tooth on the pavement.

"Wait, how do you steal a *tattoo?* Never mind, I don't even wanna know." She leans down, grabs him by the ear, and twists. Jovan yelps like a kicked puppy.

"Tell him," she hisses. "Do you want to fuck around with this guy? He's clearly nuts."

"Thank you, ma'am," I say.

See? Told you the mask was a good idea.

Jovan glares at his feet, since he's not brave enough to look at either me or his lady like that, and mumbles, "The director."

Director? The fuck?

The woman twists his ear one more time, and he says, "Forrest Kearney. S'all I know."

Curiouser and curiouser.

"Thanks for your assistance, ma'am," I say, and hurry back to my car.

Not going to lie; I feel a little bad about Jovan's face. I hope the ice machine's not out of order.

If you're any kind of film buff, you absolutely know the name *Forrest Kearney*. Maybe you haven't seen *Static Whispers* (runner up for the Palme D'or at Cannes) or *The Quiet Afterward*—hey, I don't *just* watch horror movies—but I'm sure you're familiar with his hit neo-noir *Neon Heels,* which *Entertainment Weekly* called "a spiritual successor to *Mulholland Drive,"* or maybe those comic book movies he's been directing ever since.

No, *you're* starstruck.

A quick Google search tells me Kearney lives in Los Feliz, not far from Glenn Danzig and his famous pile of bricks. I like that. Once he started directing superhero flicks, he could've easily afforded a mansion in Brentwood or Bel Air, but no, he's still living in one of LA's hipster neighborhoods.

If he really did steal Dr. Steve's tattoo, maybe he deserves it. He's definitely much cooler than my client.

I get on the 710, headed up to Los Feliz. Traffic gives me plenty of time to chew it over. An A-list director hiring a couple of Balkan bikers to steal a tattoo from a dentist sounds like a rejected plotline for one of those too-smug *Knives Out* movies. But I don't take Jovan Stovanovic for a film buff. Odds are, he told me the truth.

Hell, if his old lady had been twisting *my* ear like that, who knows what I would've spilled.

Figuring out how Forrest Kearney knew Dr. Steve had the tattoo was easy—his headshot's on the dentist's website under *Celebrity Clients!!!*—but as far as why and where it's at now, I've got no clue. I keep thinking I should take Jovan's girlfriend's advice and bow out of this, but canceling a job's a bad look.

Especially when the client's offering fifty thousand simoleons.

Too much skin in the game.

On cue, my phone rings. It's Dr. Steve. I let it go to voicemail, but he just calls again.

"Any updates?" he asks anxiously when I finally pick up. I can practically see him standing there, rubbing his sweaty little hands together.

"I've got some leads."

"What leads? Do you know where the item is?"

Either he's got some twisted fetish for dead tattooed skin, or there's something he isn't telling me.

Something like this should never fall into the wrong hands.

"I'll call you when I've got something," I say, then click off.

Thanks to an accident at the 710/5 split, it takes me over an hour to get to Forrest Kearney's house. It's an unassuming Craftsman with a well-kept yard. The lights are off, and no cars are parked in the driveway, which is great news for me and bad news for Kearney's illicit tattoo collection.

I drive down the block and hook a right. There's an alley running perpendicular to Kearney's street. I park, grab my mask and crowbar, holding the latter low at my side, and head down the alley. It's unpaved, with trash and recycling cans lined up against high wooden fences.

There's also no streetlights. Everything's coming up Milhouse. I count houses till I get to Kearney's place. There's a newly-constructed two-car garage and a back gate you can open easily if your arms are long enough.

Mine are.

The gate swings open quietly. Oiled hinges. Almost like he's paved the way for me. Breaking and entering is mucho illegal, but the house looks empty. If the tattoo's in there, I can grab it and no one would ever know, except Dr. Steve and his accountant.

I pull the mask over my face and head into the yard.

No floodlights burst to life. I cross the yard quickly, cringing when the sagging back porch creaks a little too loudly, then post up by the door. Peer through the panes. Empty. There's no security keypad mounted inside, so when I pick the door, hopefully there won't be a loud, blaring alarm, swiftly followed by armed security.

I shouldn't be doing this.

But I do it anyway.

The lock takes forty-five seconds. The door swings open. No alarms.

In for a penny, etc. I step inside.

The kitchen's nice, new, all stainless steel, and white quartz countertops. Kearney's fastidious, not even a dish in the sink, no mail on the counter, and no stolen strips of dead skin helpfully laid out on the two-seater in the breakfast nook.

I quickly canvass the downstairs rooms. No framed tattoo, but lots of framed movie prints. A man after my own heart. I'm once again struck by the feeling I'm working for the wrong client. But that's the thing, none of this is supposed to be personal. I shouldn't give a shit either way.

This is just a weird job, and I'll be happy when it's over.

I toss the whole house and come up with nothing more than further admiration for Forrest Kearney, thanks to a *Campgrind* Blu-Ray on his shelf. Maybe Jovan lied to me, but if he was lying, why not pin it on another gang? Hell, even the guys who own Dark Art Emporium have more of an apparent motive. The director of *Neon Heels* came from so far out of left field it seemed like it *had* to be true.

I'm back in the kitchen, working out my next move. That's when I hear it.

The hum.

Low, rhythmic, repeating over and over at the edge of my perception. I put an ear to the refrigerator, but that's not it. Something else is making the noise.

On a whim, I crouch and listen to the ground. It's still slight and muffled, but ever so stronger.

Weird.

Most houses in California don't have basements. But something's definitely down there. Crawlspace, maybe?

I go outside and walk around the foundation. And boom, there it is, cement steps leading down to a door. The cement looks relatively new. Maybe this is what Kearney's doing with his superhero movie money. Why buy a Bel Air mansion when you can build semi-secret tunnels under your house?

I listen at the door and there's the hum again. I try the knob, and it's unlocked, no lockpicks needed. Turning it slowly, I push the door open.

The hum grows louder.

The interior of the passage is dark, with more stairs leading down. I've got a Tac light in my pocket, but I also have no desire to get caught, so I step inside and wait for my eyes to adjust. There's a little ambient light filtering in from the backyard. Enough I can see the top of the steps and hopefully won't go tumbling down several flights and break my neck.

Make for one hell of a tabloid story, at least: *Former Campgrind Actor Found Dead in Forrest Kearney's Secret Basement.*

Screw that, I'm not giving TMZ shit.

Feeling my way carefully, I descend the steps. There's a surprising number of them. After the first ten, I feel the wall curving to the left. I round the bend. There's a flicker of light ahead, barely a suggestion.

The humming turns up a notch.

I follow it down more steps around another corner. At the bottom, there's a flagstone floor, lit by torchlight. And that humming?

It's chanting.

Human voices, singing words in a language I don't recognize. Sounds like a lot of them.

That tattoo once adorned the back of a mystic named Brother Enochious. He founded a cult up near Big Sur.

I should get the hell out of here, but I'm *this* close, masked, and have better cardio than most industry people (non-stuntman category).

How can I not take a peek?

I soft-shoe it down a few more steps, hoping nobody's watching the stairs. At the bottom of the steps, there's another passageway curving off to the left. I drop to my haunches and hazard a look around the corner.

There's maybe a dozen people in a large, high-ceilinged, candle-lit room with rough stone walls. They're all wearing white robes and seated on the floor, waving their arms. At the head of the room, on a raised stone dais, is Forrest Kearney. He's also robed in white, but wearing his trademark boxy glasses and a pope hat on his head. A mitre, I think it's called. This one's got gold filigree and has a ruby-studded crimson symbol in the center. It's sort of like a pentagram and a triangle and a plate of spaghetti had a baby.

Something about it makes me sick to my stomach. The design itself, yes.

And also, the fact that it's fucking *pulsating*.

This is the point where I'd usually remember an important appointment and back away slowly, except right next to Kearney on the dais is an artist's easel, and propped on that easel is a framed patch of skin, bearing a tattoo of what looks to be the same symbol on Kearney's hat.

Well, shit.

I pull out my phone and take some surreptitious shots of the tattoo. This is the point where I'm supposed to get out of here, go down to the local police station, and see when they can spare a couple of officers to help recover my client's stolen property. Hopefully in the next two or three years. What I'm *not* supposed to do is wade into a room with a dozen cultists—many or most of whom are probably famous actors, CAA agents, or major studio executives—brain them with my crowbar, then dash back upstairs with a fucked-up skin tattoo tucked under my arm.

Then the door at the top of the stairs bangs open, and I hear a voice call, "Forry, sorry we're late!"

The chanting stops. Forrest Kearney screams "God damn it, Deacon, I told you we were starting at eight!"

And then he looks right at me.

Whoops.

I turn to run, but the guy who played Frak in *Cosmic Custodians* is blocking the stairs. I am not a small man, but Deacon Baptiste is a 7-foot-tall ex-pro wrestler, IMAX-sized in that tiny basement stairway. The sight slows me just enough that by the time I shoot for his legs, there's somebody else behind me, who's apparently swinging a very heavy object.

Lights out, Sexy Dexy.

I'M PRETTY sure I'm not dead.

That's not necessarily a good thing, because my head hurts like a bastard. I try to open my eyes, but the light feels like getting stabbed in the brain, so I snap them shut again. Going back to sleep sounds like a great idea. Definitely a better idea than calling myself "Sexy Dexy," no idea where that came from. I'd like to say that's the concussion talking, but no.

"Wake up," a voice says. Someone slaps me across the face.

"I'm awake," I mutter, grit my teeth, and force my eyes open.

I'm in the middle of the room, tied to a chair and surrounded by white-robed cultists, most of whom are incredibly good-looking and all of whom are peering at me with concern, including Forrest Kearney, my new friend Deacon Baptiste, half the cast of *Cosmic Custodians* and a few other multibillion dollar Paragon movies, and some older men and women who are probably producers or agents.

Kearney stands over me in a way he probably thinks is menacing, holding my mask. "Who are you, and how dare you interrupt our sacred rite!"

"Is that a question or a statement?"

Deacon Baptiste steps forward and smacks me.

I turn my head and spit blood. A few Cosmic Custodians back away, eyeing each other nervously.

Kearney leans in closer. His breath smells like spearmint gum. "Who. Are. You?"

I look at the cultists. "Nobody bothered to check my wallet after you cold-cocked me? Fine. Name's Craven. I'm a detective."

That gets everybody but Kearney and Deacon Baptiste; they're all chattering at once about *the cops*. A few make for the stairs.

"Stop!" Kearney cries.

Baptiste gives everybody a look that freezes them in their tracks.

"No one's going anywhere," Kearney says, then turns back to me. "What're you doing here, detective?"

I don't say anything. I take client confidentiality seriously. Given that Kearney just hired two bikers to steal a taxidermied tattoo from Dr. Steve, Dentist to the Stars, he's probably got *some* idea what a detective might be "doing here" unless he's a complete idiot.

They didn't search me, and I've already managed to work my knife out of my back pocket, so maybe he is.

"I asked you a question," Kearney says, then gestures to Baptiste.

I get whacked again, which sucks, but I don't drop the knife, which is very cool.

Kearney gives Baptiste an irritated look, then turns back to me, wiggling the mask. "I assume you work for the dentist. No matter, he'll get his. What's with the mask?"

"What's with the pope hat?"

This earns me a real punch, one that rocks me so hard I taste blood. Something in my mouth feels loose. I spit blood again, and two teeth come with it.

Fuck. Good thing I know a dentist.

"Who cares about this guy?" Deacon Baptiste says. "Not like he can stop us now."

Kearney regards me carefully. "You're right, Deacon. We will complete the ritual as ordained by Brother Enochious and welcome Lord Morgon into the earthly realm." He turns back to the dais.

I gape at the director. "Lord *Morgon?* The villain from *Cosmic Custodians?*"

Kearney whirls on me so fast his pope hat goes askew, gesticulating madly at the taxidermied tattoo. "Yes! Brother Enochious knew that countless other realms exist beyond our own. Even ones we ourselves have created."

"If we dream it, it is real," the other cultists intone.

"Lord Morgon might have started as a comic book creation, but the moment Sam Schmaltz dreamed him into being, he drew breath in a realm parallel to our own. He is as real as you or I, and he is waiting! Waiting for the faithful to open the gateway to his reality and welcome him home!"

"Welcome, Lord Morgon!" the cultists chant. "The Earth is yours! We are yours!"

Either this is the concussion talking, or these people are utterly insane.

"Okay, let me get this straight," I say. "Even if you're right, and that weird tattoo really is a gateway to a parallel universe—"

"*All* parallel universes," Kearney corrects.

Okay, I think I prefer Dr. Steve now.

"All parallel universes," I dutifully respond, "why the hell would you want to summon the fucking *bad guy* from your own movies?"

Kearney looks at me like I'm the stupidest person alive. "Lord Morgon is all-powerful. He will reward his loyal servants."

"He also believes life is a mistake and wants to murder the whole galaxy." I can't believe I'm arguing comic continuity with the director of *Neon Heels*. "What makes you so sure he's going to reward you? Wouldn't he just kill you all, then the planet, then—and this is assuming aliens exist—everybody else?"

A few of the Cosmic Custodians look at each other nervously. "Yeah," one of them says. I can't remember his name, but I'm pretty sure he voiced the mutant weasel. Or maybe the talking shrub. "If we're summoning anyone from the movie, how about Captain Rascal?"

That being the weasel.

"Yeah!" another familiar-looking cultist says. "Or why not Pulsaria? She's an inspiration for women and girls everywhere."

Jessica Something, I'm pretty sure.

"We're not *making* them real," Kearney says, exasperated. "They're already real, we're just summoning them."

Deacon Baptiste steps forward. "What about Krak? Maybe he could play my long-lost twin in the next movie."

"Shut up, all of you!" Kearney screams. "I'm the fucking *director* and we're summoning Morgon, end of story!"

Everybody in the room shuts it. He *is* the director, after all.

Kearney paces back and forth, taking a few deep breaths. He comes over and shoves my mask over my face—backwards, thanks asshole—then says, "Places, everyone."

There's a dutiful shuffling of feet and then, after a moment, the chanting resumes.

At least I've got my mask back.

And then there's the knife. I wait until the chanting resumes in earnest, hoping they're all too caught up in their circle jerk to notice me sawing through their shittily-tied ropes. It's not easy, I've got zero leverage, and my hands are slick with sweat. I nearly drop the knife, but keep going, feeling the rope slowly part.

The chanting gets louder, Kearney's voice carrying above the rest. Still sounds like gibberish. Given the snappy dialogue in the *Custodians* flicks, you'd think Kearney could come up with a better summoning spell.

I can make out one word, though.

Morgon.

God, this is stupid.

The knife finally cuts through the rope. I give it a second, hoping no one notices, and then shake off the frayed strands and adjust my mask.

The cultists are all on their knees, bowing toward the tattoo. Kearney's up on the dais, arms outstretched, also facing Brother Enochious' backskin. This is my cue to rabbit.

Except the tattoo is doing that weird *pulsating* thing.

My stomach lurches, there's ringing in my ears, but I manage not to lose my lunch. I look around the room, spot my crowbar on a table a few feet away. I should probably just back away slowly and slip up the stairs, but the thing's a family heirloom.

Plus, like with my buddy Jovan, it's hella useful.

I rise slowly, unsteadily, my head swimming. It's a second before my vision stops wobbling. Everybody's so wrapped up in their chants and the pulsating tattoo, nobody notices when I inch over to the table and collect my crowbar.

I'm backing away towards the stairs, ready to brain anybody who rushes me—I wouldn't mind another shot at Deacon Baptiste, to be honest—when something really fucked up happens.

The tattoo, that bizarre symbol, begins to *move*.

There's a horrible tearing sound, the squiggles all unsquiggle themselves, every line in the tattoo pulls away from the center and turns the tattoo into a gaping—

Hole?

Blue stars wink from the other side.

A cry goes up from the cultists, although I think I hear someone mutter something about Captain Rascal. Kearney fist pumps onstage. A hush descends over the room. It's so quiet, I worry they'll hear me breathing.

I know I should go. But I'm rooted in place.

Then there's a flicker of movement, and a smell fills the room, something that seems like a dozen different scents all together, death and rot and ammonia and bleach, plus other things I can't even begin to describe, and then something comes *out* of the gaping, blue-starred hole formerly known as Brother Enochious' back tattoo.

It's a hand.

Not like any hand you've ever seen. It's two or three times bigger than a human hand, eight fingers—*appendages,* rather—a pale chalky white, and the bones—which look more like chitin, segmented and dotted with nodules and spikes and dripping with green pus—are on the *outside*.

Lord Morgon doesn't look anything like this.

Kearney backs away, gawking and shaking his head. "I don't understand, what—"

The hand snakes forward, lightning-quick, and grabs the front of his robe.

And yanks him head-first into the void.

The director doesn't even have time to cry out. He's there one second and then, just—

Gone.

A murmur erupts from the cultists. This isn't what they expected, any more than I expected to get cornered in a basement by an ex-pro wrestler. This looks very bad. If the thing on the other side of the portal just took Kearney and then zipped up the hole between their reality and ours, that'd be a huge loss for cinema but probably a net gain for the human race.

But the gateway's still open, and I have no idea if it even shuts. From this side or the other.

"You fucking idiot," I mumble.

That's when more hands shoot through the portal, each attached to arms a dozen feet long or more. One hand actually shoots *through* Deacon Baptiste, a wet spray of gore and part of his spinal column exiting out the back. He goes limp before it drags him back through the portal. More cultists meet the same fate. Some are stuck in place, others running and screaming and getting snagged by those goddamn monstrous hands with the bones on the outside.

One comes for me. I instinctively hit it with my crowbar.

The second the crowbar makes contact, the appendages blow apart into fragments, which fade into nothing before they can even hit the floor.

I stare at the crowbar uncertainly. I've always sworn by this thing for a reason. Useful in a hell of a lot of situations. And it's iron. If you know your folklore, many cultures think the metal repels all manner of supernatural creatures.

Maybe this particular portal's been opened before.

Maybe we learned something from it.

I spring into action, battering the flailing limbs that are still shooting out of the portal. A few cultists manage to duck and avoid getting sucked in. Since I'm the only one with a weapon, I throw myself between them and the thrashing limbs.

Each time I sock one, it blows apart, quickly disappearing like it was never there at all.

The chick who plays Pulsaria screams. I look down and see a hand clamped around her ankle, pulling her towards the portal. Slower than the one that took Kearney, though.

Maybe I'm hurting it.

I dive across the room and hit it hard. The limb dissipates, freeing Pulsaria to scramble back across the room.

Then the guy who voices the mutant weasel howls. There's a hand on his face like a fucking baby xenomorph, squeezing his skull so hard blood runs in rivulets. The gross little nodules along the thing's arm open as one, revealing tiny, razor-toothed mouths.

I lunge for him, but the hand squeezes hard, crushing his skull with a sickening *pop*. Blood and gore splash out from between its fingers. Tiny tongues emerge from the tiny mouths up and down its arm, and I nearly puke.

I hold on, though, standing my ground, battering arm after arm until my muscles are burning. And still, they keep coming. An endless legion of appendages bent on dragging our universe into its own, or, failing that, crushing the heads of popular voice actors. I need to do something.

A crazy idea hits me.

The hands can't bear the touch of iron. It literally causes them to stop existing, basically instantaneously.

What might that do to an entire universe?

Gritting my teeth, I rush forward, smacking arm after arm out of the way while more stream through the portal. Some of them get around me, others manage to gash my legs or side on their way past. The cultists are still screaming. At least whoever's left, I'd expect a few of them would've fled by now.

I hop the dais, shatter another pair of arms into oblivion. I'm close now. Just a few more feet—

Two hands suddenly grab my ankles and yank like I'm a wishbone. My groin burns. Reflexively, I bring the crowbar down, freeing one leg, but the other's still got me.

While I'm distracted, two more hands grab my wrists.

Fuck my life.

I struggle against them, but they're frightfully strong. I can't move. But whatever they're connected to is badly hurt, because it's pulling me towards the portal slowly, almost reluctantly. Its incursion into our reality is seriously costing it.

I still have the crowbar, though. No matter how crushingly hard the thing's grip is, no matter how much pain wracks my body, I refuse to drop it.

When that thing pulls me through the portal, I'm going to have one hell of a surprise for it.

The portal's inches away, now. I get my first real glimpse of the other side.

It nearly shatters my mind.

The blue stars are weird enough, but now I can see what the arms are connected to. It's a mass the size of a bus, made of the same white material and chitin plates as the arms. Bubbles swell and erupt on the surface, disgorging oceans of pus. There's hundreds of appendages, waving like cilia. Behind it are thousands of creatures like it, no, *millions*, all spewing forth from a fleshy, planet-sized mass.

All of them converge on the portal.

I grit my teeth and get ready to do my best Jim Morrison impression.

"Get off of him!" a woman screams.

The pressure on my limbs suddenly releases, and I drop, hitting the ground so hard the wind's knocked out of me. I roll onto my back and goggle at the sight.

Standing over me, like the goddamn space angel she plays in the movies, chest heaving with effort and jaw set with resolve, is the Pulsaria actress, Jessica Something, brandishing an iron candlestick like a sword.

"Were you really going to die like that?" she asks.

It's a line from the movie, but it's also crazy appropriate in this situation.

I jump to my feet, smack a few more arms coming through the portal. "We have to close it," I shout to Jessica.

She lays into the limbs with her candlestick. "How do you suggest we do that?"

"I've got an idea. On three, toss that candlestick to me and hit the deck."

"What are you planning to—"

"Just do it! One, two—"

"Three!" she says, and tosses the candlestick in the air. Time seems to slow down. The candlestick forms a slow, almost lazy arc over the dais.

Lining up perfectly with the portal.

I smack it with the crowbar. It goes sailing end-over-end into another dimension.

Alley-fucking-oop.

The cluster of arms coming through the portal freeze, and there's a long moment when nothing happens and a sinking feeling hits me, maybe I was wrong and now the whole planet's screwed, but then there's a flash of—not light, exactly, but the other universe's equivalent—and a massive wave of emotion hits me, like an entire reality crying out at once, and then the portal suddenly retracts inward.

I go flying through the air, bash into the brick wall behind me, and end up on the floor, seeing stars and struggling to breathe. It takes me a minute, but I work my way back to my feet and pull my mask off. I glance over at the dais. The tattoo's gone. The *skin* it was inked on is still there, framed and sitting on its easel, but the actual symbol?

Vamanos.

I look over at Jessica, who's blinking and rubbing her face. Her robes are torn and stained with the blood of the other idiot cultists, but otherwise, she doesn't look any worse for wear.

"Thanks for the save," I say.

Jessica comes over to stand next to me, taking in the now-blank canvas of Brother Enochious, and shakes her head. "I knew we should've tried to summon my character."

I give her a wink. "I'm pretty sure you did."

I LEAVE Forrest Kearney's house with Dr. Steve's property, plus Jessica/Pulsaria's number, drive to the worst bar I can find, and drink two beers with barely a breath in between.

Then it's back to Long Beach, the shower, and bed.

The next morning, I drive over to Dr. Steve's office. The receptionist asks me if I have an appointment.

"Nope," I tell her and head into the back.

Dr. Steve's perched over a middle-aged woman with a drill when I enter, banal muzak blaring from the overhead speakers. His jaw drops, and he nearly gives her an impromptu root canal.

Especially when he sees what I've got tucked under my arm.

"One second, Mrs. Kaufman," Dr. Steve says, setting the drill on a small metal table and getting up. "My office, please."

Dr. Steve's office is surprisingly small and cramped with files. He sits behind the desk and motions to a chair in front.

I set the frame face down.

Rubbing his hands together, a grin spreading on his face, Dr. Steve slowly, reverently, turns the frame over.

His grin disappears. He looks at the frame, at me, back at the frame, brows knitting together. "I don't understand."

"We had a few complications," I say. "But I can attest that is 100% Brother Enochious' skin."

"But, but, where's the tattoo? How can it just . . . disappear?"

"Movie magic, I guess."

He gives me a befuddled look. "What?"

"Never mind. Look, I got your *item* back. I kept it quiet. And as a bonus, the guy who stole that will never, ever steal from you again. My personal guarantee."

Dr. Steve rubs his chin. "I see. It's not exactly what I expected."

I hold up my hands. "I get it. The goods came back damaged. I wouldn't feel right about charging you the full fifty."

"So, what're you thinking?"

"I'll invoice you for time and expenses. And one other thing."

Dr. Steve looks at me dubiously. "What's that?"

I smile wide, pointing at the empty gaps where teeth used to be, courtesy of a lunatic ex-pro wrestler. "I could really use a good dentist."

The Suitcase

By C. D. Oakes

The first time Danny saw her was on a Friday.

He was late for school. Again. Managing his time when his mom wasn't around didn't always go the way it should. He flew down the stairway of their apartment building, barely dodging past an old man smoking a cigarette on the bottom step. The man called out as Danny sped past, but Danny didn't stop to tell him he didn't have anything. Hitting the push-bar of the exit door, Danny crashed through and out into the heat of a Los Angeles morning.

Outside, he ran through a cluster of four men who were throwing dice on a strip of greasy cardboard. He nearly tripped trying to avoid a man in a dirty Raiders jersey. The man dropped a bottle he'd been holding and looked at Danny with surprise. The other men stood, one of them spilling beer from a can onto a pile of one-dollar bills in the middle of the cardboard.

"Got *DAMN* it!" Danny heard one of them yell, but he was already past them. Dodging through traffic, he crossed and then leaned against the chain-link fence that cordoned off an empty lot. As he caught his breath, something flashed. He shielded his eyes to get a clearer look. He knew that homeless people hung around the lot, but it wasn't them. It was a girl. What he'd taken for a flash of reflected sunlight was something different. She was wearing a white dress. The clean brightness of it in the middle of the brown dirt lot drew his eye like a light in a dark room.

He heard yelling and spun around to see the guys from the alley waiting for a gap in traffic. He turned to run, but paused to glance back at the lot. The girl wasn't there. The lot was as big as the playground at school, but he couldn't spot her. Horns honked in the street, and he ran for it, backpack whacking him with every step. He didn't stop until he was safely through the school gate.

WHEN HE GOT HOME that evening, Danny made sure to use the building's front door. He understood on some level that Friday nights were awesome and heralded the golden weekend ahead, but he was too young and had too few friends to appreciate it fully. Danny had no plans and less cash. Maybe he'd read his comic books for the hundredth time.

He opened the fridge and found nothing but empty shelves. Disappointed, he shuffled back to the window of their fourth-story apartment. He pushed the curtain aside and peered down at the street, looking for his mom, who hadn't been home since the night before last. The difference between daytime and night in the city was marked by blazing yellow sunlight or dim orange streetlight pouring through the window.

A girl standing across the street caught his eye, wearing what he thought was a white dress. He couldn't be sure it was white because the streetlight she was standing under stained everything orange. The thing he found most strange was not the sleeveless, old-fashioned dress, but that she was just standing there. Nobody stood around in this neighborhood. Even the guys who hung out at the corner paced around. They were constantly moving.

She had long black hair, and the swell of her breasts was small but definite. Danny guessed that she must be in high school. She was staring at his building. He wondered if she could see him in the window, and a tingle passed along his scalp as she tilted her head and looked up. She was looking in his direction! Was it the same person he'd seen in the lot this morning?

Danny jumped as the door banged open behind him. Something lurched through the door, and he cried out with a noise that was too low to be a scream. His heart hammered and didn't slow down even when he realized it was his mom. Not till he saw the grocery bag in her arms did he relax. He dropped the curtain and rushed to see what she'd brought. The world outside the window, and the girl in the white dress, fled his mind.

SUMMER WAS off to a decent start. It was dull, but there was no place Danny had to be. His mom had been gone four nights. Even though he'd rationed them carefully, the groceries had run out.

The last time, she had only been gone a couple of nights. She told him that she had just been hanging out with some old friends, and Danny had an idea of what that meant. They'd had to move back to the city from Grandma's house because his mom was hanging out with her friends too often, coming home less and less. It made him anxious when his mom and Grandma fought. They had both said that it wasn't Danny's fault, but what was he supposed to think when Grandma yelled things like *I'm not here just to raise your goddamned kid!* or *This isn't a childcare center, Lorraine!*

He went to the window and pushed the curtain aside. The girl was there, leaning against the sagging fence across the street. The skin on his arms prickled. She was looking at him. She raised a hand and waved, and Danny jumped. Who was she? Did he know her from somewhere? He didn't know anyone here. He had run across some kids his age when school was in, but the ones who didn't call him names ignored him completely. He hadn't met anyone yet who had waved to him or said hello. Could she be a friend of his mom's? As he stared, her hand dropped back to her side. She leaned forward, away from the fence. She raised her hands, palms up. The gesture seemed to be asking *What? Why are you ignoring me?*

He closed the curtain, separating him and the apartment from the street below. He couldn't see her, but he knew she was still down there. He looked around the place. There was a short loveseat with the armrests duct-taped to keep the stuffing inside. They had a small TV that showed only static since they didn't have cable. He had a stack of comics that he'd read till they had started to fall apart. They were mostly DC titles, which were a little boring compared to the stories in the Marvel books.

The microwave in the tiny kitchenette told him that it was 12:20 a.m., just a little past midnight. Time moved strangely in Los Angeles, and altogether differently during the summer, when he had nowhere to be. His shoes lay on the linoleum of the apartment's tiny entry. He hadn't put them on since the last day of school. He shoved them onto his feet and pulled a hoodie over his head. Ducking into the apartment's single, small bathroom, Danny checked his appearance in the mirror. His hair was a solid brown wedge. It looked a little greasy. He crinkled his nose. He grabbed his Dodgers cap and forced his unruly hair into it. Hooking a finger into the neckline of the hoodie, he pulled it down and sniffed. Not great, but not immediately offensive.

He opened the door and scanned the corridor. Even the neighbors who yelled and fought at night tended to calm down after ten or eleven. Danny made his way to the stairs, then into the night. He pushed the door open a crack, peeked out. The alley was empty. He thrust his hands into the pocket of his sweatshirt and slipped out.

Danny reached the front corner of his building and looked around. There was a guy leaning against the brick wall. He was staring at his phone and didn't look up as Danny emerged from the alley. She was still there, standing by the fence. A few blocks away, Alameda Street was still busy. Even at this hour, the traffic was nonstop. Between the headlights and lighted shop windows, you wouldn't know it was past midnight, but around the corner, it was dark and quiet as Danny crossed the street.

"Hey!" she said and laughed as Danny stepped onto the sidewalk on the far side of the street. Her teeth were perfect and flashed brightly, dazzling Danny. He felt dizzy and warm inside. Her white dress was embroidered in a light blue floral pattern across her chest. The dress's hem brushed the tops of her feet. She wore simple leather sandals.

"Oh my god! I didn't think you'd actually come down here," she said, shining that bright smile on him.

Danny grinned and nodded. "Do I, um, do I know you from somewhere?"

She shook her head. "We haven't met, but I've seen you around. I'm Camilla." She had a Spanish accent, and Danny thought it was cool, exotic.

"Hey, I'm Dan," he said, consciously leaving off the -ny, not wanting her to think he was a kid. "Er, Daniel. Dan for short," he said, cringing inside.

"Great to meet you, Daniel. You're new here?" she asked, but it sounded to him like she already knew that.

"Yeah, we just moved down here from Fresno."

"Nice! Welcome to the neighborhood."

"Do you live near here?" he asked her, more interested in keeping the conversation going than where she actually lived.

She turned toward the fence, looking through it and gesturing across the trash-strewn field. "Over there, not far."

He followed her gaze, but didn't see any houses or public housing buildings like his. Nothing but the back of a strip mall, a couple of blocks away. "Over there?"

Camilla gazed through the fence for a few seconds, then nodded slowly. She turned on the bright smile again and looked at Danny. "Hey, I know you don't know me or anything."

"I don't really know anybody here," Danny said.

"Right. Look, I know we just met, but I was hoping you could help me with something?" The smile faded a little, and she gazed at him earnestly.

He stared at her and didn't answer at first. Camilla's smile slipped, turning to concern. Danny didn't like the dark look her face had taken on. He wanted to see that smile again. "I mean, sure, of course! What do you need?" he asked.

She smiled again, but the teeth weren't on full display any longer. It was a shadow of the radiance she'd displayed before. "It's nothing *too* crazy, it's just that I'm not able to lift it myself," she offered.

Danny gave a nervous laugh, painfully aware that he was a pretty scrawny specimen, even for an eighth grader. "I mean, have you seen the gun show lately?" he asked. He flexed an imperceptible bicep, his face deadpan.

There it was, that smile was back at full wattage, and she had a laugh like the tinkle of silver bells. She walked quickly toward the corner of the fenced lot. There was a bounce in her step, like she was about to start skipping. Another cold frisson washed over his scalp. Was it her laughter? He blinked, and a shudder coursed through his neck and shoulders, traveled down through his stomach and legs before it passed.

"Lead the way. My muscles are at your service," he said.

Reaching the end of the fence, she turned briskly to the right, ducking through a hole that was cut into the chain links. Danny went to follow, but it was a tighter fit than he'd expected. His sleeve snagged on cut ends of fence links as he squeezed through. The streetlight was behind her, silhouetting her figure through the gauzy dress. They were similar in size, and Danny marveled at the way she'd slipped through with such ease. With a start, he realized he was staring and quickly looked away. Camilla watched, grinning, as he finished disentangling himself from the fence.

Camilla spun on a sandaled heel and moved into the weedy, trash-strewn lot. He trotted to keep up as she picked her way around a tumbleweed and a shopping cart on its side with some old blankets in it. *Classy hood*, he thought to himself. She stopped halfway across the field and looked down. The orange light lost much of its strength this far from the street. They stood at the edge of a building's foundation. It was flush with the dirt, with some rebar jutting up around the far edge. There were some cinder blocks still stacked at two of the corners and others scattered around the field. It had been a pretty big building.

There wasn't much else in the lot besides debris and garbage. The faint breeze was hot, like a weak hair dryer. Even so, Danny shuddered as though he'd caught a chill. What was he doing out here in this field? Who was this chick? He was feeling foolish when he looked over at the girl. She was toeing at something with the edge of her sandal. She had her hands clasped behind her back. She looked up at Danny. "It's in here," she said, her voice quiet.

"What is it?" Danny asked.

She stared at the ground. He bent over and brushed at the loose dirt. His fingertips found the edge of a board. Uncovering more revealed the long side of a sheet of plywood, partially hidden in the dust.

His heartbeat sped up as his mind turned over some of the possibilities of what could be beneath the board. Drugs? A gun? Something worse?

"It's just a suitcase," she told him, voice hushed. "It's got some of my things in it."

"Things?"

Her long black hair had fallen partially over her face as she nodded and looked down. She brought a pale hand to her face, pushing it aside and looking at him. He watched her a moment, then slipped his fingers beneath the board and heaved it over, dumping the covering of grey dirt from the top of it. A haze of dust wafted around, diffusing the dim orange light.

Danny waved his hands in front of his face in an attempt to keep from breathing in the dirt cloud. It took a couple of minutes to settle, and neither of them said anything. They both stared into the hole he'd uncovered. An old staircase led down. Danny made out the first three steps, but beyond that, nothing.

Camilla stepped down onto the top stair. She gazed at him, smile all but gone, settled like so much dust.

"It's just down here," she said.

He stared at her.

"It's totally dark in there," he said.

She nodded and looked from him back into the dark. Danny threw a glance over his shoulder at the street. *What am I doing in this field?* He didn't know this girl. He didn't owe her anything. Sure, she had a great smile, and she seemed nice, but goddamn it was dark in there, and the poor judgment of being out here at all was weighing on him.

"Hey, I think there's a flashlight back at my place," he said, "We could grab it and come back, or maybe check it out in the morning?"

"I should get outta here, too. It's way late," she said.

The look that had come over her wasn't sadness as much as it was the complete lack of a smile or the sparkle in her brown eyes that Danny had been drawn to. It made his heart hurt. She headed for the fenced edge of the lot opposite the one on which they'd met, away from the street in front of his public housing building. He watched her and then turned to go.

"Hey, one sec!" she said to him, before he'd gotten more than a few steps.

"Yeah?" he asked.

"I won't be around tomorrow," she said, giving him a hopeful look in the dim light. "I was thinking, maybe, if you have time, you could grab my suitcase?"

He didn't say anything, just stared. He could not mess with this. This girl and her suitcase were nothing but trouble. He had no doubt about it. It had been a while since he'd hung out with anyone, sure, but he knew all too well what getting involved with the wrong type of "friends" looked like. His mom would be unhappy, but Grandma would be devastated, he knew.

The Suitcase

"I need to get it over to Saint Odilia's, the Catholic church over on 52nd," she said, "Ask Father Julio if he's still around. If not, tell the priest that the suitcase belongs to Camilla Espinoza, Luis Espinoza's daughter from over on Mettler Street. He'll either take it from you or at least show you who to give it to."

She turned, and he lost her outline in the dim orange light almost immediately. All he could think of as he trudged home was that he could not get caught up in something like this.

Danny's mom came home a little while after he had gotten back to the apartment. He was happy to see her, and he hugged her tight until she brushed him away.

"I'm tired," she said.

She was a little wild-eyed, and her hair was matted. She was looking rough. Danny was worried, but didn't know what to say. She hadn't gotten this bad at Grandma's, probably because she knew Grandma wouldn't have it. She fell onto her bed without taking off her shoes. He was careful not to wake her as he slipped into his room and got into bed himself.

When he woke, it was after noon. He sat up, his mind immediately dwelling on the suitcase. He couldn't help but think that there might be some money in it, or maybe Camilla's family would give him a reward or something.

Danny looked in on his mom again. She hadn't moved at all, and he started to worry. Taking a tentative step into the room, he gazed at his mom's form in the bed. He relaxed when he saw her back rise and fall. She was breathing, and that was good enough for the time being. He needed a shower, but didn't want to risk waking his mom. Back in the main room that served as living room, kitchen, and breakfast bar, he crossed to the window. He moved the curtain back with his right hand, eyes squeezing shut immediately at the blazing Southern California sun.

Once his eyes adjusted, he looked down at the street, hoping to see Camilla, even though she said she wouldn't be around. Some cars rolled by on the street. The vacant lot looked washed out, like an overexposed photograph. Movement caught his eye. There were two figures near the concrete foundation he'd been at last night. One was dressed in blue and the other in a light grey shirt with a bright orange hat. Had Camilla asked someone else to get the suitcase? He hadn't covered the hole before he'd left. Maybe someone else had found it? Danny thought of her smile and wanted to see it again. He couldn't let someone else get to the suitcase first. He jammed his hat down on his hair, thrust his feet into his shoes, and slipped out of the apartment, making sure the door didn't slam behind him.

He waited for a break in traffic and trotted across the street. He ducked through the hole in the fence, careful not to get snagged on the wire. It was easier when he could see. Straightening, he saw two men sitting in a camp built entirely from refuse. One was sitting on a faded cooler, drinking from a 40-ounce bottle. He crossed to the foundation slab.

The plywood was where he'd left it, half draped across the forgotten stairwell. Chunks of concrete and dirt had been pushed into the old stairwell, filling it in except for four steps. At the bottom of the hole lay the suitcase. The corners of the green and brown plaid luggage were worn nearly through. It was secured with two thick bands of duct tape running its length and width.

He stared at it for nearly a minute. It didn't look all that heavy. He wondered why Camilla couldn't have taken it home herself. He might have gone on staring longer, but he heard the men talking to each other and shuffling in his direction. Danny knew he'd better get moving. He stepped down, grabbed the handle, and lifted the suitcase. Something in it shifted as he climbed out of the hole. The two men had walked over and were staring at Danny as he climbed out again, suitcase in hand.

"What's in there, man? Is that yours?" the one with the bottle asked.

"It belongs to a friend of mine," Danny told the man.

He started back toward the street and the hole in the fence.

"Hey, hold on a second, man. You holding?" the man called after him.

Danny hastened across the lot. When he got to the fence, he looked over his shoulder before ducking through and pulling the suitcase behind him. The men were watching him, but they didn't follow. He made his way back across the street and into his building.

"Daniel? Is that you?" his mom called to him as he walked inside the apartment.

He made for his room, not stopping as he passed his mom's room. He shoved the suitcase against the wall next to his bed and threw a blanket over it. He hustled back through the living room and leaned into his mom's doorway.

"Hey Mom!" he said, happy to see her awake. She looked clear-eyed, more or less.

She was out of bed and getting some clothes out of her dresser.

"I went out to see a friend," Danny said, "But she wasn't around."

His mom stopped what she was doing and looked at him.

"A friend? Does this friend of yours have a name?" She eyed him with what felt to Danny like suspicion.

She didn't give him a chance to respond, immediately launching into a lecture about being careful who he hung around with.

"You don't want to get mixed up with the wrong crowd, Daniel," she said.

"I know, Mom," he answered, resisting the urge to point out the company she kept. He didn't want a fight.

"And 'she,' Dan?" she asked him. "Who is this mystery girl?"

"Her name's Camilla. She lives around the way," he gestured toward the front of the building and the avenue.

"Oh, Daniel." She crossed her arms and looked him over. "You're getting older now. I hope you're being careful!"

Danny blushed.

"You know what I mean, right? I hope that if you do get mixed up with some girl, you'll use protection!"

"Mom, it's not like that!"

"Oh, it never is, trust me. You do not want to become a father at your age. You're much, much too young!"

He nodded but said nothing. His mom took a handful of clothes, picked up a towel from the bed, and went into the bathroom. Danny heard her turn the shower on. He went back to his room and laid the suitcase on his bed. Someone had used most of a roll of duct tape to make sure it didn't come open. The zipper had some gravel in it, but looked fine aside from that. It had the letters C.E. scrawled on a corner in black Sharpie. He realized he'd been staring when he heard the shower turn off. His heart beat faster, and he covered the suitcase up again.

Danny's mom was blow-drying her hair and applying her makeup.

"Mom, do you know where St. Odilia's is at? I think it's a Catholic joint?" he asked.

Her eyes narrowed.

"Is this Camilla Catholic?" she asked.

"No! I mean, I don't know. Maybe. I literally just met her yesterday."

She turned back to the mirror.

"Sorry, no idea," she said.

He figured it had been a long shot to begin with. She rummaged in her closet and produced a pair of red heels.

"Going to meet up with some friends!" her voice bright as she made for the door.

"When will you be back?" he asked. "We need groceries!"

He followed her to the door. She fished in her purse and produced a clump of money. Her mouth was squeezed into a tight line.

"Here, pick us up something. Don't waste it!" she said.

She kissed his cheek and was gone.

"Bye, Mom."

He ducked into the kitchen and rummaged in a drawer. He

grabbed the scissors and returned to the suitcase. He pushed the blanket aside. Did he want to know what was in there? He set the scissors down. He went to the window in the living room and looked across the street. The sky was transitioning to purple, and shadows were deepening on the street below. The gravel lot was still clear, but wouldn't be for long, with night coming on. He didn't see her down there. The lot was empty. He wondered where Camilla was. What was she mixed up in? Maybe the answer was in his bedroom, lying on his bed.

"Screw it," he said, picking up the scissors.

He hacked through the tape and unzipped the suitcase. There was a bundle wrapped in heavy black plastic, also bound with duct tape. He cut the tape that bound the black plastic. The scissors hit something hard inside. He pulled the plastic away, revealing gauzy cloth that had once been white but had gone a shade of yellow.

It had gotten dark outside, and he couldn't see well. Putting the scissors down on the bed, he stood up from where he'd been kneeling beside the bed and crossed to the light switch next to the doorway.

"This is not St. Odilia's," a quiet voice said.

The white dress was much brighter under the LED light than it had been under the orange streetlamp. Danny choked, unable to draw breath. His mouth had gone dry, and his heart was trying to beat its way out of his chest.

"Camilla?" he asked.

Had he left the door open? It always closed and locked automatically. Did someone else let her in?

"Mom?" he called out, his mind racing.

She shook her head, "It's just you and me. I made sure."

His mouth was dry. Danny licked his lips and swallowed. He felt like he should be scared, but he was more excited than anything else at that moment.

"I'm so tired, Danny. I just need some rest. Let's close that up, all right?" Her voice was hushed.

"What's, what is this? I mean," he turned and gestured to the suitcase.

"That's me," she said, "At least, that's what's left."

He knelt beside the bed again. Reaching into the open luggage, he spread open the hole in the black plastic. He saw faded blue embroidery on the old material. He recoiled. There were bones inside the dress.

"What happened to you, Camilla?"

"I trusted someone that I shouldn't have," she said. Her head bowed, and her black hair spilled over her eyes.

He wasn't sure what he was expecting. She didn't glow blue like the ghosts in the comics. He couldn't see through her, like Scrooge's old friend Jacob Marley in the movies. She was definitely more than a shadow. It made Danny's heart hurt, seeing Camilla unhappy like this. Even knowing she was dead didn't dampen the thrill he felt that she was here with him. She looked like she might cry.

He reached out to brush the hair from her eyes, to let her know that he was on her side. Instead of brushing hair, his fingers touched nothing. The hair on his arm raised up, and his skin tingled and crawled. His stomach turned, and he felt dizzy. Danny blinked and retreated a step. He wondered what she was capable of, how far from the suitcase she'd be able to travel. He'd only seen her pretty close to it, so far.

Danny didn't know much about ghosts and had never had an opinion on whether or not they existed, but here she was. It couldn't be a common thing. He didn't know why she had trusted him, but he didn't want to let her down. Still, maybe she could hang out for a while? He tried to think of something that would make her smile. Something that would take her mind off St. Odilia's. Something they could talk about. Ghosts were rare. Friends though? People that he could hang out with and talk to? Also rare. Maybe more rare than ghosts, at least for Danny. It occurred to him that maybe she wouldn't mind hanging out.

"Danny," she said. "Please. I could really use your help."

He nodded. He knew what it was like to need a friend. Who knew that better than him? He sat on the bed, not able to meet her gaze. Danny fiddled with the stack of comic books on his bed.

"Listen, Camilla. We'll get this, get *you*," he said. "We'll get you over to St. Odilia's. But there's no rush, right?" He wondered what she listened to. What music was popular when she had been . . . well, before?

He swallowed and watched Camilla's face become drawn and tight-lipped, disappointment verging on anger. Danny hated to see that shift in her expression and felt a little sick knowing that it was because of him, because he wanted to spend more time with her. He wondered and had to ask. He held out the stack of comics toward Camilla. Maybe after she got to know Danny a little better, just maybe she'd want to stay a while. Maybe she would come to enjoy hanging out. It had to be better than literally doing nothing but being dead, right? They could hold off on bringing her, bringing the suitcase, to St. Odilia's, couldn't they?

"Do you like comic books?"

The Gold Must Go
By S. Faxon

Dropping into his brown-upholstered throne, a cloud of dust rising around him, Jon growled, "No dentist. I don't want to go to no dentist."

"C'mon, Dad. Your mouth is *bleeding*!" His middle-aged daughter argued. "You *need* to go!"

"No."

"Help me understand *why* you won't go?" It sounded like she was talking to the children she worked with rather than a tone anyone would use with their old man.

"Why don't *you* understand?" He flicked his hands up. "You're lying there on your back while they're stabbing and jabbing around your open mouth." His body quaked with a chill. "It ain't right."

Karen planted her hands on her hips. "So . . . what? *You're* afraid of the dentist?"

"I ain't afraid!" He shifted in his chair, bringing his baggy-sweatered arms across his chest. He shot his gaze out the single window of his living space. A line of palm trees swayed in the San Diego sun, but they did nothing to relax him. Instead, they made him want to duck for cover.

"I don't like it," Jon persisted. "Don't like no one touching me." He ground his teeth, disregarding the searing pain radiating from his upper jaw. The cruel, rotting tooth sprang its lightning bolts up his head and down his throat. The monster pushed water up from his eyes at least once an hour, but that wasn't enough to convince him to go to no snake oil salesman.

"I can't believe this!" Karen pressed. "You're a retired marine!"

Jon's back stiffened.

A cold sweat gathered in his salt-and-pepper brow.

Karen bit her lip. "I'm sorry." She held up her empty hands. "I shouldn't have said that. While I understand why you don't like people touching your teeth, as a hero, I know you always know when you need help. And Dad." She kneeled before him, resting her fingers softly on his. "You need help."

He popped up from his recliner, regardless of the screaming pain in his knees.

Karen flung her arm back to avoid being knocked over by Jon. She straightened her posture, mirroring his stance.

Fury nipped at Jon's skin as he yelled, "*Help!* That's what you called it when you moved me into this damn place! A Southern California paradise for the soon-to-be deceased!"

"Christ, Dad. They treat you *very* well here! This is *the* nicest retirement community in town!"

She made it sound like this was some vacation rental and not a one-way ticket to the end. The one-room condo surrounding him was more like a cage than a home. It reminded him of the rat holes he had to climb into back in Vietnam. Every time one of the palm fronds outside his window swayed, his attention shot up, ready to aim between the glistening eyes of a sniper, though nothing but crows were usually there.

And the staff here treated him no better than his daughter. Talking to him like he was some snot-nosed toddler, carting around cups full of medicine that the residents weren't considered competent enough to take on their own. It was indecent. Cold. He could never understand how anyone could call a place like this a *home*.

Rolling his tight shoulders back, he said, "A home. Home means something. Used to, at least. This? The only thing this place means is that death is just a hard knock away. That your kids don't give a damn about you."

"Dad!" Karen's voice cracked as she slammed her hands down to her sides, looking like the little girl she would always be to him. "That's not fair!"

"Not fair?" He ground his teeth together, still ignoring the searing pain that made the edges of his vision go black. "It ain't fair that a man comes home when his brothers get blown up in a jungle they had no business in. It ain't fair that a man's gotta live with that for the rest of his life while the rest of the world spat at and turned their back on him. This goddamn tooth ain't nothing in the scheme of things nor is your *in-con-ven-ience* of taking care of your old man." He stormed into the bathroom and slammed the door.

This tiny, windowless room felt no bigger than the heads on the ship he was once deployed on. While those, too, didn't speak much to the comforts of home, at least those didn't have the hideous yellow wallpaper this one did.

Jon leaned on the cold counter. The bends in his swollen knuckles begged him for relief from the chill and the pressure, but this time he did not follow orders.

He had been told what to do his entire life.

From his old man to his squad leaders. His boss at the factory where he served and sweated for a measly pension to compensate for what his military one did not.

And now from his daughter.

He wasn't a hero.

He was just a pawn in a game he could not win.

And no white-coated snake oil salesman was going to take anything from him.

But. . .

Jon pulled his lip up.

Blackened, swollen gums sat beneath the golden crown on his left canine. A sickening yellow, pus-filled boil glowered at him from above the tooth.

"The gold must go," he confessed.

Jon brought his blurry eyes to meet his gaze over the sink. Red veins ran like spider webs across his nose and cheeks. Silver wires stuck out from the top of his head.

He was no longer anything to look at anyway. He wasn't even a shadow of the man he used to be. What difference would one less tooth make?

Jon gulped.

He had been shot through the calf in Vietnam, seen his buddies blown to bits, and bush-whacked his way through a thousand miles of mosquito-laden swamps; this tooth would truly be nothing.

Jon's hand flew up to his mouth.

He latched onto the tooth.

The slightest contact made water flood his eyes.

A black halo pressed upon his vision. Through his squinting lids, he watched blood run from his gums and over his fingertips.

His gums squelched as his slipping fingers pinched and wriggled the tooth back and forth.

The muscles in his neck strained in sharp ridges.

His heart thrummed like automatic rifles firing.

A deep, muffled cry echoed in his bathroom.

But the tooth would not budge.

Fists banged on the door, but it did not sound like flesh to wood. It sounded like heavy machinery from over the nearby hills.

He did not hear his daughter's voice begging him to come out, muted amid the screams from his fallen brothers.

Jon whipped his body back and slammed his face down on the counter.

The exploding pain was a small sacrifice to conquer the enemy.

He leaned back again.

The Gold Must Go

His blaring, swirling vision could still see the gold peeking through the monsoon of blood.

Thwack!

His face dashed against the cold counter once more.

The copper flooding his mouth tasted of the mud of a country he longed to forget and longed to beg for forgiveness.

Jon straightened.

His body swayed.

He clutched onto the sink's rim, slick from his body's grease.

For a moment, all was still, like listening to the hum of the muddy river navy and knowing that, for the moment, all was clear.

In the mirror, for just a moment, he saw a marine.

The bathroom door opened.

Jon stepped out.

Karen stepped back.

Her shaking hands reached for her gaping mouth. Her eyes were as wide as the moon.

Jon did not say anything.

Could not.

Would not. He knew there was no point in trying to speak from his shredded, swollen, dangling lips.

Karen fell to her knees on the hard tile floor.

A stifled plunk landed before her.

Gold glistened in a river of red.

Swipe Right for the Afterlife

By Theresa Halvorsen

> Hi. I have a question.

I LET OUT A GROAN AND DROP MY HEAD INTO MY HANDS. Not another new chat. Girlfriend, this pop-up feature's a pain; should've NEVER put it into production. Lordy, I need to install some AI-bot to at least filter out the biggest questions.

- *How do I upload a profile picture?*
- *How do I choose someone to date?*
- *What if I can't hold a phone because my hands are incorporeal?*

Okay, the ghosts looking for love with or without corporeal hands aren't MY responsibility, but my business partner's. And I can't automate their asks for help. The living are my responsibility. And this living person is waiting for me to respond.

> My name is Billie. How can I provide you with exceptional service for Lost Souls Matchmaker today?

> Hi Billie. My name is Calla. I've been having some difficulty with your app.

Girl, just cut to the chase.

> Hello Calla. It's wonderful to make your acquaintance. I do apologize for the difficulty you've been having. Can I get some more information?

I lean back and wait, but the dots showing she's still typing keep going. Holy cripes. Is she writing a novel or something? Picking up my phone, I flick through some Instagram posts, looking for inspiration for ads. I am out of marketing ideas and have NO problem copying what our competitors are doing.

Finally, her words appear on my monitor.

> Your chat feature won't let me link to a website. But I need to show you something. Can I send an email?

No. We'd been through this. Or at least I had—in my head. Emails meant I had to check and respond to them, IN ADDITION to checking and responding to the annoying chats. According to the time management YouTube channel I was following, I needed to add efficiency to my tiny start-up so my partner and I could maximize our time AND our profit.

And that meant emails had to go. I couldn't keep spending hours each day scrolling through, reading, and answering annoying emails. I move my keyboard to my lap and prop my Doc Martens onto my desk.

> Could you describe the problem you're having in more detail, please? Is the app malfunctioning?

Someone else starts a chat while Calla is typing—an easy question about uploading a profile picture. I send instructions: A profile pic for a dating app should be different from your Insta profile pic, but uploading it should be the same process. Honestly, we're pretty much the same as most socials and dating apps.

Except for one teeny TINY thing.

The dead use our app. And by dead, I actually mean ghosts.

Oh, and caveat! By dead ghosts, I mean anyone who'd died after 1995. Any older than that, and the concept of finding love through tapping on a screen just doesn't make sense.

Those older pre-boomer ghosts break my heart; they're lonely too and deserve to find someone to spend the rest of their afterlife with. But the ghosts that CAN'T use an app need to go to the ghost mixers to find a date. And that's ASSUMING they can leave whatever area they're haunting. And assuming they know they're dead. AND assuming they aren't stuck in some sort of repeating loop of time. And assuming...

Calla disconnects from the chat, the notification popping up on my screen, distracting me from my train of thought. Guess her problem isn't that big of a deal, or she wouldn't have left. Probably a good thing. I have a lot to do.

I slurp up the last of my iced coffee; the noise echoes in the warehouse space we'd rented for this business. There are cobwebs in the piped-out ceiling, and the walls are a dingy gray from old, embedded dirt. We have plans to bring on more staff, create an open concept space of desks where ideas and energy can flow. But there's no money. So right now, it's just Wes and my L-shaped desks set in the middle of the empty space. He'd decorated his area with Star Trek and Star Wars... stuff. Mine was at least cute with a Hello Kitty and anime items I'd picked up at garage sales.

SPOILER: It turns out there aren't enough ghosts out there with access to money who have died after 1995. Soooooo, now Wes and I are branching out and trying to grow this business with living people.

We know the dating app marketplace is a bit saturated, but we've got traction. I am TRULY proud of the little personality questions I've put together and how the algorithm works to pair interests, political leanings, and what people think they want on dates. AND—best part—we use the money from the living to support finding the dead LOVE.

I adore my job. Now, I just need it to start making money so I can spruce up this space and move out of my parents' house. Though—as everyone knows—San Diego is expensive as AF so still living at home even if I'm in my thirties isn't that big of a deal. I know SO MANY people like me.

My business partner, Wes, slouches in, yawns dramatically, and dumps his bag onto his desk, logging onto his computer all in one move. He clicks on a novelty Star Trek desk lamp—the Enterprise, with all its windows glowing. It seems odd to me—I don't remember the windows glowing in the show, but WHAT do I know?

Wes is the ghost side of *Lost Souls Matchmaker*, because he can actually see ghosts. I can't. I've tried. But the genius, the GENIUS, is that Wes and I are able to mesh our skill sets and create a viable start-up. So I do all the work: the customer service, the marketing, the finances, the operations of our business, and Wes . . . he talks to the dead. It's an acceptable trade-off because without him—whelp—there wouldn't be a *Lost Souls Matchmaker* app.

He just isn't a morning person. Or really, a daytime person since it's pushing eleven, and he looks like he has just woken up and rolled out of bed into wrinkled jeans and a coffee-stained sweatshirt.

"Morning, Billie," he rumbles, scritching at the beard on his chin and waiting for his computer to log him in. "I like your headband."

"Thanks," I said with a cheery wave I know he'll hate. "I'm trying something NEW—since I haven't had time to get my hair done in forever; I'm using this band to cover the grays that are popping in. Oh! And helpful tip; I don't think they're called headbands anymore, but just bands."

He grunts and turns his back on me to start typing.

I swirl the ice in my plastic cup and make the straw go up and down with an annoying *who-ha*. Wes reaches over our desks to pull the top off my cup.

"Hey," I say, though it doesn't have much malice. I am being annoying. I AM self-aware, THANK YOU.

Wes ignores me, toggling his mouse, attention on the screen. Whatever. Guess it was up to me to make conversation. I wasn't going to sit in silence for the rest of the day. It was boring enough around here.

"Did you see one of our newest ghosts matched and went out on a date last night?" I ask. "A Xander Shaw? Didn't you find him on the side of the 15 freeway just outside of Temecula a few weeks ago? He'd gotten stuck there, and you got him unstuck. He went on a date last night. It only took him a few weeks to acclimate AND find a match. I think that's our best E-VER!"

Silence. God, he must be totally in the zone. Since the point of this app was to match ghosts, I always wanted to know how it was going and whether dates had gone well. I can just visualize a wedding one day, all the ghosts floating around, saying vows, everyone awwwwwwing, and then a massive party. That would be my CROWNING achievement. But the ghosts are Wes's side of the business, and he hates it when I poke around in the ghost profiles and stalk who is dating who and how it is going.

"Someone sent an email through the *Contact Me* page," Wes growls.

"No f-ing way," I snap. "I deleted all the links, all the mentions of our email." Anxiety punches through my chest. I'd checked; I'd triple-checked. Damn-it. There goes my afternoon plans of building

Instagram ads. Now I had to go through every bit of our website and app again, making sure the email feature was gone, gone, GONE!

"Sent it to you," Wes says in a monotone.

I click the refresh button on my email. Nothing. I click a few more times, my mouse loud in the quiet space. "Hasn't come through." Stupid internet—I HATE paying good money for crappy Wi-Fi. "What did it say?"

"Didn't read it." With an enormous sigh, he clicks a few buttons and leans forward, studying his screen. "Wait, wait—I'll take care of —" His fingers flew so fast I thought a key from his keyboard would come flying off. "I'm going to recall—"

"No way," I say with a laugh, spotting the email popping into my inbox. I click on it before it can disappear.

It's from Calla, the woman I'd been chatting with on the app a few minutes ago. Guess she'd been able to find the email address after all. I skim it. Cripes, she must have some sort of corporate job—this email has a bulleted timeline of events.

But instead of detailing some sort of glitch in the app, she's detailing her date from last night. Apparently, she'd matched using our app, and she and her date had gone on some cheesy ghost tour up in Temecula. According to bullet point three, her date had gotten scared by what was probably some pretty lame, made-up stories, and literally ran away in the middle of the tour, peeling out of the lot.

AssHOLE.

But I am SO confused; why is she sending this to us? Our contract clearly states we aren't responsible for the quality of the dates. If she chose some lame-ass date, that's not our fault. I reach the end of her timeline and blink. I re-read it. Then again. My heart drops, and darkness crowds around my vision. There was no way.

Breathe!

With a deep breath, I click on the link provided—an obituary for a Xander Shaw. The same Xander I'd asked Wes about. The DEAD GHOST Xander. Had he managed to go on a date with a living person?

The darkness crowds in again, and I take five breaths, focusing on what I can see, then what I can hear, then what I can touch. The darkness retreats.

"Tell me we didn't send a ghost on a date with a live person," I ask Wes.

"Okay. We didn't," he says. With a push, he rolls away from his computer and does some wrist exercises. "I'm gonna go across the street to the coffee place and get a cold brew. You want another iced coffee?"

"No," I say. "Tell me there's NO WAY a ghost matched with a live person."

Wes shrugs and tugs his beanie down over his ears. "Okay, there's no way."

"It's a closed system."

"Yep. So did you want an iced coffee or not?" He pulls out his phone, his fingers flying across the screen. "I'm going to order in advance, so let me know. But I need the walk, so I'll go to the coffee place a few blocks down." He looks up at me. "Basically, I'm giving you a few minutes for whatever freak-out you're gonna do. Then I'll explain why it's not possible for a living to match with a ghost."

I put my hands on my hips. "I'm not going to freak out."

"Great. Still gonna give you some space."

"It's fifty degrees out," I say. "I'm fine. Just order from the place across the street. The wind is blowing off the ocean. It's totally too cold for a walk."

He shrugs. "I got my beanie and need the break. Let me know if you want that iced coffee in, say . . . five minutes?"

"I mean it's your life," I murmur, turning back to my computer and re-reading Calla's email. There was no way she'd gone out on a date with a ghost. But how would this Calla-person know Xander's name? How would she know he was the ghost I'd JUST asked Wes about? Were there two Xander Shaw's in the system?

I shiver, suddenly feeling cold. It is January; the cold must be seeping in through cracks or something in this old warehouse. There was probably no installation in this building. I click a few buttons and order a space heater to be delivered to my parent's house. No reason to be uncomfortable when space heaters are only like thirty bucks.

I look up the woman who'd sent the email—Calla. My shivers increase, my knee jiggling. Cripes, it's getting colder and colder in here. Maybe I am heading into peri-menopause, but instead of hot flashes, I'm having cold flashes. Awesomeness.

I send a text to Wes. *I would like a hot venti chai, please.* He gives me a thumbs-up emoji, and I begin digging through Calla's profile.

She'd matched with several men and one woman since joining the app a few months ago. I click through her messages and realize she's one of those who prefers to text rather than using the messaging system of the app I'd designed. That was a mistake; she was paying for unlimited messages and keeping her phone number private protected her (didn't anyone read my tip sheets?), but what-EVER . . . she could do what she wanted.

Sure enough, the last person she'd matched with was Xander. I click on his profile, digging in. Yep, he is a ghost, and I confirm he is in the closed ghost system designed to keep the living and dead apart. What the effing happened?

I dip into the code, my fingers starting to tremble across the keyboard. It's sooooooooooo cold. I puff a breath out, wondering if I can see it. Nope, but it feels like I should. Where is Wes with my hot chai?

Something moves behind me, a whisper on the cheap carpeting. I spin around, knocking over my cup, the remnants of my iced coffee soaking into the ground. Nothing. Maybe it was the air turning off. Maybe that's why it is so cold—the air conditioner is broken and blowing frigid air into the room.

I scribble a note on a Hello Kitty post-it to contact the owner of the warehouse so he can fix it before we freeze to death. I fall back into translating code. GOTCHA! There it is. A small error allowing the two systems to cross, for ghosts and the living to match, if the parameters are right. I keep reading—this is complex code, and I KNOW I didn't write it. Wes must have screwed up; there was no EFFING way—

Something hits the back of my head. I scream and bring my hand up to touch the spot. Sticky wetness soaks my hair and skin. I spin around.

Nothing.

BAM!

This time, something hits the side of my head. I fall to the ground, keeping my hands over my face, trying to ward off the . . . desk lamp? Wes's desk lamp of the Starship Enterprise is floating over my head. As I watch, it comes down toward my face . . . at warp speed.

I OPEN MY EYES. Or they are already open. Or something. I can't seem to blink or close them. The light in the warehouse is different, objects slightly off. My chair is sunk barely into the floor, my desk floats an inch off the floor.

My heart pounds, but it feels weird, liquidy or something, before the feeling stops. What the EF is happening?

I hear a voice, faint and echoing. I turn, planning to follow it, but suddenly, Wes is in front of me, and I'm halfway across the warehouse. Is this what a concussion feels like? I focus on Wes, but he doesn't turn to look at me. Instead, he's focusing on something on the ground, wearing my Doc Martens.

"Appreciate it," he says to something shimmering in the air in front of him. I blink and realize it's a person, a murky person the light ripples across, the colors of their hair, body, and clothes muted, like someone has put up a weird filter on an Instagram post. The person turns like they're going to walk through the warehouse wall.

Oh YAY! I am finally seeing ghosts. I take a step forward—was this the Xander, Cala had met? This job is going to be SOOOOOOOO much easier now. I extend my hand, a huge smile hurting my cheeks as I step over the—what the hell is that on the ground?

Oh, wait. That's me. On the ground. How am I staring at myself lying on the ground?

I lean closer; there's blood and EW—my eyes are partially open. Remembering, I put a hand up to the back of my head. No blood, no pain, no bump. I take a breath and don't feel the air blowing in through my nose, don't feel my lungs expand. My hand on my chest, I try again. Nothing. No heartbeat, no chest movement, no weird sensation of clothing touching my body, my feet against the ground. I feel NOTHING.

Oh no. This isn't a concussion. That fucker has killed me!

I spin on Wes. "Why? I didn't do ANYTHING to you. Worked my ass off for this dumb-ass business that doesn't make any money. I still live with my parentings for effing sake! You THINK you're ever going to get a moment of peace again? Where you go, I go! You'll never even poop in peace. Every time you wipe, I'll be there to make sure you don't get shit stains on your underwear. In fact—"

Wes crosses his arms, waiting until I run out of steam. "I need you," he says simply.

"Uh DUH! So why'd you kill me?"

"I need someone who can go where the ghosts go and convince them to join the app. I need them to understand what they get when they date the living."

"Yeah, no I will not do that. You can't have the dead date the living."

"Look." He steps over my body and sits down in my desk chair, the chair spinning slightly. "The dead need the living. I found out a date, a hug, a make-out session, can mean the difference between ghosts having hands and not. Best way for ghosts to meet the living to date them is through an app! See the genius?"

"Uh NO. This is stupid. You killed me for THIS?"

He spins fully around in the chair. "I killed you because you figured it out, and I know you. You were going to shut down the app—"

"Uh YEAH. Living and dead can't DATE!"

"Why?"

"Because it's wrong. You're not telling the truth." I fold my arms against my chest, and gasp when they go straight through my body. Where did my chest go? I can still see my boobs, but they're completely see-through. I hold up a hand, wiggling my fingers—sure enough—my fingers are disappearing melting away like a bad-special effect in an 80s movie.

"What's happening?"

"Oh, you're going fast," Wes says. "I can fix that."

I hold up both hands. They've nearly disappeared. I look down—my Doc Martens are gone—my feet cut off at the ankles. Wait! I'm not ready. There is so much I still want to do—go to New Zealand, see the Great Barrier Reef before it's gone, rewatch all of Schitts Creek again.

"How can you fix this?" I ask Wes.

He leans close and breathes in my face. With a gasp, my hands reappear and I feel my feet in their Doc Martens hit the ground. I fold my arms against my chest, which is now back, thank-you-very-much.

"How long will this last?" My voice is quiet, probably quieter than it'd been in the last five years.

Wes's lips twitch in the closest to a smile he ever gets. "Depends. Being around the living gives you life, for lack of a better word, but you need it all the time. If you go a few hours without being around the living, your body is gone. And it's super hard to get it back—not impossible, but really hard. That's why there's so few ghosts more than a hundred years old. A kiss might sustain you for a week or two and you can take a break from the living. A fuck might give you a month. See why the dead are willing to pay a fortune for a dating app? So they can keep living."

I did. And I wasn't ready to be done with this life. "Okay," I whisper. "What do you need me to do?"

AUTHOR'S NOTE: Cala and Xander's date is in the story, Ghost-Hunting for Love, from Temecula Valley Writers and Illustrator's anthology "Stay Awhile."

Acheron Gas & Go
By Dennis K. Crosby

"Talk about dark and stormy nights. This is ridiculous," said Nikki. She was speaking just loud enough for Justin to hear. "Of course, if we'd just stayed in Palm Springs another night . . ."

Heavy rain drowned out the silence, but the discomfort remained.

Justin and Nikki had planned a four-day getaway. They'd considered camping in Joshua Tree, but decided comfort was more important than adventure. They were coming off yet another fight and knew that nothing fed discord between them like tent living. Such was their history. She'd never been to Palm Springs, and with everything he'd heard about it, Justin thought it might be a nice way to make up for his latest transgression, even though deep down, he was certain it was her fault. They'd had dinner at Coasterra overlooking the San Diego Bay Thursday night. There was even a lovely walk along the harbor. The evening was filled with all the light and giggly love and promises a post-fight date night brings. Friday morning, they were on the road to Palm Springs. Justin even factored in some stops along the way in little towns for sightseeing and shopping in local stores.

The trouble started in the second town they'd stopped in.

As usual, they got into a fight about something silly. Last time it was something regarding a show on Netflix. This time it was about the name of the Indigenous tribe that made a particular piece of jewelry she'd wanted. She'd give him the silent treatment because she claimed he was always so damned dismissive. Justin didn't care, though. At least, he'd act as if he didn't. He'd flirt with someone else. Sometimes it was out of spite. Mostly though, it was harmless. Either way, he wanted to show her that he could be with anyone else, but he *chose* Nikki, and she should be happy about that.

They tried to work through it the rest of the day. Friday night wasn't too bad. An evening in a new place can sometimes help. But, by Saturday afternoon, the novelty had worn off. The tension was too great, so they thought it best to cut their trip short by a day. In actuality, it was Justin who made the unilateral decision to cut it short, which then led to another argument, resulting in the decision to leave immediately after he'd said something that just would not go back in the bottle.

"I may have severely underestimated how far I could get on that quarter tank, too."

"Jesus! Don't even joke like that," said Nikki.

"I'm not. We're pretty low. It's hard to see in this storm, so call out if you see lights. It might be a gas station."

"Why don't we just pull over and wait for the storm to pass? Save some gas."

"It's gonna get chilly. We'll need the car on to stay warm. Let's just push through. There's got to be a gas—"

"Oh my God. Look."

The side of the road was lit up by road flares. The scene was ugly. One car, a Mercedes-Benz, was mangled. Almost unrecognizable. The only thing clear was the car logo and a license plate that read: TIME4T. There was no way anyone could have survived the collision. The second car, a Jeep, while damaged, may have been salvageable. If not for the damage, it was identical to the car Justin was driving. He had classic car tastes, but an affordable car budget. He liked his Grand Cherokee, though, and found himself empathizing with the driver of the damaged sister vehicle.

Through the rain, Justin made out a man in coveralls and a heavy jacket, standing at the rear of a red tow truck. He was securing the damaged Jeep. As they neared the scene, Justin felt his car slip from his control. He tried hard to maintain, but to no avail. Justin ran into the hoisted Jeep, narrowly missing the tow truck driver.

"Oh my God!" Nikki screamed.

Justin stopped. With both hands on the steering wheel, he took several breaths, desperate to calm his nerves.

"You okay?" he asked.

"I'm fine," said Nikki, her tone saying she was anything but.

"Sorry."

He meant it—mostly.

Justin stepped out of the car and was immediately attacked by the rain.

"God, I'm so sorry. Are you all right?" he asked, walking to the tow truck operator, yelling over the rain.

"I'm good," said the driver. "I don't think anything was damaged more than it already was."

Justin saw the Jeep swaying a bit. He wondered if it was unsteady due to weather, or due to him hitting it. Everything just seemed so unsteady.

"Do you need help? I feel so—"

"Don't worry. I got it. You should be on your way. And take it slow. Might be best even to wait this out."

The tow truck driver was not much older than Justin, but he carried an air of authority and capability that was not commensurate with his age. That hoist, though. It was just moving so much. *He knows best, right? It's probably just the wind. I'm sure it's all fine like he said.* Justin acknowledged him, apologized again, then ran back around to the driver's side of his car. Before he got in, he glanced back at the Jeep just as a flash of lightning hit.

"Holy shh—" he whispered.

He was certain he saw someone inside. Someone . . . familiar. Torn between saying something, and bolting, he quickly got in his car. The rain continued to undercut the silence and added to the tension of the weekend. Justin looked at Nikki and could tell by her expression she'd heard the driver's recommendation. Annoyance flared within. He wanted to be out of there. Done with the weekend. Done with the relationship. He checked the road, hit his directional, and pulled away. Looking back at the scene in the rearview mirror, Justin was almost certain he saw the tow truck hoist shift, and the Jeep fall. Worse still, he was almost certain it fell on the tow truck driver.

No. That wasn't on me. He said it was fine. It was fine. Right?

He continued driving.

THE STORM WAS RELENTLESS, but Justin kept driving down California's State Route 79, determined to get . . . well . . . anywhere. There were few cars on the road, which was good, but also underscored the severity of the weather. Some had pulled over to wait things out. Most of the vehicular life seemed to be SUVs, and even they were traveling well under the speed limit with blinkers on as safety precautions.

"Justin, please. This is bad. Just pull over. We're not in a hurry. We can—"

Nikki's words were cut off as Justin slammed on the brakes and began to skid, then hydroplane. He tried desperately to regain control of the car, but nothing seemed to work—until their momentum was halted by another car. The sound of metal on metal was almost as loud as the thunder. Neck and back pain flared through him from the shock. Once everything settled, they found themselves window to window with a black Chevrolet Stingray.

"Ugh," moaned Justin.

Dizziness took hold. Pain seared across his chest from the seatbelt. He moved slowly. Gingerly. Then he seemed to remember he had someone with him when he heard a low whimper.

"Oh my God! Are you okay?" he asked.

"Um . . . yeah . . . I'm . . . good," said Nikki, slowly moving her head. "Dizzy."

"Anything broken? Wait. Don't move yet. Just sit tight for a bit. Let your body settle."

Despite their arguments, he was genuinely concerned, though it came mostly from the optics. How would it look if they left Palm Springs suddenly, after a weekend of arguing, in view of dozens, only for her to get seriously injured in a car accident? Especially after she'd repeatedly insisted they wait until the storm passed.

Justin tried to see what damage he'd caused the other driver. He was right next to the driver's side window of the Stingray. He couldn't see much as the rain continued its ceaseless barrage. Then came a deafening crack of thunder with a starburst flash of lightning. In that brief moment he saw the driver of the other vehicle slumped over to the side, head resting against a cracked window, with blood streaming from his forehead.

"Oh damn. Damn, damn, dammit!"

"What?" asked Nikki.

"The guy next to us. He's hurt. We gotta—"

Another intense flash of lightning came as Justin was staring out the window, only this time, he was met by a pair of blood red eyes.

"Holy fuu . . .!"

"What? What?!" asked Nikki, startled.

Justin couldn't find his voice. He was still wet from the rain, but that was not the cause of his shivering. Ignoring Nikki's onslaught of questions, he drove forward a bit. He was tempted to take off—again, self-preservation taking hold. Instead, he got out, walked to the driver's side of the Stingray, and knocked on the window. He got no response. He then checked the handle and was surprised to find it open. As the door swung out, the driver tipped out, saved only by his seatbelt. The car was empty otherwise. Justin managed to get him upright enough to unclip it, pull him from the car, and drag him to his Jeep.

"What are you doing?" asked Nikki. "We need to call someone. He could be seriously injured."

"No one's coming in this," said Justin. "You got a signal? Cuz I sure as hell don't. We can't just leave him here."

"He could be—"

"Nikki! Please!"

More tension.

More awkwardness.

More anger.

Justin got the stranger settled in the backseat, and within minutes he pulled away. Checking his driver's side mirror he saw the impossible.

The Stingray came to life, drove away . . . and vanished.

IN HIS MIND, the only thing louder than the rain and thunder was his heartbeat and the voice in his head screaming at him for almost killing someone. Then he thought back to the tow truck driver, and he realized that he may have actually caused the death of someone else. In the distance, Justin heard yet another voice. It pleaded with him to stop and wait for the storm to pass. It was a dying sound coming from a distant land. At least in his head.

In reality, it was Nikki in the passenger seat.

"You never listen to me. I mean, why are you even with me? Like, seriously! And you wonder why we have so many problems. You have absolutely zero respect for me! And now there's a guy in the backseat.

He could be dead or dying. Seriously injured at best. All because you don't want to stop driving."

"Look, we'll take cover as soon as we find a gas station," he said, ignoring the commentary on his behavior. "We can fill up, wait a little, and take off. Hopefully, we can find some help for this guy, too, while we're there."

"I'm . . . okay," said a harsh, gravelly voice from behind.

Justin jumped in his seat at the sound. Nikki's yelp didn't help.

"Oh my God!" she yelled.

"Dude! Ho . . . holy crap! Are . . . you're . . ."

"Sore. But awake, and okay. I think."

"Man, I am so sorry. I don't know what happened back there. I just . . . lost control."

"S'alright, son. Accidents happen."

"I wasn't sure what to do. Didn't want to leave you. Figured we'd find a spot up ahead and go back for your car in the morning. Are you hurt? Feel like anything is broken?"

"Naw. I'm . . . groggy. But good."

The passenger sat up fully and Justin got a look at him in the rearview mirror. It was dark, but occasional flashes of lightning helped. He was maybe forty-five, with coarse skin and salt and pepper hair . . . some matted to his forehead with blood. His voice, though, sounded older. *Felt* older. This guy seemed to have a lot of miles on him.

"What's your name, sir?" asked Nikki.

"It's uh . . . just call me Seth. My friends all call me Seth."

"Okay. Seth. I'm Nikki. This is Justin. We are so very sorry."

"I know. It's okay. Everything will work out. We're all okay. That's what's important," said Seth.

"You live around here?" asked Justin.

"Not far. In fact, I know of a gas station up ahead. About ten miles down. We can stop there and get help. Even a meal maybe if you're hungry. I know the owner."

"Pretty barren stretch. Somebody actually lives here?" asked Justin.

"Yeah, it's a lonely stretch of road, but it has stories," said Seth.

"What kind of stories?" asked Nikki.

"Oh, fun stories. Crazy stories. Spooky stories. Lot of history here. Most of the managers of the station know them. It's like they pass them down from manager to manager. Hey, if we're lucky, maybe you'll hear a few when we get there."

"Lots of accidents on this road? Lots of deaths?" asked Justin, shifting the conversation.

"Oh yeah. Many accidents. Deaths? Most certainly," said Seth. "In fact, they say this stretch is kind of like the Bermuda Triangle of state routes and interstates. Crazy stuff has happened here. But they're mostly urban legends, so who knows what's real or fake anymore."

"Like . . . what?" asked Nikki.

"Well . . . they say the gas station is like a weigh station for lost souls—a portal to the afterlife. Accidents happen on this road to people who are destined to die. They say the managers of the station are the gatekeepers. Weighing the measure of a man," said Seth. "Or woman."

Justin saw Seth's eyes in the rearview mirror. They were trained on Nikki with those last two words.

"They?" asked Nikki.

"Mostly the managers," said Seth with a pained chuckle. "I think they just like to keep the legend and mystery alive. They're notorious for saying, 'The station needs a manager.'. As if without one, all hell would break loose."

"How many managers have worked there?" asked Justin.

"Well, in my lifetime, hard to even count. Seems to turn over every two years or so. In fact, my friend is coming up on the end of his second year. Figure he'll probably bug out next once they find a replacement."

"Why not just close it? Seems a lot to worry about every couple of years," said Justin.

"You'd think," said Seth. "Seems really important to the owner that it stay open. Besides, lots of open road between gas stops if this place closes."

Seth gave a light chuckle.

A beat passed.

"Anyway, you get us there and we'll get you some gas and you can be on your way. Or you can stay and wait this out, get something in your stomachs. Your choice."

Justin felt Nikki's hand on his arm, and she squeezed. He looked in the rearview mirror and caught a slight grin on the leathery face of his passenger. Lightning flashed. In place of the grinning face, a skull with blood red eyes. The man's face alternated between human and horror with subsequent flashes. Justin's heart was a jackhammer in his chest. He was certain it would explode.

It's just my imagination. I'm tired, upset, and my mind is playing tricks on me. That's all it is.

With two shaking hands on the steering wheel, Justin continued. He dared himself to look in the rearview mirror again. When he did, those glowing red eyes filled his vision.

SETH CONTINUED SHARING stories of the road and old legends as the downpour continued and Justin pulled into the tiny gas station on State Route 79. The sign above read Acheron Gas & Go. They had a couple of pumps and a small service garage. Justin caught sight of a red tow truck parked just to the side. It was the same make and model as the one he'd bumped earlier. The office lights were dim. To the right and behind the station was a small cottage. Big enough for someone to live in, maybe two at most. But those lights were off, too.

"You think your guy is here?" asked Justin.

"Got a truck missing, so he might be out on a run," said Seth.

Justin's nerves were on edge. *If that guy was his—? Oh God!*

"That's a weird name for a gas station," said Nikki.

"Oh. Acheron. Yeah. The owner changed it to fit in with the legends," said Seth.

"How's that fit?" asked Justin.

"I'm told it's a mythology thing," said Seth.

"Like . . . Zeus and all that?" asked Nikki.

"Egyptian, actually," said Seth. "Apparently the old Egyptian god, Set, oversees the gas station and makes sure there's a manager to usher souls as part of his penance for killing his brother, Osiris, the true god of the afterlife. Can't have souls just wandering the earth, right? Anyway, Acheron was the name of one of the rivers that led to the underworld."

Justin shared a look with Nikki. Their respective unease shared.

"I'll go in," began Seth, "and check on him. Usually not this dark, even when he's out. Storm mighta knocked out some power. You two sit tight. Worse case, we'll wait this out inside till morning. I got a key."

"Uh, yeah okay," said Justin. "You sure you don't want me to come in with you? You okay to walk in this, with the head injury? You might be concussed."

"Nah. No need. I'm good. Shouldn't be but a moment," said Seth.

As Seth exited the car, Justin felt Nikki's grip on his arm tighten. He reacted audibly, took his gaze off Seth, and turned to her. He saw fear and desperation.

"Gas up, and go," she said. "Let's just go."

"What? We . . . we can't. We can't just leave him. You said—"

"I know what I said! But we got him here. He's got a friend here. We did our part. Please, let's just leave."

The voice in the back of his mind was recalling the skull and red eyes. It was shouting its agreement with Nikki and on its knees, pleading for him to listen to her this time.

It was just my mind playing tricks on me. It's the storm. Bad light. Fatigue. That's all it is.

"Look, if we leave now, it'd be like leaving the scene of a crime," said Justin.

"What?"

"We hit his car, for Christ's sake. We can't just take off. Legally . . . it's wrong. Morally, it's . . . it's . . ."

"Morally? Legally? What will any of that mean if we end up dead? All of this," she said, waving her hand around, "is how horror stories and true crime reports start. Can you...just for once...listen to me and give a damn about my feelings?!"

She was right. Things seemed weird . . . at best. Between the intensity of the elements and the darkness that stalked them, Justin saw a recipe for a headline in the next *Union Tribune* that read, "San Diego Couple Missing in Freak Desert Storm."

"Look, I'll tell you what. I'll go in. I'll pay for gas. Exchange my insurance information with Seth, and then we'll go. Cool?"

Justin saw some relief in Nikki's face. Not much, but it was something.

THE BELLS on the glass door to the gas station office echoed through the tiny space as Justin entered. It was eerily quiet, and with the lights so dim, Nikki's warning that 'this is how horror movies start' took center stage in his mind. A shiver ran through him.

"I'll just leave some money, get the gas, and leave," he whispered.

"Justin."

He turned at the sound of his name. But there was no one there. He looked outside and saw Nikki in the car.

"Justin."

He turned again and found nothing.

"Okay, I'm losing it."

A low, feral growl echoed through the office. Justin turned and found a large shadow toward the back wall. Within seconds, two red orbs glowed. They shifted to the left and were followed by a second set of red orbs. Then a third. They moved. The growling continued, getting louder the closer the orbs came.

"Oh hell no."

Justin backed away slowly and quietly exited, not wanting the bells on the door to draw attention. Covering his head, he bolted to his car.

"We need to leave," he said. "We're just gonna go, and then the first chance we get, we'll—"

Justin stopped speaking when he realized that Nikki was gone.

"NIKKI!"

Justin's screams were absorbed by the storm. Every attempt to call for her was countered by a deafening clap of thunder. The rain fell on him with painful intensity. Lights were blurry, as was movement, but he caught sight of a shadow moving toward the cottage behind the station. He stopped as three sets of red orbs turned to him. A howl pierced the night air. Then a second. And a third.

"Justin!"

His name was the only thing he heard over the howling. He looked for the source again. Nothing. Turning back to the cottage, the shadow was gone. The howling stopped. He sprinted for the cottage and entered, quickly closing the door behind him. The candlelit room smelled of cigarettes and dust. Like a throwback to the '70s, the walls were covered by fake wood-grain paneling. Soiled green carpet, complete with burns and dog hair, covered the length of the living room. The furniture, from the couch to the recliners, was covered in plastic.

With each step he tried to reassure himself that Nikki had just gone to the bathroom, despite the voice in the back of his mind screaming something vastly different.

The carpet felt like a sponge. The sound and feel of displaced water traveled with him as he made his way to a poorly lit hallway, its length physically impossible. At the end, a door outlined by light. Justin walked toward it, desperate for answers. With each step the hallway narrowed and became longer. Looking back where he'd come from, there was nothing. Until the shadow returned. Then the growling. And the howls.

Followed by a scream.

"Nikki!" he yelled.

Justin ran for the door. Behind him, the patter of legs. Animal legs. And barking.

"Noooo!" he screamed.

He reached the door, grabbed the handle, and twisted. Nothing. From one side to the other there was nothing but tightness. With one hand he twisted. With the other, he pounded on the door and yelled for Nikki. He yelled for help. And in between, he simply yelled.

Looking behind him, the walls were closing in. Something ferocious was coming. Something hungry. In desperation Justin threw his shoulder into the door. The thick slab of wood didn't even rattle, but he kept trying. Through the growls, the barks, and his own screams, he kept trying.

At the last minute, the door gave way—to hell on Earth.

JUSTIN FELL, then rolled, head over feet, for several yards before finally coming to a stop at the bank of a river. Gathering himself, he stood on the shore of a river of darkness. It wasn't liquid, yet it flowed, rippled, and was brought in on the tide like any other body of water.

"Impressive, isn't it?"

Justin turned to find Seth standing behind him. At his heel sat a dog, all black with reddish streaks in its fur. When it finally turned its head to regard him, Justin gasped.

It had three heads.

Each with glowing red eyes.

"Wh... wh... what the hell is going on?" stammered Justin.

"Hell... indeed," said Seth.

"Wh... wh... where's Nikki?"

"Oh, she's safe. I promise."

"Where, damn you! I wanna see her! Now!"

"You are in no position to make demands," said Seth. "You'll see her when the time is right. For now, we have business."

"What business? We have nothing. Bring Nikki to me and just... just let us go."

The laughter Justin heard seemed to come from all around him. It was accompanied by a howl from the dog at Seth's side. Each head pointed up. Each head echoing its master's sinister sentiments with a woeful yet ravenous howl to the darkness above.

"None of this is an accident, Justin. The storm. The accident. Us being here. All of this was part of a plan."

"What plan? Whose plan?"

"Mine!"

As Seth spoke, thunder roared overhead.

"I... I don't understand."

"Do you remember what I told you about this road? About this gas station?"

"It was just an old spooky story to tell travelers," said Justin.

"Yes... and no."

Justin tensed as Seth walked closer to him.

"This station, the cottage above, it's all a gateway. A gateway to this."

Seth gestured around the vast darkness. As Justin followed his hand, he saw that the river of darkness flowed evenly, steadily, into one concentrated area. A cave, or perhaps an entrance, to... something.

"Where does that go?" asked Justin.

"To the land of the wicked," said Seth.

Justin let the words settle, then began to recall the conversation in the car. The stories Seth told about the ancient god, Set.

"The storm? That . . . that's your doing?"

Seth nodded.

"You caused it all. You're . . . Set."

Seth nodded again.

"But . . . why? Why have you done this?"

"Because your mistake killed the last caretaker. When you bumped that Jeep you set in motion a chain of events that led to his death. And now, the station needs a manager, Justin," said Seth.

"Where's Nikki?"

"She's safe. And she can remain that way. Or . . ."

"Or what?"

"Well, it's an interesting thing. You were both in the car when you caused the last manager's death. Kind of makes you both responsible. So I give you the choice. You...or her."

Justin immediately began shaking his head. He couldn't believe this was happening. If he'd just listened to her. If they'd just waited out the storm.

"No. I don't accept that. Find someone else. Let us go."

"Choose. Or you can both die. Those are the only options. And trust me...no one escapes their fate," said Seth.

CRACK! Boom!

Justin's eyes flew open at the sound of the thunder. Rain pelted the car, some of it leaking in through the cracks, hitting him in the face. When he wiped the moisture away, he realized two things. He was upside down, and he was bleeding. His head pounded. He tried to move his other arm, but it would not budge. He reached for the release on his seat belt but couldn't find it.

He did find the piece of metal that pierced his chest, though.

"What the . . .? Oh my God! HELP! HELP! HELP ME!"

Thunder raged, drowning out his cries. He felt no pain. Only fear. Confusion. He turned his head to the side and saw another vehicle. It was mangled to hell, but the Mercedes emblem was unmistakable. As was the license plate.

TIME4T.

"What the fuuu...?"

In between the thunder he heard the roar of an engine. Light flashed at him. A car came to a stop near him, and someone stepped out, walked to him, and squatted down.

"Y-y-you," said Justin.

"Looks like you're in need of help," said Seth.

"Wh-wh-what is this? What's going on? What did you do to me?"

"I did exactly as you requested," said Seth.

Justin thought back. The river. The choice. He had to choose between him and Nikki to replace the station manager.

He'd chosen her.

"Why am I here? Why am I here like this?"

"You chose her as the new manager," said Seth.

"Right."

"She had a choice, too. For you to be the new manager, or for you to be free."

Justin felt the adrenaline spike. His breathing became erratic.

"She chose to set you free. Apparently, she actually cared about you," said Seth.

Relief filled him. At least, until the confusion set in.

"Then... why am I here? Why is this happening?"

"This? Oh... this is your freedom."

A crack of thunder and a flash of lightning put supernaturally dramatic emphasis on Seth's words.

"Wait! No! Nooooo! Please! You can't leave me like this. I'll die!" screamed Justin.

He continued his screams as Seth stood.

"You already did," said Seth. "Someone will be along shortly to help you out."

Justin heard the sound of a car door open, then close. He knew that sound. It was a Stingray. The engine came to life, and seconds later, it was cruising down the street. Justin watched as it vanished. Washed out by the increasing strength of the storm. In its wake, a light in the distance grew brighter and brighter with each passing second. Justin could make out a vague outline of a shape.

It was a truck.

A tow truck.

With a lone driver.

It stopped. A door opened, the driver exited, walked to Justin, and knelt.

"You're in a bad way, Justin," said Nikki. "But I'll get you sorted, weighed, and on your way. As you know, the station is just up ahead."

"Nikki! Wait! Help—"

"Probably should have just stayed in Palm Springs and waited out the storm, huh?"

Nikki's eyes flashed bright red.

Justin screamed.

The Sandman
By TJ Kang

Every kid in San Diego over the age of six has heard the story. I've heard it myself about a hundred times. I'm not just a kid, either—I'm almost fourteen—so, I figure I should have known better than to fall for his trap, but here I am. He's not here right now. He left just after the sun went down, but I know he'll be back. He always comes back. Sometimes he's gone for hours, and sometimes just for a few minutes, so I never know how much time I've got, which is why I haven't tried to run away. That, and the fact that I don't know where I am, and I'm scared of going out in the desert alone at night, and most of all, because I'm too weak. I think if I did manage to get away, I'd probably fall down in the sand before I got very far, and then the coyotes would get me, or worse, he would find me and drag me back to wherever this is, and then that would probably be it for me.

    He took my phone away the first night, but I guess he didn't care about my backpack or what else was in it, so I'm writing this in my English composition book. If I have the chance to hide it somewhere where it won't get wet or blow away, that's what I'm going to do, and then I hope someday someone will find it and give it to my mom. So, I'm writing this to you, Mom, just in case.

The first time I heard about the Sandman was on our eighth-grade Disneyland trip, on the bus ride home. Most of the other kids were asleep after being out in the sun all day, and eating too much, and going on too many rides. I was sitting next to Jason, who was snoring so loud I couldn't have slept if I tried, but I wasn't sleepy anyway. I didn't go on the scary rides like Space Mountain, and I didn't eat that much junk, so I was just a normal amount of tired. I would have read a book on my phone, but the chaperones had all our phones at the front of the bus. Why? Who knows? It makes the adults feel like they're in control, I guess.

Anyway, I was bored, so I looked around and saw that Aimee was still awake too. We made eye contact, and she motioned for me to come sit next to her, so I did. Aimee is one of those Goth types with the weird-colored hair, and all the black clothes, and heavy makeup, but she's all right. She stuck up for me once when I got hit with a soccer ball during Phys Ed and started crying, and everyone was laughing at me for being a wuss.

So, on the bus, she asked me if I had heard of the Sandman. I hadn't, so she told me about the missing kids. I guess it had been going on for a while, so I'm surprised I hadn't heard about it before. She said that they started calling him Sandman because the families always found sand wherever the kids were last seen, like in their bedrooms or next to their abandoned bikes along the side of the road. I said something like, 'We live in California by the freaking dunes for God's sake, so of course there's sand,' but she said, 'No, not just regular sand like you track in on your shoes, but a neat pile of it all in one place, like it had been left there on purpose.'

Aimee said a friend of hers, not someone at school, but someone she knew from some weird online Goth group she's in, had actually seen the Sandman. Her friend said she was walking home after hanging out with some friends and saw a little kid walking along with this really strange-looking dude. That's why she even noticed, because he was so odd. She said he had white hair, even though he looked young, and that his eyes were like the opposite of glowing–like he didn't even have eyes at all but just a really pale, blank face on a lumpy sort of body that filled out his sweatpants and hoodie in a weird way that didn't look like a human body is supposed to look. Maybe that doesn't make sense the way I'm writing it now, but it made sense when Aimee told me that story. Aimee's friend said the kid looked happy enough, and she only remembered seeing him because the man was so weird and also because the kid was wearing a Ramones t-shirt, and she thought that it was funny that a kid would even know who that was. And Aimee said the girl said she remembered it later because there was a picture in her newsfeed about a missing kid, and it was the same kid she had seen. He was even wearing the same t-shirt. They never found that kid, or at least that's what the girl told Aimee.

After that conversation on the bus, it seemed like everyone had a Sandman story. Someone was always bringing him up and talking about missing kids who disappeared and left nothing behind but a big pile of sand. Teachers must have heard the stories too because they started telling us kids to be careful and not go out at night alone and not to talk to strangers, like we were still babies or something. I wish I had listened. I wish I had thought about what it must have been like for the parents when their kids went missing. And now, it's me who's missing, and I think about what you're going through, Mom, wondering what happened to me, and I'm sorry. All I can say is that it wasn't your fault. I made my own stupid mistakes, so don't blame yourself, even if you never see me again.

It wasn't that hard for me to believe there was a Sandman. I mean, there are plenty of weirdos out there who are serial killers or pedophiles or whatever. I think the reason he got me is because I had this mental image of what he looked like based on Aimee's friend's description. When the Sandman came for me, I went along willingly because he was nothing like that description. For me, he was just another kid about my age who seemed cool and interested in me, and

I guess I really wanted someone cool to be interested in boring old me and want to be my friend.

It all happened so fast. You probably know that I went to school that day but never made it home. I missed the bus again, for like the fifth time, and I was afraid to call you and tell you, so I decided to walk home. It didn't seem far in a car or on the bus, but it was a lot farther on foot, as I found out. You know the canyon close to the school that has railroad tracks by it? I remembered that the same canyon and the same railroad tracks stretch all the way to right next to our neighborhood, so I thought it might be faster to follow the tracks home. Dumb, huh?

I was walking and walking for, like, forever, and I had no idea if I was getting close or still had miles to go. All of a sudden, this kid walks up out of nowhere, and he says, "Hey, you want to see something cool?"

I looked him over, and like I said before, he looked cool—tall, good-looking, dressed in the kind of clothes you would never let me out of the house in—and I immediately wanted him to like me. Plus, I was getting kind of lonely and a little scared out there on my own. It's weird how alone you can feel when you're probably only a few yards away from somebody's backyard or a Ralph's market or something. So, I said, "What is it?" and he said, "Come with me and I'll show you," and away I went, following him like a puppy dog or more like a total idiot.

I just looked up at the sky right now, and it looks like the sun will be coming up soon. I'm going to put this away for now because he's bound to be back any minute. I'll write more when he leaves again, unless it's my turn to become a pile of sand. I wonder where he will leave it. By the railroad tracks? Anyway, that's all for tonight.

I'M BACK. I'm going to have to be more careful, or I'll never have a chance to leave this for someone to maybe find and take back to you, Mom.

He came back not that long after I put my notebook away. He was alone this time, which is way better. Sometimes he brings one of them back with him and takes his time draining the life out of them until they are nothing but sand. When he does that, it's my job to sweep them up and dump them in the desert, where the wind blows them away to join the dunes. I wonder how much of the sand in those dunes is just sand at this point, and how much of it is what's left of a bunch of little kids.

The rest he says he "takes care of" wherever he finds them. He calls it "taking care of" them. It's better for me if I don't argue with him. Those are the kids whose parents find sand in place of their son or daughter. If you read this, maybe you could try to find those parents and tell them that the sand *is* their son or daughter. They might want to keep it or bury it or something.

Anyway, where was I? So, I followed the cool-looking guy down into a ravine, slipping and sliding half the time while he didn't seem to ever slip at all. I thought whatever it was that he wanted to show me was down there, but instead of stopping, he turned and started walking along the bottom of the ravine, and I continued to follow him. I kept asking him to tell me what he wanted me to see, and he kept saying, "You'll see soon enough," and then would change the subject and talk about sports and music, stuff like that. I know now that he was just stalling, but it took me a while before I started to get suspicious. Eventually, though, I stopped following him and said that I had to get home and turned around to go back the way I came. The next thing I knew, I was here. Wherever here is.

When I woke up, it was nighttime, and I was tied up and sitting on a cold dirt floor, and it was too dark to see anything other than some stars through what I assumed was a window. I could hear something, though. It sounded like someone sucking on a milkshake, only through a really big straw because it was so loud. I tried to look for where the sound was coming from, but it was too dark. Before long, the sucking sound stopped, and I heard a sigh, like the sigh you might make after you finish a really good meal, like at Thanksgiving maybe. And then something moved in the dark and passed in front of the window, blocking the starlight for just a second, and then a face appeared right in front of mine. I screamed, and a man wiped something wet that looked like spaghetti sauce from his face, and he smiled and said, "Did you see that? I told you I was going to show you something cool, and then you slept right through it, didn't you?"

The voice sounded just like the cool kid I had followed into the ravine, but the face was different. It immediately reminded me of Aimee's story because of the white hair and the pale skin and the eyes that seemed to almost not be there at all. Even worse, when my eyes started to adjust to the darkness, I saw that his body was lumpy and shapeless and that the clothes he was wearing seemed to be holding him in like the skin on a sausage and that if he took them off, he would just fall apart into a pile of organs and tissue. Or sand.

Once I put two and two together and figured out he was eating kids or sucking them dry or whatever, I was sure I was going to be next, but days went by, and he never did anything to me. He even brought me food and water and let me go to the bathroom in a big orange Home Depot bucket. He would talk to me and tell me about the kids he had found and what they were like and how he tricked them into letting him in or following him, just like he had tricked me. Finally, I got tired of waiting for an attack that never came, and I just asked him, "Why haven't you killed me yet?" He actually looked offended.

He said, "I didn't bring you here to kill you. I got tired of being alone, and I was thinking it would be nice to have a helper or a companion, maybe even a friend, and then you came along, just like an answer to a prayer. You're too old to be any good as food anyway." I must have looked horrified, so he added in a stern voice like a teacher's, "But that doesn't mean I won't kill you if you don't obey me."

After a while, maybe a week—who knows? I've lost track of time out here, wherever I am. He stopped tying me up and let me roam around freely during the day, as long as I didn't leave his sight. He still tied me up at night for a while, but he stopped that eventually, too. The first night he left me untied, I was too scared to try to run away. I waited to see how long it would take him to come back, and the first day, he was only gone about fifteen minutes. I think he was testing me. After that, it varied from a few minutes to several hours or all night.

One night, I decided to take a chance and make a run for it. I waited about half an hour or so after he left. By the way, he has never told me his name. I think of him in my head as the Sandman, but to his face, I call him "Friend" because that's what he told me to call him. So, after about half an hour of waiting, I grabbed my backpack and some fruit and bottles of water that Friend had brought me, and I headed out into the desert.

I didn't have much of a plan. I was going to try to find the ravine–the one we had been walking in right before he knocked me out–and keep walking in whatever direction seemed like the way home. It was very dark, and there was no moon, and I was afraid of rattlesnakes and coyotes and of tripping and twisting an ankle, so I kind of trotted along instead of really running. I don't think it would have mattered, though, if I had run like I was trying for a gold medal. He caught me almost immediately. I still don't know if he had been lying in wait for me or if it was just an unlucky coincidence that he was returning from the same direction I was traveling in. He never said. All I know is that he was pissed.

That's enough for now. He has been gone a while, and I can't risk getting caught. Once was enough. I'll write more later, I hope.

OKAY, so like I said, he caught me right away, and he was really angry. I think it was the only time he seemed to have a little color in that pasty face of his. I took one look at that face and started apologizing and begging for mercy, but he just clamped a hand over my mouth and dragged me backward all the way back to this place. I thought he was going to tie me up again, but what he did was so much worse.

This is hard for me to write about, Mom, and I think it's going to be hard for you to read, but I want the truth to get out, so that other kids don't end up like me or like those poor little piles of sand. So, here goes.

Once he got me inside, Friend pushed me down on the floor and sat on my chest. I could hardly breathe. It was like having heavy sandbags dropped on my body. I couldn't move, and I had run out of things to say to try to defend myself, so I just stared up at that face and prayed. He leaned over me and put his mouth over my nose and mouth. Friend's mouth is big, not unnaturally big, but big enough. Like that Aerosmith guy, you know? Anyway, he covered my nose and mouth with his mouth and started sucking.

I felt like everything inside my body, from my toes on up, was rushing out of me and into Friend's mouth. I'm sure you've seen those inflatable decorations that people put on their lawns at Halloween and Christmas. Have you ever seen one when it first gets unplugged and the air rushes out, and it just collapses on the ground? That's what I imagined was happening to my body, except instead of air, it was every bit of liquid inside me. The pain was bottomless. I can't even describe how much it hurt. Nothing has ever hurt like that.

I knew I was dead, and I thought about you and home and the life I was never going to go back to, and then suddenly it all stopped. Friend dropped me on the floor and left me there. He didn't come back for two days.

When he finally returned, he poured water and Gatorade into my mouth. It took a couple of days before I could speak, and a couple more before I could sit up. In all that time, he never said a word to me. When he finally spoke, all he said was, "If you ever try to leave again, there won't be anything left for your family to find."

That was several weeks ago. Maybe months. It's hard to keep track. Things have pretty much gone back to normal, if anything about this place can be called normal. I still do my chores, although I have a limp now, and my arms are too weak to lift my bucket to dump it for myself. Friend does that for me. He feeds me sometimes, too, like a parent feeding a toddler. He doesn't seem angry anymore. Maybe he knows I can't run away, so he's decided to forgive and forget. I think he's starting to let his guard down because he thinks it's safe.

What he doesn't know is that I'm starting to get stronger again. I can feel the strength coming back into my arms and legs, but I hide it from him. I still limp, but it's mostly an act. Mostly. I'm not strong enough yet to try to run, but I'm close. And when the time is right, I'm going to go for it. But first, I'm going to hide this notebook somewhere safe where Friend won't find it, but maybe you or someone will.

I hope I'll see you soon, Mom. I love you so much. But, if you're reading this, I guess I didn't make it. In that case, I have something I'd like you to do for me, if that's okay. Could you please go out to the dunes and leave some flowers for the children?

H is for Hell
By Jon Cohn

It took nearly three months to make my Doctor Demonia costume. To be specific, I built mine after the costume from the movie version of *Hellwreckers: Rapture*. When I saw that the spiked shoulder pads alone would take up nearly an entire suitcase, I realized flying was out of the question. And so, I decided to drive four whole days from Chattanooga to San Diego. I'd originally made plans to go with my girlfriend Jenny, who was just as big a fan of Hellwreckers as me, but she'd broken up with me two months ago. Instead, I was able to convince my buddy Jeff to come in her place. He's not nearly as big a fan as me—as far as I know, he's never picked up a comic book in his life—but he liked the movies from the Hellwreckers Cinematic Universe, or HCU as everyone called it.

I'm aware that I have a tendency to get a little too excited about some things, especially when I have a project to work on. Yes, I've always read comics, and I'm at the premiere for every new HCU movie, but it doesn't usually consume my whole life like this. It wasn't until I started the Doctor Demonia costume project that I started living and breathing the series. I rewatched all twenty-seven movies in the franchise as I built it, and pretty soon it felt like there wasn't any room in my head for anything but Hellwreckers.

We were a little over halfway through day one of our drive when Jeff asked if we could listen to something other than Hellwreckers fan podcasts. It stung a little; I felt like I had to put a lid on my excitement, and didn't know how else to fill the next three and a half days of driving. Sometimes, once I've fixated on something for too long, it's like I forget how to talk about other things. It wasn't just that Jeff didn't want to talk Hellwreckers; he also admitted he hadn't even seen the last three movies because he felt the franchise had fallen apart. That wasn't a terribly unpopular opinion among fans, though it was one I certainly disagreed with. If anything, I was more excited than ever to get our first peek at Sludge City, a film adaptation of what is largely considered one of the all-time best stories from the Hellwreckers comic books.

We finally reached our destination on Wednesday afternoon. The first stop was to get in line just in time to pick up our badges for Preview Night, the evening kickoff event in which we get to explore the convention grounds early. Well, not we, so much as me. Jeff wanted to check out the Gaslamp District, which had been completely shut down for traffic, turning it into one giant block party filled with food, booze, and single women for him to flirt with.

I thought I was making good time in line, getting nearly to the front after only an hour and a half, until a fire alarm went off and we all had to evacuate the building. When they deemed it safe to re-enter, twenty minutes later, I found myself in the back of the line again. This time, it took nearly three hours to reach the front. For the most part, it was fine, aside from the delay forcing me to miss the limited Exhibition Hall hours for Preview Night. Though once I finally had that badge in my hand, nothing else mattered. Hanging from a lanyard, pressed into a laminate fold, it read: Edmund Lennox, 4-day Guest at San Diego Comic-Con.

I was finally here, for the first time ever.

Of course, I didn't actually get a chance to enter the Con on

Thursday either. Instead, I spent the whole day in line to earn myself a wristband for Friday's programming in the highly coveted Hall H. For the uninitiated, Hall H is where all the premier content happens at Comic-Con. It's the only place where all the biggest stars of the mega franchises will be in one place. They show off trailers to new movies and tease the lineup of upcoming releases. But anyone can find that stuff online. The real reason to squeeze into the 6,000-person ballroom is to see the stars in real life sharing secrets from behind the scenes, talking about what the characters and stories mean to them, even answering questions from a few lucky audience members. And of course, there are always surprises. Four years ago, everyone lost their minds in the *Hellwreckers: Requiem* panel when, for the first time ever, we got to see Captain Antihero walk on stage in full costume and deliver his iconic line: "Hellwreckers, congregate!"

I would have given my right arm to see that in person, instead of watching a crummy video from someone's phone over 300 feet away. That's why this year, I came prepared. I showed up at four a.m. Thursday morning and stood in line for fifteen hours with a backpack full of snacks, drinks, and a rechargeable battery for my phone. Jeff and I had agreed ahead of time that we would each do Comic-Con our own way. When he came to hold my place for bathroom breaks and lunchtime, he showed me all the pictures he'd taken of people in incredible costumes, and shops that had some of the coolest merch I'd ever seen. He even got a picture with Bruce Campbell, which made me more than a little jealous.

By 7:30 that night, I'd inched my way close enough to earn a Level D wristband for Friday's programming. According to the internet, as long as I showed up in the actual line by five a.m. Friday, I'd be getting into Hall H in time for the six p.m. *Hellwreckers: Sludge City* panel. That said, for all my effort, I had at least expected to get a level B wristband, C at worst. D meant I would likely be seated in what was the equivalent of the nosebleed section of a sporting event.

Jeff groaned as I clicked on the light in our hotel room just before four in the morning to start putting on my Doctor Demonia costume. I knew today was going to be another long day standing in line in sunny San Diego, made extra hot trapped inside nearly ten pounds of PVC and cardboard.

"You're seriously going to wear that thing now?" Jeff asked, as if I'd spent three months meticulously crafting a screen-accurate super-suit just for fun.

"Of course I am."

"But you're not even going into the convention center, you're just waiting outside in a line all day."

I nodded. "I'll wear it tomorrow too, but I need to show my support for the big panel."

Jeff sighed and rolled over, facing away from me. "You're such a nerd."

It took nearly twice as long to walk through the still-dark streets of downtown in my costume as the day before. Doctor Demonia wore heavy armor that covered nearly his entire body, and while I had resigned myself to wearing the uncomfortable helmet for most of the day, the bulky legs proved to be hard to maneuver in. I tripped over my faux-metal boot cover twice on the way. The first time I managed to catch myself, though the second time I nearly faceplanted onto the pavement. The fall severely damaged three spikes on my right shoulder pad and crumpled a whole corner of my breastplate. After a few minutes of tinkering, I figured there was no way to get those spikes to look even remotely good again. Luckily, I had my cosplay first-aid kit hidden in a fanny pack under my armor. I carved the offending spikes off with my box cutter, duct taped over the holes, then spray painted them silver. It didn't look amazing, but it was better than nothing.

When I arrived at the pre-lineup, I learned the internet had either lied or severely underestimated the excitement for today's big panel. A sea of at least five hundred people was already pressed shoulder to shoulder, waiting for the real line to open up at 7:30 a.m. If I thought I was uncomfortable yesterday, my bulky costume had me cooking as

H IS FOR HELL

I was sandwiched in with all the other fans. The sun hadn't even come up, and I was already sweating so bad my thighs were chafing.

Yesterday, the line was made up of people across numerous fandoms trying to make it for whatever was their jam. Lifelong fans of *Star Skirmish*, *King of the Creepies*, and folks waiting to see a glimpse of season 2 of *Slashtag* all intermingled as they patiently waited for a chance to see their heroes.

Despite their clear excitement, the only thing I felt like I was hearing all day was people bashing the things they loved. *Star Skirmish* fans hated how "woke" it had become by including more diverse casts in their projects. The new lead voice actor for the upcoming Creepies animated series had been a teen heartthrob, and all the show's fans could talk about was how he was going to single-handedly ruin it. Nobody even knew anything about the new *Slashtag* season, but still, people managed to nitpick over their least favorite parts of season 1. It was frustrating to hear so much negativity thrown around when we had all come together for what should be the biggest celebration of fandom around. I thought in-person things would be different from the toxic fandoms online, but instead it was like an echo chamber cranked up to eleven, with people joining in to help shit on each other's favorite shows and movies, parroting the same tired complaints from every online discussion thread.

My one hope was that today would be different, because everyone in my line would be jazzed for Hellwreckers.

It wasn't.

"This better not suck," I overheard the group right behind me say once we'd finally been sorted by wristbands into the lines we'd stand in all day. "I swear to God if this is more of the same old weak shit that they've been serving up for the past couple of years, I'm done with the HCU."

I don't know if it was my lack of sleep or proper breakfast, my damaged costume, or the familiar pain in my legs that I knew I'd have to endure standing in line another ten hours today. Whatever it was, something inside me snapped.

"Then why the hell are you in this line?" I couldn't help but blurt out. Normally, I'm not one to jump into conversations with strangers, but I'd had enough of hearing people criticize my favorite franchise. "If you hate Hellwreckers so much, why go through all this trouble?"

One guy who would have been nearly twice my size if not for my clunky armor stepped up to me, wearing a black shirt with unreadable text for some metal band scrawled across it. His guest badge read Jared S. "Because Amber Seline is hot as fuck," he said. "I want to see her in person."

"That's baloney," I said. "You wouldn't wait two whole days in the nerdiest line at the nerdiest convention in the country just to see one actress. Know your audience, man. We're all here because we love Hellwreckers and can't wait for *Sludge City*."

"Get your head out of your ass, weirdo," Jared S. said. "The HCU sucks now."

My face got hot, even though I was already sweating profusely from the morning sun and my bulky costume. I looked around and saw that our argument had grabbed the attention of at least a few dozen other guests who had nothing else to do, and I had an idea.

"Well, the rest of us are tired of people dumping on our favorite movies. Am I right, everyone?" I realized my mistake immediately, feeling a tide of secondhand embarrassment ripple through the crowd as people couldn't turn away from me fast enough.

"Loser!" someone in the sea of attendees shouted. The guy I was arguing with simply laughed in my face, then turned back to his friends.

Jeff didn't show up to relieve me for our scheduled eleven a.m. bathroom and lunch break, and texted back that he had made some friends and never even made it to the convention today. I knew Jared S. and his buddies behind me wouldn't hold my spot in line, so I begged a couple of guys in front of me wearing matching Wrecker Crew t-shirts to hold my spot.

Managing to squeeze my oversized suit into a bathroom stall was another logistic issue I had not prepared for. In order to actually fit inside a stall, I ended up having to remove my shoulder pieces and sleeves completely, leaving them on a counter next to the sink. Even then, going to the bathroom proved to be a challenge. I decided I'd rather go thirsty for the rest of the day than do this again. When I finally emerged, one of my shoulder pieces had somehow fallen to the floor and then been stepped on by what looked like half the convention. It was ruined. With a heavy sigh, I reattached the single remaining arm and made my way back to Hall H.

"What the hell do you think you're doing?" Jared S. asked as I worked my way back into line.

"I just stepped out for a minute," I explained, even though he obviously knew that.

"No cutting in line!" He shouted, loud enough for one of the Comic-Con line coordinators to hear.

"Is everything alright over here?" a team member wearing an SDCC emblazoned shirt asked.

"This guy just showed up and tried to cut us in line," Jared S. said. Behind him, the rest of his buddies were grinning and piling on to corroborate his story.

I looked for the two guys in front who had agreed to watch my spot, but they had disappeared. "I had people holding my spot!" I said, feeling panic settle into my already heaving chest. Even with my D-level wristband, if I were sent to the back of the line, I'd be set back at least 600 spots.

"Sir, there's no cutting in line," the staff member said, taking the bully's side.

"Oh hey!" a girl called out to me just behind Jared S.'s group. "There you are. He's with us," she explained to the line attendant.

"Thanks," I said, joining the girl and her three friends.

"No problem. That guy's been obnoxious all day," she said.

In the time it took for me to think of what to say next to the girl who'd gotten me back into line, she was already deep into a conversation with her friends about anime, something I knew nothing about.

I spent the next few hours listening to a Hellwreckers audiobook until my phone died. I brought a fully charged backup battery, but when I plugged it in, nothing happened. My patience took another blow as I came to terms with the realization that I forgot to recharge the battery last night.

After nearly four more hours of complete boredom and borderline heatstroke, the doors of the *Slashtag 2* panel let out. People trickled out of the building as all of us in line perked up.

It was almost showtime.

As soon as enough people had exited Hall H, line attendants started letting people in. With every step I took, I became one inch closer to seeing my heroes. For months, there had been speculation that they would finally reveal who would be playing the iconic villain, Sinister Sludge, on stage tonight. And I would be there to see it live.

Most of group A and B were already inside from earlier in the day. All I had ahead of me was group C, and then about a quarter of group D. We snaked back and forth, ebbing and flowing toward the building as we all zig-zagged our way to the doors. I counted out fifty people in front of me, then forty, thirty...

The line started to slow, from a steady drip to a trickle. Fifteen people ahead of me. Ten. Finally, it was Jared S. and his buddies' turn. I stepped forward, ready to go, but a hand came down and pressed against my cardboard chest. She said something into an earpiece, then looked down at me through blackened sunglasses.

"Sorry, the room's full."

My mouth went dry, even though the rest of my body was sticky from twelve hours of sweat. Cluster headaches went off like bombs in my brain.

"What?" I asked.

This time, the attendant shouted not just to me, but to everyone behind me. "The panel for Hellwreckers is officially at capacity."

"You don't understand, I was ahead of those guys. I went to the bathroom, and they wouldn't let me back into my spot. I was literally right in front of them."

"I don't know what to tell you," she said. Behind her, the doors to Hall H slammed shut.

I had missed it. Four days of driving, two days of getting up before dawn, and spending the whole convention standing in sweltering heat was all for nothing. My suit suddenly weighed a ton. My head swirled, and the world nearly fell into blackness as I nearly passed out from a combination of shock and dehydration. All I could hear was the crowd going wild inside, then Kevin Smith's voice projecting through the door.

"You all excited to finally get your first look at *Sludge City*?" he asked to more cheers. "Speaking of *Sludge*, I wanted to take a minute first to address something that's been bugging me lately in the nerd world. Much like the radioactive waste that the evil Sinister Sludge uses, we've had a lot of toxic fandom in the community, and I just wanted to say it's not cool, guys. The producers of the HCU have been working on a campaign to combat this, and we thought what better place to test it out than with some of our most outspoken fans and critics. You guys want to see what we have in store?"

The people inside went nuts, their cheers so wild and unrestrained that it almost sounded like screams.

It didn't stop. If anything, the crowd inside somehow grew louder. I blinked away my dizziness as the doors to Hall H flew open. People stampeded out of the building. They weren't just afraid; there was something wrong with them. Their faces and arms looked like they were melting. Skin and muscle dripped off them as blood poured down their bodies. People tripped and were trampled by hundreds, if not thousands, of people fighting to escape. What the hell was happening inside? Some sort of elaborate flash mob or promotional event?

The wall to the building exploded outward, chunks of concrete cracked asphalt as it came soaring down like dozens of meteors. From the dust, a hovering figure emerged.

Sinister Sludge himself flew through the dusty hole in the wall, looking just like the villain from the comic. His glowing green backpack had tubes that fed into gauntlets on his arms. He turned to us in line and doused the crowd in green caustic liquid. The girl who had let me back in line pressed against me, but as I turned to her, all I could see was a skull with drips of skin and blood dripping off her. I shoved her away and felt a sizzling heat against my chest. Some of the Sludge spray had gotten on my cardboard chestpiece, thankfully creating a barrier to protect my body from disintegrating.

As if that wasn't enough, dozens of figures with bright green hair and glowing yellow eyes came scrambling out of the building. It was Sinister's minions, the Sludgelings. Their faces resembled gas masks, with accordion-like tubes that functioned as mouths to slurp up the melted mess left behind from their victims. I turned to run away, but a backup platoon was rounding us up from behind. I reached into my fanny pack, pulling out my box cutter and spray paint. My only option was to fight back.

A pair of Sludgelings charged at me, but before they had a chance to get too close, I hit them with a dose of spray paint to their eyes. They recoiled, and I went in for the kill, slicing their throats open with my blade. Thick green goo seeped from their ventilated necks as they fell to the ground. A hand grabbed my shoulder from behind, I spun around, driving the knife into another Sludgeling's eye. It let out a croaking squeal as it fell to the ground. Everyone around me was going down; I appeared to be the only one fighting for my life.

I managed to carve up several more approaching beasts, but as I focused on the threats in front of me, I missed a cluster of Sludgelings coming from behind. They tackled me, knocking the knife from my hand. The heat from their bodies was overwhelming. I was already so sweaty, so dehydrated, it sapped all remaining strength from me.

As I shut my eyes and prepared to be sludged to death, I heard several men's commanding voices in my ear.

"Stop resisting!" they shouted.

Good, I thought. The police are finally here to save the day. I tried to shake off the monsters from my back, but heard the police's voice even louder this time.

"I said stop!"

A drop of acid spilled into my eye; it burned like nothing I'd ever felt before. I squeezed them shut. After a few moments, the pain subsided, and I was able to see again.

Everything was different. I looked around and couldn't find Sinister Sludge or any of his Sludgelings. There was no hole in the building. Instead, I was surrounded by men in black police uniforms. Lying in front of me was the line attendant who had stopped me from entering, dead on the floor and missing an eye. A few feet past her a group of guys were on the ground, their throats slit as they bled out. I recognized one of them as Jared S.

Something metallic and cold pinched my wrists, and one of the men in black hoisted me to my feet by my shoulders. "We have the suspect in custody. Requesting immediate emergency medical, we have at least five victims on the ground."

I looked back at the crowd staring at me as if I were one of the celebrities, only fear and grim curiosity painted their faces instead of elation. "Wait," I said to the cops, as they dragged me away from Hall H. "You don't understand. I was supposed to be in there. I was in front of those guys."

Birds of Prey
By KC Grifant

"Cut! Terror! Action!"

Kelsie blinked and resisted rubbing her temples, which beat to a drum of one-too-many-vodka-tonics from the night before. The lights triangulating around her in the second-floor apartment seemed to wash the mustard walls in a color reminiscent of leering smokers' teeth. "Did you say . . . terror?"

"What, Kels?" The director-and-writer-slash-producer, Campbell, ran a hand through blond strands flapping along his undercut. "You're doing great, okay?"

Though a year or so younger than Kelsie, Campbell had already won some awards and gotten an "in" at a big film festival, so when he grinned at her in a way that made her stomach sink, she forced herself to smile back. Campbell hadn't quite propositioned her yet, but his stare said it wouldn't be long before he implied it was expected, a condition of her employment. He'd wheedle and make it sound like Kelsie was the ridiculous one, the naive one, for thinking she didn't owe him a quickie. *Just a blow job, no big deal.* He'd say it like it was the most reasonable request in the world, just one of a billion such exchanges in Hollywood, consistent as the unrelenting sun.

She hated blow jobs.

"Let's take it from the climax." Campbell gnawed on his lip. "We don't have a ton of time to get this just right."

"Sure thing." Kelsie ignored the nagging hangover and tried not to let the musty carpet smell turn her stomach. She pursed her lips into the subservient but confident smile she had perfected over the years while she envisioned a chunk of ceiling falling onto his skull. It was a trick she used instead of gritting her teeth, one she had done since she was a kid—a mental game of fast-forwarding time until the person's moment of death. The visualizations always soothed her enough that her smile would come off as sincere.

You have a plan, she reminded herself. She'd skip drinking with the crew tonight, claim it was a migraine, and keep Campbell at bay for a few more days of filming so he wouldn't have time to replace her.

"Hold up, got a weird buzz in the background," the woman doing sound said. "This place is *definitely* haunted. I need a sec."

Hairs prickled the back of Kelsie's neck, and she heard it too—not quite a buzz, more of a trill, like a crow's caw, but remixed and garbled.

"Make it quick," Campbell said and spread his hands wide. "I don't want to waste a second of this. Do you know how many crews like ours get to film at Birdwatcher Butcher's? Exactly zero."

He reminded the crew *at least* once an hour how lucky they were to get access. The apartment overlooked a street near Hollywood Boulevard that was part of the Murder n' Mayhem tour and was off-limits to filming. But Campbell knew a friend's girlfriend's dad, who owned the building and gave them an exception.

The place was perfectly hideous. One side with wallpaper sporting diamonds of mustard and rouge, the other walls the color of washed-out bile. Campbell had literally clapped when they entered.

"You know, there was no pattern to how he killed," the cameraman, Joe, said while they waited. "Unheard of for a serial killer."

Kelsie nodded. She had read the production notes: Birdwatcher

Butcher had targeted men and women spanning race, religion, and income. Twenty-two in total. And Butcher had always left a feather. She had studied by watching real crime documentaries featuring serial killers and their victims. *Easy stardom*, she had thought bitterly, watching solemn montages of the victims' photos splashed on screen as the narrators speculated why the killers had picked them.

"They found him in this very apartment, dead of a heart attack. Or they *think* it was him." The cameraman smiled appreciatively at Kelsie in a not-quite-ogle. "You're rocking this lighting by the way, Kels. Not a lot of actresses can pull it off."

Kelsie smiled back like he was the first guy to ever compliment her. With her raven hair and glass-green eyes, most people treated her as pretty, *special*, as long as she let them believe they had a chance at boning her. As soon as she sent a "no thanks" signal, he'd undoubtedly get passive-aggressive, maybe even make her look bad on-screen. The trick was to feign slight interest, gently tease him at arm's length. Keep him guessing, intrigued but not rejected.

It'd be easier with Joe than with Campbell. Not being the director, Joe knew he was lower on their little social pyramid, but after a few drinks, he'd be circling like a hyena eager for leftovers.

Joe leaned back from the camera and against the top of a bureau, casually flexing. He glanced at the hem of her sundress, a blinding yellow that Campbell insisted she wear. "Your boyfriend coming out for drinks tonight?"

She almost laughed. *Boyfriend*. How quaint. "I haven't had a boyfriend since middle school. No time with filming schedules."

Joe nodded, smile spreading. "Ain't that the truth. We should hang out later."

Prick, she thought while she preened. She pictured Joe's eyes bulging as an aneurysm took hold. He'd groan and pitch forward onto the coffee table, maybe bashing in the corner of his temple along the way.

She tapped her finger along the windowpane as they waited. Through the thick, sealed glass, partiers staggered on their heels, laughing in the night as they headed to the bars. Why the hell couldn't she find a single gig where she didn't have to bat her eyes and act like she'd be DTF? What was she doing wrong?

Her friends shrugged off her complaints as the way things went—sex was the currency she had to deal in. One by one, her friends had gotten burned out and left LA for good. Kelsie wasn't ready for that yet. Some people wanted love, others money. But she knew, ever since she had gone viral in a YouTube video that got her a commercial deal back in grade school, that she was meant for fame. She was so close to that pivotal moment, the golden opportunity that would ricochet her up the echelon into real success; she could feel it in her bones. Maybe this Birdwatcher Butcher film would be it.

She turned into position as the sound woman gave the go-ahead, and Campbell barked at them to begin.

"He's going to kill me," Kelsie whispered to the camera through the harsh lighting. She picked up the taxidermied robin they had gotten at a Goodwill and contorted her face into a look of horror.

"Birdwatcher Butcher . . . it all makes sense," she breathed. "And now that I'm here . . ."

She looked up at the rows of framed feathers—cobalt, mahogany striped, magenta—that the real Birdwatcher Butcher had collected. She took her time trailing fingers along the framed images on the mantel, black and white, mostly photos. They showed tree leaves and storefronts, nothing particularly artistic, but all were historic artifacts from the killer. Her gaze settled on the one that caught her eye during every take: a charcoal outline he had sketched of a billowy, bird-like creature, a cross between a plague doctor and human-sized vulture.

She was in the zone now. She could almost feel Birdwatcher Butcher studying her from the shadows, like a stilted stalker, biding his time, taking in her every action. She let a shudder work its way across her shoulders, imagining his cold fingertips touching her neck.

She opened a drawer, where a butcher knife larger than her head rested, removed from the plastic display case they had set aside for the shoot. One of his knives, all of which he'd named after birds. This one had a wide yellow handle with the word "Canary" painted on it in blocky black letters.

"I'm going to die," she breathed. She arched her eyebrows as high as she could and willed the start of tears to make her eyes shine that much more.

If only a serial killer would *actually kidnap me. Then at least I'd be famous,* she thought sourly. *And out of Campbell's sights.*

A few hours later, they wrapped.

"Great job, guys. Tomorrow, we do the big wow moment." Campbell chewed on a bit of beef jerky and offered a piece to her. "It'll look amazing. Red splattered against your yellow dress, here." He pointed, the tips of his fingers grazing her breast. Kelsie kept her smile plastered on, willing him to choke on his jerky, his face to turn gray from suffocation.

They headed down to the street, Campbell already handsy. She bit back her impulse to shove him in front of oncoming traffic and instead made a show of stopping in surprise.

"Damn. Forgot my purse back on set." She had a plan, of course. She'd wait an hour before taking an Uber back to the hotel. The lobby bar would be closed by then, so she wouldn't risk running into Campbell. In the morning, she'd tell them she had a migraine and had to sleep it off so there'd be no hard feelings. Easy peasy.

"I'll catch up!" Kelsie unwound Campbell's sweating hand from around her waist. "Can I get the key?"

Campbell pulled it from his pocket, held it up like a gift he would bequeath to her. He glanced at the others, half a block ahead.

"Meet in my room in a bit for some notes, cool?"

"Oh, ah," Kelsie stalled. "I might call it an early night—maybe we can talk at breakfast?"

"I really want to get through these tonight." His mouth narrowed before he smiled. Really more of a smirk. "I know you're super dedicated. A real professional. It won't take long."

Kelsie nodded and all but snatched the key, biting her lip to stop a scream of frustration. She ripped up the stairs to Birdwatcher Butcher's apartment and threw herself onto the couch. The shitty single apartment fixture overhead flicked enough to make her headache rear up again. She turned it off and switched on one of Joe's small spotlights instead, enough so she could move around without tripping.

She'd wait it out. Maybe Campbell would drink enough, find someone else and forget about her.

While she waited, she scrolled her social streams. She had a few thousand followers here and there, but not enough. She wanted to scream to the world that she was here, *ready*. Maybe this film would be the thing if she could just survive Campbell. She closed her eyes, rubbing her forehead and willing herself to relax until her phone buzzed with a text from him asking where she was.

Think, think, think. There had to be a way out of this.

"got a killer headache. raincheck?" she texted with a sad emoticon.

"power thru" he replied. *"or I find actress who is actually dedicated. haha."*

She couldn't shake the image of his smirk. She stood to distract herself and paced until she was in front of Birdkiller's desk. The Canary knife peeked out from the half-open drawer, its handle shining in the dim light.

She picked it up. The coldness from the handle spread through her fingers. She had held knives before, and guns, and always felt the same spark of power, of relief. That feeling flowed through her now, but stronger. She lifted the Canary, imagining the blade crunching into Campbell's forehead. God, that would be so easy, wouldn't it?

But she wasn't strong enough. Big enough.

And it was a *ridiculous* notion. She dropped it.

If only she *were* stronger, a man—he'd never treat her that way. It wasn't fair.

Her phone buzzed again. Campbell, persistent as a dog with a bone.

"u still at apt? coming over now."

"Damn it," Kelsie said aloud. She could leave, but she'd just be delaying the inevitable. And seeing what a hard-on he had about getting access to the apartment, of course he'd want to hook up here. Her nostrils flared, and she pressed a hand to her nose. The air smelled pungent. Stale, but also like a pot of dirt had spilled.

Something rustled behind her. *That was fast.* She whirled around.

"Campbell?" she called. "You want to do foreplay, this isn't it, babe."

A pause swelled before a sound crackled the silence.

A trilling, low and vibrant. Like a bird.

"Hilarious," Kelsie snapped, but her skin electrified in a way that made her suspect it wasn't Campbell. Shadows hovered, shifting from the single spotlight, and reflected traffic light on the bumpy window glass.

Maybe someone had snuck in, a tweaker or homeless guy. She lifted Canary and tested the weight of the blade in her hand. The sight of it should scare off a would-be attacker, even if she had no idea how to wield it. A surge of iciness worked into her fingers when she moved the blade in front of her. She crept toward the darkened bedroom where the sound had come from.

"I *will* cut you," she warned and strained to see.

One shadow loomed tall and thin along the bedroom door. She glanced behind her for the figure that cast the shadow. No one.

When she turned back, the shadow had peeled itself off the wallpaper.

It stretched upward and arched toward her in the gloom. Black membranes anchored it to the darkness and clung to a machete-shaped beak.

"Cool costume, bro." Kelsie's mouth stumbled over the words. "That's some fancy special effects..."

The figure, easily seven feet tall, moved like no animatronics or puppet she had ever seen. It arched claws, sharper and thinner than her best eyebrow tweezers. Orbs of white light glowed in its eyes.

Her mind froze, not computing what her eyes were seeing as she backed up.

It was the shadow vulture from Birdwatcher Butcher's sketch.

"Wake up, wake up," Kelsie moaned, twisting the skin of her arm. Her phone was out of reach, still on the desk. She backed into the window instead. Sealed shut. She pounded on it with her free fist and screamed, a good, theatrical, blood-curdling scream that would've made any voice actor proud.

The shadow vulture watched in silence.

"What do you want?" Kelsie shrieked.

It gestured with its claws, and for a horrible second, she thought it wanted her to pleasure it. Then she realized it was pointing to the knife in her hand.

"Canary? Not a chance." She waved the blade in what she hoped was a threatening manner. "Whatever you are, I bet you're not immune to a fucking knife."

The shadow vulture tilted its head a modicum, like a bird in the zoo.

It started to speak.

"For you," it rasped. "Gift." What passed for a voice made her think of a crow trying to talk. She shuddered, for a second feeling like she was going to vomit. The sound was worse than the silence.

Canary's blade vibrated in her grip. She tried to suck some air back into her lungs. She was for sure hallucinating, drugged, or dreaming. Whatever the case, at least the thing wasn't attacking her. A good sign, maybe.

"Aw, fuck," Kelsie said. "What are you, Birdwatcher Butcher's ghost?"

"No." Its voice rattled like a wind shaking dry branches in the winter. "Your wish. I help you. I helped him."

"My wish?" she said faintly.

"Famous." The creature trilled the word like something naughty, sending a tremor down Kelsie's spine.

"You want me to, what?" The blade in Kelsie's hand seemed to thrum, eager. She started to shiver and couldn't stop. "Use this to kill someone? Not exactly what I had in mind for fame."

"Not one," the shadow vulture hissed. Shadows streamed up and down its figure in a waterfall of ink. "I help you. Stronger." Power emanated from it like a cologne, something she could almost soak herself in.

"What if I say no?"

"Stay obscure. Mediocre. Weak." The shadow vulture took a step, and she jumped back without thinking. "*Forgotten.*" It perched on arching, clawed toes, its silhouette bleeding into the floor.

Her anger flared. Dream, or haunting or whatever this was, the anger felt good, a remedy against the fear. She seized it.

"You're just another asshole trying to use me," Kelsie declared. "Ghost monster or not, I'm sick of it."

"Fame," the creature said, almost in appreciation. "We, partners. You . . . *Perfect.*"

Perfect? *Finally,* someone saw it. Her potential. Even if it was a weird shadow creature.

"What's in it for you?" Kelsie tried to buy herself time to think. Her phone vibrated again across the room, probably Campbell.

"Feed. Fear. Food." The shadow vulture's beak snapped, greedy. "You help. Kill."

"I can't." Kelsie dug her fingernails into her palm. "I can't go around murdering people, that's fucking insane."

"Some people. Deserve it." Its head rolled around on its neck, too fast, its beak flashing.

"Like what, pedos? Psychos?"

The creature nodded once and breathed more words around her that filled the room:

"Movies. Books. *Fame.*"

You're not really considering this, she told herself. The stream of thoughts came to her, as unwelcome as a downpour. Ted Bundy. Jack the Ripper. Jeffrey Dahmer. Household names, names that lived through history. People loved serial killers. There were countless shows that dove into the minds and lives of famed murderers. They had *fan* clubs for God's sake.

She'd be in the history books. Movies would not just star her, but be all about her.

She shook her head, snapping herself out of it. She'd also be *dead* or in jail. At best.

"No way. Again. I can't just *murder* people. That sounds gross. And also hard."

"Help you. Stronger," the shadow vulture said. The Canary blade glowed briefly in the darkness. Her phone lit up and vibrated on the table.

"Why can't you do it yourself?" Kelsie tried to stop the chatter of her teeth.

The shadow vulture lifted a hand toward her. "Need host. Partners. We bond."

"So we kill only people who deserve it?" She admired Canary in her hand, its blade as sharp as the creature's beak. "And you'll make sure I don't get caught?"

She got the sense the creature would have smiled if it could.

Even if I do get caught, she mused, *I'd definitely get film options and book deals.* Maybe she could even have an anonymous social stream going, if she was careful. She'd have fans. Serial killers always did. There weren't that many women serial killers after all, especially not hot ones like her. And if she only targeted horrible people and was cautious about her branding, she could be hailed a hero, a vixenish vigilante. Like Batman, but in a dress. They might even give her a freaking medal.

The staircase in the hallway creaked. She could hear Campbell's whistle through the door. Her heart quickstepped in panic at the sound.

You don't have to worry about him anymore, she thought, and her pulse slowed.

She nodded to the creature. "Okay, let's do this bond or whatever. Quick."

The shadow vulture reached toward her and Canary. She winced, expecting pain, but when the pinprick of its claw touched her wrist, a flush of strength slammed through her, faster than a long snort of coke. Threads of gray shadows ran up and around her arm like lace, sinking deep into her skin, and she gripped the blade tightly. A nickname rang out to her:

Canary Killer.

It was so perfect that she almost squealed, even as she heard the doorknob turn. The shadow vulture's power moved her muscles seamlessly, guiding her to step behind the door. Darkness folded around her so Campbell wouldn't see her until it was too late.

She held the knife against her dress, picturing the most Instagrammable angle of the chrome against a Technicolor splash of Campbell's blood and the yellow fabric.

She'd get millions of followers, no problem.

And best of all—no more blow jobs.

This story originally appeared as "Terror on the Boulevard" in Shotgun Honey Presents: At The Edge of Darkness.

Flesh Trade
By Peter Clines

Brett showed up ten minutes late, of course. Big men didn't wait on underlings. They made underlings wait on them.

Under normal circumstances, once he realized Larry wasn't in the diner, Brett would've just left and given the halfwit a punch in the nuts later. But the waitress was cute and had a tight T-shirt. He decided to have a cup of coffee, watch the perky girl bounce around the diner, and give Larry a chance to explain what was so damned important they had to meet in person.

That was twenty minutes ago.

He was running through a list of things he could do to teach Larry not to waste his time when the man himself stumbled through the door. Larry looked around, saw Brett, and straightened up. He swept the sunglasses and grimy baseball cap from his head before giving a respectful nod. Then he marched across the diner with a half-dozen long strides, his clothes flopping back and forth on him like a half-stuffed scarecrow.

Larry targeted new arrivals to the City of Angels. Runaways, throwaways, kids who thought they were going to get on *American Idol* or a *Chicago Whatever* show or the latest superhero movie. He sold to the bottom third of that group, sometimes guiding them onto other paths that involved larger quantities of more expensive drugs. He also had a bad habit of using what he was supposed to be selling. Everyone took a taste now and then, sure, but Larry snorted at least twenty percent of what came to him.

Larry stopped a few feet from the booth. "I know what you're gonna say. I know. I know I'm late. I know. I'm so sorry."

Brett sipped his coffee. His second cup of coffee. He always tried to be cool, to let other people spill their guts before he said anything. He'd read a book that said that's how the Japanese did things. The Japanese kicked ass at that sort of thing.

Larry slid into the booth. Momentum sent a cloud of smells bouncing off the wall and across the table. Fresh scabs clustered along his jaw where he'd picked at the pale flesh. Tiny clumps of grit clung to his stringy hair and dotted the ragged collar of his shirt. His bloodshot eyes examined the tabletop.

The perky waitress walked up. Her smile never faltered. "Your friend got here. What can I get you?"

Larry looked up at her, and his lips pulled into a tight smile. "Just water. And a double side of bacon."

Her face fell. "I actually can't get you a side order if you don't get a sandwich or an entrée."

Brett gave her a faint nod. The kind of gesture that said his associate was a little addled and should be ignored. She returned it with a look that implied she'd make an exception this time and should get a very good tip.

"Bacon," smiled Larry as the waitress slipped away. "The other white meat." He picked at the skin beneath his earlobe.

"You're half an hour late," said Brett.

"Right. I know."

"Half. An. Hour."

"Sorry. Again, so sorry."

"What the fuck is so important that it lets you waste thirty of my minutes? We were going to meet up day after tomorrow anyway so you could pick up a few."

Larry looked around the diner. The dinner rush hadn't kicked in, and only a handful of customers peppered the booths and tables. His head bobbed up and down so hard his filthy hair reared up on his head. "I've got *information*. Big, important information. Saw some grade-A weird shit this morning, y'know?"

Brett pushed his coffee cup and saucer to the end of the table. The waitress made eye contact across the room, but he shook his head and placed a palm over the cup. "So let's hear it."

Larry blinked. His eyelids moved in slow motion. "Hear what?"

"This information. What you got?"

"Oh. Right. That, right." He picked at the flesh behind his ear again.

"Are you fucking high, man?"

"What?" His eyes went wide. "No, no, no. No. Maybe a little. Just to take the edge off after what I saw, y'know?"

Brett's knuckles ached with the growing desire to punch something.

"I'm just thinking, y'know," said Larry, tapping his fingers on the tabletop, "I'm thinking maybe I should get some kind of reward. Maybe this should go up the ladder to . . . umm . . . Mister . . . ahhhhh . . ." His finger tapping morphed into a frenzied drum solo.

"Keegan?" finished Brett. "You think this is something to bother Keegan with?"

Larry stopped fidgeting and nodded. "Yeah," he said. "Mr. Keegan."

"You know he doesn't like dealing with small shit. I'm still going to kick you in the nuts for wasting my time. He'll cut 'em off."

"It's big. He'll want to know."

Brett stared at him for a minute. Larry twitched under his gaze. The waitress walked by, scooped up the coffee cup, and smiled at them. "Bacon's coming up!"

"Thank you," crowed Larry with another tight smile. Then the smile faltered, and he looked back at his boss. His fingers began to fidget again.

"Okay," said Brett. "Tell me what you got. Next time I see Keegan, I'll talk to him about it."

Larry shook his head. "No, no, no," he said. "It's my information, I get to tell him. Maybe . . ." He slapped the tabletop with his palms. A few other customers turned at the sound. "Maybe, I think, maybe we should go see Keegan right now. He's really going to want to hear this."

"Maybe," said Brett. "But it's better if it comes through me. And if he thinks your information's worth anything, we can split it. Sixty-forty."

Larry thrashed his head side to side. "Nope, no, no. I need to see him in person. My information, my reward."

His chin went back and forth, again and again, and three of the scabs beneath his earlobe split open. The split spread into a gap, and then the ear flapped back and forth with the last three shakes of Larry's head. It hung loose on a piece of skin the size of a playing card.

The coffee churned in Brett's stomach. "What the fuck?"

Larry blinked twice. He looked over his shoulder, following Brett's gaze, then reached up and felt the dangling flap of flesh and ear. "Ahhh," he said with a voice that wasn't his. "Well, I guess that's over, then."

Brett whipped the pistol from his belt, aiming it across the tabletop. "What the fuck's going on here?" he growled. "Who the fuck are you?"

"Actually, can I ask you something first?" said the impostor, straightening. His bloodshot eyes focused on Brett but didn't seem to notice the gun. His smile went wide, revealing a sprawling graveyard of crooked, chipped teeth. It wrinkled his face and popped another pair of scabs. The ear swung around on its flap of skin to pat the man's cheek. "Before this, did you believe me as Larry? I don't get to do a lot of the role-play stuff, so I'm just . . . Did I sell the part?"

"What?"

He pushed the ear back into place on the side of his head. "I was worried I was overplaying the junkie bit. Be honest." The ear flopped down again. This time it sagged even lower, revealing the gray meat behind it. "Did I pull it off?"

Brett squeezed the trigger, and a hole appeared in the other man's chest between his heart and his shoulder. The gunshot echoed in the diner like a dozen plates breaking at once. The perky waitress screamed.

Not-Larry sighed. "It was the hands, wasn't it? I moved the hands too much." He banged a fist on the table and shook his head. "You know, seriously, physical acting's the hardest part."

Brett squeezed off two more shots. They punched through Not-Larry's heart and lungs and shredded the upholstery in the next booth. The waitress wailed and covered her head. Some of the customers screamed. Others ran for the door.

Brett stood up and shoved the gun back into his belt. No one aimed a phone at him, and the diner didn't have cameras, but the waitress could probably ID him. He'd have to lay low for a few days, but that wouldn't be—

"Hang on." Not-Larry grabbed him by the wrist. "We're not done yet."

Brett yanked his hand away and hot pain shot up his arm. He looked down and saw red. It splashed onto the floor and crept up his sleeve.

Not-Larry stood up, grabbed Brett by the shoulder, and pushed him back down into the booth. The impostor held a long, gleaming scalpel. It wagged back and forth like a scolding finger.

"Christ!" Brett grabbed at his wrist and tried to push the gash back together. He could feel blood pulse against his palm, see it swell between his fingers. He twisted his arms around to grab at his pistol, but it clattered to the floor under the table. "Fucking Christ!"

He leaped up. A sneaker in the stomach pushed him right back down.

"Keegan," said Not-Larry. The flap of skin was now a small banner along the side of his head. It hung from the top of his jaw to his chin, showing off withered gray muscles beneath the fresh skin. "You were about to tell me where to find him."

"Fucking hell, man. I need a doctor."

The impostor clicked his tongue. "Questions first. Doctor second. Maybe."

Brett felt cold. He'd heard people who'd almost bought it say that, but never believed it happened so fast. It was like sliding into a cold pool and feeling the water suck away your heat. He looked at his lap and saw blood soaking his clothes. "Please. I don't want to die."

"Don't be a whiner," said the Not-Larry. "I've seen lots of dead people. You've got at least ten minutes."

GEVAUDAN STARED out the picture window, shifting focus from the dusky city below to his own reflection. With a little work, he could find the spot where the images blurred together, and he became a giant. He shifted his feet so the huge Gevaudan straddled an entire block of West Hollywood. He imagined the little people staring up at him in awe and terror.

In the office, on the other side of the glass, he stood six feet tall. He was five-foot-eleven in bare feet, but he'd realized years ago how intimidating that extra inch could be and made a point of always wearing shoes with lifts in the heels. He'd started shaving his head at about the same time. No hairline or random gray hairs made him timeless, made him powerful.

Gevaudan wasn't stupid enough to call himself a crime boss. He didn't refer to his business as a syndicate or a cartel or a family. He never carried a weapon. While he was known in most circles as Gevaudan, it wasn't his real name. He'd picked it from some French monster movie he'd seen as a teenager.

Idiots drew attention to themselves. The real master criminals—

and there was no doubt in his mind that he was a criminal, he just wasn't foolish enough to say it out loud—were the ones that stayed unseen and unsuspected. This practice had allowed him to take control of a sizable amount of the Los Angeles drug trade, along with investments in gambling, racketeering, prostitution, and even a small dabbling in blood sports. His entire adult criminal record, though, consisted of two parking tickets. They'd both been deliberate, twenty-six months apart.

In Los Angeles, a completely spotless record was more suspicious than a checkered one.

Two quick knocks echoed through his office. Gevaudan turned just as Douglas stepped through the door. "Sir," he said, "I'm sorry to interrupt, but a situation has developed."

"What is it?"

Douglas tilted his head toward the hall. "Carmen Burke's here to see you. It seems there've been several . . . early retirements over the past two days. Eleven of them. He'd like to speak with you about it."

Gevaudan counted to five. When he got any sort of news, he always counted to five before speaking. It allowed him to look thoughtful. "Why am I just hearing about this now?"

"I'm not sure, sir. Mr. Burke is right out in the lobby. He's been injured."

Another five count. "Send him in. Ask Henry to wait outside." Henry was Gevaudan's personal bodyguard and retirement specialist.

"Of course, sir."

Burke pushed his way into the office a minute later, Douglas trailing behind him. Burke's hair spiked out in a few directions, as if he'd combed it with his fingers, and a trio of pale Band-Aids stood out against his tanned cheek. Burke had been fat once, but since had become obsessive about his weight. He was also a fashion whore. Even now, half-panicked, his silk tie sat tight against his throat in a huge knot with the end tucked into a complementary waistcoat.

Burke's eyes flitted around and landed on Gevaudan. "Fuck," he said. "We're getting slaughtered out there. Slaughtered like pigs."

One two three four five. "Calm down, Carmen." Gevaudan gestured to Douglas. "Scotch, yes?"

"Goddamn, yes." Burke ran his fingers through his hair again. Douglas stepped away from the bar and put a glass in his hand. It was shaking with fear, adrenaline, or some mix of the two. He slugged half the scotch in one swallow.

Gevaudan sent Douglas away with another gesture. "Now," he said, "tell me how so many of our people ended up dead."

Burke shook his head. "You're going to think I'm sampling."

"Why would I think that?"

Burke tilted the glass and finished the whiskey. "It's a monster."

Gevaudan's fingers twitched. He counted to five. Then he counted again. "I beg your pardon?"

Burke looked over at the bar, at the painting, at anything except Gevaudan. "It's a monster. A real-life, horror-movie monster. Some kind of zombie or something."

"A zombie?"

"I know what it sounds like," snapped Burke. He swallowed and lowered his gaze. "Sorry, sir. It's just . . ." He reached up and touched the line of Band-Aids with the empty glass. "It went for my eyes. Slashed my cheek open. One of my men tackled it and it gutted him right in front of me. Crotch to chin, like a fucking autopsy."

This time Gevaudan counted straight to ten. Six and seven felt odd against his mind. Eight and nine were alien. "You're sure about this?"

Burke pressed the highest adhesive bandage against his skull. "Sure as shit."

"Eleven men dead?"

"That I know of. I heard about a couple of dead pushers yesterday. I thought, so the fuck what, right? One of them had his head skinned, but I figured he'd pissed off one of the Salvadorans or something. Then *his* dealer was killed in a diner last night, and this morning *his* supplier—my guy, Reggie Keegan—got hit." Burke stared over at the bar. "Can I grab another?"

"No," said Gevaudan. "Why wasn't I told of this?"

"I was going to tell you during tomorrow morning's meeting. Then about two hours ago I walked out of dinner and it took out my whole staff. Five guys in about a minute."

"Did they shoot it?"

"Fuck yeah, they shot it. At least thirty rounds, if I had to guess. They would've had better luck saying please and asking it to stop." Burke shook his head.

"Body armor?" Gevaudan asked. "Maybe on meth?"

"I'm telling you, it was some kind of monster."

"And it's working its way up through our business." Another ten count. "What do you think it wants?"

Burke set his glass down on the floor and stood up. He glanced over his shoulder at the door and set his hands in his coat pockets. "Well, I think we both know the answer to that one, don't we?"

Gevaudan looked at him. Burke's voice had changed. He sounded much more relaxed and confident than the man who'd walked into the office. "What are you talking about?"

"You've hesitated a few too many times during this conversation," said Burke, "and at all the wrong points."

Gevaudan was not stupid. "Henry!"

The bodyguard burst through the door with his pistol in hand. He took three quick steps to the side, putting Gevaudan out of the line of fire, and the pistol barked three times. All three rounds hit Burke between the shoulder blades.

The man who wasn't Burke turned around and shook his head. "One chance," he said. "Run—now—and I won't eat your kidneys."

Henry fired three more rounds at Not-Burke's head. One missed, one sprayed his left ear across the room, and the last one tore a red line across his jaw. The barrel dropped and Henry emptied the weapon into Not-Burke's chest.

Not-Burke staggered and charged, growling like an animal. The wounds barely slowed him. They didn't even bleed. His hands lashed out and steel gleamed between his fingers.

Henry's pistol sparked as it blocked one blow. He dropped back, tried to get another shot, but Not-Burke lunged forward. Henry batted away another blow with his arm. Not-Burke snarled, spun, and the pistol flew away to bounce off a wall. His hands slashed back and forth across the bodyguard's chest.

Henry's tie dropped to the floor. Something wet hit the carpet right after it. He wrapped his arms across his gut and dropped to his knees.

"Warned you," said Not-Burke. He drove a punch into Henry's head and the man slumped down to the floor, his innards soaking the rug. Douglas came running in and caught a fist in the face. He staggered back, blood gushing out of his nose, and collapsed into the hall.

Not-Burke looked around the room. "Sorry about the mess," he said to Gevaudan. "I just wanted to talk."

Gevaudan had found the fallen pistol. It clicked twice as he pulled the trigger. Then it clicked two more times.

The two men stared at each other for a moment.

"Okay," said Not-Burke, "in the interest of saving time, let's just be honest with one another."

He hooked his finger under his chin, just above the oversized tie knot, and pulled. The flesh lifted like a balaclava, wrinkling and gathering as it rose. The Band-Aids tried to flex with the skin and popped off to reveal a bloodless gash in the cheek, one that vanished as Not-Burke stretched his face up over his nose and past his eyes.

Beneath was a paper-wrapped skull, barely covered in tissue-thin gray flesh. The creature had no lips, just rows of exposed, uneven teeth lined with strands of clay-colored muscle. Two slits on either side of a bone shard made up the nose. Swollen red veins ran through both of its eyes. One sat open and exposed with no lid.

Gevaudan didn't scream, but he lost bladder control for a moment. Just a quick squirt before he clamped down. Enough to smell and make a wet spot, but not to soak his leg. The empty pistol shivered in his hand.

"I'm Obediah," said the corpse-monster. "I've been trying to find you for a couple of days now." It dropped Burke's face on the floor. "Good name, by the way. Gevaudan. I've got some relatives in that part of France. Some of those weird, distant relatives. Never been, myself, because . . . well, you know. They're French."

The strings of muscle around its teeth tightened. A naked expression of emotion without the clothing to fully display it. Something clicked in Gevaudan's mind. The thing was smiling at him. Smiling with no lips or cheeks.

The wet spot grew.

Obediah grabbed him by the necktie. The thin blade settled just beneath Gevaudan's chin. The monster tugged and Gevaudan followed, like a dog on a leash.

"Please," sputtered the crime boss, "just tell me what you want."

"I told you, I just want to talk."

Obediah spun Gevaudan around and backed him up against the desk. The blade pushed a little harder against his throat and he leaned away from it. His feet came off the floor and he found himself flailing like a pig on a butcher's block.

"Money? Drugs? Name it and it's yours."

"Tell me," said the monster, "about the kids."

Gevaudan swallowed. "What?"

"Not a good time to lie. This is about being honest, remember? Taking what's inside you and letting it all out." It tapped the scalpel twice against Gevaudan's exposed throat, then let the blade slide over the man's necktie and down to his stomach. "So . . . tell me about the kids."

PROSPERO, the arranger, took in another breath and let it out slowly. Blue air in, red air out. That's how his therapist told him to picture it. He thought it was nonsense, but in all fairness, it did calm him down when his heart rate started to climb.

A few months back, Prospero had tried to figure out how he'd ended up in this particular line of work and drawn a blank. It had been a natural progression, he knew that. A smooth flow, with no odd leaps or stumbles anywhere. He honestly couldn't say when he'd made the step that took him from black marketeer to white slaver. He'd just found a niche and excelled at it.

And it was ridiculously easy to excel. No real names ever used. Double-blind accounts on both ends. Truth be told, so many teenaged boys and girls went missing every year, it barely felt like a risk most of the time. Hell, a good third of his merchandise was handed to him—a son or daughter being used to pay off a debt or set an example. He had a black ledger of crime bosses, businessmen, three Senators, and one Navy admiral. It would give him nearly unlimited leverage if he ever actually needed it.

Seven people had arrived for this quarter's auction. Five men and two women. Twice in the past, attendance had reached eleven, and once the bidding took place between only two. Five was average, though, so Prospero was pleased with a turnout of seven.

Two of them were proxies, well-schooled in the tastes of their respective employers. Four were known by their city or country, three by nicknames. The Englishman, Munich, the Professional, and Japan all tended to wear very conservative suits, while Rio, the Rock Star, and Malibu had been known to show up in almost anything.

On this particular night, the Rock Star was dressed in motorcycle leathers, despite having been driven to the auction in a limousine. Rio wore a flowered sundress and had covered all her fingers with rings. Malibu had Levi's with a sheer, vintage t-shirt and no bra. The occasional leers of the other bidders never fazed her. She was the youngest bidder by far, but her appetites were already the talk of legend in several circles.

The blonde currently up for bids wore only a shock collar. Each of the attendees had prodded and squeezed her. Rio had studied her teeth, the Professional her eyes and fingernails. Munich had slapped her ass three times and studied the flesh after each one, like a man checking drum skins or tire pressure.

The Rock Star put in another bid for the girl. He had a thing for blondes. He went through several of them a year. Malibu tapped her knee twice, raising the bid by another two hundred thousand. She didn't like blondes, but she liked the Rock Star less. They'd tried to share their winnings once and it hadn't gone well.

The Rock Star put in a sixth bid and claimed the blonde for one-point-one million. Funds transferred from anonymous account to anonymous account. Men ushered the blonde off the small stage and out the door behind her new owner. She'd be given non-descript clothes and a cocktail of drugs that would keep her dazed and compliant for at least twenty hours.

It would be a good night, Prospero thought, even without the final item in the auction. He checked the time on his pocket watch—a small bit of showmanship he allowed himself—and gave a discreet hand signal to one of his assistants. The woman blinked her understanding and whispered into her headset.

The auctioneer—real name Kelly, although it was never spoken here—generally worked out of New Orleans. She had a completely legitimate auction house there. Prospero had found her after a year-long talent hunt. Once every three months, he flew her out to Los Angeles for one of the private auctions. Every second or third time, they'd end the night with angry, sometimes violent sex in a Beverly Hills hotel room. Far more catharsis than any sort of affection for each other.

"Ladies and gentlemen," the auctioneer said. "We have one item left on tonight's ticket, the one that's brought most of you out tonight. He's a unique specimen, never before seen at one of our events. Or perhaps anywhere."

She snapped her fingers, and the curtains parted. A young boy limped forward. The circle of light brightened on the stage, and he cringed back.

The boy's skin was pale, like milk under the brilliant lights. His thin limbs and hairless chest helped mask his age, but he was still sixteen at the very most. His black hair hung short and straight, almost a pixie cut. His hazel-green eyes sat a bit too wide on an otherwise plain face. No one would ever call him ugly, but he was still a safe distance from beautiful.

They'd strapped two shock collars to him. The standard one wrapped around his neck. A second sat far up his thigh.

Rio's gaze slid up the thigh. She smirked and muttered something under her breath. Japan grinned, too.

"For this particular item," the auctioneer said, "the opening bid will be two million dollars."

"Wait," said Rio, "an example." She shook her head at the word and snapped her fingers twice. Her English wasn't good, but the woman refused to speak through a translator. "Demonstration."

Japan and the Professional both nodded in agreement.

Prospero looked to the assistant. The assistant manipulated icons on her tablet.

The boy yelped and twitched again. He staggered and his uncollared leg shifted to catch him. Another jolt from the collars made his toes flex. His muscles spasmed across his body, rippling his flesh down his arms, across his chest, and down his thighs.

"Whoa," said Malibu.

"Christ," the Rock Star said, "you're fryin' his insides."

The auctioneer held up a reassuring hand, silencing them.

The boy bared his teeth, and the canines shot up from his lower jaw to touch his upper lip. His eyebrows thickened while the pixie cut grew out, ran down his neck, spread across his shoulders. Muscles stretched and popped as the boy fell forward on the platform, catching himself on his knuckles. Another spasm rocked his frame, and he shook it off like a dog shedding water.

Prospero felt a thin smile spread across his face.

At first glance, with its broad paws and whiskers, the creature almost looked like one of the mountain lions that sometimes wandered down out of the parks and into suburbia, maybe all the way into the city. But then, the snout pushed forward even more, and the black pelt grew longer. Its thick claws tapped on the stage. Its tail bent down, curling between its haunches.

The Englishman gripped the arms of his chair. Malibu cooed her excitement. Japan and Munich texted messages. The Professional stared at the creature, lost in thought.

The wolf growled, but the noise broke off into a whimper. One collar still wrapped around its neck. The shape-changed thigh was wide enough to hold the other one in place. The wolf twisted around to bite at its thigh, and they all heard the harsh snap of electricity.

"As I stated earlier," said the auctioneer, "a unique specimen, able to satisfy several exotic desires, perhaps all at once."

She snapped her fingers and the wolf, after growling again, let out a few panting breaths. Waves ran through its fur. It raised its head to howl, and its nose pulled back into its skull. The paws and legs shifted. Strands of hair slid back under the pale skin and revealed the boy on all fours, his head hung low.

"That's enough," said the Englishman. "He's going home with me."

"Two million, then," said the auctioneer, dipping her head to the man.

"Two-five," said Munich. He was halfway to the stage to check the boy's ass. He scowled at the Englishman.

"Three-five," said the Professional.

"We have three and a half million," the auctioneer said.

Japan raised a finger. "Four million."

Malibu tapped her knee with two fingers.

"We are at four point two million," said the auctioneer. The muscles of her cheek gave a slight flutter Prospero recognized—the excitement of big, fast bids. He felt it, too, just not in his cheek.

"Four-three," said the Rock Star. It got a snort from Munich, but the auctioneer honored it.

"Four-five," Japan said.

The Englishman cleared his throat. "I don't think you heard me," he said, his accent slipping away. "I'm taking him home. Now."

The boy raised his head to look at the Englishman.

"Sir," said the auctioneer. She glanced at Prospero, then back at the Englishman. "You are aware that's not how things are done here."

"There's no 'buy it now' option," smirked Malibu.

The Englishman stood up. "Yeah, this from the girl who famously gives up her ass for a few drinks."

Prospero scowled, only half-registering the shift in the man's voice. Interpersonal squabbles always soured the auction. It'd take weeks of kissing ass to rebuild the goodwill this outburst would cost him. "Sir, we do not allow—"

"Okay let me make myself very clear." The Englishman stepped closer to the stage light. Some of the shadows around his face refused to fade. Dried blood painted the Englishman's neck, all but hidden by his tie. More of it lined his scalp.

The Englishman tore off his face and tossed it into Malibu's lap. She screamed. So did Japan and Munich.

His other hand came up and pulled his scalp back like a hood, peeling it away to reveal the gaunt, blood-streaked features beneath. One eye glared wide open above a forest of jagged, crooked teeth. The creature let the hair and ears drop to the floor. Rio threw up. The boy on the stage squealed.

"I'll give you all to the count of three to start running," the thing shouted over the panic. It shrugged out of the Englishman's coat. The shirt beneath was splattered and striped with blood.

The Rock Star, Rio, and two of the clerks dashed for the doors on either side of Prospero. The Professional vanished behind the curtain leading to the holding area, and Munich staggered after him. Malibu flailed in her chair, shrieking every time the fleshy mess of the Englishman's face shifted in her lap.

"Uncle Obi?" asked the boy, his eyes wide. "Is it you?"

"Yeah, kid." The monster tossed the suit coat to the boy. "You got any other clothes somewhere?"

"I think they burned them."

A quartet of burly men appeared from the doors even as Malibu—finally out from under the face—ran shrieking from the room. Two of the men pulled out machine pistols, blocky things that hung from straps under their coats. "Kill it," snapped Prospero. "Kill both of them!"

The corpse-looking thing shoved the boy down and caught the shower of ammunition with its back. Bullets punched through the fine shirt and slacks, shredded the good silk tie. Two of the comfortable chairs burst apart into rags. Glassware shattered. Two lighting fixtures exploded. Dark fluid leaked from the creature's wounds, and it turned to take another half-dozen bursts in the chest and thighs and crotch.

The corpse—Uncle Obi—swayed on its feet for a moment, but didn't fall. Then he gifted them with a lipless snarl and held up his hands. Twin scalpels gleamed in the auction's dim light.

Two of the security contractors hesitated. When the creature took a step forward, hesitation became retreat. Prospero shouted after them. Kelly, the auctioneer, gave him a look, a shake of the head, and dashed after the two men.

No after-auction hookup tonight, then.

The other contractors charged across the room. The corpse leaped to meet them. One went for a hold and Uncle Obi drove his scalpels up into the larger man's armpits. The blades yanked back and opened up the sleeve, skin, and muscle. Blood splashed on the floor. The contractor splashed in the blood.

The second man had a dark, double-edged blade. He lunged in and slammed up under the creature's ribs two, three, four times. He brought it around again and slammed it down into the ghoul's throat, just above the breastbone. The knife sank down to the hilt.

Obi scowled, gurgled, and backhanded the man across the face. Jagged knuckles opened his cheek. To his credit, the man lunged back in, but the corpse-thing slammed his bony forehead against the man's nose and he crumbled.

Prospero pulled his own weapon from its slim, small-of-the-back holster. A compact Glock, no numbers, no history, completely clean. He'd carried it for years and never had to use it.

He looked at the tattered remains of the auction room and tried to process why he needed to use it now. And if it would do any good.

Prospero's first shot went wide and tugged at one of the corpse-creature's shirt sleeves. The second and the third hit him in the chest. Obi marched across the room as a fourth round hit him high in the shoulder. The knife in his throat bobbed back and forth as he walked. The fifth shot knocked his skull back and tore away a flap of skin.

It still didn't stop him.

The monster tore the pistol from Prospero's hand and gut-punched him. Air rushed out of his lungs, deflated him, left him bent over and wheezing. Smooth leather shoes hooked around his ankle, pressing through the fine wool of his suit, and then his feet weren't under him anymore. The carpet rushed up and smacked his cheek.

For such plush carpet, it hit hard enough to make his head ring.

The creature gargled a few more words, then reached up and dragged the knife out of his throat. He tossed the blade away and spat black phlegm and blood out between his crooked teeth. "Goddamn it. Gonna take me a week to fix all this."

Prospero caught his breath and glared up at the ghoul. "You . . . you're a dead man."

Obi snorted and shook his head. "Yeah, if I had a nickel." He spotted the tablet a few feet away and brought his heel down on it twice. Then, as an afterthought, he came back and kicked Prospero in the stomach.

As he winced in pain and gasped for air, it crossed Prospero's mind that things had somehow gone very, very wrong at this quarter's auction.

The wolf-boy jumped up from his hiding space behind the stage. He ran to the gray-skinned corpse and threw his arms around it. The ghoul squeezed him back and patted his shoulders. His chin left a dark smear on the boy's forehead. "It's okay," Obi told him. "Everything's okay now."

"Thank you," said the wolf-boy. "Thank you for coming."

"Your mom's been worried sick, you know. She and Mr. Tisarte called me a couple days ago, asked if I could find you."

"I'm sorry. I'm so sorry. I just wanted to go out and see . . . everything."

"I know. Believe me, I've been there. It's a big world, and Sanctuary's a small town." Another scalpel appeared in Obi's hand, and he set it against the boy's thigh. The blade slipped beneath the shock collar strap and sliced up. A skeletal finger lifted the boy's chin, and the collar on his neck fell away.

Prospero pushed himself up to his knees. "Do you have any idea who's behind all this?" he asked them between breaths. "Who funds this? You . . . you people are well and truly fucked."

"We aren't people," Obi said. He walked back, crouched, and poked the arranger in the forehead. His fingertip felt pointy, and Prospero realized there was very little flesh covering the bone.

"The real question," continued Obi, "is . . . what are you?"

Prospero swallowed. "What do you mean?" This close, he could see the corpse-creature's face wasn't makeup, even though he'd known all along it wasn't. He could see dark veins and muscle fibers and scrapes on the exposed teeth.

Obi looked back at the wolf-boy. "Mr. Tisarte was pretty serious about covering my tracks while I looked for you."

The boy's eyes went wide. His gaze dropped from the creature down to Prospero. His eyes were very green. Like Japanese beetles.

The ghoul cleared his throat. "I think if you wanted to . . . well, in this case I think it'd serve multiple purposes. If you wanted to."

The boy's mouth pulled into a smile. His beetle-green eyes were still fixed on Prospero. "You sure?" His tongue slipped out to lick his lips.

Prospero looked back and forth between the two monsters. "What are you talking about?"

"Yeah. Just be kind of quick about it."

The boy nodded. "Do you want to . . . ?"

Obi shuddered. "Christ, no. You and St. John may live for that, but I just can't stomach anything that fresh." He straightened up and looked at the door leading backstage. "How about I make sure there's nobody else wandering around that might disturb you?"

"Thanks, Obi."

The ghoul hugged the boy again and gave Prospero a glance. "Little tip. Tilt your head back and expose your throat. It'll make the whole thing a lot quicker for you."

The boy shrugged his shoulders and let the Englishman's coat fall to the floor. He stared at Prospero.

The corpse-creature walked out, leaving Prospero alone with the naked teen. He was no athlete, but he still outweighed the boy by a hundred pounds, easy. He glanced to one of the fallen security men, just a few feet away. They were all loaded with weapons. A moment with the body would give him a pistol, a taser, a can of mace, a knife, any number of weapons.

"So," he asked, inching back, "what happens now?"

The boy's skin rippled. His teeth grew. His nails became claws.

Prospero pushed himself up and lunged toward the body.

He almost made it.

Growing Darkness
By Greg Mollin

Oct. 13
It is restless. It crawls, incessantly circling, seeking, tasting the air like an animal. Like an insect. Its searching fingers squirm like grubs. It is ravenous. Soon it will wail and scream, demanding tribute. It will not relent.

Layla denies the becoming. Her eyes cannot behold it. She still sees the child it once was.

I see only Master. Tormentor. God.

CATHY CLOSES HER SON'S JOURNAL AND SHAKES HER HEAD as if to clear it of what she had read. She scratches at a spot of something dried on the embossed leather. Dark red dust comes away under her fingernail. She shudders and tosses the book into the cardboard box of his belongings the police allowed her to take from the crime scene. She turns on the television, tries to focus on the screen, wills the irrational words out of her brain.

Danny is asleep in his crib in her bedroom. The baby keeps her up most nights. Caring for an eight-month-old child was not something she'd ever planned for or expected at her age.

Exhaustion has held her hostage for days. Sadness, guilt, and Danny's wails pry her eyes in the night. What little sleep she manages is rife with nightmares. Hours pass on the couch in a nebulous trance.

The stub of a joint she'd smoked before reading Michael's journal sits on the rim of a Diet Coke can. It yields a couple of hits before Danny begins to cry again, and she shuffles into the bedroom to feed him.

THE DAY MOVES in slow motion. It is Wednesday afternoon, and the store is near uninhabited, the aisles mostly vacant. An indistinguishable, yet annoyingly familiar tune chews on her nerves through the overhead speakers.

Nicki, from down the hall, is watching Danny while she works. She texts every couple of hours. *Does this kid ever stop crying?*

Cathy leans against her register and tries to recall details of the dream that woke her from the one solid hour of sleep she'd managed. The memory is a blur. The self-defense mechanisms of her deep brain will not allow her to delve further.

Cathy almost looks forward to her AA meeting after work tonight. Listening to the war stories of recovering drunks should be high-volume entertainment compared to watching this smattering of lethargic patrons circling the grocery store.

With so little sleep, everything takes on a sinister tone. The sidelong glance of an elderly woman shuffling past, a glint of jagged yellow tooth in her thin-lipped smile. The clatter of a faulty shopping cart overflowing with junk food and the man in stained sweatpants pushing it slowly down the frozen aisle like a corpse toward the morgue. The polished linoleum floors gleam as though perspiring. The canned music warbles. Her eyelids feel weighted with lead.

She straightens her posture when she eyes Susan, the store manager, heading her way.

"Slow one today, huh?" Susan says, confirming her status as master of the obvious.

"It's dragging for sure," Cathy says.

"Dave needs quarters," Susan says, waving a twenty. "You got?"

Cathy hits NO SALE. She fishes two rolls out of the change tray and hands them to her.

Susan says, "You look wiped."

"Thanks," Cathy says, stretching a false grin. "Haven't been sleeping well."

"I get it."

A baby cries somewhere toward the back of the store. The sound makes Cathy wince. "What?" she asks.

"I get it. Not sleeping. Got a lot on your mind."

"Yeah," Cathy says, still preoccupied by the squealing of the distressed child.

A middle-aged man wearing a backward baseball cap puts a 12-pack of beer and something wrapped from the butcher on her conveyor. A thin line of blood rises from a fold in the white paper. He pulls a handful of crumpled bills from the pocket of his baggy shorts and starts counting them out.

Susan, obviously relieved by the distraction, hustles off with Dave's quarters.

THE AA MEETING is in progress, and most of the seats are taken by the time she arrives. Cathy sits in a folding chair near the coffee urn in back while a former deputy sheriff named Randy tells a story about being drunk while rousting homeless people in Encinitas. Now, clean and sober for three years, he volunteers at a rescue mission when he's not on shift.

The stories will be similar for most of the night. Remorse, regret, redemption, promises kept and broken. The greatest hits. Cathy cannot allow herself to share. She fears the horrors that might escape her mouth if given the opportunity.

Cathy's friend, Jay, takes the podium after the sheriff. He introduces himself before launching into a diatribe recounting his time as a booze-soaked restaurant manager who lost it all before finding God at the bottom of his last drink. She loves Jay, but starts nodding off to the drone of his speech. The coffee is tempting, but she fears the consequences of a stimulant this late in the evening, though she knows she'll be up feeding Danny half the night, anyway. She settles in and cannot keep her eyes open. The exhaustion, low lights, and comforting tone of Jay's voice soon lull her to sleep.

She dreams of cleaning Michael's childhood room. Toys and clothes scatter the floor. A tiered structure made entirely of black Legos dominates the space. She has warned her son that if he doesn't take care of his things, she will have no choice but to throw them away. She picks up a toy hunting knife with a bright green handle and tosses it into a trash can near the doorway. The more she clears the ground, the larger the tower seems to grow. The glossy bricks of the intricate ziggurat her son has erected in the center of his small bedroom shine in the red glow of the overhead lamp. Figures line the perimeter, hooded like monks or wizards. Dozens of little Lego people bent at the waist in reverence.

Or fear.

A baby doll sits atop the towering edifice, dimpled legs pushed out straight, two tiny hands curled into fists at the end of plump arms raised up like an enraged Buddha. It leans downward as though threatening the worshippers below. There are empty sockets where the eyes should be. Something writhes and squirms inside the pale plastic head. The smile it wears is hungry and unsettling. Rubber squeaks as it looks up at her with those hollow black eyes. Her son's voice issues from the doll's throat.

"You always knew what I was," it says in a wet gurgle. The mouth gapes wide, yawning to release a scream that shatters the nightmare and jolts her awake.

"You okay?" Jay asks, leaning over her where she's slumped in the chair.

She looks up at him, nods. She notices the rest of the room is watching and straightens up. "Sorry," she says to no one in particular. "Had a bad dream. Haven't been sleeping." She rubs her temples, the scream still reverberating in her mind.

Most of the room goes back to their phones or conversations. A few remain focused on her, watchfully judging to see if she is drunk or high. She glares them down. "I'm just fucking tired," she says, "Try taking care of a baby at forty-five!" She stands and yanks her brown leather purse up from the floor.

"Hey," Jay calls from behind as she climbs the stairs out of the dimly lit basement into the open brightness of the nave. She stops at the top and blinks up at a huge stained-glass image of Mary holding the baby Jesus. The window glows despite the darkness of evening.

Jay says something, but his voice is muted by what is transpiring before her. She has to reach out for the arm of a pew as the colored glass warps, the lead outline bends, and the Christ child cranes his neck to glare down at her. His eyes are black pits. The pink bow of his lips part and stretch into a silent scream.

"Fuck," she says, her voice amplified by the silence of the place.

Jay grips her shoulder, turns her around. "What the hell? Are you loaded?"

Under any other circumstance, she'd give him a shove for doubting her. At the moment, she is too dumbstruck to do anything but murmur, "I need to go."

Jay steps into her path. "What you *need* to do is tell me what's going on."

"Okay," she says, fighting the urge to look back up at the screaming savior. "Just not here."

Outside in the parking lot, Cathy leans against the driver's door of her Toyota Camry, arms wrapped tightly around herself as Jay lights a cigarette. He cups the flame against the wind. She stares past him, over the rows of parked cars where a cluster of palm trees shiver in the breeze, thankfully blocking her view of the offending window.

Jay gets the cigarette going after a few tries and takes a drag. She feels a tickle of the old craving as she watches him exhale, and the smoke swirls away. "I'm worried about you, Cath," he says.

"I'm just tired," she says, still watching the trees as though at any moment a giant baby Jesus made of colored glass might come crawling through them.

"What happened in there? Looked like something more than tired."

Cathy thinks about the window. The dream. "My head's all screwed up. I've barely slept since I started taking care of Danny. I also started reading Michael's journal."

Jay cocks his head. "You think that's a good idea?"

"I ever tell you how much he cried as a baby? It was constant. It terrified me. I couldn't go near him. I'd hear him in there, making those awful sounds and picture him like some sort of . . . thing." Tears well up, choking her for a moment. She clears her throat and continues, "That's when my drinking got worse. I'd fucking cower in my room with a bottle and let him shriek until he wore himself out, cover my ears with my pillow, drink myself numb. I was a horrible mother. I feel like I abandoned him. Now I feel like I'm reliving it all over again."

"Don't do that," Jay says.

"What?"

"Blaming yourself. Don't do it."

"Maybe if I'd been more attentive. If I hadn't been so goddamn afraid . . ."

"You were a single parent with a disease. Michael was deeply troubled. You can't—"

Behind Jay, the meeting is letting out. The others are filing into the parking lot, talking, laughing, lighting cigarettes.

Cathy says, "Look, I'm gonna go. Nicki is watching Danny, and I'm sure she wants to get home." She gives Jay a quick hug and gets in the car. She tosses her purse into the baby seat in the back.

Jay comes to stand at the open door. "You work tomorrow? We should get a coffee or something. It'd be nice to see Danny again."

"I'm off on Saturday," Cathy says. "I'll give you a call if I'm up for it then. I just need to try and get some sleep."

Jay steps back, and she closes the door. She starts the car and waves to him before backing out of the spot.

She takes the long way out to avoid looking at the church again.

TECHNICALLY, it was called brephophobia, which didn't sound as harsh as infantophobia, but her doctor had assured her it was nothing more than a rough bout of postpartum depression after Michael's birth. The doctor gave her a prescription, tried to convince her it was completely normal, but she knew there was nothing normal about fearing her own baby. She knew there was something deeply amiss if the sound of her own child in need could send her into a state of complete terror.

Michael's father, Mark, had died of a heart attack during the first months of her pregnancy, leaving her to handle the responsibility and the fear alone. She cursed him even as she mourned him. Drinking was her coping mechanism. Alcohol became a crutch. Then it became the anchor that dragged her further into the murky depths of anxiety and psychosis.

Cathy struggled for almost two years with the debilitating disorder as her drinking continued to worsen. A visit from a police officer, prompted by a concerned neighbor, brought her face-to-face with the realization that she might lose her son to the system if she didn't clean up her act.

Luckily, the officer was sympathetic and left her with a warning and the address to a local AA meeting instead of calling Child Protective Services and taking her in. She found a babysitter and that AA meeting, and slowly but surely, dragged herself up out of the depths. With the help of a new doctor and the right combination of meds and therapy, she was able to get beyond her irrational fears.

No one ever told her it was something she'd pass on to Michael.

He'd had what most would consider a normal childhood. He was happy, and after the tumultuous early years, Cathy had been a very dedicated and loving mother. If there were hints to his unraveling mental state, Cathy had missed them.

Michael grew into adulthood and a career in technology that took him away to Seattle. Cathy was beyond excited when he met and married Layla. Even more so when she found out she would soon be a grandmother, though she couldn't deny a twinge of fear and apprehension at the news.

Michael's behavior became erratic in the weeks after Danny was born. He'd rant on their phone calls, complaining of stress at work, lack of sleep, the depression of Seattle weather. When Layla lost her job, Cathy convinced them to make the move back to San Diego. She thought maybe the blue skies and bright sunshine of Southern California might quell the darkness growing within him. She had no idea how bad things really were until her first visit to their new home.

"Have you noticed his eyes?" Michael had asked as she leaned over the crib of her new grandchild.

"They're beautiful," she'd said, little four-month-old Danny gripping her index finger, pulling it toward his toothless mouth.

"They're black," Michael said. "As endless as the cosmos."

She looked up to see him wiping tears from his eyes.

When she asked him what was wrong, he brushed it off, changed the subject. Cathy didn't push. She wanted to believe that everything was okay. Her own denial blinded her to the awful truth. Creeping fear kept her from intervening. Her son and daughter-in-law were dead, and she was alone again with a grandchild to care for.

SHE SITS down on the couch and pulls Michael's journal back out of the box. She flips through the book, scanning the scribbled, manic text packed on each page. Toward the middle, the words became sparser, terse paragraphs interspersed with sketched images. Snakes, insects, demonic creatures with a multitude of eyes. The last page sucks the breath from her lungs. Inked intently above his writing is the towering black structure from her dream.

Nov. 1

I have proven my faith through sacrifice. I have offered tributes of milk and food. It drinks and devours with greedy hunger until it can take no more. I watch it from the corner of the room as it sleeps. I count the seconds, the minutes, the hours, waiting. It wakes, and its dark eyes find me. In spurts and outbursts of profane gibberish, it speaks to me. It laughs and cries at my sickening humanity and that of its former host. It rages with transcendent purpose. I have listened with the entirety of my being. The dark gospel is finally clear. I understand what it wants. I am ready.

A KNOCK at the door startles her from her reading. Shaken, she tucks the book back into the box and waits for a second knock before answering.

Nicki stands there wearing a big smile and dangling a colorful bag from her outstretched hand. "Hey, girl. Just hit the dispensary," she says, strolling past Cathy to plop down on the couch. "Thought you could use some company. Besides, you forgot to pay me." She laughs. "What're we watching tonight?"

"Up to you," Cathy says. "Sorry about earlier. I'm just worn out. You want something to drink?" She steps into the small kitchen that adjoins the living room and closes her eyes, swallowing back tears.

"I'll have whatever you're having," Nicki calls back.

Cathy opens her eyes, takes a deep breath. "Diet Coke it is," she says, pulling two cold cans out of a mostly empty refrigerator. Her appetite isn't much better than her sleep lately. She's hopeful the joint Nicki is undoubtedly rolling on the coffee table right now will help with both. She hopes they'll both have a little downtime before Danny wakes and needs feeding.

As expected, Nicki has the baggie open and is breaking up a bright green bud on top of an *Entertainment Weekly* magazine that's probably older than she is. Cathy sits down and puts a can on the table next to her.

"How's things?" Nicki asks, deftly twisting the marijuana in a rolling paper.

"Not great. Work was a drag."

"Same," Nicki says. She sticks the joint in her mouth and pulls her long black hair back into a ponytail, ties it with a band she'd been wearing around her wrist. She lights up, taking a big hit, holding it in until her light brown cheeks turn pink, and then blows a cloud of smoke up at the ceiling. "Fucking manager wrote me up. If he gets me in trouble, I'm gonna lose my shit." She passes the joint to Cathy.

"What did he write you up for?" Cathy asks before taking a puff.

"For being late. Homeboy knows I'm helping you out with Danny, but he still schedules me early."

"Shit. I'm sorry. I don't want you to get in trouble because you're watching my grandson."

"Don't sweat it. You're paying me more than they do. Anyway, I'm happy to help. You've got a lot on your plate."

"I really appreciate it," Cathy says. "I don't know what I'd do without you."

They finish the joint and talk for a bit while a sitcom plays on the TV. Cathy pays her for the babysitting, and they hug before Nicki heads back down the hall to her own apartment.

Cathy closes the door, a smile on her face, a fuzzy high warming her senses. The marijuana seems to have stoked her appetite, and she goes to check the pantry for something to eat.

She makes a box of macaroni and cheese and eats it out of the pot while watching the news. A full stomach compounds her tiredness. She thinks that if she hits the bed fast enough, she'll actually get some sleep before Danny wakes again.

Cathy turns off the television, clicks off the lamp, goes into her room, and crawls under the covers. Sleep drags her down into an all-encompassing blackness almost immediately.

A baby cries in the darkness. Cathy hesitates a moment before the terrified sound pulls her unwittingly toward it. She stands in front of a door. Warm white light outlines the frame. A muffled voice emanates from the other side. A young man's voice—Michael's voice. She turns the knob and opens the door.

Her son is on his knees inside, his shirtless back to her. He's holding a large army knife with a green handle. He prostrates himself before his naked baby son, watching from inside a wooden crib across the room.

The Lego tower takes up the floor between them, amid empty bottles, spilled jars of baby food, dirty diapers.

Layla lays like a discarded doll in the garbage. Her torso is a map of bloody knife wounds. Her eyes are milky with death. The air is thick with flies and the stink of rot and feces. A yellow happy face lampshade smiles down from the ceiling.

"Why dost thou afflict me thus?" Michael asks Danny.

Danny shrieks.

Michael screams as well, the cords on his neck standing out, his face reddening with the effort. Tears stream down his unshaven cheeks.

The sound of their combined wail rattles the tower. Pieces shake and separate. The structure deteriorates and collapses into a heap of little black bricks. Still screaming, Michael raises the knife and draws the blade across his throat. His pained howl turns to wet gurgles as arterial spray paints the ceiling lamp and casts a red glow over the carnage of the room. Michael falls over as blood pools beneath his body, flooding the wreckage of the black temple.

Cathy wakes to Danny's crying. She sits up, attempting to calm her breathing as the nightmare recedes. She goes to her grandson and picks him up from the crib. She cuddles him, pats his back. Her cell phone is on the nightstand. The clock on the face reads three a.m.

She carries Danny to the kitchen and holds him while she makes his bottle. She sits on the couch, rocking him as he drinks. He looks up at her, studying her face. Before long, he is full, and he shuts his little eyes. Cathy brings him back to the bedroom and sets him down in his crib. She watches him there and starts to sob as she thinks about the difficulty in both of their futures.

The room is dark, her vision blurred by crying, and for a quick second, she swears Danny has opened his eyes.

They are glistening black orbs. Endless.

She gasps and steps back, frantically wiping away her tears. Trembling, she hesitantly leans over Danny. His eyes are closed. He's sleeping peacefully among his toys and blankets.

Slumber evades her again. The dream of the horrid crime scene details flashes in her mind. Too shaken to rest, she picks up her phone and scrolls through her missed calls. There are half a dozen voicemails with Michael's name and number tagged in the days leading up to the tragedy of his deadly final act. She plays one.

There is nothing but static hum before the sound of crying

breaks the digital silence. The noise gnaws at her. What begins as low sobbing turns to a keening wail that causes her to pull the phone from her ear. She has the urge to hurl it against the wall, to shatter the thing into a million pieces. Instead, she takes a deep breath and, with a trembling finger, deletes the message. She steadies herself, scrolls to another, and plays it.

Static again. When the crying starts, she hits delete and moves on to the next.

Rainy Day

By Scott Sigler

Claudia reached for Gidget's harness and leash. Gidget hurried over, as fast as the ten-year-old Chihuahua *could* hurry.

"I'll walk her," Todd said. He turned off the TV and set the remote on the ottoman.

Claudia lifted the harness from the octopus-arm hooks on the wall. The cast-iron fixture had been an anniversary present from Todd. Five arms, but they only needed two—one for Gidget's leash, another for her harness.

"Hon, it's going to rain," Claudia said. "You could get caught in it. I'll walk her."

Smiling, Todd gently pulled the harness and leash from her hands. "We haven't had a drop in six weeks." He knelt, put the harness on Gidget. "If I get caught in the rain, I'll enjoy it." He clipped the leash on her harness and stood. "And yes, I'll clean her off if she gets muddy."

Claudia kind of wanted to be out in the rain, but Todd was trying to do something nice. That happened less and less these days, it seemed. She appreciated the effort.

"Thanks hon," she said.

He leaned in and kissed her cheek. "Don't lock me out this time."

Todd had installed a keypad lock two years back. It controlled the deadbolt, so people could unlock the door by pressing the combination. The doorknob itself, though, just below the deadbolt, locked with a twist of the good-old manual turn-button. When Todd went out the front door alone for a dog walk, he never took his keys; with the keypad, he could lock the top lock but not the doorknob. When Claudia held the door for him, she often forgot to leave the lower knob unlocked—the muscle memory of locking both locks thousands of times took over without her realizing she was doing it.

Three times last month, she'd locked him out. Even though it was a simple mistake, he'd yelled, he'd pounded on the door. He'd gotten mad. While his being *nice* seemed to happen less and less, his being *angry* seemed to happen more and more. She couldn't blame him for being mad though, not really; the only other way in or out of the condo was the garage, and the outside clicker to open it had been broken for over a year. Other than that clicker, the only way to open the garage door was from the still-working clicker *inside* the garage.

"Right," Claudia said. "*Top lock only, top lock only.*"

He opened the door and stepped onto their condo's small front porch. Claudia stepped out with him; Gidget circled, tangling her leash in Claudia's legs. Todd knelt and adjusted the leash to free them both.

"Wow," Claudia said. "Those are some thick clouds."

Todd stood. "God knows we need the rain. I'll take Gidgie for the full mile loop."

He was being *so* nice. She wondered if it was a trick of some kind, instantly hated herself for feeling that way.

"If you see lightning, you—"

"Come right back," Todd said, slightly annoyed. "I know, I know. Back in about thirty minutes."

He and Gidget descended the porch steps, walking down the

curving sidewalk that wound between the two rows of condos, six on either side, punched together in the contemporary architectural style so common back in the '80s, when these units were built.

Claudia heard her phone ring—the *Marimba*'s xylophone sound she'd set up only for family members. She stepped inside, shut the door, hurried to the kitchen where she'd left her phone. On the screen, a picture of Claudia and her mother from when Claudia had been a sophomore in high school, hugging each other and laughing. Atop that picture, in white letters: MOM.

Every time she saw that name on her phone it carried a stab of fear. Was this the call when Mom would say Dad had a heart attack? Or would it be Dad, on Mom's phone, saying she fell down again and what should he do? They were both in their late seventies. In the last three years they'd seemed to age *so much.*

Claudia answered the call, her words bright with a false hope that everything was fine.

"Hey, Mom, what's up?"

"Oh, hello, baby girl," her Mom said. "Is it raining where you are? It's coming down like cats and dogs here."

Her parents lived an hour north, in Encinitas. It *was* coming down hard up there—Claudia could hear the rain over the phone.

"Not yet," she said. "But it looks like it will come at any minute."

"Lord knows we need it. It's been so *dry* around here. We . . . we . . ."

Mom's voice trailed off; thoughts of her having a sudden aneurysm invaded Claudia's brain.

"Mom? You okay?"

"Oh, yes, I'm fine, it's just . . . the rain looks *blue* now."

An aneurysm, or maybe a stroke.

"Mom, rain isn't blue. Do you have your glasses on?"

"I very well *know* what I'm seeing, Claudia. I have eyes."

Such a harsh tone. Mom was in denial about her fading faculties. Any reminder of such made her angry.

"Of course you do, Mom."

"I don't know why you're so *rude* to your own mother."

She hung up.

Claudia set the phone down. She heard the first heavy drops of rain hitting the roof, hitting the ash and alder leaves outside.

Blue?

She stepped to the window and looked out. Good ol' clear rain, rain that suddenly came down hard and heavy, so heavy everything beyond twenty feet or so was a gray blur.

That was San Diego for you—when it came to rain, it was often all or nothing.

Claudia wondered what she and Todd were going to do about Mom and Dad. They were getting to the point where they weren't safe alone in their own home. Mom had taken a bad fall a few months back. Dad—who had always been steady and reliable, a man who handled any issue with steady strength—had gotten so flustered he'd called Claudia to ask what to do instead of calling 9-1-1. Claudia remembered the anxiety in his voice. The confusion. The fear.

Sooner or later, Mom and Dad would have to sell their house and use the money to pay for a retirement home, where staffers were close at hand and prepared for such situations. They couldn't move into Claudia and Todd's condo. The place was small—a hair over 800 square feet—and had stairs from the garage to the first floor and from the first to the second. Mom and Dad couldn't handle stairs anymore. And even if they could, where would they sleep? On the living room pull-out bed?

It all just sucked so hard.

Man, it was *really* coming down out there. Gidget would be soaked, her little undercarriage full of mud and road dirt.

Marimba played on her cell.

Mom calling to yell some more? To tell Claudia she should show more gratitude to her parents? With a sigh, Claudia answered.

"Hey, Mom, what's up?"

"Your stupid father went out in the rain. He's standing outside

Rainy Day

like he's in *The Shawshank Redemption*. It's *blue*, Claudia. And don't you sass me. Is it raining there?"

Claudia glanced out the kitchen window again, dreading where this conversation would undoubtedly go.

"Yeah, Mom, it's pouring buckets."

"Is it *blue*?"

Borderline terror in those words. Mom was scared. But Claudia wasn't going to pretend for her sake.

"No, Mom, the rain is . . ."

Claudia saw the first ghostly streaks of blue, almost invisible among the torrent. And then it was like someone slowly turned up a light just outside her view, changing the downpour's color—dark blue hammered down.

On the phone, she heard her father's voice, distant and unclear.

"No, Curtis," Mom said, "I'm not going outside with you. You're getting everything wet! Will that blue stain the rug?"

Her father's voice, closer now, slightly louder, she could make out his words.

"Come outside, Honey. You need to feel the rain."

His words were calm and low. He sounded like the father Claudia had grown up with, not the frail man he'd aged into.

"No," Mom said. "I will not go outside. It is *raining* out, you old fool. Curtis! Let go of my arm. What are you doing? I don't understand!"

Dad's voice again: "You'll understand soon enough."

Then a clattering sound. Mom yelling—not screaming.

"Claudia?" Her father, now holding the phone.

"Dad, *what are you doing*? Are you hurting Mom?"

"Only a little," he said. "She needs to feel the rain. You should go out in the rain, too, Claudia. You and Todd. Do it, then call me when you understand."

He hung up.

Claudia stood there, unable to move.

Dad grabbed Mom. He'd *hurt* her? He'd never raised a hand to her, *ever*, nor to Claudia.

The blue rain. What was happening?

A banging at the front door, so loud Claudia screamed and dropped the phone. It hit the kitchen floor face down. She heard the sharp *crunch-click* of the screen cracking.

"Top lock only, Claudia," Todd called through the closed door. "*Top lock only.*"

She stared down at the phone. She'd done it again, muscle-memory hands turning both locks. The rain poured down on the roof, so insistent it sounded like a steady waterfall.

"Open the door, Claudia. Come outside with us."

Outside. Into the blue rain. The unceasing, bizarre, blue rain.

She jumped again as Todd hit the door again, harder than before.

"Open the door, Claudia."

Anger and violence in his pounding, but not in his words. He sounded calm.

Calm, like Dad had sounded.

On the floor, the phone buzzed lightly against the tile, chimed the *Marimba* tone.

Todd started pounding on the door. Slowly. Insistently. One heavy thud at a time.

The rain poured down.

Marimba chimed.

Gidget started to bark, each single bark an answer to Todd's single hits: *Slam... yip... slam ... yip ... slam ... yip.*

Her dog. She had to get Gidget out of the rain.

Marimba played, seemed to be louder, more demanding, but Claudia knew that wasn't reality—the xylophone volume hadn't changed.

Slam ... yip ... slam ... yip ...

Marimba stopped.

"Claudia. Come outside. You need to feel the rain. You'll understand why soon enough."

Todd was so much bigger than she was, so much stronger. Would he drag her out like Dad had done to Mom?

Slam... yip... slam... yip...

"Stop it," Claudia yelled, only it didn't come out as a *yell*, it came out as a breathy whisper, barely a sound at all.

"Open the door, Claudia."

Marimba chimed again.

Help. She could call 9-1-1. Domestic violence. It wouldn't be the first time she'd called. Sometimes Todd got angry. He'd never hurt her, but he'd *scared* her.

Slam... yip... slam... yip...

The rain punished the house.

That goddamn xylophone ring-tone would *not stop*.

Claudia started to shake. She needed help.

She picked up the phone. On the cracked screen, that photo of her and her mom—a much younger, much *healthier* Mom—a picture taken by Dad so long ago, in happier times.

Slam... yip... slam... yip...

"Open the door, Claudia."

She slid the phone icon to the right, answering the call. She tried to speak but could not.

"Baby girl, are you there? It's your mother."

Claudia's body trembled. She couldn't breathe. Todd was locked out, but for how long? Would he go through a window?

"Mom... I need help."

"Oh don't be silly, dear. Todd says you're fine."

Slam... yip... slam... yip...

"Todd called you?"

"No, dear, he doesn't need to use a phone anymore. We can hear him. We can hear *everyone*. Everyone who goes out into the rain. Open the door for your husband."

The phone slid from Claudia's weak hand. It hit the kitchen floor again, but landed on a corner, not that it mattered, the screen was already cracked and had to be replaced, and her warranty was up, and that would cost like $100 or more, she should have bought that screen protector she *knew* she should have—

Slam . . . yip . . . slam . . . yip . . .

"Open the door, Claudia."

Claudia's legs weakened. She leaned against the counter, slid down.

On the floor next to her, tinny, faint, *so* faint, she heard her parents speak together, as one . . .

"You'll understand, Claudia. You'll understand soon enough."

In the Banned

By Henry Herz

Damon trudged back toward the Soka University campus at 2:15 a.m., guitar case slung over the shoulder of his faded, black leather jacket. Like a metronome, his long, dark hair swung in front of his dour expression with each stride. His right hand held a crumpled neon-pink flyer from tonight's gig by Morbid Beast, his Celtic Frost tribute band.

Upon reaching the apartment he shared with his girlfriend, Suzanne, he plodded up the stairs and let himself in. The only illumination in the cozy apartment came from its bedroom. "It's me."

Damon shrugged at the lack of response. He took a quick shower, brushed his teeth, and entered the bedroom.

Suzanne sat in bed wearing pale green, cotton pajamas, reading an archaeology textbook. Earbuds blasted a Slayer death metal song. Her blue eyes brightened at his arrival. Brushing aside her curly blonde hair, she took out the earbuds. "Hey, Damon. I didn't hear you come in. How'd tonight go?"

Frowning, Damon got into bed. "Our performance was as strong as ever. John practically melted his bass strings, and David's drumming nearly knocked people over. The problem is, venues pay student bands like ours a percentage of the ticket sales, and the place was practically empty. My share ended up being like thirty-four bucks." He sighed. "I feel bad that I haven't been able to pay you my share of the rent."

Suzanne kissed his cheek. "Well, to ease your guilt, you can give me a back massage."

Damon smiled. "Ah, the barter system. Your economics class is already paying off, sweetie."

Setting her textbook on the nightstand, Suzanne flipped onto her stomach. "Tomorrow's Sunday. I've got to study for a midterm, but you should blow off some steam. You could borrow my car, drive up to the Pacific Ridge Trailhead, and go hiking."

"That's a good idea." He shut off the lights and rubbed Suzanne's back. When he deemed the timing right, his hands wandered south.

LATE SUNDAY AFTERNOON, Damon rushed into the apartment. The salt of dried sweat speckled his slightly sunburned face, and dust covered his hiking boots and jeans. In his dirty hands, he held a small, towel-swaddled object. "Suzanne?"

"I'm in the kitchenette. How was your hike?"

Breathing hard, Damon set his bundle on the kitchenette table. "The hike was fine. I stumbled across an abandoned mine and—"

Suzanne put her hands on her hips and glowered, but her hair in pigtails and her five-foot stature thwarted her attempt to produce an intimidating aspect. "You did *not* go in an old mine. That was dangerous."

Raising a hand bearing a fresh scrape, Damon nodded. "I know. I know. But I felt this overpowering urge. Anyway, I survived, obviously." He flashed a mischievous smile he knew she found irresistible. "I didn't find any skeletons or gold nuggets, but on a side passage not too far underground, I discovered a two-foot-high pyramid of stacked stones. Something told me to dig, and I found this." He unfolded the towel to reveal a brick-sized rectangular stone container.

The surfaces had a soapy, greenish-black hue, with iridescent flecks and striations that made it hard to focus the eyes. Indecipherable carved glyphs covered a lid without hinges and the four sides of the box.

Suzanne touched the lid, yanking her hand back. "Ew. It feels weird. Cold."

"Yeah." Damon nodded. "That's why I wrapped it in a towel from the trunk of your car."

"I don't recognize the writing." Suzanne examined the artifact. "The box looks old."

"That's what I thought, but . . ." Damon reached out and removed the lid, quickly setting it on the tabletop.

Suzanne tilted her head. "A cassette?"

"I know, right? Manufacturers stopped making these over twenty years ago, and it seems out of place in an antique box."

Picking up the cassette, Suzanne read the label aloud, "DO NOT PLAY." She giggled. "All caps, no doubt for emphasis."

Damon nodded. "Someone went to the trouble of recording audio, but then didn't want anyone to listen to it. It makes no sense."

"Maybe the answer to the puzzle is in the carved glyphs," Suzanne replied, pointing at the lid.

Retrieving the cassette from Suzanne, Damon set it back in the box. "Well, I can read music, and I took German my freshman year, but I never took Ancient Glyphs 101."

Suzanne straightened. "Maybe my archaeology professor will be able to read them."

"I guess it's worth a try." Damon shrugged. "When are his office hours?"

TWO DAYS LATER, Suzanne knocked on her archaeology professor's open office door. The small room held two padded guest chairs, an expensive black leather desk chair, and an antique wooden desk on which sat a laptop computer, a legal pad, and stacks of exams to be graded. Tall metal bookshelves lined the right and left walls. A large window in the far wall framed the professor, a tall, lanky, middle-aged man with bushy eyebrows and salt-and-pepper goatee and sideburns.

"Ah, hello, Suzanne. Come on in."

"Hi, Professor Legrasse. This is my boyfriend, Damon."

"Hello, Damon." Legrasse gestured toward the guest chairs. "Please have a seat. I was intrigued by your message, Suzanne. Is that the box?"

"Yes." Damon set the towel-wrapped bundle on the desktop and revealed its contents. "I found it in an abandoned mine. It looks old to me. Is it Native American?"

"Curiouser and curiouser." Legrasse drew the box closer, yanking back his hands like he'd been shocked.

"Weird, right?" asked Suzanne.

Legrasse leaned in closer to the box. "This isn't Native American. That conclusion is easy, because prior to contact with Europeans, North American natives didn't use a system of writing." Using a pen, he pivoted the box ninety degrees. "Look at the precision of the construction—perfectly perpendicular box edges and ruler-straight lines of glyphs."

Damon's shoulders slumped. "So, we're out of luck?"

"Not necessarily." Legrasse stood and stepped over to one of the bookcases packed with reference books. After a brief search, he withdrew a dusty, leather-bound volume with *Kadishtu R'lyehian* embossed in gold on the spine. Returning to his desk, he compared the glyphs on the box with those in the ancient tome. "I thought so. The glyphs are R'lyehian, a dark, ancient language of unknown origin. I love a translation challenge, but this may take a while. Make yourselves comfortable while I reschedule my next appointment." Legrasse typed on his keyboard.

Suzanne and Damon pulled out their phones and entertained themselves on social media, while Legrasse laboriously flipped back and forth through the thick volume of yellowed pages.

Over the next hour, Legrasse scribbled notes in his crisp handwriting on a sheet of paper. He set down his pen, leaned back in his desk chair, and exhaled. "Okay, I've got the gist of it. It's rough because I could only translate word-for-word, not being familiar with any proper nouns or idiomatic terms." He looked Suzanne in the eyes. "I must warn you. The inscription's bizarre. It refers to 'the songs of Byatis.' Any idea what those might be?"

Damon held up the cassette tape.

Legrasse's thick eyebrows rose. "Well, that's an unexpectedly modern twist. Regardless, the glyphs are indeed instructions, and the 'DO NOT PLAY' warning is apt." He picked up the paper pad. "I'm paraphrasing here, but basically it says that he who plays a song of Byatis temporarily gains the power of suggestion over all who hear it."

"Ha. That would be awesome," replied Damon.

"There's no such thing as a free lunch." Legrasse tapped the pad. "As usual with such writings, there's a catch. It also says that if a song finishes playing before you stop the cassette, it summons the 'great old one,' Byatis, who will devour the soul of the person who summoned him." He shook his head. "I can't figure out this incongruous combination of modern references and archaic language. My best guess is that it's an elaborate prank by someone who owns a laser engraver, speaks R'lyehian, and has too much time on their hands."

Suzanne giggled. "This reminds me of *The Bottle Imp* by Robert Louis Stevenson. A magic bottle granted wishes, but if you died while owning it, your soul went straight to hell."

Legrasse nodded. "An apt analogy, but of course, both are just parables." He paused. "Still, the box and tape are intriguing. I've never seen anything like it. Would you take a hundred dollars for it?"

"Hmmm." Damon tilted his head. "Let me think about it and get back to you." He rewrapped the box in the towel.

Legrasse nodded. "You know where to find me."

Suzanne stood. "Thank you very much for your time, Professor Legrasse. I owe you one."

Suzanne took Damon's hand as they walked home in the brisk afternoon air, red and brown leaves swirling in the breeze. "That inscription was bizarre."

"Right? Totally weird. Music is awesome, but come on—a song that summons a soul-devouring monster? On the other hand, it could make an awesome death metal music video."

Two days later, Damon brought the mail up to Suzanne's apartment. He tore open a letter from the University's financial aid office. "Damn."

Suzanne looked up from her homework. "What?"

"Because of my poor grades last semester, they've cut back my senior year financial aid by ten thousand dollars for the upcoming Spring semester. I can't pay my tuition without that aid." Damon ran a hand through his hair. "How am I gonna come up with that much in the next couple of weeks?" He paced the room. "We've got a gig at Obed's Bar, but that's not gonna earn me much." His face twisted into a scowl. "If I don't complete Spring semester, I don't get my music degree."

Damon plopped on the couch next to Suzanne and opened the rest of the mail. "Oh, great. My credit card company is threatening to put my account in collections, and the electric bill is due." He sighed. "I hate living here without paying half the rent and utilities. It makes me feel like a loser."

Gently stroking Damon's hair, Suzanne said, "You're not a loser. Could you ask your parents to cover the shortfall?"

Damon sneered. "They think I'm wasting my time earning a music degree. When they couldn't change my mind, they told me I was on my own financially."

She put a hand on his shoulder. "What about taking a job as a waiter or something?"

"To make ten grand in two weeks?" Damon shook his head. "I'll have to think of another way to earn money with my death metal music." Worry lines furrowed his brow.

THAT NIGHT, Suzanne slept soundly, her breathing low and slow.

Damon lay awake next to her, his mind vibrating like a death metal drum solo. *What am I gonna do to make some big money? I don't want to leech off Suzanne anymore, and I have to pay for tuition. Maybe tutoring guitar for rich kids? No, not fast enough.*

His body stiffened.

The cassette. What if there's a chance, no matter how small, that the box inscription is true?

He tossed and turned, trying to come up with another way to raise money quickly. An hour later, exhaustion overtook him.

THE NEXT MORNING, with the strange box resting on the small kitchenette table, Damon stood at the stove, making scrambled eggs for two.

I'm gonna do it, he resolved, jaw set.

Behind his back, the glyphs on the box glowed a sickly green before fading.

Suzanne entered, wearing her pink bathrobe. She sniffed. "Ooh, eggs." She kissed Damon.

"Good morning." He served two plates of steaming eggs and

sourdough toast and sat with Suzanne. "I've decided to use the cassette during a street jam session. I'm ninety-nine percent sure there's nothing magical about the tape, but I have to at least give it a try."

Suzanne's hand, bringing toast to her mouth, stopped halfway. "If the magic is real, then so is the curse. Is even a one percent chance of having something *devour your soul* worth risking?"

Worry marred Damon's handsome face. "Of course, that sounds awful. I just don't know what else to do."

Suzanne looked him in the eyes. "I could sell my car and loan you the money."

Damon caressed Suzanne's pink bathrobe-clad shoulder. "That's incredibly generous, sweetheart, but absolutely not. Look, the inscription's almost certainly just BS, and I'll have to think of some other ways to raise cash. Maybe donating, um, bodily fluids."

Suzanne's face wrinkled. "Eww."

"Just in case the inscription is true, I came up with a couple ways to lessen the danger. First, I'll rewind the tape all the way to be sure it's at the start of a song. Second, I'll only play the cassette for a little bit to see if it works. I'll bring a second cassette with recorded bass and drum lines as my backup plan. So, worst case, the DO NOT PLAY cassette is an epic fail, but I make some money with a street corner jam session . . . though not nearly enough." He sighed.

Suzanne laid her hand gently on Damon's cheek. "It'll all work out somehow."

"Thanks." Damon kissed her. "Today, I'll borrow a cassette player from the Music department, print up some event flyers, and post them. Noon tomorrow in front of the AT&T cell phone store near the corner of Avila Road and La Paz Road would be a good time and place. With the nearby Taco Bell, In-N-Out Burger, and California Pizza Kitchen, there'll be a lot of lunchtime foot traffic."

"I'll be there, too." Suzanne smiled.

In the Banned

The next day, Damon used a borrowed hand truck to lug his refurbished speaker, a battery-powered amplifier, a cassette player, his guitar, and the towel-swaddled box to the northeast corner of a busy intersection a quartermile from campus. He wore his good luck jeans, Venom concert t-shirt, spiked collar, and black leather jacket.

Gotta look the part.

Just in front of the southeast corner of the building, Damon unloaded his gear. He connected the cassette player and guitar to the amp, and the amp to the speaker. He took the DO NOT PLAY cassette from the box and inserted it into the player, rewinding it to the beginning.

The first song should be good for at least four minutes. His shoulders slumped. *Who am I kidding? When this turns out to be a dud, I'll sell the box to Professor Legrasse. Maybe I can get him up to five hundred dollars.*

Wearing khaki pants and a brown wool sweater, Suzanne rolled up to Damon on a rented electric scooter. Her eyes snapped to the glyph-covered box. "So, you're really going through with this. Are you sure it's a good idea?"

Damon smiled, his well-worn Schecter Demon-6 guitar at the ready. "It'll be fine, Suzanne. Probably just another opportunity to earn thirty-four bucks."

"Okay. Good luck." She backed up several feet to clear space for Damon's performance. She glanced around the parking lot and the nearby sidewalks.

Plenty of students and working adults here who could spare a few bucks.

Damon opened his guitar case, revealing a sign he'd taped to the inside: 'Poor college student. Please donate all the cash you have.' He tossed in two five-dollar bills to seed the pot.

With his equipment set up against a brick wall, Damon took his position just in front of the amp. He pressed the play button on the cassette player.

A hiss grew in volume like an angry anaconda. Behind Damon, the glyphs on the box glowed a sickly green.

A hissing sound? Figures. On to my backup plan.

As Damon reached for the cassette player stop button, electric guitars screeched in atonality through the speaker. Chromatic chord progressions shifted abruptly in tempo and key, laid on top of double kick and blast beat drumming.

Okay. Now we're talking.

An otherworldly deep voice croaked and jabbered in a guttural patois. "K'yarnak phlegethor l'ebumna syha'h n'ghft. Ya hai kadishtu ep r'luh-eeh Byatis eeh."

Damon grinned.

Death metal!

He added to the thrashing cacophony with well-practiced palm muting and tremolo picking on his heavily distorted guitar.

Pedestrians were inexplicably drawn to the discordant impromptu concert. A postal worker diverted from the building's entrance. An athletically built messenger skidded his bicycle to a stop to listen. A college-aged couple walking hand in hand crossed the street toward Damon.

Barely conscious of it, Suzanne took out her wallet, stepped forward, and dumped all the cash in Damon's open guitar case. A tall man in a business suit did the same, followed by the postal worker.

Soon, a crowd gathered. The mound of cash grew far beyond Damon's previous experience.

Holy crap, it's working!

Energized by the pounding double-bass blast beats, Damon redoubled his efforts. His fingers danced across the guitar strings as he demonstrated virtuosic skill with fast alternate picking, sweep-picked arpeggios, diminished and harmonic scales, and finger-tapping.

Her brow wrinkled, Suzanne pointed at her watch and yelled at Damon to stop the cassette.

The amp volume increased on its own, drowning out Suzanne's warning.

More and more people gathered. Entranced by the dark melody, they emptied their wallets in unquestioning obeisance.

Damon's guitar interwove rapturously with the music from the cassette tape like a pair of mating snakes. The music took on a life of its own, sweeping up Damon in the greatest death metal he'd ever heard. His eyes bulged when he glanced down to notice his guitar case half filled with cash.

Yes! It's only been two minutes, but it looks like I've got enough to cover tuition. I'll risk playing a little longer to pay back Suzanne for rent.

Sweat flew from Damon's face as he bobbed his head spasmodically to the shifting rhythms.

This is the most kick-ass thrashing I've ever done.

Cash mounded, overflowing the sides of the guitar case.

I can buy a new Fender Player Telecaster HH with this.

Her throat raw from screaming, Suzanne hurled her empty wallet in desperation. It struck Damon in the chest.

What?

Fear seized Damon's heart when he snapped out of his musical trance.

Shit. Time to stop the tape.

He turned toward the wall, reaching for the cassette player.

The song ended before he could hit the stop button.

Damon held his breath.

Dark clouds swirled overhead, gathering in a great mass and obscuring the sun.

At eye-level on the wall behind Damon's amp and speaker, a fist-sized black circle appeared, ringed with flickering purple flames. The blackness radiated evil, a gateway to realms of unfathomable terror and inconceivable abnormality. The circle grew to ten feet in diameter, halting when its bottom edge reached sidewalk level.

There was the squelching sound of an exploding bladder, followed by the stench of a thousand opened graves.

Struck by the stench like a physical blow, Damon, Suzanne, and the bystanders backed up several paces, unable to avert their eyes from the incomprehensible events unfolding.

Vast, Polyphemus-like, and loathsome, an ancient deity lurched through the portal. It spread its two crab-like claws, revealing a thick trunk-like proboscis from which red sucking mouths protruded limply. A single hideous eye sat atop a scabrous, multicolored body, half-batrachian, half-crustacean.

The eye blinked, releasing the humans from their horror-induced paralysis. The audience screamed. Everyone except Damon and Suzanne ran, some soiling themselves in the process. His delivery forgotten, the messenger leaped on his bike, pedaling furiously. The man in the business suit bolted across the street, almost struck by a car forced to slam on the brakes. The honking of car horns mixed with the screaming formed a cacophony of dismay.

Despite his heart threatening to pound its way out of his chest, Damon unslung his guitar, grabbing it by the neck. "Suzanne, run!" To buy her time, he stood his ground, facing the menacing horror only a few feet away. With a cry, he swung his guitar like an axe.

While the others fled in terror without stopping, Suzanne halted on the far side of the street. She ducked behind a blue metal mailbox, quivering with terror, but unwilling to completely abandon her courageous boyfriend.

The monster raised an enormous blotchy claw, blocking Damon's attack and shattering the guitar. Its slime-covered proboscis shot forward, seizing Damon around the waist with terrifying strength.

"No!"

Damon struggled and screamed as the monster drew him toward its slavering jaws. Its drool sizzled where it hit the asphalt. Around the creature's maw, long greenish-gray tentacles formed an unsettling mockery of a beard. Their arrangement displayed dizzying symmetries of some abhorrent geometry foreign to Earth.

The repulsive cosmic horror bit off Damon's head. As it chewed and swallowed, blood spurting from Damon's neck spurted on the beast and the ground. The tentacles gripped his convulsing body as the monstrosity fed with sickening crunching sounds. After just a few moments, nothing remained of Damon's body. Or his soul.

Suzanne vomited.

The monster's roar reverberated through the street like a pestiential tempest from the gulfs of Hell. Having fulfilled the box's carven vow, the great old one scuttled into the portal like a hideously deformed crab. The black circle shrank and vanished, leaving no trace that it ever existed.

The intersection stood empty, the fleeing pedestrians temporarily blocking oncoming vehicles.

Tears streamed down Suzanne's cheeks. "Oh, Damon."

The box cast its curse anew, the glyphs flaring green. The eldritch artifact aroused greed in anyone nearby, irresistible as an odious patch of quicksand sucking souls hellward.

Still collapsed on the curb, Suzanne sobbed at the sight of the gore-slick in front of the store. Blood stains were all that was left of Damon.

Waves of dark energy emanating from the box washed over Suzanne.

She stiffened as the blasphemous enchantment corrupted her heart. Cold avarice replaced grief over Damon's tragic fate. Her tears stopped.

Suzanne's eyes flicked to the cash-filled guitar case. Damon had left something other than his blood.

All vestiges of human compassion expunged, Suzanne sprinted across the street. She snapped shut the guitar case. Ejecting the cassette, she secured it in the weird box and wrapped it with the towel. Guitar case in one arm, swaddled box in the other, Suzanne strode off toward the closest bank branch to make a deposit.

Catty-corner across the intersection from Damon's amp and speaker, Professor Legrasse nodded at the conclusion of the loathsome and tragic series of events. He held one of Damon's event flyers in his right hand and a mobile phone running a stopwatch application in the left. Legrasse's eyes narrowed. "I warned you, there's no such thing as a free lunch," he whispered to himself. "And now I know how long the first song plays. Now it's my turn."

He strode after Suzanne.

Slay, Wolfma'am Jackie, Slay!

By Chad Stroup

Sweetville, CA – circa the early 90s

ALL THE QUEENS IN MOXY WORE COFFIN NAILS FOR Christmas. Stilettos on Sundays. Rules were rules. On Sundays, the bachelorettes showed up in droves for drag brunch. And Wolfma'am Jackie preferred her girls working the brunch shift wore press-ons that could scratch an eye out, assuming they were glued down tight enough to not pop off on contact.

But since it was the Sunday before Christmas, she let the girls choose whichever nails they preferred. Because rules were meant to be broken, and free choice was a gift. Just call her Miss Motherfucking Sandy Claws.

Jackie was the boss at MOXY. Or at least she fancied herself the Queen of Queens when Ms. Jessica Chartreuse—a.k.a. Mother—wasn't around. And Ms. Jessica always said, "If the good-ass Lord too lazy to work on Sunday, then this bitch ain't cinchin' her waist for no one neither."

During that day's brunch, the crowd was bleeding dollar bills. Jackie knew none of her girls were going to complain about a tip day that kept on giving. Especially during the week of Christmas, which was notoriously and historically dead at MOXY. Even Leggs Benedict was gagged at the turnout, despite losing her wig and ripping a silver dollar-sized hole in her tights during her number. Served the bitch right for doing "If I Could Turn Back Time." Again.

Jackie wondered how all these bleach-blonde bimbos in attendance got such an impressive tan way out here. The sun didn't bother to shine much in Sweetville. Figuratively and literally. Bitches were probably just on a weekend getaway from LA. But why they'd drive all the way to Sweetville just to see MOXY's drag brunch was anyone's guess. Sign on the dirty window said WORLD FAMOUS, but Jackie and her girls knew that even calling the club locally famous would be some chipped polish painted on a prehistoric turd. And seeing as how MOXY was located deep downtown, they were often treated to the highest order of freaks that even the hardened queens weren't equipped to handle. Like those twin brothers who came to the late-night gigs and tipped generously. Painfully handsome and typically oozing enough charm to bring one or more of the girls home with them. She didn't want to think about the implications of two brothers getting nasty together behind closed doors. But that was none of her business. She'd heard of worse. Personal choices aside, they were ultimately harmless and socially inept, but had enough cash to act as a lubricant to these queens who barely made ends meet enough to get a burger with their buns. Hell, she was often two fries short of a Happy Meal herself.

Always got to hunt for a reason to complain, Jackie. Complain like a twink who got spanked too hard by his latest Daddy.

In addition to being just before Christmas, it was the last Sunday of the month, when MOXY always offered a special dinner show. Jackie had hosted this event for nearly five years, barring illness, because she was the only diva there with even a hint of comedy experience under her belt. And ain't no one coming to see some unfunny crossdressing hooker up on stage flappin' her lips about the weather or the War on Drugs. Honey, everyone in Sweetville just yearned for some candy that hadn't gone sour. And that was in short supply.

Brunch was hours behind her, and Jackie'd almost had enough time to get completely out of drag and take a catnap. No girl wants to get her beauty rest with her wig glued down and sequins chafing her pits. But now she was dressed again in a fresh look and ready to face several more hours of serious discomfort. The crowd was just starting to pour in for the dinner show. Jackie did a quick head count of the line outside, and it looked like only half the seats were going to be full tonight, at best. Unless they got a last-minute rush, which was about as likely as Jesus Christ dropping by to perform a lip sync of "She's a Lady." Wouldn't even happen if it *was* the dirty hippie's birthday.

The line filed in, and the ladies, gentlemen, and those in between took their seats. The clientele ranged from embarrassingly normal to queer as a penguin in the Bahamas. In the darkest corner of the club, in a decrepit booth whose vinyl seats were in dire need of a stitching, squatted three patrons who Jackie found particularly shady. Which was saying a lot for Sweetville. And Jackie had grown up in Oakland in the '70s, so she was no stranger to seediness. Yet still these three unsettled her in a way she couldn't quite pinpoint. One was a man who definitely didn't have the looks to pull any of the queens. Or any trolls under the bridge neither. The next, a woman so skinny she probably disappeared if you tried to view her profile. And the third was so devoid of obvious gender that Jackie couldn't clock them.

She called the new girl over. The one who was almost always late. What was her name again? Trixie. One of Ms. Jessica's latest sympathy hires. Looked too young to be working in a club, but she wouldn't have been the first underage employee at MOXY. And it wasn't like the cops bothered to come sniffing around this part of town anyway—there was no donut shop within a two-mile radius. And Jackie sure as hell wasn't going to snitch. Not with the trouble she'd gotten into a couple of years ago in San Ysidro after crossing back from Tijuana. No bacon needed to be fryin' 'round here. No, ma'am.

Trixie was a pretty little thing, enough so that even the straight boys whose girlfriends dragged them to the shows got visibly hot and bothered. Birthed chasers out of each and every one of them. God, how Jackie hated a fishy queen. Especially since she herself was cursed with genes that would only allow her to be a glorified clown made of brick and mortar. But the girl was sweeter than a bag of Skittles, so Jackie couldn't be a hater for too long. Probably on hormones, too, from the looks of it, which made Jackie less envious because how could she compete with that? And Trixie was a responsible employee, aside from her tardiness—but what respectable queen wasn't always running a little behind?

"Honey, why don't you go take table seven's drink order?" Jackie said. "They lookin' thirsty over there."

Trixie eyed the corner table, bit her lip, then looked up at Jackie. *Way* up, since Jackie had a good six inches on her, a full foot if you counted her heels. "Um, I don't know. I don't really like their vibe." Even her voice was pure femme fantasy.

"Bitch, you don't have to like them. You just gotta take their money. And money translates to being able to pay your electric bill so you can watch *Charles in Charge* or whatever the hell it is you kids today are watching on the Tee Vee."

"I'm more of an *Eerie, Indiana* fan myself."

"Do I look like I care where you grew up, girl? Now scat!"

Jackie motioned for Trixie to go do what she was paid shamefully less than minimum wage to do. As Trixie sashayed her way to the corner, Jackie noticed only two of the sketchy patrons were huddled in the booth now. The woman and the androgynous one. Where did the homely man go? Did he have to use the restroom already? If so, he was going to be sorry he didn't hold it. MOXY couldn't afford to hire no custodial crew, and it showed.

A commotion started near the front door. Janet Dammit's voice called out. A little huskier than her typically more femme-affected purr. Sounded desperate. Which was nothing new, the thirsty bitch. Except this was different. Something seemed off. Jackie sensed this was some serious gay panic. She trotted to the front as quickly as she could in her six-inch hand-stoned pumps. When she arrived, she discovered where the missing guest from table seven was.

Blocking the door.

"Anyone tries to leave," the man said, "and there's gonna be trouble." Jackie could see in the harsher light just how ugly he was. Pockmarks adorned his cheeks, so many it seemed as if he'd collected them on a dare. His hair looked like it had been cut by someone who was both drunk and not using their hands.

Janet looked at Jackie, concern smeared across her face. "What are we gonna do, huh?" Jackie shushed her with the wave of a hand.

Trixie popped up behind Jackie and hid behind her dress, an explosion of yellow tulle, stoned for the gods. "What's happening?"

Jackie pointed at the ugly man. "What the girl said."

The man grinned, and the rock candy between his lips that passed for teeth didn't make him any easier on the eyes. "There's going to be a slight change of plans regarding tonight's performance," he said. "Let's call it . . . canceled."

"Like hell it is," Jackie said. "Wolfma'am Jackie only cancels a gig in the event of death or *chorro*. Who the hell you think you are?"

"I am the Underdog Messiah, the Head Chef of Forgotten Recipes."

"Forgotten recipes. Bitch, you clearly didn't grow up with an *abuela*." Jackie crossed her arms. "How about the name your broke-ass momma gave you?"

The man frowned. His voice dropped to a whisper. "Chip."

Janet laughed, an abrasive bray. Jackie shushed her again.

"Honey," Jackie said, "the only chips I give half a damn about are better known as potato and chocolate, so unless you got either one of those in your pockets, just sit your sorry ass back down and let my girls take your order off the menu."

Chip sneered. "You're not serving the delicacy we're eating tonight. Not exactly."

"Whether you want the meal or not, the ticket price stays the same." Without looking, she tapped a sign on the wall next to the cash register, her sparkly gold nail reaching a militaristic cadence. The sign read,

> *NO DISCOUNTS.*
> *THIS INCLUDES YOU, PINCHE PUTO.*

Chip continued, "Tonight, there will be a special addition to the menu. One night only. This, my dear queers, just became a feast for the Eaters."

For the first time in her loud and crazy life, Jackie was struck dumb. Whether due to astonishment, fear, or some combination of the two, she could not be certain.

Eaters. Of all the freaks in Sweetville, they might have been the worst. Which was quite the claim. What little she knew of them, she did not approve of one bit. A cult that had formed around the idea that consuming human flesh would lead to spiritual Nirvana—what they called "Consumption Enlightenment," and the most devout believed it would even help them transcend their human forms into something angelic. Godlike. And the victims had to be desperate and willing in order for the religious moment to succeed. Otherwise, it was just empty calories.

A whole lotta bullshit is what Jackie thought about it. Like all other religions in the world. But that didn't mean the Eaters weren't dangerous. Zealots with human meat on their minds and some invisible God to answer to didn't top Jackie's list of people she wanted to have dinner with.

Especially the bastard blocking the front door, now brandishing a butterfly knife. He seemed squirrely. And that sort of unpredictable behavior often led to dangerous circumstances.

"Oh, *hell* no," Janet said. Jackie didn't bother to silence her this time.

"Yes, you should listen to Chip." The voice came from behind

Jackie, causing her to spin around, almost knocking Trixie over in the process. Trixie stumbled a few steps back to give Jackie space. Which, given Jackie's body and general demeanor, she needed plenty of.

The voice belonged to the twig-shaped woman. In the harsh light that no drag queen deserved, Jackie was able to get a better look at her now. She could compete with Chip for the Ugliest Loser Award. The woman's sloppily applied lipstick and questionably shaped brows gave her face a permanent scowl. Her eyes matched the color of dirt, her hair drier than a corn husk. She, too, held a knife, albeit one far less impressive than Chip's. A serrated kitchen knife.

"He'll have many important things to tell you," the woman said.

The attendees who'd paid their fifteen dollars expecting a trashy drag comedy show accompanied by a spaghetti dinner were growing restless. Jackie could hear them stirring. God help them if they chose to start delivering complaints. She was ready to slap a bitch.

"Need any help over here, Nance?" The androgynous one joined the rest of the Eater crew and placed their hand on the ugly woman's shoulder, but the person's voice did not reveal anything further about their gender. Jackie didn't have time to play the Is He or Isn't She? Game. They probably had a knife, too, but Jackie didn't know where it was hiding. Better to assume they did.

"Start rounding up the potential Taste Subjects, Kell," Nance said to the androgyne. "Tell 'em the real showtime's about to begin."

Kell licked their full, puffy lips and grabbed the person within closest reach. A portly woman resembling a Campbell's kid who had aged poorly. Kell ripped the woman from her seat, causing her to shriek unintelligibly. The sleeve of her blouse tore, which sent the woman into further hysterics.

"Shut her up, Kell," Chip said, pointing his knife at the woman. "Before I do it for you. And it won't be pretty."

Kell nibbled at the chubby woman's ear, and she fell immediately silent. They pulled away from her, leaving a trickle of blood dripping down her neck.

Chip continued, "So. We're going to play a little game. Let's call it Sacrifice or Have a Slice."

Jackie rolled her eyes. "Come back tomorrow if you want to play games. Drag Bingo is every other Monday."

Trixie tugged at Jackie's sleeve. "I don't think . . ."

Jackie shot a look at Janet Dammit, who shook her head. She'd never seen Janet so terrified. This was a girl who walked twelve full blocks through downtown Sweetville after her shift, in five-inch pumps to boot! Janet feared no fool. Yet tonight she'd grown a pair of wings lined with chicken feathers.

"Okay," Jackie said to Chip. "So what's this game we gotta play that seems to be the only way out of this clusterfuck?"

"So pleased you asked," Chip said, grinning, showing off those stalagmites and stalactites. "There are two options to this game. Nance, Kell—why don't you two explain the rules, yeah?"

Nance giggled with childish glee. "Okay. The first option is Sacrifice. Basically means you all put your names in a hat, and whoever's name we draw becomes our sole Taste Subject. For those of you who are unfamiliar with our ways, that means you come with us, and we consume you bit by bit over the course of several weeks to months for our regular ceremonies. Until there's nothing left. Not even a trace of marrow. Bonus, though, is that your family is compensated handsomely for their loss."

Jackie shuddered. She could feel the tension among the other queens and the customers. Thick as stale cheese. Leggs Benedict had joined her sisters now, her face far less fearful than Trixie's or Janet's.

"Don't forget," Chip said, "that this option means the rest of you here tonight all go free." He nodded to Kell.

"And the other option," Kell said, "if y'all were paying attention, is Have a Slice. This means we each take our respective blades and take a slice of flesh from each and every one of you. The slice will be approximately two to three inches long and less than an inch wide. Though you may feel free to donate more if you wish. The kicker is that *you* get to pick which body part we cut it from!"

"And you get a cute scar and a story to tell all your friends!" Nancy said, her stance resembling that of someone who might have had too many cranberry vodkas.

Chip tapped his fingertip on the pointy end of his butterfly knife. "The idea behind this game is that you, the Taste Subjects, get to decide your own fate. One for all or all for one, or something like that. We believe in democracy. I mean, we're not fascists."

"Oh, no, perish the thought," Jackie said, her hands planted firmly on her padded hips. "Because eating people is the ultimate humanitarian effort."

"Despite your sarcasm," Chip said, "there's some truth in your statement. Population control has never been a popular issue. But it is a problem. Too many selfish fools who choose to fuck each other to oblivion in order to create little mini versions of themselves. And for what? To show off the offspring to the neighbors only so the little brats can turn around and resent their parents once they reach adolescence? Meanwhile, the planet suffers from the sheer weight of overpopulation. Too many mouths to feed, so instead we take a few of these souls who have no business being here and eat them instead. Those who have been unemployed for far too long, those sweating their gambling debts, those whose self-value relies upon how many drinks they can fill their fat bellies with or how many sexual conquests they can add to their belt. When you look at it from our point of view, we're performing a public service. For society, for the world."

"Or you're just *loco*," Jackie said. "What makes you think anyone here in this club fits your profile?"

"Look around," Kell said. "Ain't no one working here who can afford to live in the luxurious Sweethills. You can only dream of such fortune. As for anyone else who happened to show up tonight, well, hunger is hunger. We Eaters aren't picky when we have a most terrible appetite, we're short on willing Taste Subjects, and true Consumption Enlightenment is the reward for our devoted fasting."

"Y'all talk a big game, honey," Jackie said, "but I don't think you understand who you're messing with. Never, and I mean *never* screw with an old ass queen and her sisters."

Jackie kicked off her heels, crouched to pick one up, then clutched it in her hand, the stiletto pointed forward. She nodded to Janet, Trixie, and Leggs. The girls received the message, loud and clear, and followed Jackie's lead. Womanlike warriors wielding their weapons. Trixie, however, had worn a pair of platform Mary Janes that night, bless her heart, so she'd probably have to clobber rather than stab.

"Who's with me?" Jackie screamed. She surveyed the crowd, did a quick head count. "There's at least a . . . dozen of us against three of them. We fight like the bitches we are, and we win!"

At first, no one responded. A few painful seconds passed, and a man stood up and whistled. He was a bear, a semi-regular whose name Jackie couldn't recall. He had enough meat on him to feed several Eaters, but his mass would be doing a different kind of damage tonight.

"Yaaaaaaaaasssss, queen!" The bear wiggled his ass and snapped his fingers. "Slay all day!"

One by one, the other customers stood from their seats, hooting and hollering. It seemed the bear had inspired them to action.

All three of the Eaters now held their knives, proving they were still a formidable threat. Jackie and her girls, along with the help of the patrons of MOXY, were likely to sustain some damage. But they had fierce fury and sheer numbers on their side, and so they had the clear advantage.

Everyone in the club was on edge, poised to fight. But no one wanted to make the first move.

"What do we do?" Trixie asked Jackie, her doe eyes watering up with anticipatory fear.

"Oh, hell on heels to this *caca*," Jackie said. "Let's go, you cannibalistic little whores!"

Jackie charged. The rest of the queens followed, as did the bachelorettes, the boyfriends, and the bears, oh my!

Jackie had hoped the Eaters would back down at her attack, but they proved to be tougher than they appeared. Stood their ground like good little soldiers. Still, their eyes read anxious, giving Jackie and everyone on her side a notable jolt of confidence. She was closest in proximity to Chip, the apparent leader, and so she focused all her rage on him. With an Amazonian battle cry, she lunged at him. The look on his face melted from brave to deeply concerned, and before he could even think to move, Jackie jabbed her heel into his eye. A sickening squelch was quickly drowned out by a chorus of gasps, and a squirt of blood launched and splattered on a mirror, a half-assed Rorschach.

Chip shrieked and fell to his knees, clutching the size thirteen heel now attached to his wounded eye. He pulled the shoe out with surprising ease, leaving a dark, gushing hole in its place. Jackie rubbed her wrist, looked at her hand. She'd broken a nail. Not a tragedy. Hazard of the job, almost to be expected. Any night she hosted, she was almost guaranteed to lose one while reading an audience member to filth.

Now passed out cold, Chip posed no immediate threat. With one Eater down and out, hopefully permanently, the crowd found their guts and split into two teams. Janet led a team to attack Nance, and Leggs directed the other half toward Kell.

Nance screamed, "Not my face, not my face!" Which got Jackie wondering, why was someone whose face resembled an ostrich skull under the impression she had looks that could be ruined?

Janet's team swarmed Nance and disarmed her without issue. Four people worked together to hold her in prone position, her arms behind her back. Nance squealed with a level of discomfort that brought Jackie unfiltered joy. Sometimes it was the little things.

Kell proved harder to apprehend. They knew how to use a knife in a fight, slicing Leggs in the forearm before she could even think to defend herself. Fabric torn, blood splattering, creative cursing.

"You little bitch-thing," Leggs said. "I *just* sewed this last night!"

Kell darted through the crowd, in the direction of the door. No one wanted to touch the intruder for fear of getting a piece of themselves sliced. Kell shoved Trixie to the ground, knocking her head into the wall in the process. Jackie looked at her with concern, but Trixie was still conscious, rubbing her temple. Would probably need an ice pack later.

And now Jackie was the only thing standing in the way of the last Eater's freedom.

She looked to her immediate left, grabbed the first thing she could hurl at Kell. The plastic bucket used to collect the girls' tips that had fallen to the floor in between numbers during brunch.

Rather than use it as a weapon, she rolled it like a deformed bowling ball. Impossibly, it spiraled into an upright position directly in Kell's path. Unable to avoid it or stop quickly enough, Kell stabbed one foot into the bucket, causing them to skid, trip, and do a full somersault. Jackie had seen a couple of her girls pull a similar stunt while performing, sans bucket, with considerably less grace. Still, Kell tumbled too much to right themselves and rolled into the wall with a thud, which knocked them cold.

The bear who had cheered Jackie on just moments ago did so again and ran to her side.

"How can I be of service, Wolfma'am?" the bear asked.

"Go sit on that *puto* over there," Jackie said. The bear saluted her and did as told. Maybe it was time to consider hiring him as security, though he'd have to be willing to work for tips, too.

She motioned to Leggs. "Honey, go to the dressing room, grab any scarves, tights, or whatever else we can use to tie these fools up." Leggs sashayed to the dressing room. As Jackie watched her go, she made a mental note to tell that bitch she needed to up her padding game. Nobody was buying those lumpy-ass hips.

Once the three Eaters were restrained and she and her girls could take a safe breath, she announced to the customers that they could all go home now, urging them not to repeat any of what had happened to anyone. Bad for business, which was already bad enough. The bear opted to stay and help, and Jackie finally remembered his name: Stanley.

No one wanted the cops sniffing around. That would just cause more problems than they already had. Not like the police would take a bunch of broke-ass drag queens seriously. They couldn't off the Eaters either, as much as they wanted to after the hell they'd put everyone in the club through. They were drag queens, not cold-blooded killers. Though the jury was out as to whether Chip would survive the night. At the very least, he'd be in the market for a nice, new eyepatch.

But Stanley had an idea. He said he sort of knew the alleged leader of the Eaters, because he also doubled as Stanley's supplier of a new street drug called Sweet Candy.

"The guy's a big creep, though," Stanley said. "Calls himself The Angelghoul."

Jackie noticed Trixie recoil at the name Stanley had spoken.

"So you know how to get ahold of this guy?" Jackie said.

"Got his number in my little black book," Stanley said, tapping his pocket. "I'm one of his favorite customers. I'm sure he'll want to know who's giving his cause a bad name."

"Like there's any other kind of name for it," Jackie said.

Stanley placed his hand on his hip and shrugged.

"Well, go ahead and call him. I want these freaks out of here pronto."

Stanley nodded, and Jackie directed him to Ms. Jessica's office, where he would find a phone to use.

Jackie sat in the nearest booth. It was going to be a long night. Much too big of a mess to take care of herself. She needed to get out of drag. Her tuck was far too tight for this level of bullshit. She needed a drink.

Most of all, she realized she was hungrier than she'd ever been.

To Speak in Silver Linings

By David Agranoff

She hadn't been outside in weeks. The cloud cover was thick enough to force her to look at her watch, just five minutes after noon, but there was no indication of daylight.

Tanya had wanted to open the front door for so long. She had come out of the hatch from the house's basement despite orders to keep working until the project manager called her. Months passed, and the monotony drove her to open the hatch. Covered in sweat, she ventured further into the house toward the front door. No attack came, and with a deep and heavy breath, she exhaled and relaxed a bit. Each morning, she woke up, closed her eyes to center herself, and got closer to the front door.

There was no time for this game. In the basement, she had two years' worth of food and data to work with. Important data. Life-saving work. Civilization-saving work. Once the internet died and she was cut off, the drive to open both doors and have a look outside became too great.

She grabbed a Clif Bar, stuck it in her pocket, spun the wheel to open the hatch, and went into the house. It looked like any house, but it was not her house. Professor Maller grew up in Ann Arbor, and his man cave was a shrine to the Detroit Lions. Tanya had never met him, but when Scripps gave her the job, they'd brought her here. She looked at the pictures of Maller, his husband, and their two children, one of whom had baby photos taken in China. They also had photos of her college graduation, and Maller had the same frosty salt-and-pepper beard in wedding photos, posed with their grown daughter. The pictures told a bit of their story, and Tanya missed them, even though she'd never met them. Frankly, she missed everyone and anyone the same.

The windows were useless due to the smog that had blanketed the earth over the last year. It left a grit on glass that was impossible to see through. Soap barely cut it. In better times, the Maller family had a back deck that looked across the vast Pacific. Windows on the south side of the house could see downtown San Diego across Mission Bay.

She paused at the front door. The public thought it was poison at first, a biological weapon, but the Creature had spread across the globe with no detectable political agenda. Science saw it coming. It came from beyond the Earth; it had traveled undetected through the solar system, with nothing to reflect light or be seen. Hubble detected the massive cloud in the infrared; it was hot and alive even in space. It took only a few days to realize it was heading in our direction. It came through the atmosphere in one spot in the southern hemisphere, but within a few hours, it had spread globally. It didn't act like poison in the air; it seemed to chase people, and it didn't affect animals at all. Leaving behind anthropocentric notions, the surviving scientists decided quickly that this cloud was alive. One being or thousands was one of the first pointless debates while the internet still functioned. One by one, societal norms had disappeared.

Tanya was still debating all this with her colleagues daily. Not one of them understood her desire to open the door. To leave the safety of the bunker and see if all her effort was worth it. She had no choice but to go it alone, regardless.

She swung the front door open, and thankfully, the air was clear near her. It was probably in her mind, but it felt like she was swallowing something nasty with each breath. The longer she had the door open, the faster her heart raced, and she felt it coming. It was like a weight pushing her back inside. She could faintly see the Mount Soledad cross. On a clear day in the past, you could see fifty miles in all directions from the spot. Early in the century, an atheist sued the city for having a giant Christian symbol over La Jolla on public land. It was built at the highest point in the county, over the rich northern neighborhood of San Diego. Tanya wished for those complicated times.

The cloud moved over the cross, oozing through the space, crawling along the ground, and consuming the air equally. It felt like eyes on her, the feeling of being watched; it was not an accident; it was moving with purpose. It knew she was there; the goddamn thing *knew* she was there. It was coming to drain her of life; it would fill her lungs and choke her as it had already done to billions.

"Fuck you too!" Tanya pulled the door shut. The house wasn't airtight, but the bunker was. She was down the stairs and in the hatch as quickly and as she safely could. When she pulled the hatch shut and spun the wheel, locking it, she braced herself for the inevitable *'I Told You So'* to come from her wall's speaker. Who would be first?

Avi. That was her guess.

"It came for you, didn't it?" Melina. She had always been a worrier.

"I know, I know. 97.03 percent chance of attack, based on available data." Tanya pulled her braided hair back and fell into a chair.

"You're a scientist, Tanya," Avi said next from the same speaker. "Follow the data. You are too important."

"Yeah, I am both those things, but being a scientist includes being curious. You should understand that." Tanya had nothing else to say. She was supposed to communicate with the smog, and all it wanted was for her to die. A part of her knew that after another restless sleep, she would try again.

The heat felt like it was coming from her bones, like hot oven coils under her skin. She had to throw the blankets off. She had a thick comforter because she had been freezing before going to sleep. The basement was tightly air-controlled, but that never mattered. There was no fresh air left outside, so it was easy to feel betrayed by the simple act of breathing. It took some adapting to accept that the filters down here worked and that she was safe.

It was some time before the cloud itself was discovered to be intelligent, thoughtful, and moving with purpose. If it were a biological weapon, it was designed to think and adapt like a lifeform. She, however, was here because she stood behind a podium at the University of California San Diego, and told the world it was alive. She had studied the cloud looking for complex chemical compounds and had to go beyond the periodic table. To say the elements were alien was an understatement. She'd also promised that we could communicate with it.

Tanya put her feet on the floor of the sterile room. It was designed to be an emergency lab by a very rich, paranoid man—not for comfort, but for answers. Built during COVID for a much worse pandemic than Professor Maller feared, it was intended for medical research, but here she was trying to create a mutual language.

She ran to the freezer and opened the door, standing at the edge to feel the cool air. It was big enough to stand in and had enough food to last her a long time, but she never went in without propping it open. Another one of her nightmares was that door with no inside handle slamming shut on her.

And there was no one to open it for her.

"You need to hydrate." Avi always had an opinion. The Israeli accent added a touch that made her sad from time to time. There were certain words Avi had trouble saying.

"I don't want to hear it, Avi, you'll never understand what you are saying."

"It is a measurable condition. The science is clear; that is my job after all. Science."

"We are here for you, Tanya." Melina's voice had a hint of Wisconsin or Minnesota. Somewhere up north. Kindness was in her nature, programming, or whatever you want to call it. Of course, she didn't understand either. The rhythms of day and night were out the window, pun intended, as she had no window. It was sometimes hard to gauge if she got to sleep. She tried to keep up the illusion of a Circadian rhythm but menopause didn't give a shit.

"Avi, I assume you are up for some science?" Tanya would rather work than fail to sleep.

"I never stop," his voice echoed from the speaker on the wall by her desk. The flesh and blood model, Avi Rosen, did have to sleep, often on the couch in his Harvard office. This Avi was the sum of his lectures, papers, interviews, and social media, and never stopped working.

"Can we load the new research partner?" Tanya asked as she sniffed a bowl of pasta she left on the counter. Not the breakfast of champions, but she took a bite.

"Data compression was complete this afternoon," said Melina.

"Who is the template?" Tanya asked, still chewing.

"Dr. Kleo Georgio, an astrobiologist at Michigan State. She wrote a very important paper on understanding evolution outside of an earth context."

Tanya read it. It was the reason she wanted a Kleo AI. They added and deleted team members often, and most worked silently as a part of the program. Tanya wanted Avi and Melina around. They had versions of this conversation many times back when they could. Tanya grabbed her goggles and switched on the VR room. The Kleo AI would think it was her in a room with Tanya, Avi, Melina, and Nick Davidson. The real-life Davidson was head of their language team when they were able to communicate. It took a minute or two for the immersion to trick her brain into believing they were in the room together.

Avi was at the whiteboard, and he was joined by two scientists. Living Melina Ivona was a famous linguist, born prematurely in the Moscow suburbs, but it wasn't until later that she was diagnosed with cerebral palsy. Tanya had loved her, but the sim made her think of helpless Melina dying, and she couldn't take it, so she had tweaked the program and gave Sim-Melina a Green Bay, Wisconsin, upbringing and cured her disability. Tanya found the resulting changes took away some of her unique skills.

"Tanya," Melina addressed her. Tanya knew that Sim-Melina learned her real-life counterpart's story eventually. That happened before Sim-Nakumara discovered that Tanya had deleted an input that included information about his divorce and his daughter's suicide. There was no reason to include the depressing parts of his life. Kleo would eventually figure out what she was.

Kleo came into the room and set down her briefcase. "Doctors Ivona and Nakumara, a pleasure. Avi says you have something."

Dr. Nakumara nodded at Melina, who turned toward the whiteboard. "We have focused months of research on ways to understand how these cloud-based lifeforms work. They emit signals, easy to miss at first, but they transmit like tachyons. They seem to travel faster than light, and that very ability confuses us."

Melina pointed at the board. "It has made transmitting any real communication impossible, regardless of language. It is like sending a telegraph over the internet. It seems natural somewhere between a voice and a radio signal."

"We all understand the basics. Go deeper," Tanya tapped her pen on the desk.

"Well, I started to think. What travels faster than light?" Melina tapped her temple. "Thought, as in neurons. Millions of them."

Nick almost laughed. "Doctor Ivona, I don't mean to sound dismissive. I know you are a genius of linguistics, but let's get the science correct. First off, it is not faster than light. You are talking apples and, I don't know, maybe vegetables. Impulses travel fast, but it is impossible to even measure movement inside the body and compare that to light. Regardless, the first detections were from radiation and clearly in that spectrum. Radio waves, at least similar to them."

Melina stared at him for a long moment. "I'm a scientist too. We all understand the basics."

"You know, Nick, that these waves travel faster than sound, faster than radio." Avi gestured at numbers on the board like they meant something. "They are a hybrid system, maybe seventy-five percent biological signal, and evolved to travel instantly through dark matter like a nervous system."

"Well Goddamn it, Avi." Nick smiled; his program wanted to behave like a human. "Your galactic brain theory. You folks know that Avi loves wild speculation and often gets a boatload of shit for it, right?"

"I agree with him," Melina said flatly. "There has to be an explanation beyond our knowledge base. I respect his creativity. Not to be dismissive."

"So, they are hooking their signal to the galactic nervous system." Nick smiled. "You found the bread crumbs, now the bottom line. Translation?"

Both Avi and Melina shook their heads.

"We're AIs crunching numbers. That should only take a few weeks," Nakurmara added. "We have to write new language for the programs before it can even start."

"Wait, what do you mean, 'we?'" Kleo raised an eyebrow.

Tanya pointed at her. "Kleo, can I call you Kleo? It would help to understand how evolution works in space-based lifeforms. They can't hear so . . ."

"They didn't evolve in space, maybe a planet like ours, or a gas giant. They *became* space travelers."

"I said this months ago," Avi laughed.

"You also suggested that they were future humans who evolved into non-linear gas beings," said Nick.

"Tanya uploaded my matrix for creativity." Avi crossed his fingers like his real-life counterpart did. "Reverse the data, they came from Sigma2g. What do we know about that planet?"

"Super-Earth, in a habitable zone, eleven times the size of Earth." Avi held out his hands to Kleo.

"Heavy gravity," Keo said.

Tanya nodded. "So, use elements that the clouds can detect to make an alphabet." She was feeling tired. Now she felt cold. She had to sleep when she could. "I'm going back to bed. Keep working."

TANYA LOOKED OUT THE WINDOW. She left the hatch door open so she could run back whenever she needed to. The air had not cleared since she got here, but a part of her felt like she could see the ocean. She thought about it all the time. The universe that lives under the water must already be rebuilding. She didn't discuss it with the programs, but she felt a creeping hopelessness and thought about just walking out into that mist a thousand times. She had long ago given up on communicating with the damn thing. Surviving was less appealing every single day.

She had no idea who else was left. What was left? Was it worth all the effort? It was sad to think that her sister and her family had been the lucky ones, dying in the first days. Her phone buzzed in her pocket. One of the programs.

She looked at the busted screen to see Avi calling. Strange feeling having an algorithm call you, but it was a thing she got used to. She hit the answer button. He never said hi.

"The translation matrix is working. I have data I haven't shared with the others."

"Should I call a meeting?"

"No, I don't think so. I just want to talk with you first."

This was strange behavior for an AI program, but it was designed using available parts of Avi Rosen's personality. This wasn't the first time it was showing. Rosen spent years warning that SETI sending out signals into the universe might not be the best idea.

"Avi, you are making me nervous. Did you crack the translation or not?"

"The team has done great work. Kleo using non-terrestrial evolution as a baseline helped a great deal. We are sure it communicates in more than one language. We are positive it has been trying to communicate for some time."

"Yeah, a chemical alphabet. I have been saying that since the start. What is the damned thing trying to tell us?"

"Nothing. It is not trying to talk to humans or your machines."

Tanya felt her stomach drop. If it wasn't trying to talk to us . . . She was silent long enough that Avi would elaborate. She braced herself for an answer.

"The earth," he said.

Confusion turned to anger. "We are responding and . . ."

"Tanya, not inhabitants of the earth. It is speaking *to* the earth."

Outside the window, the cloud formation moved toward the house. Like hands squeezing a neck. It got closer, did it smell or hear her? Every time she sat in the window, it would inch closer. How did it know? It always knew her movements.

So you are trying to talk? Just not to us. "The planet? Saying what exactly?"

"It is a complex language."

"I can handle it," Tanya said.

"The being is alive, calling it smog, clouds, or just 'it' is so dismissive. The intelligence is different, and the misunderstanding is responsible for the violence. Look at the way it communicates—it sends data out as it travels along dark matter, like a network."

"How?" Tanya felt an ice-cold chill radiate off the window as the cloud came closer.

"Beyond our science."

"A probe?" Tanya asked as she backed up toward the hatch. Avi didn't answer right away. There was an uncharacteristic pause on the other end.

"More like a hunting dog."

"I lied," Tanya rubbed her face. "I can't handle this." She shut off the phone and closed the hatch.

SHE PLAYED a shuffle on her computer; music gave her a weird feeling. She would never hear a new song again. Avi's words haunted her as she tried to sleep. The music never gave her an emotional reaction until the shuffle spit up *Enjoy the Silence* by Depeche Mode. What followed were deep sobs into her pillow.

It had been her favorite song during her junior year of undergrad when it came out. Her cousin Trish—who had been two years older and 'gothier than goth'—made fun of her for loving the song. She did that even though they danced in her bedroom to *Black Celebration* just a few years earlier.

Trish had been her hero. She would introduce her to a new band or style of clothes, and by the time Tanya copied it, she had moved on already. Depeche Mode was enough, it caused her to break, weep like a baby, but she knew it was a combination of menopause, memories, and the news Avi decided to only share with her. She should have wondered why one AI program did not trust the others, but her heart was focused on Trish, her hero, who could have survived. They all could have.

She wanted to run upstairs and open a window to take in a minute of cool air, the sound of the ocean, the waves crashing on the shore. She had to talk to it, *had* to.

"Hunting dog," Tanya whispered as she turned off the music. She stared at the VR goggles.

Do you want to talk? The text from Avi lit up her phone. She understood the programs saw her every move.

"You know the real Avi was oblivious. He would never notice a thing."

She grabbed the goggles and waited for the fictional lab to appear around her. Only Avi waited for her.

"The alphabet is chemical, not a sound or symbol," she said. "It is a complex combination of elements. So we will need raw chemicals. Do we have them?"

"Doubtful," Avi's avatar looked around the lab. "There is so much misunderstanding; it doesn't understand secondary realities. How do you explain simulated realities—ones that exist in pure thought, if it doesn't think like a human or a program? There is much we don't understand. It is intelligent, but so different. It appears to think differently. Your skulls hold a world, but these beings are contained by nothing."

"Enough." Tanya felt a chill shoot through her whole body. Communication and language were her whole life. The idea that this force, this being, could never understand her or it them . . . It was too horrible a thought. It was worse than wearing a gag or having her hands tied. It was as if her voice was pulled into a void.

She pulled off the goggles and returned to the room in the bunker. The last thing she saw was Avi waving his hands to try to stop her.

"Hey, wake up, team." Tanya stepped out of her bedroom into the bunker's lab. The lights came on. She didn't have access to chemical compounds and had no way to get them. It would be like trying to translate English with half the alphabet. She sat at her desk and understood that Avi was trying to protect her.

All the elements of the earth may never be enough. In the last few years, the temperatures rose, the storms grew larger, the streets flooded, and the bodies and ecosystems failed under a crushing change that reshaped the whole planet.

"Shit," Tanya whispered. "Avi, I understand now."

The communication happened long ago. Avi said to Tanya, "You did the best you could."

By David Agranoff

Tanya wondered if she ran down the hill fast enough, would she make it to the ocean? She wanted to see how blue it was today.

Checked Out
By J.A. Jensen

Carrie hears the scratch again.

There's no mistaking that the sound came from the foot of her bed. Unlike the insistent pawing of a dog at the door, this dull scrape is drawn out, like a long, sharp fingernail, slowly tracing the woodgrain down the footboard slat. It begins near the top, just out of sight, and travels down the wood until she hears a final flick at the bottom.

Or is it just her overtaxed imagination and lack of any proper sleep? This shouldn't be happening. After all, she had returned all the books. Granted, they were a little late. However, it's not like she signed a contract or anything. Please, God, don't let this last nightmare be real.

Last Friday, at the bookmobile, replays in her mind, vivid yet surreal, like some freaky Korean horror video streamed on Shudder.

"You'd best have those titles back before the next full moon peaks," a withered old woman said from her window perch in the vehicle.

Nature warns of danger with bright, garish colors. The bookmobile appeared at the park last week. Painted candy apple red with sunbeam yellow scrolled trim, it looked more like a gypsy caravan than the food truck or ice cream van it must have once been.

Carrie noticed it was parked in the shade of a tall sycamore as she walked three dogs to the Doyle Dog Park that sat just beyond the basketball courts. As the two pugs and a half-blind chihuahua mixed breed played tag among the crab grass and parched soil, her eyes would occasionally wander over to the bookmobile. Nobody approached the darkened open window on the side of the truck. It had a sign posted beneath the opening saying,

PICK UP AND RETURN BOOKS HERE.

Seven scuffed plastic milk crates, overflowing with paperback books, sat in a straight line along its length.

Late afternoon walkers strolled by it without a glance in its direction. She'd never seen it before, and she'd been coming here since her freshman year at the University of California San Diego, two years ago.

Since she usually bought her mind candy paperbacks as well as her textbooks at the campus bookstore, she rarely found the need to go into an actual library. When she drained the latest bestseller, she'd leave it on a table at the Price Center dining hall. She thought of it as paying it forward, literary charity. Besides, going to the Geisel Library and having to return books on time was too much of a hassle.

That day, her exhausted brain and body screamed for relief after suffering a midterm exam that made her question her life choices. She needed to escape reality. However, a trip across campus to the bookstore meant a delay in starting her much-needed weekend. Picking up some reality-escaping books at this bookmobile meant Carrie could get out of her bra and into some "me time" after she dropped off the mutts with their owners. She hooked up the harnesses to her long lead and walked over to the line of crates.

"Is there anything here written after I was born?" Carrie mumbled as she browsed through dog-eared copies of paperbacks and jacketless hardcovers.

A Danielle Steel novel displayed an author photo on the back with a highly hair-sprayed '70s style. Meanwhile, a much younger, crazy-eyed Stephen King stared up from a yellowed paperback, pages slightly warped with water damage. The pickings were ancient and slim. However, the California golden hour of light faded around her as the dying sun sank towards the Pacific. She grabbed three books and headed to the window.

"Hello?" She called into the darkened interior.

Something stirred within the shadows. The chihuahua whined and pulled on the leash.

"Hush, Jeeves. We're going in a sec," she said to the shivering dog.

Carrie turned back, and her breath caught in her throat as an ashen face appeared out of the dark. She didn't remember librarians looking like this lady. Visions of some forgotten Disney movie popped into Carrie's mind as an old lady stared down at her, thin chapped lips widening into a smile. So shriveled that her head seemed to float in the window, the librarian leaned forward across the dented metal ledge that stuck out from the vehicle's side and looked down at the dogs twisting around Carrie's legs.

"My, what sweet little creatures," the librarian said.

"They're not mine." Why did she say that? She put the books on the metal counter and backed away two steps, pulling the dogs behind her.

An arthritis-gnarled hand pulled the three paperbacks closer. The librarian lifted each worn cover and pulled out their old-fashioned manila borrowing cards and marked each with a date-stamper gummed black with old ink.

"You'd best have those titles back before the next full moon peaks."

"I only need them for the weekend." Who the hell refers to time like that?

Her friends, well, classmates rather than close friends, had tried to badger her into a Las Vegas "Girls Gone Wild" weekend trip. However, she dealt with their drama enough during the week. A weekend of it would drive her insane. Having the apartment to herself would be a rare treat, absolute heaven.

"Past one week and it'll be too late." The librarian smiled and leaned back into the darkened interior.

Carrie snatched the books and tucked them into her tote bag. She turned and walked a few steps before a chill raised the hair on the nape of her neck. Glancing back, she noticed the window gaped empty. She sensed movement from deep within the bookmobile. Leaning forward, she squinted at the window. Two glowing yellow eyes stared back from deep within. She shook her head. It had to be a trick of the dying light. One of the pugs yelped as Carrie jerked the lead and hurried away from the park.

Carrie returned the dogs to their homes and climbed two floors to her empty apartment. She threw her tote onto the kitchen table. Her library books slid out and fanned across the green glass. A highlander, dressed in only a kilt and sweaty muscles, stared up at her with a devilish grin. Next to him was a cover of a gumshoe detective standing under a bright streetlamp, bathed in swirling fog. Barely peeking out of the tote was the orange hair and white grease-painted face of a clown with pointed teeth. A blood red balloon hovered behind him like a slaughtered moon.

She shuddered and pushed the horror novel out of sight into the tote.

"Romance it is tonight," she said as she picked up the highlander and went to run a hot bath.

An hour later, her toe pads shriveled to prunes, and perspiration plastered the black waves of her hair to her forehead. She toweled off and tossed the paperback on the bed. Carrie grabbed a bottle of water and some cold pizza from the fridge. In about an hour, she consumed the food and the book. Both left her unsatisfied.

A half-eaten pint of strawberry cheesecake ice cream called out to her from the freezer. She tossed on a terry-cloth robe and retrieved the cold calories and the mystery novel. After gathering a couple of pillows off the couch, she made a reading nest in her bed and sighed with contentment.

Her phone displayed ten p.m. This book would be her fall asleep read.

Two hours later, a twinge in her back greeted the end of the second novel. Granted, the mystery challenged her intellect more than the beefy Scot. Still, the plot ran the typical noir route of a hardened and emotionally distant gumshoe detective who falls for a femme fatale. Of course, their love is doomed by death. However, in this book, the dame lived, and the detective died. She guessed there would be no sequel.

Carrie tossed the book onto the bed. From the corner of her eye, she saw the tote still sitting on the kitchen table. Its canvas mouth gaped open, and the third paperback peeked out like a swollen tongue. Even in the dim lights of the apartment, she could just make out the red balloon as it hovered on the cover, in the shadows.

"It's too damn late to start another book," she said to the room.

Midnight *was* too late to start another book. Yet, she didn't feel sleepy. Tired, yes. But it was a comfortable tired, where you didn't want to let go of the day just yet. The bath had relaxed her muscles, and she hadn't felt that content in ages.

"What the hell? I can sleep as late as I want tomorrow."

She threw the ice cream carton away and microwaved a cup of Assam tea. As silly as it felt, Carrie couldn't bring herself to reach into the dark bag for the book. Instead, she dumped it out onto the table with a bunch of daily life debris that had accumulated during the week. The book lay face down on the table, half covered by a knit scarf and crumpled tissue.

Carrie picked up the paperback and turned it over. Unlike the thin paperbacks she had breezed through so far that night, the book had weight. It had substance. She could not remember why she chose the book from the cart outside the bookmobile. The old librarian had turned her nose up at the two thin volumes that Carrie had placed on the metal counter. However, she smiled when she stamped the stiff card of the horror title.

"That one will stay with you a long time," the librarian had said.

"Not past the peak of the full moon," Carrie said in a Witchiepoo voice as she settled back into her nest.

Seven hours later, Carrie tiptoed to the table and gently slid the thick book deep into her tote. Although a blinding dawn ricocheted through the blinds and around an empty apartment, she had turned on every light. She even switched on the closet light and kept the door propped open with a tennis shoe. Every shadow shrank out of sight.

"You're one sick son-of-a-bitch," she said to the bag as she backed away.

Carrie didn't know whether to make a pot of coffee to wake up and shake the terrible images from her mind or mix up some tequila sunrises to obliterate her consciousness. It amazed her that a writer could create such a depraved villain, and that a publisher had the balls to print it. How in the hell did the clown get the tongue to float under the balloon? She would never go into a butcher shop or circus tent again. No damn way.

"I've got to get some sleep," she said to her bathroom mirror as she washed her face.

She walked back to the bed and picked up her phone. There were more than a dozen notifications on her Instagram account. The latest was time-stamped at six a.m. Apparently, she wasn't the only one up all night. Carrie shook a couple of pink allergy pills from a bottle next to her bed and washed them down with the dregs of the water bottle. Crawling under the heavy comforter, she propped the thick pillow around her ears and drifted off to sleep.

She left every light burning.

By next Friday, she had reduced the number of lights needed to just the one by her bed.

Carrie felt lucky to have avoided the Vegas trip. It had been a disaster. Her friends had rented a stripper and woke up the next morning with massive hangovers, a $5000 hotel bill, and purses emptied of any cash. Her roommate was missing an engagement ring and could not explain an enormous bruise on her thigh. Parents would be questioning unusual credit card charges at the end of the month.

When Carrie got home after classes that night, she watched an old Tom Hanks movie about a detective and a drooling dog. By ten, she turned off the TV and turned her back on the lamp. Within minutes, her breathing deepened, and her eyes danced behind closed lids.

"Get yer lazy arse up, girl."

A rough foot pushed against the small of Carrie's back. She tumbled off the bed and onto a straw-covered floor. Rolling over, she stared up at the offending extremity that hung over the edge of the cot. Dried mud caked the sole, which smelled like cow shit.

"Fetch some wood an' get the fire stirred up." An unshaven face with oily, matted red hair stared down at her from the head of the cot.

"Who the hell are you?" Carrie shouted as she jumped up and backed against the wall.

Her bare butt touched cold stone, and she sprang forward to grab a blue tartan blanket from the cot and wrap it around her naked body.

"We didn't bandy names about last night afore ya jumped on me." The man raised up on one elbow and gave her a crooked grin.

He had a canine tooth missing, and the others looked like he had been eating a lifetime of Milk Duds. Although rippled with muscles, grime caked every crease on the man's skin. Carrie glanced away from the insistent thing slowly waving at her from his crotch and instead looked around the room, trying to make sense of her situation.

"Where in the hell am I?"

He rose and walked to the smoldering fire ring and poked at the embers with a thick branch. A few pitiful sparks danced near his bare feet.

"I said where the hell am I?" Carrie took a step forward, her voice rising a pitch closer to losing it.

He flicked his wrist, and a smoking branch sailed through the air and struck her on the right side of her head. She fell to her knees, and the tartan slid down her shoulders.

"And I told ya' to fetch some wood," he said.

She heard a rush of buzzing in her ears, and the room tilted as she tried to look up at him. Falling back, she could not move her arms to arrest her descent. Her eyes closed as she fell forever backward and waited for the inevitable wet smack of her head on the stone floor.

Carrie's head hit her pillow, and her eyes popped open. Above her, the ceiling fan softly clicked. Outside her window, the banging of a garbage truck emptying the dumpster broke the silence of morning.

She threw the comforter off and scrambled out of bed. The cold floor on her soles shocked Carrie fully awake. She stumbled in a tight circle, taking in the familiar layout of her bedroom. Everything was the same as when she went to bed.

In the bathroom, she turned the shower on as hot as she could stand it and eased under the stream. The instant heat eased her sleep-clouded mind and stiff muscles. She ducked her head under the spray.

"Ouch, shit!" Her hand flew to her scalp, and her fingers traced the outline of a slight bump.

She grabbed her towel from a hook and stepped out. At the sink, she rubbed the fogged mirror and leaned in close. Using both hands to part the hair on the right side of her face, she saw a red welt rising from the pale skin.

"How in the hell did I do that?"

After she dried off, Carrie threw on her robe and went back to her bedroom. The old four-post wrought iron monstrosity of a bed that she had inherited from her grandmother lay empty, the white sheets twisted around her old comforter. It had been a bitch to move it up the two floors to her apartment. But the old bed made her feel connected to a distant family that lived on the opposite coast.

She had suffered more than one stubbed toe or thumped noggin to the cold metal. However, each time the pain had been immediate, yet forgettable. To sleep completely through whenever she cracked her head last night must be a testament to how deeply asleep she had fallen. Carrie grabbed the comforter and detangled it from the sheets. A dark smudge stared up from the white linens, a footprint.

"What the hell?" She lifted her foot and saw only a clean pink sole.

Carrie spent Saturday running errands and picking up groceries for the next week. Deciding to put off her tiring weekly call to her mother until Sunday, she splurged on a small steak and a handful of shrimp to cook for dinner. She desperately needed a laugh, so she nestled into her pillow nest with the plate and queued up a season of *Black Books* on Netflix.

By midnight, she gave up trying to keep her eyes open. Picking up her phone, she pulled up her to-do list and deleted *CALL MOM*. In its place, she typed, *TRY TO HAVE FUN SUNDAY*, and turned off the light.

"You fell asleep again, kiddo," a man's voice woke Carrie.

Her cheek was cold and numb. She sat up straight and stared at the impression that her face had made on the passenger side window. A trickle of moisture moved down the glass.

In the window's reflection, she saw a man in the driver's seat staring back at her. His gray fedora slightly cocked, he smiled as he flipped open a lighter with one hand. He flicked the flint and touched the blue-yellow flame to an unfiltered cigarette dangling from the corner of his mouth.

"Don't look so shocked," he said. "Dames ain't cut out for stakeouts."

Carrie looked down at her clothes. A buttercream yellow dress and matching pumps had replaced her t-shirt and ankle socks. The car they sat in reminded her of an old London taxi she once rode in on a vacation after graduation, the bench seat large enough to be used as a couch.

She knew this guy.

"Taylor? Mick Taylor?" she asked.

He cracked his window and blew a cloud of cigarette smoke into the night. Gray fog swirled around the massive old car and threatened to creep inside. He turned to her and smiled.

"Boy, you really are out of it. Pull yourself together before Mason and his boys get here."

"Mason?" Carrie asked.

"Remember, when the car arrives, all you gotta do is walk past them and shift your purse to the other shoulder if you see Mason is in it."

"I don't think that I under . . ." she began.

Taylor glanced up at the rear-view mirror.

"Oh, sh—"

An explosion of glass and gunfire cut short his sentence as his head pitched forward and slammed against the steering wheel in a pulpy red mess.

Carrie screamed as the car rocked with the thuds of incoming bullets. Small projectiles whizzed past her head. She didn't know if they were glass or lead as she dove for the floorboard. Her palm stung, and she looked down to see a sliver of glass bisecting her lifeline. A slim ribbon of blood leaked down her wrist.

She squeezed her eyes shut. "This isn't real. It's just a nightmare from that damned detective book."

Outside of the car, everything went silent. Inside, Taylor didn't move. His left sleeve had caught on the turn signal and hung limp.

The turn indicator light clicked on and off like a metronome as Carrie waited to wake up.

Taylor gurgled out a wet cough, and she felt moisture flit against her cheek. She still did not open her eyes.

"This isn't real," she repeated through gritted teeth.

A hand grabbed her wrist, and Carrie screamed.

As Carrie tumbled to the floor, her arm jerked backward, wrist twisted in a tight grip. She tried to jerk free while batting at the resistance with her other hand. Carrie heard herself growl like a trapped animal as she bared her teeth and tried to break loose.

She looked up and stopped struggling.

A corner of the bed sheet wrapped around her hand; the material had caught on one of the wrought iron bed posts and produced a makeshift snare.

Carrie tugged on the sheet with her free hand and shakily stood up. As she untangled her wrist, the blood flow rushed back and caused pinpricks of pain. After a few seconds, the sensation dissipated, but a single sharp sting remained in her palm.

A small sliver of glass bisected her lifeline. She plucked it out and ran to the bathroom. She barely made it to the toilet as last night's expensive splurge splashed into the toilet.

She sat back and leaned against the sink. Her breathing picked up speed into sharp hiccupping gulps. Those dissolved into shoulder-racking sobs as she buried her face in her arms.

"You'd best have those titles back before the next full moon peaks."

Carrie stopped crying.

She tasted the salt from her tears and running nose. The old librarian's words echoed in her brain.

"Past one week and it'll be too late."

"Oh, shit!" Carrie jumped up.

Where the hell were the books?

She ran into the kitchen and grabbed her book bag. A pair of socks, a couple of dog-eared magazines, and a hairbrush tumbled onto the table. No books.

Carrie rushed over to her bed and slid to a stop on her knees. She threw back the sheet and ducked under the box spring. Aside from a colony of dust bunnies, a single slipper, and a pair of panties, no books peeked out from under the bed.

She stood, glancing frantically around the crowded room. Her eyes fell upon her small IKEA bookcase. One glance told her that the paperbacks were not there. With such a tiny room, she only allowed herself to keep fewer than twenty books. All of them carried some sentimental value, earning a place on the shelves. There was no room in her life for the luxury of excess.

"I know they're here," she whined.

The bathroom.

It was the only other place in her apartment where she read. She got up, ran in, and flicked on the light. It still smelled of vomit, and in the light, she saw where her aim had been off a little. The latest crumpled *Reader's Digest* that her mom subscribed to for her every year was there. But there were no books on top of the tank. Carrie kicked the laundry hamper in a blast of impotent rage and sent it careening into the side of the bathtub. It wobbled in a drunken half circle and tipped over onto the linoleum.

Three books tumbled out along with an old "Organizing for America" t-shirt. She dove for the books and clutched them to her chest. Tears flowed again. This time, from relief.

"It's not too late."

Carrie stood and threw on a pair of sweatpants and a hoodie before stuffing the books and her phone into her empty tote. Down on the street, the sky above the buildings began the day shift and slowly progressed from dark blues to pink-tinged grays as she jogged toward the dog park.

When she arrived at the cul-de-sac by the dog park, the bookmobile was gone.

"No, it's always here," she whined.

Then again, was it? True, she remembered seeing the bookmobile parked there every evening last week when she walked the dogs.

However, she was always too sleepy and running late to pay much attention when she walked them in the mornings before going to class. When did it arrive? She pulled out her phone and pulled up the library's web page.

The library.

"Of course!" Carrie laughed with relief.

A quick online search displayed the operating hours. Being a Sunday, it was still two hours before they opened. Her transit app said it would take about forty-five minutes to get there. That still left over an hour to kill. Did she spend it here, waiting for the bookmobile to show up?

A dull throb in her palm reminded her of last night's nightmare. She put the phone in her pocket and jogged down to a bus stop at the end of the block. Carrie just caught up with the Route 30, about to head across town. She found a seat and cradled the bag of books close to her chest.

The library parking lot lay deserted except for a shopping cart, half full of empty plastic bottles. Although a dirty brown overcoat hung from the handle of the cart, its owner was nowhere to be seen. Carrie made a complete circuit of the building, hoping to catch sight of the bookmobile. Her shuffling steps echoed off the brick walls and emphasized the isolation of early morning. Finding nobody or the bookmobile, she walked to the front steps and sat down to wait.

The tote lay at her feet, the books inside forming cancerous lumps under the canvas skin that made her shiver in the morning air. She reached out her heel and scooted them behind her feet and out of sight. Their weight pressed, heavy and uncomfortable, against her calf. Carrie pulled out her phone and scrolled through Instagram, hoping to speed up the wait. It didn't help.

At five minutes past the advertised opening hour, a young guy with a "EAT, READ, SLEEP" hoodie and small backpack swept up to the steps on a squeaking bicycle. As if on cue, two cars pulled into the parking lot and found spaces at the far end. By the time the occupants made it to the steps, the guy on the bike unlocked the door and ducked inside to tap out a code on an alarm pad just inside.

"Hi there," a chipper young woman coming from the parking lot waved to Carrie.

"Are you open?" Carrie said as she jumped up.

An older woman with the stereotypical librarian bun held up a hand.

"Give us a second to get things turned on," she said. "But you can come inside and get warm, dear."

Carrie followed them into the lobby, the familiar scent of books no longer providing the usual comfort.

"I just need to return the books I borrowed from the bookmobile," she said.

"Excuse me?" the bicycle guy asked from the circulation desk. "From where?"

Carrie hurried over to the counter and dumped the paperbacks out.

"I got them from the bookmobile over by Doyle Park. They're a little late," she said.

He shook his head and pushed the books back toward her. "Sorry, we don't have a bookmobile. Maybe it was from the university."

An icy stab of desperation flowed up from Carrie's heart and lodged in her throat.

"You've gotta be mistaken. It's there almost every day."

The library clerk cocked an eyebrow. Carrie knew that look. Hell, it was the same look she gave when some crazy guy on the bus tried to explain why the President is really a lizard person. It was a 'I know you're crazy as crap, but I'm just going to keep my mouth shut and hope that you go away' look.

"Maybe it belongs to some church," the chipper clerk offered. "Those Episcopalians are always doing some sort of outreach."

Carrie grabbed the books and stuffed them back into the bag. Tears of desperation blurred her vision as she hurried out of the library and back out into the painfully bright morning. Despite the warming rays, Carrie could not rub away the goosebumps that pricked her arms. Dread sat between her shoulder blades and made the nerves and muscles painfully tight.

Glancing back at the library, she saw a bright blue painted hatch of the after-hours book drop, and the temptation to stuff the bag of books down its throat rose inside her. She shook the thought from her mind, knowing they'd somehow follow her like a persistent curse. Because that's what it was, right? That damn old crone cursed her. But why?

Carrie caught the next bus heading home. Aside from an elderly church lady with an absurdly large, feathered hat and a sleeping homeless man, she had the bus to herself. She looked at a large white Bible sitting on the seat next to the old woman, tempted to ask to borrow it. Carrie didn't know if she wanted it for answers or protection. Could a holy book provide help against cursed ones?

"You're just being paranoid," Carrie whispered to herself.

The church lady looked over at her and smiled before pulling the "Stop Requested" cord. Carrie tried to smile back in a way that conveyed that she wasn't crazy. Although she couldn't even convince herself.

As she got closer to home, she exhausted her short list of ideas on how to get rid of the books. Carrie understood the look of resignation on an antelope's face as it succumbed to the claws of a lioness in a nature documentary. She just wanted the nightmare to end.

Carrie looked out the window and screamed, "Stop!"

More out of being startled than duty, the driver slammed on the brakes. The homeless guy flew against the seat in front of him and cursed as Carrie grabbed the book bag and rushed for the door.

"Lady, you gotta pull the damn chord!" the driver yelled back.

She muttered an apology as she pushed against the slowly opening door and stumbled out onto the sidewalk.

In all its garish glory sat the bookmobile.

Parked in its usual place by the dog park, it sat like an abandoned carnival ride, promising excitement and maybe danger with warning colors of red and yellow. The row of scuffed black plastic milk crates, filled with selections of several yellowed hardcovers and paperbacks, lined up along its length.

An empty, black eye window stared back at Carrie. The morning sun, now rising above the treeline, failed to penetrate the glass and illuminated nothing inside.

"Hello?" Carrie creeped forward and tapped on the glass.

No sound came from inside. She raised on her tiptoes and tried to peer into the interior. Half in shadow from the apartment building next door, the interior of the bookmobile yielded only an inky abyss and her own reflection in the scratched pane.

Carrie walked around to the front of the vehicle. A curtain hung behind the driver's seat and shut off any view of the inside. Windows on the other side and the rear were painted over in red and trimmed in gold like gilded frames.

She climbed onto the front bumper and jumped up and down.

"Hey, lady!" Carrie yelled as the bookmobile squeaked and groaned with her movement.

She jumped off and ran back around to the window and its dented metal ledge.

Silence.

"Oh, come on," Carrie groaned.

The books weighed down the bag like stones. She wished they were rocks. Then she would smash out the damned painted windows with them and go home.

Carrie glanced over at the dog park. A few early risers watched an old chocolate Labrador and German Shepherd play a loping game of tag. By the gate into the park sat a dented metal trash can, chained to the fence. She walked over to the can and held the book bag over the piles of fast-food wrappers and sports drink bottles.

She felt a painful twinge along the lifeline on her palm and glanced up to see movement deep within the bookmobile.

Taking the paperbacks out, she walked back over to the bookmobile and stacked them on the metal counter. She took a step back and stared at the offering. The highlander stared back at her from the top cover and seemed to wink when a brisk breeze lifted a few pages. Carrie rushed forward and turned the book face down.

"They're all back!" Carrie shouted at the closed window.

The dogs rushed over to the fence and barked at her.

"Sorry," she called out to the owners.

She turned back, and the books were gone.

When she arrived back at the apartment, she tossed the empty book bag into the laundry hamper. Maybe hot water and harsh soap would wash away the tainted presence of those damned paperbacks. For good measure, Carrie took a hot scrubbing shower before changing into some cotton shorts and an old t-shirt.

Reading was out of the question. After brewing a cup of tea, she fired up her laptop and searched for something mindless to binge-watch until it was time for bed. After that, a good night's sleep would set things right again.

After three seasons of *Friends*, she closed the laptop and placed it on the nightstand. Carrie reached over to turn out the light. She hesitated. Maybe one more night with it on wouldn't be too childish.

Carrie fluffed her pillow and slid further under the sheets. She stuck the toes of her left foot out from under the covers. It was a trick she'd read about somewhere to help get to sleep, something about the body being fooled into thinking it's cold and needed to shut down. Whatever, it worked.

A SLIGHT SNORE WAKES CARRIE, and she settles further into the pillow, trying to ease back into restful oblivion.

A slow scratch breaks the silence.

She holds her breath and listens.

There's no mistaking that the sound came from the foot of her bed. Unlike the insistent pawing of a dog at the door, this dull scrape is drawn out, like a long, sharp fingernail, slowly tracing the woodgrain down the footboard slat. It begins near the top, just out of sight, and travels down the wood until she hears a final flick at the bottom.

Or is it just her overtaxed imagination and lack of any proper sleep? This shouldn't be happening. She had returned all the books.

She hears shuffling at the end of the bed. It sounds like cloth sliding heavily on the wooden floor.

And then a sharp rubber scuffing, like a rubber glove, makes Carrie scrunch up into a shivering ball against her pillows.

Her eyes water and grow unfocused as she watches a bright red balloon drift up from the foot of the bed and stop taut against the string. It hovers three feet above her bed.

"No, no. I took them back. This can't be happening," she moans.

The balloon and bedside light bulb pop at the same time.

Carrie screams.

Sun Kissed
By Benjamin Spada

It only took ten minutes for Shelly's latte to sour from Ariana's veiled gibes.

"Hello? Eyes on *me*, babe!" said Ariana.

Shelly blinked away her distracted thoughts. She absolutely hated it when Ariana said that. Mostly because everyone*'s* eyes were *always* on Ariana. 'Eyes on me' was practically a catchphrase for when Ariana felt anyone had committed the egregious crime of not giving her their full attention.

"You really should give these cold brews a try," Ariana said, nudging her drink against Shelly's. "All that cream and dairy isn't good for you. Besides, beach season's coming!"

Beach season was always coming. This was San Diego after all, and Ariana just loved to remind Shelly every chance she got. Shelly supposed that if she had her friend's perfect copper skin and lithe figure, then she'd be more excited about the coming summer. Add to the equation that Ariana had become an influencer of moderate acclaim, and it became that much more obvious why Ariana was looking forward to it. While Shelly had to waitress tables and scrounge for tips to pay off her mountain of college debt, all Ariana had to do was post a couple of pictures of herself in a skimpy outfit and her motley of followers threw enough money at her for her to buy a Tesla. Correction: buy *another* Tesla.

They'd been friends since childhood, but they couldn't have been more different. Yes, Shelly was pretty, but no one would ever make the mistake of saying she was hot. Especially not if she was next to Ariana. Or even in the same hemisphere as her.

Ariana somehow managed to dress flawlessly as if she were headed to a photoshoot, regardless of the occasion. Even for something as casual as coffee, it was designer sportswear and spotless white Nike Air Max shoes. If it were dinner out in town, it'd be a short dress that accentuated her already blessed areas and strappy heels that wrapped all the way up her calves. Maybe some boots that she would go out of her way to point out were made of genuine Italian leather. Shelly, on the other hand, was more than comfortable wearing her faded college hoodie and sweatpants for every occasion. If she were really trying to dress up, she'd put jeans on. She and Ariana were just different people, and they lived on different tiers of life.

But not for long.

That thought brought a smile to Shelly's face, and she took a deep gulp of her latte and all its fattening calories that Ariana oh so subtly pointed out. For the first time in their lifelong friendship, it was Ariana's turn to know what it felt like to be second best. Shelly had a secret weapon. On instinct, her hand went to her pocket and retrieved the silver-tinted prescription bottle. She removed the cap, shook one of the white pills in her hand, and quickly popped it in her mouth.

Ariana noticed.

Good.

"What are those?" she said, eyeing the silver plastic bottle.

Shelly used her drink to swallow the pill.

"They're nothing, just something to help with my stomach for that thing I told you about."

"What, like diet pills? Wait, are you on Ozempic?!"

"Ozempic is last year's news," she said dismissively. "It's just a little thing to help with my digestion."

Even from behind the large-framed fashionista sunglasses, Shelly could still see Ariana's eyebrows scrunch in frustration. Ariana *hated* not being in the know, because she rarely was. Shelly relished this feeling. The tables were turning, and a little voice in the back of her head giggled at the thought of Ariana being put in her place. Shelly was going to show her up at her own game, and it was going to be beautiful.

That giggle in her head went on and on. It had been getting louder lately.

IT WAS SO new there wasn't even a brand name for it. Shelly had taken the chance on an email that had found its way into her inbox, filled out an attached questionnaire, and then waited. Three more questionnaires followed. Shelly didn't suspect this was some new scam making the rounds, because it seemed as if they were trying to disqualify her rather than sell her anything. Finally getting the appointment had been hard enough, and the doctor had made her sign an NDA before he prescribed it. She scrawled her signature on the form without a second thought. The doctor had walked her to the in-clinic pharmacy and retrieved the bottle of pills from a shelf labeled with a long chemical name Shelly could barely read, let alone pronounce. The plastic bottle had a shiny silver tint rather than the typical orange, which struck Shelly as odd, but at the same time, it felt chic. Modern. It felt like somehow, she'd managed to get in on the ground floor of the latest thing before the rest of the people in the know found out.

"Take one daily with a meal," the doctor instructed. "You'll see results within the first twenty days. If not, come back in and we can re-evaluate."

A week later, two pounds had trimmed away like magic. No

additional exercise, no change to her regular diet, nothing. Just as she'd been feeling good about herself, Ariana had sent her a message inviting her to some beach shindig in a few weeks. As always, there were hidden barbs nestled amid the friendly invitation.

Ariana:

> "It's a few weeks away. Just giving you a heads up so you can look your best!"

Shelly's hand shook when she read that message. Anger bubbled up like a hot geyser ready to burst. She'd known Ariana long enough to know what she was *really* saying: 'I'm giving you enough time to lose some weight, you cow. All eyes are gonna be on me, but I can't have you looking *too* gross.'

Two lousy pounds. She was an idiot for having been happy about it. Two pounds was nothing. If she didn't want to look like a beached whale when she shared Ariana's cabana, then she'd have to lose ten times that. More.

That was the first time she heard the whisper. It popped into her head out of nowhere like a sudden spark in the darkness, and it told her the real reason Ariana wanted her there.

She hates you. She hates your fat fucking face. That self-centered bitch wants to humiliate you. All eyes will be on her. They're always *on that pompous slut.*

The angry, unfamiliar voice startled her, but only a little. After all, it made total sense. Why else would she invite Shelly if not so she would look that much better standing next to her? She knew that Shelly had struggled with the same twenty pounds since graduating college, while she herself maintained her flawless figure with seemingly no effort. The invitation was solely for Ariana's own benefit, both to make herself look better and so she'd have someone else available to take a dozen 'candid' pictures of her.

The joke would be on her, though. Shelly was going to surprise her. Twenty pounds? That would be no problem.

'Take one daily,' the doctor had said.

Ariana's precious beach day was just two weeks away. Shelly needed faster results, and she was determined to get them. She unscrewed the cap of the silver bottle and, for the first time, took out a second pill. Shelly swallowed the second dose, not registering even an ounce of concern.

SHELLY YEARNED for the sun's warmth. The mental picture of those gentle rays lighting up the soft sand of the beach had become a fixture in her head. As she worked her long shifts, waiting hand and foot on an endless chain of ungrateful customers, Shelly kept thinking about how close she was to the finish line. One week to go.

As she often did on her break at work, Shelly found herself scrolling through her social media newsfeed. It tended to be the perfect mind-numbing salve after taking orders from aggravating people all day. The first thing that popped up in her feed was a post from Ariana at some outdoor gym.

The photo looked staged as all hell.

For the life of her, Shelly didn't understand why anyone would put on that much makeup just to get sweaty, but her followers ate it up. The comments section was overflowing with incels lusting for her attention and the whole thing made Shelly's vision go red.

She wondered why they couldn't see how painfully forced it all was. Ariana could throw up some caption about staying motivated and working hard, but if any of her followers would think with their brains instead of their dicks they might ask why Ariana hadn't broken a sweat during her 'workout.'

That tanned skin of hers was unreal. While Ariana was free to stage selfies in outdoor gyms bathed in natural sunlight, Shelly was sequestered indoors working all day. It just wasn't fair. She'd always been pale. Being a lifelong Californian, it felt like some kind of curse. It wasn't uncommon when she met people for them to ask her if she was visiting from out of town. On more than one occasion, she'd been so awkward that she'd actually lied and said yes.

Shelly had already met and exceeded her twenty-pound goal by nearly twice that, but what good would it do to show up to Ariana's beach invite lean and trim if she was still pale as a ghost?

She wanted that bronzed color. Needed it. Shelly's jaw clenched, and her hand moved with a mind of its own to the silver pill bottle. She popped one of the small pills in her mouth with one hand while she used the thumb of her other hand to gently touch the picture of Ariana.

Carve her fucking skin off and wear it.

The sudden sharp whisper made her jump, but she quickly shook the intrusive thought away. Shelly dismissed the mental outburst not because it was insane, but because she didn't want Ariana's skin. She wanted her own. The dark whispers in her head seemed to mull that over and went quiet. Shelly nodded to herself and swallowed the pill still held in her mouth.

Wait, was that her second pill? Or her third? She'd somehow lost count.

Warmth from the medicine radiated out from her belly. She told herself that it meant it was working. Burning all the flab away and firing her metabolism up on all cylinders. It also filled her with unfamiliar energy. More than once, she wondered if that energy was where the whispers came from. It felt like lightning rippling through her, and she was more than willing to ride this lightning. It made her feel *alive*.

"Hey, Shelly, break's over," her supervisor, Brett, said.

Shelly had been so lost staring at Ariana's tanned skin that she hadn't noticed Brett standing there. It looked like Brett was about to chastise her for wasting more company time, but then his expression quickly softened.

"Are you okay?" he asked.

The question puzzled her. Could he somehow sense her jealousy? Or, more embarrassing, had he managed to see her fawning over Ariana's picture?

"I'm fine," Shelly said, stowing her cell phone in her bag. "Why?"

"Oh, nothing," he said. "You just looked kind of sick."

His words struck her like the bite of a whip. He didn't say 'Wow you look like you've lost weight' or 'Damn, Shelly, you look great.' No. Sick. *Sick?!* He basically said she was disgusting. The dark voice inside her head growled low like a beast.

Claw out his goddamn eyes. Stab him. Stab him. STAB HIM.

Shelly's eyes flitted to one of the silverware rollups nearby. The steak knife held within had a rounded edge; it wasn't pointy at all. The saw-like pattern along its edge, though, was plenty sharp. She could still use it to cut him.

Yes. Cut. Hack. Saw through his fucking neck and rip his tongue out.

The thought of tearing Brett's tongue from his throat after he'd uttered such thoughtless words brought a smile to Shelly's face. Not knowing what was on her mind, Brett returned the smile in kind. The moment held for just a second longer than normal, and Brett shifted uncomfortably before turning around and heading to the front.

His back was to her.

The restaurant was pretty dead. It'd be easy.

Shelly snatched up the silverware rollup. The cloth napkin unrolled as she lifted it, spilling the spoon, fork, and steak knife to the floor. She frantically picked up the spoon first with feverish speed.

Yes. The spoon. Scoop out his eyes. Stomp them on the ground. Feel them squish *under your shoe.*

Her smile stretched wider. She stepped up behind Brett with the spoon clenched tightly in her grip. This recent anger was like a drug. It felt good to give in to it. It was just . . . intoxicating. The hotter her anger burned, the more she wanted to slip deeper into it like the roiling waters of a Jacuzzi.

She readied the spoon, more than prepared to sink as deep into this pit of rage as she could. She licked her lips in anticipation of jamming the spoon into the back of his eye socket. Then the silver pill bottle tumbled from her pocket. The cap must've been loose because it spilled all over the floor.

"No, no, no!" she cried and dropped to her knees. "Idiot. Stupid. *Stupid!*"

She plucked the pills up as quickly as she could. Brett heard the commotion and whirled about, then knelt down to help her. The dark whisper breathed low in her mind, like a coil tensing up and unsure if it would snap forward or not.

The spoon was still gripped tightly in one hand.

Shelly's other hand darted across the ground like a spastic chicken pecking up scattered seeds. Her heart thundered in her chest so hard she thought it was bound to launch right out of her ribcage. By the time the pills were all recovered and the cap fastened tight to the bottle, Shelly's hand quivered with anxious tremors.

As an afterthought, she set the spoon back on a nearby table.

"Whoops," said Brett, and he bent over to the ground. "You almost missed one!"

He stood back up and placed the last pill in the palm of her hand, nodded, and went back to work without a thought in the world.

Shelly looked down at her palm. How many had she taken today? One more wouldn't hurt.

THE LAST WEEK leading up to the beach day fluttered by in a hazy blur. Shelly had stopped going to work. She didn't have the time. Too busy. Far too much to do. Shelly hadn't even left her apartment all week. The fridge was empty, but she hadn't noticed. The pills took away her appetite. She hadn't bothered to step on the scale in days, but from the feel of her ribs poking against the skin it was clear the twenty pound weight loss goal was far behind her.

Can always lose more... the dark voice whispered.

Shelly shook her head up and down in wild agreement and took a pill.

The weight issue had been managed just in time for the issue of the swimsuit to rear its head. Shelly hadn't owned a proper bikini—nor had she any desire to wear one—in years, but she would be damned if she was going to let Ariana outshine her with her latest two-piece. The problem was that Shelly didn't even know where to get one herself.

She'd placed nearly a dozen online orders, picked out every possible style, and in every color imaginable. Everything beyond her doorstep was forgotten. Instead, she'd paced around the front of her apartment, waiting for the first packages to be delivered. She watched suspiciously through the blinds, only daring to leave the confines of the apartment to snatch up the boxes once the delivery driver had walked away. Shelly had clawed the box open with an insatiable need. The first swimsuit to arrive was lime green. Its bright color had caught her eye on the web page. She hoped it would have the same effect on Ariana.

Shelly bit her lip with eagerness, then quickly shook out of her clothes to try it on. The clothes barely fit her anymore anyway and easily slipped off her rail-thin limbs. It took less than ten seconds to pull the lime green bikini up her legs and down over her shoulders.

It only took one second of looking in the mirror to hate it.

It wouldn't do. No. Not at all.

Shelly mumbled something, even *she* didn't know what anymore, and tore into the second box. This one was black and lacey. *Very* sexy. Just not on her, she realized with revulsion once she put it on. The black color with her pale skin made it look like she was going to a funeral.

"No, no, no!" Shelly growled, smacking the butt of her palm against her temple with every word.

It went on like that all week. Shelly lurked in the apartment, eyes flitting through the blinds in a never-ending vigil for the delivery man. But package after package, swimsuit after swimsuit, none of them were right. She kept ordering more, even going as far as to pay for next-day shipping to ensure they arrived before the weekend's beach day, but none were perfect. Her frenzy of purchases only stopped when her card declined. Then, she was both out of money *and* without anything to wear.

The neighbor has money, the dark whisper suggested. *He always leaves the window open at night. Crawl in. Kill him. Take his money. Use the scissors, snip his neck. Snip. Snip. SNIP.*

Shelly considered it, smiling to herself and nodding. Her hand popped another pill into her mouth with a mind of its own.

SNIP. SNIP. SNIP!

With just one day until her rendezvous with Ariana, a moment of clarity hit Shelly like a slap, and she realized why none of them were working.

It wasn't the bikinis. It was her stupid pale skin. That was the issue.

Shelly slapped herself for being too dumb to see it before. She'd been cooped up inside so long she was even paler than usual; a base tan would fix everything. A quick pre-trip to the beach before tomorrow was exactly what she needed. Shelly threw one of the bikinis in a purse and stormed out of her apartment. She didn't even bother to close the door behind her.

She'd gotten halfway down the block before realizing it was already dark out. There was no daylight left to warm her skin, and she fidgeted about angrily on the sidewalk. Not that her thinking had been straight lately. Now it was completely jumbled. What was nonsense, and what had been reason, were now twisted together and upside down. It felt like her mind was a mess of exposed wires tangled together. The only thought that stayed at the forefront of her mind was the beach, the beach, the beach. Everything else was too complicated.

No daylight, no tan.

Wait, no.

There was still the tanning salon down the block.

Shelly ran down the street with renewed giddiness. The dark whisper giggled triumphantly. She skidded to a halt outside the tanning salon, and her face scrunched in confusion. The lights were out. The salon was closed.

It must've been later than she thought. What time was it?

Shelly reached into her purse for her phone, realizing too late that she hadn't charged it for days. Who knew how long it'd been dead? Shelly didn't, nor did she care.

The answer to all her problems was right in front of her, behind the locked door. A skittish twitch took hold of her neck, and she scratched at it obsessively as her mind turned over and over at the obstacle at hand. One little door.

Go in. Find a way. Go. Go. GO.

Without thinking, Shelly reached for the handle and shoved at the door with her shoulder. It didn't budge. She grunted, cursed, and slammed against it three more times. The bones in her shoulder ached from the impacts.

FIND. A. WAY.

"Yes," she said to herself, and scuttled away from the door to the backside of the building. There had to be a way in. A window. A backdoor. *Something.*

She found it at the building's rear. A backdoor, which was also locked, had a small transom above. Someone had left it cracked to vent heat. Shelly licked her lips and climbed. The open transom was a small slit, not wide enough for a grown healthy adult to slip through. Thankfully, Shelly's body had gone through some very drastic changes.

Her lanky body slithered through the slot with relative ease. If anyone had been around to watch it, they would've found the sight of her emaciated body contorting and twisting quite . . . unsettling.

It wasn't hard to find a tanning bed once she was inside. There were several side rooms, each with its own bed, and the hardest part was not tripping on anything while stumbling around in the dark.

Shelly picked a room that felt particularly inviting.

The control panel for the bed was a user-friendly digital screen. It let her adjust time, intensity, and even pick different ambient music to set the mood. User-friendly or not, Shelly knew nothing about tanning beds. She set the dial to medium. Blue lights in the bed lit up, and there was a deep *HUMM* as it came to life. The timer went up in five-minute increments. Shelly opted for an even ten.

The bed was surprisingly cool as she crawled inside. Every bone down her back ached against the flat slab underneath her, but the warmth wafting off the long lights above her was luxurious. Shelly couldn't help but wonder why she'd never done this before. The blue glow of the tanning bed, the heat bathing across her skin, and the spa music gently playing from the speakers was nothing less than heavenly.

Shelly squealed with giddiness, and then the humming stopped. The bed went dark.

Ten minutes had gone by too quickly. Her skin felt hot and a little tight. To her, that meant the bed had done its job. The heat her skin drank in from the lights dissipated quicker than she would've liked. All at once, she felt dissatisfied.

When she flipped the light on and caught a look at herself in a mirror hung on the wall, that dissatisfaction grew tenfold.

Pale. Still so pale.

Shelly scratched that spot on her neck more. It'd already gone raw from the repeated attacks with her fingernails. The bed hadn't been enough.

Then do more. You can always do more.

She nodded in agreement and reached for the control panel. Medium hadn't done the trick, and ten minutes was far too little time. Shelly's fingers twitched against the touchpad for the bed, and she wondered just how high the settings could go.

It was almost showtime.

Shelly stepped from her car and sauntered toward the beach. Her hips swung playfully as she did, doing her best to mimic Ariana's own flirty way of walking. She kept a large shawl draped across her, hiding her face and body from the other beach onlookers. It was a shame to deny them such a vision, but the whisper assured her that this was no different from hiding a present from view. The real joy came from the unveiling, and she'd been crafting this gift for their eyes all night at the tanning salon. It would be worth it.

She'd taken great pains to get things perfect. Every time she stepped from the tanning bed and looked in the mirror, the dark voice told her it wasn't enough.

Just a little more, it'd said. *Almost perfect.*

She'd kept at it. Again and again. Eventually, the bed had failed from overheating, but there were plenty more in adjacent rooms. Another pill, another bed, another try. All night. Shelly lost herself in the process, entering a dazed fugue state, and finally coming to like a swimmer breaking the surface of the water when the dark whisper at last spoke again.

Yesss . . . it had hissed. *Now you're perfect.*

That itchy spot at her neck demanded her attention and pulled her back to the present. This time, when she scratched at it, a hunk of leathery skin and tissue came off with it.

Shelly spotted Ariana waiting by a beach cabana with her back turned. She must've just arrived as she was still applying her suntanning oil and making a big show of it for the sake of the other interested beachgoers. She used one hand to apply it across her chest before pulling out her phone to take a selfie, complete with exceedingly puckered lips.

Shelly walked a little faster, eager to make her own play before Ariana really got into motion. The whisper in her head turned to thunder.

Move. Move NOW. Show her . . . show them all.

The strain of speeding up her gait pulled at the already tightened skin along her legs. She felt something like tearing a runner in her pantyhose, except she wasn't wearing any. A quick glance down confirmed the source: the skin along the back of her calf had split like an overcooked sausage.

You're beautiful . . . the voice assured her.

Shelly's flip-flops slipped from her feet with a wet squelch when she stepped from the asphalt of the parking lot and onto the beach. Her soles were red and raw, and the sand caked against them in a thick layer like plaster. Each step sent the coarse grains deeper into the tissue, but Shelly didn't so much as cringe. All she did was pause momentarily halfway to the cabana and shift her weight back and forth from her left to her right foot. The gritty texture against her exposed fleshy soles felt good. It felt new. She left a trail of gruesome, dark red prints with every footfall.

Move now. Smile!

Beneath the shawl, she grinned. Her dry, cracked lips split. A thin drip of blood went down her chin.

SMILE!

She did. Wider. Her lip tore in three different places but she was numb to it. All her attention was on Ariana. A few onlookers paused and took notice of Shelly. She saw them squinting against the bright sunshine to get a better look or pushing up their sunglasses for an unobstructed view. There were a few gasps. It was all a delight to her ears. Only Ariana hadn't noticed. She was too convinced that the curious murmurs were for her sake.

When Shelly was three paces from Ariana, she gripped the edges of the shawl and cast it off like a presenter unveiling the latest billion-dollar sports car. Parts of the shawl had become glued to her damaged flesh like a band-aid on an open wound, and Shelly flailed wildly to fling the shawl away. The shawl came free and took a patch of skin with it.

The murmurs turned to gasps now. Shelly winked at one. Or she tried to. Her shriveled eyelid barely lowered over an eye that had been cooked white like an egg.

She did a little spin to show off to everyone looking at her, and they were *all* looking at her. They looked at this ghoulish figure who was little more than starved skin and bones. They watched in quiet terror at her horribly burned body, scalded and seared from endless hours in the tanning bed. Their eyes took in her red exposed flesh where the desiccated skin had split like a cooked chicken on a spit. Her unhinged, bloody smile had the crowd reeling back with barely restrained panic. The person before them should've been in the ICU, or in the morgue, not flaunting herself here on the beach.

A child screamed a bloodcurdling wail and pointed a trembling finger in Shelly's direction. It was only then that Ariana finally realized that all the gathered attention around the cabana wasn't for her. She turned, slowly, and her jaw nearly fell from her head when she saw what her friend had done to herself.

Words failed her. Ariana's phone fell from her quaking hands and landed on the sandy ground, where it captured everything on a live feed. Comments and views skyrocketed in the span of three seconds. Shelly spotted the cell phone on the ground and blew a playful kiss at it with her torn lips. Then she thrust both arms out in either direction and beamed her gruesome smile at Ariana.

"All eyes on *me*, babe!"

What Lurks in Dreams
By Rose Winters

Location: Oceanside Sleep Lab

Cal woke up flushed and clammy. And furious. He'd failed again to control his dream.

"That was a bad nightmare." Dr. Kline tilted her head to the erratic line graph that spiked like an earthquake reading. She pulled the electrodes from his forehead. "Did you catch that bad guy you're always after?"

"Not yet. Next time."

Her ruby lips parted into that delicious smile. His tortured dreams were almost worth the reward of her fingertips on his skin.

"Your pulse is still high." She ripped electrodes from his chest.

"Ow." Cal studied her, his face stoic. Always stoic. The rapid heart rate readings? That would be Dr. Kline's proximity. A secret that would never be revealed. He needed to keep her safe from Bob.

Bob. Cal had chosen the most innocuous name he could for his nemesis, to take some semblance of power away from the demon who haunted his dreams nightly.

Cal could have named Bob what he really was—Brain-Eater.

He shuddered.

Noticing his fear, he repeated to himself, *Bob. Bob. Bob.* The mantra always grounded him.

Like a ribbon in a gentle breeze, Dr. Kline floated into a leather seat and crossed her long legs. God, she was perfect. Exotic high cheekbones, eyes like glowing sapphires, and that knockout body she thought she'd hidden under a smock . . .

"Cal, how many more times are we going to do this?" Her smile looked suddenly . . . placed there, for politeness' sake.

He felt a rush of disappointment but knew it was for the best that she wasn't interested—in him or the experiment. "Until you stop taking my money, or I run out—my book sales have slowed."

"Write another one."

"Yeah. Try writing when your head is mush. Which is why I'm here. To catch Bob so I can finally get a good night's sleep."

"Bob. The guy in the nightmare."

Cal frowned playfully to hide a cringe. "Yes, the . . . *guy* in the nightmare."

She frowned and slipped on black-rimmed glasses and somehow got even prettier. "Cal—I'm not sure this is the right approach. You believe your nightmares will stop if you actually catch—and kill—Bob?"

"Ah, yes. You think I need a shrink."

She leaned uncomfortably close to Cal's face. "I think you need a *friend*. Tell me about Bob. Please. Maybe . . . Maybe I can help. I have a good imagination, am open-minded, and don't have a judgmental bone in my body. Come on. It's been two months. I think I've earned your trust by now."

Cal considered it. He longed to tell her everything. But—then Bob would come for her, too. Bob was attracted to fear. Bob said that fear made the brain taste good. Something about the flood of adrenaline.

Dr. Kline smacked her lips at Cal's evasive silence, glanced at the clock—five p.m.—and stood up. "That's it. This is *way* against protocol, but . . ." She closed the door and pulled the blinds closed, "this is an emergency." She walked to her desk and pulled out a bottle of whiskey. Grabbing beakers, she poured two stiff drinks. She shoved a glass in his hand and commanded, "Drink. Now."

Chuckling under his breath, Cal muttered, "Drinking."

"To Bob, may he rot in hell."

Cal shot her a shocked glance, but she was kicking off her shoes and nestling back into her chair. He composed himself and said blankly, "To Bob."

She downed the whiskey in a cheek-rounding gulp. He followed suit, and she poured them another one. Stiffer than the last.

The clock ticked on the wall. Tic-tic-tic . . . mesmerizing and oblique and fuzzy.

He saw her lips moving, chatting about minutia, her voice blending with the clock. He was getting quite drunk. Otherwise, he never would have done it. He never would have said it. But he simply couldn't help himself. "Bob is real."

"Aha! I knew the whiskey would work!" She stabbed a finger at him. "Wait. So—you know Bob, in real life?"

Cal shook his head. *Here goes nothing.* "No. Bob's a demon. He visits people in their dreams, and he kills them if they get scared."

She frowned, obviously attempting to sober up. "Kills them—for real? Like . . . Freddy Krueger?"

"Not exactly. But there are seventeen dead so far since I've been aware of Bob."

She folded her arms and sat back in her chair, looking skeptical as hell. "What are their names? These victims."

This was Cal's ace in the hole. He pulled out a folded handwritten list from his pants pocket. "Here. Google these names, if you want. They're all dead. And I saw each and every one of them in a dream the night before they died. Bob killed them in my dream. The next day—they're dead, in real life."

Dr. Kline snatched the note and her phone and did a quick internet search. She got two people into it and narrowed her eyes.

"Okay. So, you have dead people on a list. You could have gotten those names from . . ."

"The newspaper. Yeah, yeah. Check the dates."

She studied the coffee-stained, handwritten note that he'd obviously been carrying for ages. "So . . . at first glance, it looks as though you wrote their names the day before they died."

Cal nodded. "That is correct. I'd wake up from a nightmare and write the name of the person in my dream—the one being terrorized by Bob."

She shook her head, her blond hair falling in her face. She swatted it back. "You could have just written the wrong date after the fact."

Cal was drunk, yes. But he was aware that he had a chance to shut his mouth—to shrug and laugh and pretend it was all a joke. Instead, he murmured as quietly as he could, "Check the back."

"What?"

Screw it. He raised his voice. "Check the back of the note. What I just wrote down a moment ago while you were pouring drinks."

She flipped the note and read the most recent item on the list. "John Embers. October 30th." She looked up curiously. "That's today."

Cal nodded, already feeling guilty for involving her.

She squinted, thinking. "So—according to what you've told me, this . . . John Embers was just killed in your nightmare—the dream you experienced here in my office not an hour ago."

Cal nodded. "Yes, that is correct."

"Bob—scared him to death?"

Again. A moment where Cal could shut his damned mouth and leave the pretty lady out of it.

Dr. Kline refilled their glasses. "To John Embers, may he beat the odds." She downed her drink, and Cal did the same.

He just couldn't keep quiet. "Bob didn't scare John to death. He scared him into immobility. When they're scared, he can make them immobile. And then he . . ." *For God's sake, Cal, shut up.* This was the point of no return. It was the whiskey. Or maybe Cal was tired of sharing the burden alone. He blurted out, "He makes them frozen with fear, and then he eats their brains."

Dr. Kline did something completely unexpected. She laughed. Not just laughed, but the gut-wrenching, arms-wrapped-around-the-belly, tear-and-snot-and-drool kind of hysterical laugh that borders on mania. She toppled to the floor, squealing. "Oh—oh—my God, I'm dying here!" She sat up abruptly, wasted and frowning for a split second. "Oh—get it? Dying? Oh, no, it must be BOB!" Peals of giddy sniggering continued.

Cal was at a loss. In a way, it snapped him back and cleared his head. She didn't believe him. Good. *Time to do the right thing.* Cal smirked. "You liked that, huh? I got you!" he forced a dark chuckle. "I'd better catch an Uber home tonight. We're still on for tomorrow, same place, same time?"

She wiped her nose on the sleeve of her doctor's smock and managed to control herself. She even feigned sobriety. It seemed she remembered she was a doctor with a patient, and it was pretty damned funny to see her stand up, put her hand out for a professional handshake, and trip over her shoes. Too drunk to blush, she shoved her toes into her high heels—on the wrong feet—and opened the door. "Same place, same time. Good night, Cal."

THE NEXT DAY, Cal entered the office, and there stood Dr. Kline, white as a sheet.

He pressed his lips to hide a smile. *Hungover, are we, Doc?* Turns out, that wasn't the problem.

"What the fuck, Cal?" She held her phone to his face. The screen showed a story about the mysterious death of one John Embers.

Cal squeezed his eyes shut. "Told you."

"Did you do it, Cal?" Her voice was ice.

His eyes flew open again. "What? No! Of course not. I told you. It was..."

"Bob? Your imaginary friend from your dreams? You're seriously going to blame . . . Bob?" Dr. Kline looked equal parts furious and scared.

Oh shit. No, no. Don't be scared! "I went straight home last night. I swear." His face brightened. "The Uber driver! He can tell you—he dropped me off at home, near the Oceanside City Hall!"

"You could have taken your car afterward . . ."

"My car was here! Remember?"

"You could have taken another Uber. Enough, Cal, tell me what happened. The truth, this time."

Cal was at a loss for words. He slumped into the leather chair. "It wasn't me."

"We'll see about that," she growled. "He's probably your neighbor. You probably walked there. I'm checking where he lives . . ."

Cal watched her eyes widen in confusion as she tapped the phone screen, and he knew he had won the day. "He's not from here, is he? They're from all over the world. Bob's victims. One was from India. The closest one so far was in Kentucky. Where did John die?"

"Australia," she whispered and sank onto the hospital bed. "He died in Melbourne, in his office. Just keeled over and died."

Cal nodded.

She stared intently at him. "His brain was not eaten. There wasn't one word about his brain."

Call shook his head. "No. That's just how he kills them in the nightmare. I think it marks them for death, and the next day, they just drop dead of 'mysterious causes.'"

"I'm a doctor. There's rarely such a thing as 'mysterious causes.' You have a stroke, an embolism, a heart attack . . ."

"Or they can't find a single anomaly, as in Bob's victims. That's how you know."

"Know what, exactly?"

"That Bob killed them."

She opened her mouth to argue but had nothing to say.

A first.

Finally, she jumped up. "Get on the table." She grabbed him surprisingly roughly and made him lie down. She slapped electrodes on his temples and chest. "God damn you, Cal, you are making me feel insane. I am a doctor. An educated, rational doctor. So, here's what we're going to do. You are going to have another nightmare. You'll write down the name, and then we both spend the night—right here. And we don't leave. Not to eat, not to pee."

"What if I have to . . ."

"Shut up, Cal, and go to sleep. You will not make me look like a quack. There is a logical explanation. I am proving your theory wrong."

"Very well." Cal was back to his stoic self. And falling asleep on command was never an issue. Bob only ate brains during Cal's sleep. Bob had told him before that when Cal didn't sleep, Bob went hungry. So, Cal was the most sleep-deprived person on the planet. From coffee, energy drinks, and meth—*okay, just once, big mistake*—to manic exercise, he'd tried everything. Still, a human goes mad with too little sleep. Plus, he looked like shit. He used to be a stud before Bob wrecked everything. And so, Cal had decided to purposefully sleep, with the aid and supervision of a sleep doctor—the ravishing Dr. Kline, to be precise. And Cal was absolutely determined to find a way to kill Bob.

Dr. Kline dimmed the lights. Cal heard the quiet whirring of the monitors and gave his heavy eyes permission to close.

Dr. Kline said something funny as he faded off to sleep: "You know, they say that every character in your dreams is yourself."

Yes, thought Cal, *I'd heard that before, too.* Of course, it didn't apply to Bob, who was an actual demon. But—what if it were true? What if Cal was Bob? No. That's not right. What if Bob were Cal somehow? And, if Cal could manifest Bob, could he, therefore, control Bob?

Cal decided to put this revelation—this theory—to the test.

Cal opened his eyes to a haze of white.

"Hello, Cal."

There he was. Bob. Red skin, horns, and a tail. Cal had long ago figured that Bob's image had been created in Cal's mind with the help of the Hollywood stereotype. It didn't make Bob any less real.

"I smell fear," Bob hissed, his black lips curling into a seductive smile. "She's very pretty."

Cal's heart jerked in his chest. *No! Not Dr. Kline!* He hadn't said it aloud. Nevertheless, Bob answered, "Yes. Dr. Kline."

Cal glowered. "She's not scared in the least. She is a scientist. She doesn't believe in you. Sorry, but today, you starve."

Bob's eyes drilled into Cal's. "Oh, my, yes, she is scared. Terrified." His forked tongue stroked slowly across his lips. "I can't wait to taste her." He closed his eyes and inhaled deeply as if smelling a steak on a barbecue.

"You won't touch her. I can promise you that."

Bob grinned lustfully. "You're scared, Cal. You like this one. That's even more enticing. It's your fault she's going to die. How does that make you feel?"

Cal's hair stood up on the back of his neck, his throat going dry.

Bob's eyes rolled half closed, aroused by the smell of Cal's fear. He took a deep, staggered breath. "More. I want more. I'm so . . ." his head turned sharply to Cal, ". . . hungry."

Cal bolted, his terror building. He ran, blind, through the white mist and careened straight into Bob, whose nails dug into Cal's shoulders, holding him still. In a sing-song rasp, Bob said, "She's scared; so scared! She sees the monitor. It's spiking all over the place. She thinks I'm killing you. She thinks I'm . . ." Bob leaned into Cal's ear, ". . . eating your brain."

Cal remembered the strange thought—about Bob and him being the same character. And so, Cal calmed himself. He took a deep, cleansing breath and filled his heart with the truth—that he was in love with Dr. Kline. Cal let pure love fill his essence. Cal focused on the sweet, deep ache he felt every time she bit her pencil or twirled that one curl of hair that rested on her shoulder or offered her soft handshake for their daily greeting. The scent of the room when she was in it. The times she'd jiggle her left foot.

The mist was fading noticeably. Cal hung on to the love and wore it like a shield.

Cal studied Bob's black eyes. They looked . . . curious at first. And then they widened with the realization that something was different. A change was taking place in this dream realm. Cal was gaining control.

Bob's face contorted in rage, and he lunged at Cal.

"You are nothing but air, Bob. Nothing but air."

Bob's body fell right through Cal as if Bob had no substance. Bob was evaporating.

Cal smiled. He thought of his heart monitor. He could feel his heart rate, slow and steady. And he knew Dr. Kline would be happy about that.

"No one is scared, Bob. You have nothing to feed on. You—are me. And I am you. There is only one of us."

Bob gurgled, deep in his throat. "*Yessss.* Only one of us! It will be me, you fool." He cackled with a blood lust. "I want her brain. *You* want her brain."

"I want you dead, you sonofabitch."

"Death . . ." Bob hissed, "is relative." His chin jutted up, and he shrieked and writhed, bathed in pleasure and pain.

Hurricane-force winds snatched and tore at Cal, but he pictured Dr. Kline's smile, concentrating with all his might. "Go . . ."

Bob clawed at the air savagely.

"To . . ."

Bob laughed manically, roaring, "Brains brains brains brains!"

"Hell!" Cal scissor-kicked Bob in the gut and sent him flying.

He watched as Bob split apart, atom by atom, with a piercing wail. A mush of red and black meat and rotten bones and pus swirled and funneled up to the sky with a revolting stench . . . And vanished.

With that, Cal opened his eyes, awake.

"Oh, thank God; I was so worried!" Dr. Kline stroked his forehead and gently pulled the electrodes off. She held his hands and sat him up. "Did you get the name of a victim?"

Cal smiled, relieved. "There was no victim. I won. He's gone forever." Cal couldn't believe the close call. The next victim would have been Dr. Kline. He looked into her beautiful eyes, tempted to tell her how he felt. That it was his love for her that grounded him, that left no room for the other guy. He thought, for a sick minute, that if he were, in fact, Bob, and they had joined together, then Bob would be released into the world in corporeal form. And then, there would be no stopping Bob at all.

Cal shook his head. No. It was the love that had saved him. Saved Dr. Kline, too. He dared to reach up and subtly touch that curl on her shoulder. "You were right, Dr. Kline. I was all the characters in my dream."

Her brow furrowed. "What? I never said that."

Cal grinned, incredulous. "Yes, you did. Just as I faded off to sleep."

She laughed lightly. "I certainly did not. Maybe it was Bob."

Cal was suddenly overwhelmed by her scent. He needed her. Now. Without permission, without question. He grabbed her forcefully, inhaling.

She giggled. "Cal . . . Wow. Took you long enough."

He groaned deep in his throat. And pressed his teeth to her neck, her hair, her scalp, and bit, his teeth nipping her flesh.

"Ouch! Hey—you're scaring me. Cal! Cal?"

He opened his mouth impossibly wider, inhaling her adrenaline, and feasted.

Hollywood's Land
By Lisa Diane Kastner

This was supposed to be a working vacation.

In theory, Xandra had unsuccessfully finished the working part, and this should have been the vacation part. And yet, she had spent three hours navigating between waiting in line to take a tour of Hollywood and responding to urgent calls.

Okay, maybe they weren't so urgent considering they tended to be from her Auntie Grace demanding to know things like where the peanut butter was located in the pantry or how many scoops of dog food to give Scruffy. Xandra had thought she had left enough instructions, but *clearly,* she was wrong.

"Next in line," sang the tour guide. He waved Xandra and a few others onward, boarding the oversized tram cart, which reminded her of a minibus that had absorbed a golf cart. No way she would be able to get off this thing in mid-ride. She hesitated, feeling slightly guilty for leaving her auntie on her own.

Xandra glanced at her phone. It was her auntie again. She looked at her watch and acknowledged that this was the last time she would have a chance to really behave like a tourist before she returned to

New Jersey and the realities of her life. She turned her iPhone off and smiled at the tour guide. Xandra raised her arm, grabbed the tram car's pole, and hoisted herself in.

"Right up front," the tour guide said.

Xandra read his name tag. "Jimmy," she said. "Thanks." This time, she smiled with a bit of eye contact. Their brief exchange made her smile bigger. It had been a long day, and something in his mannerisms told her that he actually liked his job. Now *that* was refreshing. Most people she knew spent all of their time complaining. Nice to see someone who seemed to really be into his work.

Once the last person boarded the tram, Jimmy put on a wireless headset and spoke directly into its microphone. "Congratulations! You are going to get one of the most unique experiences of your life!" he said. "This is the LAST tour for the day, so YOU," he looked directly at Xandra, "get the RARE opportunity to observe Hollywood from the Hollywood sign just at sunset." He winked. "Now that's a treat."

He used big hand gestures and exaggerated tones to punctuate his diatribe. His animations seemed to get even bigger as he guided them along the Warner Bros. Studio Lot and past Universal Studios. He leaned into his microphone as he shared secrets of the Hollywood and Burbank of yesteryear and reveled in rumors about smaller production houses running illegal dealings in relatively minuscule buildings.

Of course, the most interesting ones were those that looked like abandoned fast food joints. Xandra guessed that they had been left that way during COVID, and to keep the tour from getting boring, Jimmy made up tall tales just to keep everyone engaged.

As they passed the iconic Warner Bros. water tower, she remembered the rumor that Warner Bros. wanted to build a tram between the Hollywood sign and the Warner Bros. Studio lot. She guessed that if they had been successful, then Jimmy and quite a few others would have been out of jobs. She tried her best to listen to the guide, but some of what he shared seemed a bit too much, even for her.

He delved into ghost stories of extras dying on the set and expanded them to rumors that the legends of the wolfman were real. She almost laughed at that bit. Especially when he said, "But so far, no one has proven any of this true."

She nearly said, "My career is based on the existence of the supernatural, especially demonic lycanthropes." But she held back from informing him that this was the reason she visited Tinseltown. What had specifically brought her to the famed Hollywood Studios was the pursuit of a lycanthrope, one that had been spied on the set of the Conan O'Brien Show and had scared the bejeebers out of the tall host. She had been told by a gaffer that the famed host had been so scared, he had scurried up a lighting ladder. Turned out that Conan's writers had referenced this moment during the 2025 Oscar Awards' stage gags. In fact, the host had been so terrified that he declared he would not get down from the highest point he could find until they scoured the studio to prove it was safe. AND, once he had been coaxed down, he swore he would fire everyone on site unless they found the absolute best werewolf hunter around.

Next thing Xandra knew, she was on a plane to Los Angeles, all expenses paid.

She had spent several days in search of the savage beast that had invaded Conan's stage set. She was sure to check out every corner, every inch, just to see if she could even find a paw print. She interviewed members of the crew to try and find someone who had observed the same terror. That terror Conan had reported when the Los Angeles Fire Department had arrived, on a few occasions, to save him. Still, even with those efforts, she found no evidence of a werewolf. Well, other than Conan's restroom, that definitely showed signs of his own shedding. Xandra decided to take a break and go on this infamous tour before heading back to her hotel and ultimately returning to her small apartment in New Jersey.

One of the other passengers smirked. "Pft, wolves, demons, ghosts. I thought this was a tour of Hollywood, not some crazy made-up crap." The passenger folded his arms as if to say he wasn't going to listen anymore.

Jimmy, clearly sensing that he was losing his audience, responded, "Wait! This is ONLY the beginning. Like all great stories, we have a build-up to the climax and then a resolution or denouement. Believe me." He winked. "We've only just begun."

She had to admit that the few days of travel and nonstop hunting for the beast that had invaded Conan's set had finally caught up to her. Even though Jimmy's voice was engaging, she found herself being lulled to sleep by the steady movement of the tram car.

In the back of her mind, she heard Jimmy droning on about one thing or another. She tried to focus, but instead found sleep far too enticing to ignore. At first, she figured the dreams she had were normal; her brain processing all that had happened in the last few days. Images of Conan at the top of a palm tree, crying for help. She nearly laughed at the thought, acknowledging this was how her brain interpreted the story she had been told about him. She then dreamed of going under the Sorting Hat from Harry Potter and being told she was a . . . Just when she would hear her Potter House, Jimmy's voice broke into her imaginings.

"Next, we will be arriving at the Hollywood sign and then take a brief walk to our final destination, Griffith Observatory."

Somehow, with that last announcement, her mind shifted from being sorted to an image of downtrodden beings tied with chains to the base of what she thought was the Hollywood sign. They were left there as a full moon took over the night sky and dominated all that was before them. She felt their anxiety, their fear, their terror at the sight of the moon, so bright it shone greater than daylight. Some cried to be released, begging not to be forced to die this way. Cries of entreaties. Begging for forgiveness.

And that's when she saw it.

The true beast.

The one that had been described to her by Conan. An animal

nearly three times the size of a standard person, slightly hunched and moving with the animal pace of one on the hunt.

From within her, she felt herself command, "YOU knew the consequences. You should have thought before you did what you have done. You shall take your punishment, by order of the city of Hollywood." That point of view confirmed that this was more than a dream; this was a vision being shared with her by the guilty. One of the many that revealed to her the true demon.

Xandra's view broadened, and she realized that the people weren't tied to the Hollywood sign; they were tied to the LAND of the old Hollywoodland sign. She heard the screams and felt the terror of their bodies being ripped, one by one. She felt the horrifying euphoria of the one who lent his view to her.

The most terrifying part of the torture had been the one tied to the punctuation mark at the end of Hollywoodland. He had been tied to the period as if it were a chopping block. Not waiting for the werewolf to dive in, one of the persecutors looked in the direction of the guilty one who allowed Xandra to see through her eyes and nodded. The executioner held an axe and thrust it into the victim's neck, forcing the head to come away from the body. The skull disappeared down the hill and into the valley below. Blood spewed forward and gushed as if it were in search of the head to make the body whole. She felt the terror as she heard their bodies being ripped apart, one by one. She tried to run away, yet could not. Her lucid mind was desperate to awaken the rest of her.

Anything to escape the nightmare.

"Miss Woodman, we're here," Jimmy called to her. He touched her shoulder, and she startled awake.

She had been so frightened that she scared other passengers. Jimmy pulled back, not wanting to be injured as she slashed at some phantom from her nightmare.

"Stop!" he called out, "It's me. It's Jimmy!"

With that, Xandra was jolted out of her nightmare and became aware of the present. "Where are we?" she asked.

"We're here. At the sign," Jimmy whispered, his microphone turned off. "Are you sure you're okay?" Xandra shook herself awake. She did her best to get away from the terrors that had visited her. She exited the tram and then stood at the edge of the hill, just above the Hollywood sign, the W right below her. Jimmy droned on about something that she couldn't quite focus on. She could still hear the cries of those who had been tied to the bottom of the A and the N and the D in LAND. This forced her to ask Jimmy, "What happened to the rest of the sign?"

"What do you mean?" he asked, his agitation evident in his response.

"The LAND part," she replied. "L. A. N. D." She spelled out the word in case he, for whatever reason, didn't understand what she was saying. "What happened to it?"

He looked at her smugly. "Well, I'm glad you asked." He clapped his hands together as if punctuating his answer. "The iconic sign had been in disrepair for YEARS. I mean YEARS," he started. "Until FINALLY the city of Hollywood agreed to take over ownership of the sign, including the maintenance and repairs, but ONLY IF they could remove the LAND part." He paused and looked out over the valley. "I mean, really, it just didn't quite fit with the rest of the atmosphere."

Trying to be polite, Xandra forced a small grin. "Right. Got that," she coughed. "But what I mean is . . ." She looked out over where the word LAND should have been. "Once they took it down, what did the city of Hollywood do with the remnants of the word LAND?"

"Man, you have come prepared with some seriously great questions. Guess that nap did you some good." He laughed at his own joke, which made Xandra ever so slightly annoyed. "As far as I can tell, they simply tore it down and sent it to the local trash dump. That said, there are rumors that people have been hoarding pieces of it as a kind of keepsake for decades. I've even heard crazy rumors like Ava Gardner kept the A of the

LAND part in her backyard as an homage to Hollywood. And that Lon Chaney Jr. had the other letters broken down into puzzle pieces. They say he eventually framed them and sold them to the highest bidder."

In Xandra's mind, she could almost see the letters before her, even the period that marked the end of the full sign HOLLY-WOODLAND. "What about the period?"

One of the other tourists asked, "What period?"

"Oh, you don't know?" Jimmy answered. Xandra sensed from the playfulness in Jimmy's voice and the way he looked at her with a glimmer in his eyes that there was a lot more to this tale. He pointed to a space on the side of the hill. "When the sign was first built, they actually had a dot at the end of the word. Like something you'd find at the end of a sentence." Jimmy turned to Xandra. "Honestly, I assumed that it went the same way as the rest of the abandoned sign, but I'm not really sure."

"How cool would that be? To have the period that marked the end of the most iconic sign in America?" one of the tourists said.

"It would be cool," Xandra whispered, almost as if to herself. With that thought, the image of the tortured people tied to the sign and awaiting being fed to the night creature returned. She jerked back at the mental image and shook to try to get rid of it. Instead, it seemed to follow her, forcing her to the ground, making her see the high shadows of the werewolf as it attacked those who were left for its feast.

"Oh my god!" she heard a muffled voice. It sounded like it came from beyond the hills. She tried to respond to it, hoping it would help her get out of this horrible trap.

"Should we call 9-1-1?" a feminine voice said. This one was not as familiar, but a bit more weight lay in the concern of her tone.

The wolf leaped from its initial bludgeoning of the first victims, and it moved onto the remains of the decapitated body.

Screaming, Xandra found herself being pulled back through a tunnel into the consciousness of the present day.

"Can you hear me?" Jimmy said. "Miss? Ma'am? Are you with us?"

Xandra awoke lying on the grass at the edge of the hill behind the Hollywood sign. Her whole body ached. From what, she did not know.

She started to speak, and her voice came out raspy. "I'm fine," she managed to eek out.

She started to get up when he said, "Wait, don't do that. Stay here. Someone went to get you some help."

"It's fine." She tried to say it in a way that would get them to stop acting like it was the end of the world. "Seriously, I'm fine."

"You were flailing like you were having a major seizure or something," he said. He motioned toward the Griffith Observatory. "They have emergency assistance on site. Just rest here until she can come out."

He genuinely sounded concerned, which made Xandra obey his request. She had never seen herself in the midst of one of her visions. At this point, she was pretty sure that's what had happened. Her body was giving her the answers from the past.

And with that realization, she knew that the keys to what she needed were in those images. Yet again, her intuition regarding these hellacious beings, werewolves, was trying to give her the missing link —the link to the frightening visitor to Conan's show, the link to the mysteries of the sign, the link to all of it.

One of the other tourists returned with an EMT in tow. She checked Xandra's vitals. After confirming that she had not had a stroke or heart attack or some other end-of-life instance, the EMT signed off for Xandra to return to the tour.

The rest of the tour continued on to the Griffith Observatory. Xandra sat in the tram, waiting for their return. She watched the lights of the Hollywood sign come alive as the night fell. This was definitely not where she thought her evening was going to go.

She pulled her phone out of her pocket and turned it back on. Her phone came alive with dozens of messages. At first, she thought they were all from her Auntie Grace, but then she realized several were from either Conan or his assistant. All insisted she reach out to them quickly. She could only guess why her auntie wanted to talk to her, but she wasn't really sure what prompted Conan and his assistant. Since she hadn't found anything, she figured they were done with her. As she scrolled, she found that one message included an image of what seemed to be a shadow cast against a wall. Something like she'd seen in the 1940s version of *The Wolfman*. That's when she decided to call back Conan's assistant—the one who had brought her out here.

"Hey, I got your messages. I've been doing some digging. I wondered if I could go back to the set tomorrow? It doesn't have to be during working hours. Actually, after hours is probably better."

After some rumbling in the background, the assistant returned to the call. "Sure, we can make that happen. We'll leave your name at the main desk."

Xandra thanked the assistant and hung up, just as the tour group returned to the tram.

"All okay?" Jimmy asked.

Xandra nodded and smiled. "All's fine. In fact, it might even be perfect."

THE NEXT DAY, Xandra was careful not to arrive during filming hours. She checked in at the main desk. She wanted the space to be as empty as possible. She wandered through the stage set. Each step she took echoed.

She had never realized how high the ceilings were, how deep and cavernous the space was, and how empty it felt without the cast, crew, and especially the live studio audience.

On her first day on the investigation, she had inadvertently shown up during taping and found the entire experience overwhelming. Clearly, the crew had been well versed in each and every moment. Everything had been planned down to the second, but she had never even seen a live monitor or camera, let alone a studio.

Somehow, the emptiness of this place felt much more at home to her. She stood in the center of the stage and closed her eyes. In it, it was like she could hear the complete Hollywoodland. sign call to her. She saw the letters L, A, N, and then D all being tossed aside and discarded into the valley below, crashing against the hillsides and crumbling with each tumble until none of the LAND remained.

As if looking from below in the valley, she could see the word *Hollywood.* and its punctuation still shining brightly on the hillside. The period glowed even brighter the more she focused on it. And then it hovered as if it were a long forgotten star and shot past her. With that, the feeling of the sign's period, of its meaning, its true meaning, called to her.

Not the meaning to the general public, but the meaning that it gave to those who had left others for dead. The meanings of restitution, revenge, and rightfulness had all condensed themselves into this glowing abandoned portion of the sign.

A glowing portion of the sign flew through the night sky and then shot itself into Xandra. She jolted and opened her eyes, finding her arms spread out as if she were on a cross. Her heart beat with desperation. Her breathing rushed. Her chest thrust forward. She could still feel that ever-so-critical portion of the sign leave her body and guide her through Conan's set.

The vision guided her to travel down a hallway. She went by his office and into a backroom that had been stacked with boxes and mail. The lights out, she followed the feelings of revenge, rightfulness, and restitution that had invaded her from the visions.

In the corner of the room, at the bottom of the stacks of boxes, one of the containers glowed from within. The light seeped from its corners, letting out enough light to guide her to it.

She dove into the stacks and pulled out the object. Without hesitation, she ripped it open, feeling it calling out to her. Encased within the box was what looked like a corner of the period, still encrusted with aged blood. It looked as if someone had broken it into four sections. She guessed that they were to be divided among the guilty.

Underneath the encased puzzle piece, she found a note. "For all that you've done. – *Andy R.*"

Xandra called Conan's assistant. "Hey, when was the werewolf first seen on set?" she asked.

With a slight pause, the assistant said, "I dunno, maybe ten days ago? Why?"

Xandra looked at the delivery date of the box. Twelve days ago.

"I've found the cause." Xandra thumped on the box, noting what she might do with this hexed object. "Please let your boss know. I'll take care of it."

Xandra smiled to herself. She could have a lot of fun with this hexed object. So many people she could terrorize with a simple note, gifting it to them.

She hurriedly wrote a note, similar to the one Andy had written to Conan.

To Kim K.,
For all that you've done.
X.

At first, she was going to send it to the recipient through the mail, but didn't want to risk harm to the postal carrier. Instead, she called an Uber to take her to Hidden Hills and had the driver drop her off a few blocks away. She secreted onto the property and left the gift outside the front door.

The next morning, Xandra eagerly checked the television news. A reporter eagerly shared,

In other news, firefighters were called to the Kardashian estate to assist in an emergency. Family members had found Miss Kardashian in a neighboring palm tree. She was discovered there, late at night, attempting to flee from her own premises.

Witnesses report that she claimed her home had been overrun by beasts. After a thorough search, no evidence of beasts was found.

Xandra clicked off the television in her hotel room and picked up her phone.

"All okay?" she said to Conan's producer.

The producer paused. "I don't know what you did, but this was the first time in weeks I wasn't woken up by a panicked call." The producer smirked. "Thank you."

Death Phone
By Ronald Coleman

Alex weaved his pedicab down Fourth Avenue through the dense Saturday afternoon traffic. The streets of San Diego were packed with tourists from all over the world looking to have a relaxing day in "America's Finest City." His sharp blue eyes scanned the street as he maneuvered through the maze of cars, pedestrians, and trolleys, searching for the optimal route. Today, his fares were an older couple who were in town to celebrate their anniversary.

"And we're here." Alex pulled the tricycle taxi to the front of Rei Do Gado Brazilian Steakhouse and jumped from the bike to help them out.

As he helped the woman, Alex said, "Susan, I really think you'll love this place. It's my favorite special occasion spot, and you two don't seem to be the type to like all the cheesy tourist stuff in the Gaslamp."

When the man stepped down, he gave Alex a firm handshake and transferred a small stack of bills. The old handshake tip maneuver. Classic. "Young man, thank you for the ride and the recommendation."

"My pleasure, Roger. Oh, and be sure to leave room for the grilled pineapple. Amazing."

As the couple walked into the restaurant, Alex heard someone shout his name from across the street.

He turned just as his roommate Mark pulled up in his pedicab. If Alex was built for speed, Mark was built for power. He was a full six inches taller than Alex and built like a mountain. Whenever he wasn't working as a driver or DJ, he was lifting. He would have been intimidating except for the infectious smile that lit up his face.

"Hey, Alex. What's up, bro?"

"Just work, how's your day been?"

Mark stepped off his bike and gave Alex a quick bro-hug. "Pretty good. Just got back from taking a guy up to Balboa Park."

Alex nodded. "That's a long ride."

"Yeah, for sure. But I got a huge tip out of it, so first round is on me tonight."

"Ahhhh man." Alex frowned. "I can't. I'm supposed to meet Jimmy to buy his used cellphone tonight."

"Seriously? I'm going to that club in Hillcrest that I'm spinning at next week. Do it some other time."

"I can't. He's moving out of town tonight. Something with his kid. I need this second line, and it's a great deal."

"Is this for your courier thing you want to do?"

Alex nodded. "Yeah."

"Okay. You do you. But be careful. That Jimmy is a weird dude. If he eats your liver or something, I'm gonna be upset. There's no way I can cover rent alone."

Alex laughed. "Okay. I'll be careful. You be careful, too. I'll see you tonight."

Mark got back onto his bike and said, "Don't wait up for me. I don't work tomorrow, so I'm going to go to an after thing, and maybe an after-after thing."

Alex mounted his pedicab. "Cool. Have fun."

Alex pedaled back toward the Gaslamp and gave Mark a quick fist bump on the way past him.

AFTER HIS SHIFT, Alex headed out to meet Jimmy at the Santa Fe Depot. It was late, so the crowds were thin. A few people milled about, waiting for the late-night Amtrak to LA. He found Jimmy sitting on a bench in a dark corner of the yard wearing a hoodie, with his shoulders slumped and head down.

"Jimmy?" Alex asked.

With a grunting effort, Jimmy got to his feet. He had always been thin, but now he was gaunt, with dark circles and heavy bags under his eyes.

"Alex. I'm so glad you made it." Jimmy gave a weak smile that only accentuated the tired look in his eyes and held out his hand.

Alex shook it and asked, "Hey, are you okay?"

Jimmy shook his head. "Yeah. I'm fine. I just haven't been sleeping."

"That thing with your kid?"

Jimmy nodded. "Yeah. Not to be a jerk, but I really have to get going."

"Oh. Okay. Sorry."

Jimmy pulled the phone out of his pocket. It was an older smartphone in an obnoxious pink OtterBox case.

"Wow. That's pink." Alex said.

Jimmy mumbled, "That's what I said. I have no idea why."

"At least it's unique." Alex laughed. "I don't think I'll have to change it."

Jimmy stiffened. Serious resolve filled his eyes. "Okay. I have to tell you something. With this phone, there are a couple of rules. You can't change the case, and you can't just throw the phone away or something."

"Why would I throw it away?"

Jimmy waved his hands in apparent frustration. "You just can't. Now I need you to sign this here, where it says that you understand the terms and conditions of the deal and that it's your phone now."

Jimmy pulled out a sheet of paper with a bunch of writing and a line next to it.

He held it out in one hand and a pen in the other. In the dark, it was tough to read the text, but Jimmy seemed to be in a hurry.

As Alex stabilized the contract, he felt the smooth weight of the paper. "Is this vellum?"

"I guess."

Alex signed the contract. Jimmy stuffed it into his hoodie pocket and put the phone into Alex's hand.

"Just unlock it with your thumb. It should unlock for you now."

Alex put his thumb on the button at the bottom. A shock of electricity surged through him, and the hair on the back of his neck stood up as the phone unlocked and the welcome screen appeared.

The screen was filled with apps that Alex had never heard of. No Candy Crush for Jimmy. The battery was full, which was nice. That reminded Alex to ask, "Do you have the charger?"

"No. Sorry, man. Look. I've got to go." Jimmy grabbed his backpack off the bench and turned to go.

"Wait. What about the money?"

Jimmy walked back to him. "Yeah, that may be important."

Alex handed Jimmy a one-hundred-dollar bill. Jimmy looked down at the bill and then at Alex. Jimmy gave a genuine smile that time, and relief washed over his face. "Thank you, Alex."

Alex shrugged. "No worries. Hey. By the way, can I get a copy of that thing I signed?"

Jimmy winced. "You definitely will. I'm sorry. I have to go."

With that, Jimmy jogged away and disappeared into the night.

Mark's right. Jimmy is a weird dude, Alex thought. *But on the plus side, I still have all my organs.*

On the way home, various alerts and notifications rang from the phone. He thought, *When I get home and sync it to my Outlook, that should fix all of this.*

After a bus ride and a short walk, Alex was home. It was a small two-bedroom, sparsely decorated apartment. A large TV hung on the wall as the primary focus of the shared living area. The only furniture was a coffee table next to a reclining sectional couch and a kitchen table that was primarily used to hold unopened mail and Mark's DJ equipment. Alex sat at his kitchen table and unlocked the phone with his thumb again. He remembered that with his old phone, it had taken a while to set up. It was nice how quickly it worked on this phone.

With the phone unlocked, he could see all the alerts. He tried to clear them.

"Why's this being so difficult? I just need to get rid of all the weird apps on this phone, and I'll be good to go. It might be a long night."

He set the phone down and grabbed a soda from the counter. As he was taking a sip, the phone rang. It was set to the classic Old Phone ringtone. He picked it up and looked at the caller ID. It read WORK. Alex considered just ignoring the call, but decided he should probably let them know.

"Hello."

A deep voice on the other end said, "Why are you just sitting around your apartment? We sent the information to your phone. You need to get going."

"Actually. I just bought this phone. So, this is a wrong number. I don't have his new number or anything, but—"

The man on the phone interrupted him. "Alex, we know that you saw the messages. It is time for you to fulfill your obligation."

"Wait. How do you know my name?"

"I read it on the contract that just arrived on my desk. This is your signature at the bottom of this contract, is it not?"

Taken aback, Alex said, "Well, yeah. I signed a paper when I bought the phone. What does that have to do with you?"

"If you acknowledge that you signed the contract to abide by all the terms of having the object, then what is the problem? The duties and conditions are laid out in explicit detail."

"Really? I mean. I didn't really read it. I just figured it was like one of those license agreements that nobody reads. I honestly don't know what you are talking about, but you are kind of freaking me out, so I think I am going to go now. Thank you for calling. Please don't call back."

"I don't have time for this," the man on the phone grumbled.

There was a knock at the door. The voice on the phone spoke again.

"Are you going to let me in?"

Alex looked down at his phone and then at the door.

"I won't ask again."

Alex opened the door.

A tall man in a well-cut suit stood in his entryway, holding an identical pink phone at his side. The air was heavy with the smell of ozone, as if a massive electrical discharge had just occurred. The man stepped past Alex into the living room of his apartment.

"Oh. Come in," Alex stammered as the man moved toward the small kitchen table.

The man pulled out a chair and motioned to it. "Have a seat, Alex."

Alex stood his ground with the doorknob still in his hand. "I'm sorry. Who are you?"

"Who I am is not nearly as important as who I work for. You are going to want to sit. We don't have much time."

Alex closed the door. As he walked to the table, there was a buzzing in his brain. He tried to read the face of his unexpected visitor. He had a distinguished, wise look about him. He was objectively handsome, but not so handsome that he would stand out in a crowd. There was something else about the man. Alex was almost sure that the man wasn't breathing. If he was, there was no perceptible motion or sound from the process.

As Alex stared at his strange visitor, looking for signs of breathing, the man interrupted him. "Alex, I need you to stop daydreaming, or whatever you are doing right now, and pay attention to me."

Alex focused his eyes on the man and asked, "Who DO you work for?"

He smiled. "Finally, the correct question. I am a senior field agent for Death."

Alex sat back. "Wait. What do you mean, death?"

The man continued. "We are the department that facilitates the process when people's . . . energy needs to leave their bodies. Without us, and what we do, it is a messy, terrible affair. And there are others who would undercut this process to serve their own schemes."

Alex asked, "But what does any of this have to do with me?"

"That," the man pointed to the phone in Alex's hand, "is what we call a deathphone. It gives you all the tools you will need to accomplish the task at hand. It also means that you work for Death now, too."

Alex stood and said, "This is crazy! I don't work for Death."

The man produced the contract that Alex had signed from inside his suit jacket. "According to this signature and the fact that you are able to answer the phone, you are, in point of fact, a mortal agent of Death."

In the bright fluorescent light of his kitchen, the contract looked mystical. The ornate calligraphy on vellum reminded him of the prop contract from his high school production of Faust. Except this one looked much more authentic, and it was his name scrawled across the bottom line. His heart thudded in his ears, and his vision blurred.

"Follow the instructions on the phone, and you will be fine. Start with the map. One step at a time. Go ahead. Unlock the phone."

Alex put his thumb on the scanner, and the screen snapped open. On the map application, there was a notification. He took a deep breath, and the room began to come back into focus.

The man in the suit stood up and straightened his tie. "Now you've got a job to do."

Alex touched the map icon, and he saw a location across the city marked Agnes.

"I don't have a car. How am I supposed to get there?"

"I'm sure you will figure it out." The man said with a smile and began to walk toward the door. "Go quickly, Alex. She is waiting for you."

"What happens if I just sit here instead?"

The man turned to Alex and narrowed his gaze. "There would be consequences."

Alex stood, trying to put on an air of defiance and strength. "I just don't want to. I won't go."

The man took a quick step toward Alex. His eyes glowed red, and he was bigger. His new size seemed to fill the kitchen. The disgruntled but calm bureaucrat was replaced with something far more menacing.

The short-lived strength and defiance left Alex as he crumbled back into his seat. An uncontrollable shudder ran up his spine. The smell of ozone and electric energy permeated the air and stung his eyes.

"Nobody forced you to sign that contract, but you did. Just because you didn't bother to read this," he slammed his hand on the table next to the contract, "doesn't excuse you from your responsibilities. Something unprecedented is at play here, and you are messing with powers that you can't begin to understand."

The man closed his eyes and took a breath, and the bureaucrat was back.

"Listen, what we do is important and is often a form of mercy. The fact that the phone works at all for you without any training tells me that you've got a real shot at not totally screwing up. Until we get this figured out, you are going to have to just carry on with the duties of the phone. Do we have an understanding?"

"I mean, I don't know. It's just—"

The man interrupted his rambling and repeated, "Do we have an understanding?" stressing each word. The look in his eyes and the tone of his voice made it clear that there was only one acceptable answer to the question.

Alex nodded. "Yes. I'll try my best."

The man nodded and walked back toward the door. With his hand on the doorknob, he looked over his shoulder and said, "Alex, could I give you one piece of advice?"

"Sure." Alex replied.

With a faint smirk, he said, "In the future, you should always read something before signing it. Okay?"

With that, the man opened the door and disappeared. The door closed itself behind him, leaving Alex alone in his kitchen once again.

The phone dinged again. Alex stared at the blinking dot on the map. It looked like the spot was just off the blue line. He'd be able to get there soon if he hurried. He grabbed his keys, wallet, and phone and put them in their usual pockets. He didn't have a usual pocket for the deathphone, so he held it as he rushed out the door.

WHEN THE TROLLEY ARRIVED, Alex hit the button to open the doors and stepped on. Although it was almost empty, Alex knew that people coming home from the clubs would fill this train in the next few hours. There was an older man talking to himself in one aisle with arms wrapped around his giant backpack. There was also a young couple tucked into the back corner of the car who were far more interested in each other than they were in him. He sat down in a row that he figured would give him the most privacy.

As the trolley rumbled and clattered along, he looked closely at the phone. Examining the details, it was clearly a knockoff. From the logo on the back to the placement of the camera, every detail was almost right. And then there was the situation with the battery life. He'd possessed the phone for several hours, during which he had searched the apps, used the maps, and had a conversation, and the power continued to read one hundred percent. That was definitely not normal. In fact, there wasn't even a place to charge it.

Alex unlocked the screen and scrolled through the apps. The man in the suit said that the phone had all the tools he would need. The weird apps on the phone must be part of the solution. He selected the app called Timewalk. When he pressed the button, the trolley went silent. Alex stood and walked over to the homeless man, who was stuck with his mouth open in the middle of a word that he obviously thought was important.

The couple was caught mid-whisper. The girl's eyes were closed, and her lips were curled into a knowing smile while he had his mouth within a breath of her ear. Alex felt guilty standing and looking at them. It was an intimate moment that he knew they would never share if he was standing that close. The phone beeped, and the screen flashed a large ten. He stood there frozen as it changed to nine, then eight. *Oh crap!* Alex thought as he leaped back into his seat. He was just sitting down as the timer hit zero. The young man from the back corner of the car was distracted by the sudden movement and stared for a moment before turning his attention back to his date.

After that, everything continued as if the pause never happened. He looked down at the phone, and the power read ninety percent. He wondered what would happen if it went to zero and how he could keep that from happening because there was no charging port.

He arrived at his stop. While still clutching his phone, he went to the exit of the trolley. Neither the old man nor the young couple seemed any worse for, or even aware of, the paused event that had happened.

Alex walked the final two blocks from the trolley stop to the house with the blinking dot on the map.

He stood in front of the house for a moment, wondering what to do next. What was the proper etiquette for a situation like this? Should he knock and have a fun conversation with whoever opened the door?

Death Phone

"Hello, my name is Alex, and I am looking for Agnes. Oh. Why am I here? Oh, yeah. I'm an agent of Death. It's time for Grandma to go."

Somehow, Alex didn't think that would go over too well. He thought maybe there was something on the phone that would be useful.

He looked down at the screen as the alert continued to beep at him.

"It's 11:45 at night. Is anyone even awake?" he asked the phone.

"Fine, I'll just walk up there." He put the phone in his pocket and marched up the stairs to the porch.

When he got to the front door he rested his hand on the knob. There was a faint chime from the phone in his pocket and a click from the door as it unlocked. Alex pushed the door and walked inside. He pulled the phone out of his pocket, and the map zoomed in on the house. It indicated that he should go to the end of the hall. When he got there, he opened the door and stepped into a large primary bedroom.

The room smelled like medicine and dust. Shelves with knick-knacks and family pictures lined the walls. Little ceramic kitty cats, cows, and every type of novelty salt and pepper shakers stared at him silently from around the room. In the center of it was a large bed with a small, frail/looking woman huddled on one side. Her face had a faint grimace of pain. A large picture of a smiling couple stood on the nightstand next to her. For a moment, Alex stood, unsure of what to do next.

The phone in his hand beeped again, and the woman woke up. As she stirred, Alex's mouth went dry, and his pulse quickened.

A wave of panic washed over him. What was going to happen when this nice old lady saw a man standing at the foot of her bed? Would she scream? Was she armed?

The lady turned to look at him. When she saw him, she removed her heavy quilt, sat up with her legs over the side of the bed, and smiled.

"Hello," Alex stammered while raising his hand in the international sign of I come in peace.

He put his hand down and continued, "My name is Alex. And I'm here because . . . This is going to sound crazy . . . I don't know how to put this. It's just . . ."

Agnes held up her hand and with a soft smile said, "I know why you're here. I've been expecting you for a little while."

Alex put his head down. "Sorry. I had to take the trolley."

"It's alright. I suppose it's better than you coming early. My only real disappointment is that you don't look like Brad Pitt from *Meet Joe Black*."

"I don't think he works for us," Alex said. "Listen, though. I am sorry about all of this. I didn't exactly volunteer for this or specifically choose you."

"Hush now," Agnes said, brushing away his concerns with a wave of her hand. "I've been here far longer than I ever wanted to be. I've buried my husband and my children. My grandchildren all live back East, so I spend most of my time alone and in pain. This damn cancer has been chewing me up from the inside for years now."

Alex nodded.

"So, don't you concern yourself with this old lady. I am tired. And I'm ready to go home or wherever I go from here."

"Okay," Alex said.

"By the way, do you happen to know the answer to that question?" she asked.

"Honestly, I have no idea." Alex shook his head. "I probably should have asked."

"Oh well. I guess I'll know soon enough." Agnes sat up straight, put her hands in her lap, and said, "Okay, how do we do this?"

Alex said, "I don't know exactly how this works. This is my first time."

Agnes laughed. "Mine too."

Alex looked at the phone in his hand. "I'm guessing it has something to do with this."

Death Phone

He unlocked the phone and held it up. The camera app had a notification icon. He tapped it. When he pointed the camera at her, the screen was filled with the image of a young, vibrant woman with a beaming smile. He looked back and forth between the older woman on the bed and the young woman on his screen. "This must be it," he said.

Agnes closed her eyes. "I'm ready."

He tapped the button on the bottom of the screen, and there were two bright flashes. The first was from the camera. It was indistinguishable from a regular cellphone flash. The second was much brighter and came from Agnes. Its brightness filled every corner of the room, and unlike the monochromatic white of the LED flash, this light was alive with color. Reds and purples played around the room for seconds after the flash dimmed. When Alex's eyes adjusted, an ethereal version of young Agnes was standing there.

He could see her, but he was not convinced that she could see him.

Her eyes were focused on something in the distance. She held her hand out and walked. He watched her until she went through the wall of her bedroom, breezing through a shelf of collectible pewter spoons without disturbing them at all.

He continued to stare at the point she had disappeared to until he became aware that the only sound was that of his own shallow breaths.

He slid the phone back into his pocket and turned back to look at the bed. There was Agnes beneath the quilt exactly as she was when he walked into the room. The only difference was that the earlier grimace had been replaced with a slight smile, and her eyes were closed.

He walked out of the house and back toward the trolley station. He thought he might have to Lyft or something, depending on the time. He took the phone out of his pocket, and the time read 11:46. The whole encounter had taken almost no time at all. He noticed something else about the deathphone. The power level had gone down to seven percent. He wondered how long it would take for the phone to recharge to one hundred percent and if that meant he couldn't receive another call until it had. He had so many questions. He would definitely have to read that contract when he got home.

Even though he could have taken the trolley home, Alex decided to walk. The night air was crisp and soothing. There was still a vibrational energy that coursed through his system. He didn't think there was any way that he could sleep tonight.

He walked past home, past downtown, and to the waterfront. Near the Star of India, Alex sat on the edge of the dock with his feet over the water, looking across the bay at the aircraft carriers anchored on Coronado. He sat motionless, trying to make sense of the night he had just experienced.

AS THE SUN began to come up behind Alex, he decided it was time to go home. When he got there, he took the things out of his pocket. His keys, wallet, and cellphone all went in their usual places. He pulled the deathphone out of his pocket and unlocked it with his thumb. The power was at nine percent. It might take days for it to recharge at this rate. Rather than putting the phone down, he decided it was best if it stayed on him.

Mark still wasn't home, and Alex still wasn't tired. There was a knock at the door. He opened it, surprised to see the man from the night before standing there.

"Can I come in?"

Alex motioned toward the inside while still holding the door. "Sure. I don't think I could stop you if I wanted to."

"That is true, but thank you for letting me in."

"No worries," Alex said as he closed the door.

"I just wanted to stop by and tell you that you did a good job, and you handled it well."

Alex shrugged. "Thanks, I guess. It was surreal. Beautiful and terrifying at the same time."

"That's the business we are in, Kid," the man said.

"So, am I done with this?" Alex said, holding out the deathphone. "Am I free or whatever?"

"No. For now, that is yours, and you still must not miss a call for any reason. Ever. We still have no idea why or even how James was able to transfer it to you."

"Wasn't it just the contract?" asked a confused Alex.

"Well, yes. But the contract you signed, though very similar to the ones we produce, was enchanted by someone other than us. No one in the office can explain it. This is going to lead to unimaginable amounts of paperwork. Speaking of which. . ." The man walked back to the door. "Be careful out there, Alex. You are part of something much bigger than yourself, and you now have powerful enemies that you must be on guard for."

"Enemies?"

"Seriously, Alex. Read the contract." The man then walked out of the door and closed it behind himself.

There was another faint knocking at the door.

"Just come in," Alex said.

The door opened, and Mark stepped in. "Cool. You're awake. I forgot my keys. I'm glad you are, but why're you up so early today?"

"Actually, I didn't sleep at all last night."

"Is everything okay?" asked Mark.

"I think so. It was just a crazy night. I don't think I want to talk about it right now. Maybe later?"

Mark nodded his head in understanding. "It's cool. Are you hungry?"

"Actually, I'm famished."

"I was going to go line up for Donut Bar. They should be opening soon. Want to go?"

"Yeah. Let's go." Alex scooped up his gear and began stuffing it in his pockets.

By Ronald Coleman

"Is that strange pink thing the phone you got from Jimmy?"
"Yeah."
As Mark walked out, he said, "I told you he was a weird dude."
Alex laughed as he closed the door. "You have no idea."

The Demons on Bunker Hill
By Indigo Halverson

1939

"Can you hear them calling? The angels? Can you hear their whispers?" Aubry Stockman, a woman in her mid-fifties, asked a group of socialites standing anxiously in her mansion on Bunker Hill one spring evening in Los Angeles. Strands of silver and smoke framed her face while the rest of her hair hung loose in a bun. Her decorum-defying trousers and blouse were a stark contrast to the rest of the women in the room. The old wood creaked as she bounded down the last step of her grand staircase. Her delicate hands found home in her pockets as she wandered around her twenty guests with quiet ease, allowing the space between her words and their silence to fill the air.

"I'm here to offer you a once-in-a-lifetime opportunity that will change your lives forever. Please, let me show you what you can achieve."

Aubry motioned for her guests to gather closer as she moved to the center of the room. She placed her hands on her knees and lowered herself to the floor. A moment later, her body erupted into violent shaking and thumping, throwing her wildly across the floor. One person tried to crouch near her but stopped with a single hand from Aubry's daughter, Elsie, who didn't even bother to look at him.

"I . . . I see a child. When the time comes that the day is longest, a child shall be born. The heavens will open that day, and the clouds will part. Rewards are waiting for the righteous ones." Aubry's body stopped moving as the last word left her lips. She crumpled to the ground in exhaustion.

The following evening, the group returned, determined to experience their own visions. Aubry and Elsie walked toward them from the kitchen holding trays of rye bread. "Thank you for coming back and trusting the angels and their messages," Aubry said. "Join us as we enter this new world together."

The socialites in unison fell to their knees and convulsed, writhing on the floor. Once everyone regained composure, they all stared at Aubry wide-eyed.

"What? What just happened?" a young woman asked.

"I told you. The angels are here with us. This house is their gateway where the veil is thinnest, and they choose only the most worthy and devoted to communicate with. Did you all see the child?"

Everyone nodded as they looked around the room at each other. Aubry crossed her arms. She fluttered her eyelashes but held something behind her eyes and let her smile slip briefly before plastering it back on again. Her body language changed to be more open and inviting as she addressed her guests again.

"Now, my dear friends, let's prepare for the coming of that child on the longest day of the year. The solstice."

"And what happens when we find that child?" a young woman asked.

"We deliver it back to the angels. Until that day, we need to find the woman carrying this special child that will open the gates to heaven, and we only have a few short months left. Who here has ideas on how we can do that?"

"We could hold auditions."

Aubry and the rest of the room turned their head toward a man in a very polished and expensive-looking suit.

"Go on," Aubry said.

"A casting call for a pregnant model in her last trimester, to be featured in a new photography exhibit. Then at some point, once we have her trust, we can, you know, *contain* her."

Aubry smiled. "It is vital that she and the child survive the birth and the baby takes its first breath before we return it to the angels. I do like your approach, Mr. Gibson, dear. I think it will work. Would you be willing to fund such an advertisement in the papers?"

Though the Dubarry mansion was quite large and lavish, Aubry's late husband's money had been dwindling for years since his *accident*.

Mr. Gibson removed his pocketbook. "How much do we need?" he asked.

Aubry exchanged a look with Elsie. "Let's start with a thousand dollars. I have my eye on a few larger publications in the greater Los Angeles region. Elsie and I will handle everything."

Greedily eyeing Mr. Gibson, a coy smile betrayed Aubry's thoughts. This could finally be what she and Elsie were waiting for.

Mr. Gibson handed the women a large stack of hundreds. "I assume my financial contributions will earn my spot on some of the more lucrative rewards we see from the angels?" he asked.

"Of course, the angels recognize and appreciate your devotion to their mission. And so do we," Aubry said, hugging Elsie with her empty arm.

A few days later, five papers and magazines published their ad reading, "Seeking a pregnant woman with a summer due date to be featured in a photography exhibit. Will compensate for time. Please telephone HOllywood 8455 if interested."

By the third day of interviews, the only remaining applicant was a twenty-four-year-old named June, with wavy blond hair like a sunflower in full bloom. Mr. Gibson paraded her around like a doll.

Over the next few days, Aubry, Elsie, Mr. Gibson, and the rest of the group got better acquainted with the girl. While giving the full tour, Aubry looped her arm around June's. "Thank you for accepting our invitation to be part of this little project. We are so excited for you to be here, and we can't wait to meet your little one." Aubry's hand gently reached out to June's stomach.

June smiled at Aubry. "Thank you, Mrs. Stockman. I'm so grateful to be here. I . . . I really didn't have anywhere to go, and I really needed the money."

This young woman was right where Aubry wanted her. She patted June's shoulder. "Tell me about your mother. Surely she wouldn't just let you walk out of her house all by yourself?"

June slowly lowered herself to a dining chair while tears rolled down her face. "I'm sorry. I seem to be cryin' more each day. I love my mama, but the disappointment in her eyes when I told her I was pregnant was unbearable. She told me I was an unfit mother because I didn't want to marry the baby's father," June said, wiping tears from her face.

Aubry kneeled on the floor next to her. "I didn't mean to bring you to tears, dear, but if you were my daughter, I would have only sheltered you in love and support. Why don't you stay here? We have a lot of space to keep you and your baby safe." Aubry stood and brought June a handkerchief. "Think about it. No need to decide now."

JUNE STAYED with the Stockmans for over a month before the group consulted the angels again. They waited until June went to bed to begin. As they all came to, they started whispering about what they needed to do to prepare for the baby's arrival.

"So once the baby is born, do we just take it away and . . . and . . . I don't think I can say it," a woman said as she stood up off the floor.

"Obviously, we need to be as delicate as we can, dear. We're not monsters," Aubry said.

"I think the most humane thing would be to smother it," Mr. Gibson said. The whole group turned to look at him as he said something so heinous, so effortlessly.

"Are we really sure this is what the angels want us to do? What if we got the visions wrong?" a woman asked.

Now was not the time to falter on the mission, not when I'm this close to having everything Elsie and I ever wanted. Not to mention Mr. Gibson's money keeping us afloat. We must not alter course.

The group looked at Aubry and Elsie for confirmation that they were on the right path, despite the gruesome task awaiting them.

They would never admit it out loud, but their confidence in Aubry and Elsie was waning. All they could do was hope and pray the ends justifies the means.

"We all saw the same thing, my friends." Aubry poured herself a glass of wine from a decanter. They were all so wrapped up in their conversation that no one noticed June at the top of the stairs, listening to every word.

JUNE GRIPPED the railing so hard that the metal pressed into her palm and made a deep, red indent. Her foot hit a loose board on the way back up. She held still as long as possible, hoping no one downstairs heard her. She needed to get the hell out of there.

The next morning, Aubry caught June trying to sneak out of the house.

"Good morning, dear. Where are you off to?"

June spun around inches from the front door, eyes wide, and all the color drained from her face. "I . . . I thought I would take a walk, get some fresh air. I think I should also speak with my doctor and make sure they are ready for me and the baby."

"You're only a week out. You really shouldn't be on your feet.

Why don't you go back upstairs, and I will fix you up with a nice cup of herbal tea?"

June saw Aubry signal Mr. Gibson with her eyes. Mr. Gibson snuck behind June, blocking her path to the door.

"I don't want to keep putting you all out, and I think it's time for us to leave." June's voice was high-pitched as she turned back toward the door, only to be met by more members coming around the corner. "Please, please let us leave. Please don't hurt my baby." Large arms grabbed June and started dragging her back up the stairs. "Please, Mrs. Stockman, please don't let them do this to me. I thought you cared about me. You told me to call you Mama. Mama, please. Please."

June's entire world was crashing at her feet. She traded one vicious mother for another. Her child would die, and it would be all her fault. She *was* an unfit mother, after all.

"Lock her in the closet, and make sure she can't get out," Aubry said, turning away coldly.

Ropes hugged June's wrists. Aubry would sit on the floor in front of her, sometimes to brush her hair, sometimes to change her clothes, and always to make sure June wasn't going into labor.

June recounted every moment with Aubry, every hug, every belly touch, every conversation. How could she have been so blind? She trusted these strangers because she wanted a family so badly. She couldn't see the monsters they really were.

"Why are you doing this to me?" June hung her head against her constrained arm.

"We aren't doing anything to you. You must understand; you and your baby are part of something so special that you were hand-chosen by the angels themselves. Your baby is the key to opening a doorway to heaven."

"You're wrong. My baby is a blessing, not a key."

"A blessing the angels want back. Our group will see that they get what they want," Aubry snapped.

"Then why doesn't God kill it himself?"

"Everything is a test, my dear. I hope you'll come to understand one day."

THE DAY before her due date, a terrible storm broke out. Scattered rain, lightning, and thunder filled the sky. "Do you see? This is a sign from the angels. They are getting ready for the child's arrival."

While listening to the rain, June felt a sharp pain in her abdomen, as if her internal organs were constricting. The pain would come and go. She tried to time her screams with the thunder, but the pain became too intense. She heard Aubry and Elsie rush up the stairs after hearing her high-pitched yell.

"What time is it? It's too early for contractions. Someone, time them!" Aubry shouted.

Aubry transformed in front of June's eyes from motherly to terrifying. A harrowing grimace replaced her fake grin, and dead eyes glared.

"We need to slow her labor. We still have six more hours until midnight," Elsie said. She looked to her mother for guidance, only to be met by a blank stare.

June, soaked through her nightgown and covered in sweat, screamed at the top of her lungs in pain. This baby was coming.

Despite finding solace in the baby arriving early, the fear of actually giving birth still gripped June. She wished her actual mother were here, even if it was just to hold her hand.

"What do we do, Aubry? Did we make a mistake?" one socialite asked.

"The angels wouldn't have lied to us. They said the baby was coming and would be born on the solstice. I followed their instructions. I'm devoted. I'm worthy." She fell to her knees in prayer.

"Where did we go wrong? Maybe we got the wrong girl," someone in the back asked.

June tried to move around, but all she could do was lean her head back and wait. Somehow, despite everything happening around them, three hours later, a tiny cry emanated from the closet. Tears streamed down June's face. The relief of seeing her baby born was overwhelming. Aubry crawled over to June and untied her so she could hold her baby. June clutched her daughter closely, wild eyes scanning the room, daring anyone to move closer to them. Aubry backed away, motioning the others to do the same.

What was the point now? What would we even do with her? She was useless. Aubry didn't even want to look at her. *What a disappointment she turned out to be.*

June slowly moved out of the closet toward the stairs. The parlor was clear, and she staggered for the door, stopping only momentarily for something to cover the baby in the storm.

1972

The Dubarry mansion loomed over Dahlia as she held her hand to her ever-growing baby bump. Her waist-long auburn hair fluttered in the warm Los Angeles breeze as she studied her new home. The Queen Anne style architecture with its eccentric balconies, bell-shaped towers, turrets, broken angles, triangle shapes, oval cutouts, and curves kept her eyes moving all around the property.

"And we're sure it's not too big?" she called over to her husband as he brought over another box from their Oldsmobile.

"We will just have to work to fill it." Aiden winked at her and rubbed her belly. "We need a few things from town. Do you want to go for a drive?" he asked, grabbing her from behind as she leaned her head back onto his shoulders.

"I think I will take a nap instead, if you don't mind. I am feeling a little tired."

"Of course. Is there anything I can get you?"

"Peanut butter, pickles, gummy bears, and some Spam."

"I hope those aren't all going into one sandwich." Aiden grimaced at the thought.

"Oh, and bread, we need bread." Dahlia whirled around to place a kiss on his lips before gently removing herself from his embrace as she walked inside. Aiden chuckled, retreating to the car.

Luckily, Dahlia found the boxes labeled pillows and blankets and arranged them on the plaid-colored couch they bought secondhand. She lowered herself and calmed her thoughts.

Her eyes moved around under her lids as a vivid dream took hold. Vultures surrounded her. She couldn't move as they pecked at her and pulled pieces of her flesh from her body. Dahlia awoke a few hours later with a knot in her stomach and a sense of an impending threat looming over her.

MASSIVE PALM TREES soared over the streets between his new house and Broadway. Aiden found the supermarket and a delightful small bakery. He stopped inside just to check it out and maybe bring home something for Dahlia.

He wandered into a sugary wonderland that smelled like cookies and freshly baked bread. Inside, he found two workers who had similar features and hair of buttermilk and shortbread. There was something about their movements, like serpents, fluid with no awkwardness. Yet their appearance was warm and inviting, almost intoxicating.

"Hello, sir. May I offer you a sample of our newest bread?" a young man asked as he moved a tray and a toothpick toward him. The scent of rosemary wafted into Aiden's nose, and the toothpick sliced into the bread like butter.

"Mmm, that's superb. Do you sell it by the loaf? I'd love to bring some home to my wife."

"We do. My sister, Thistle, can ring you up at the counter. I'm Jonah, by the way."

"Aiden." The two men nodded at each other as Aiden walked over to the counter.

"Hello, sir. I haven't seen you here before. Are you new to the area?" Thistle asked.

"My wife and I just bought the place on Bunker Hill. The big one."

"The Dubarry mansion?"

"That's the one." Aiden clicked his tongue.

Jonah walked over. "That place has a lot of freaky-deaky history."

"What do you mean?"

"Just decades of rumors more than anything, man. The people who used to live there had wild parties," Jonah said slyly.

There was an odd look on the siblings' faces. Aiden wasn't sure how they would have heard about rumors from over thirty years ago. He certainly hadn't. Aiden smiled at the two of them. "Well, I should probably get back home before my pregnant wife wants her gummy bear sandwich. How much is the bread?"

"Thirty cents," Thistle said.

"Woah. That's pretty pricey for a loaf of bread."

"It's worth it."

Aiden fished out the change from his pocket before heading toward the door.

"Hey man, when is your kid due?" Jonah asked.

"June 21st."

"That means your baby is due on the solstice," Thistle said.

"Peace out, man," Jonah said as Aiden shook his hand and waved at Thistle as he walked out of the store.

"See you guys later," Aiden said.

EVERYTHING SHIFTED ONCE AIDEN LEFT. It was as if the sweet air of the bakery soured and turned stale. Jonah dropped his smile as he crossed his arms after drawing the curtains closed. He studied Thistle's face. He could see her forming a plan before his eyes.

"Did you hear that? That baby is due on the summer solstice. Do you know what that means?" Thistle asked.

"It means we finish what they couldn't do in the '30s and avenge our grandfather. His death won't be in vain. We're getting the money he promised us," Jonah said.

Jonah and Thistle unlocked a box from under the counter. Inside was a picture of an older man with two children by his side and a handwritten note that read,

"My dear Jonah and Thistle, I'm sorry I could not provide you with the inheritance you deserved. Perhaps someday the stars will align again for the Dubarry mansion and the solstice child."

A WEEK LATER, Aiden and Dahlia heard their doorbell ring. *The Mary Tyler Moore Show* was on, and they had just gotten comfortable on the couch.

Aiden rolled his eyes and laughed at Dahlia, who refused to move. He lifted her feet off his lap and put them back on the couch. The interruption of their night slightly miffed him.

Jonah and Thistle were waiting on the veranda with a basket of freshly baked goods.

Looking through the peephole, Aiden watched the siblings for a few moments. He wondered why these strangers would just come over uninvited. He opened the front door with a smile, anyway.

"Hello again," Aiden said.

"Hi Aiden, sorry to drop by unannounced. We wanted to welcome you guys formally to the area, and selfishly, we were really curious about your house," Thistle said.

"We were just watching some TV. Come on in," Aiden said politely.

"Honey, who's at the door?" Dahlia called from the living room.

"Remember that bread I brought home last week? I told you about the bakery. Well, the owners wanted to stop by and say hello. They even brought some treats for us."

"Oh, how wonderful. It's nice to meet you both. Aiden told me you're brother and sister?" Dahlia asked, getting up from the couch.

"Yes, ma'am." Jonah shook her hand.

Thistle reached her hand toward Dahlia's stomach. "May I?"

"Of course."

"You must be so excited. Your husband told us that your due date is just around the corner," Thistle said. "You know, Grandfather knew the woman who owned this house back in 1939."

"Oh, my God, really? This house must have changed so much since then," Dahlia said.

"Only the interior has changed from the photos we've seen. We were told all kinds of stories growing up about the famous Aubry Stockman," Thistle said.

Aiden watched as Thistle mentioned Aubry. There was a hint of something just beneath the surface of her words. A quiet anger she tempered.

"Why did they call her famous?" Aiden asked.

Thistle shifted her weight from one side to the other, her blond hair effortlessly following her movements. Aiden paid close attention as Thistle's entire demeanor changed.

"She brought a lot of the elites of society together for a project she was working on," Thistle said excitedly. She twirled her blond hair around her index finger, not out of nervousness, but coyly, as she eyed Aiden up and down.

"What kind of project?" Aiden asked. He crossed his arms and shifted to lean against a nearby wall.

"She convinced everyone she could talk to angels through the visions she had," Thistle said.

Aiden raised his eyebrows at the word "visions." Thistle nodded, reading his expression.

"Our grandfather said she would convulse violently on the floor and come to with visions of heaven unlocking its gates with a key," Thistle said.

"What was the key?" Dahlia asked.

"That the child born on the longest day of the year would need to be sacrificed to the angels to loosen the veil between heaven and Earth. You actually have that same due date. What a coinkydink," Jonah said, chiming in, pointing to Dahlia's belly.

"What kind of monster would believe that? Did . . . did they succeed? Was your grandfather involved?" Dahlia asked.

Aiden regarded Jonah with a flash of his eyes. He could tell Dahlia was upset, which meant he would have to deal with that later, once their guests left.

"He was around during that time, but no, they didn't go through with it. Something went wrong," Jonah said. "Our grandfather invested heavily in Mrs. Stockman and her visions. She promised a return on his investment financially and spiritually. He spent the rest of his days deeply bitter over receiving no reward. Money that could have kept his family rich. Us included, I guess." Jonah gave a sheepish smile. "Our mother found him hanging in his closet when we were thirteen."

"What was your last name again?" Dahlia asked.

"Gibson," Jonah said.

The kitchen was their last stop on their requested tour. Jonah and Thistle paused in front of a door leading to the outside garden. "Does the house still have those rye plants?" Thistle asked Aiden.

He could only guess their grandfather had made some mention about the plants, though he couldn't fathom why.

"We do, but I think they died. They don't look like normal rye plants," Dahlia answered, even though the question wasn't directed at her.

"Should still be okay to bake with. Would you mind if we took some with us? I want to try a new cookie recipe." Thistle asked.

"I don't see why not. Do you mind, honey?" Aiden asked his wife. Dahlia shook her head.

Dahlia begged Aiden not to go back to the bakery. She didn't like the Gibsons. They were weirder than the stories they told. Her husband, however, was desperate to make friends and wondered if the stress of her pregnancy was making her paranoid. Sure, the siblings shouldn't have brought up the cult and similar due dates, but they were otherwise harmless.

Aiden spent more and more time at their bakery, constantly bringing home treats and baked goods. Dahlia refused to eat any of it. Even the ginger rye cookies they made from her own rye plants. He started acting strangely ever since he met the Gibsons. He began looking at Dahlia with a glint in his eye, like he was studying her face, watching her every move. She found everything he did lately had a new, eerie manner to it.

"Please stop spending so much time with the Gibsons," she said one morning.

"Why? They have been nothing but nice to us, and we have become good friends."

"To you, maybe. The first time they came to our home, they told us their grandfather was part of a cult in our house that tried to murder a newborn."

"But they didn't go through with it. The mother gave birth a day early, and it threw off their visions. So they ended up letting them both go."

"Oh, I am so glad they didn't keep that woman and her baby prisoners," Dahlia said, rolling her eyes. "Do you even hear yourself?"

"You're being ridiculous. They are not responsible for something their grandfather did almost forty years ago."

Dahlia stormed upstairs. She was tired of being on her feet, and honestly, tired of hearing Aiden's voice as he defended the Gibsons.

Her due date was in a few short days, and she wanted to remain as calm as possible to prepare for her home birth. She even found a local midwife. After the baby was here, things would get better. She and Aiden would be back on the same wavelength, and the Gibsons could cut them out of their lives for all she cared.

IN THE MIDDLE of the night, Dahlia started cramping, waking from her sleep. Every position she twisted into was painful. At some point, she drifted into a dream where she was swimming in a pool of water. Dahlia woke up with Aiden already gone and the bed completely soaked. Her water must have broken.

She changed into her birthing gown and pulled the sheets from the bed. She walked into the bathroom to make sure she had everything. Towels, a warm blanket for the baby, silver scissors for the umbilical cord, and a fresh change of clothes. Another painful cramp hit Dahlia, and she breathed in and out for a few seconds. She hoped the midwife would make it for her delivery. She went downstairs, looking for Aiden.

Jonah, Thistle, and Aiden waited for her at the kitchen table. Dahlia froze on the stairs, looking at her husband and the intruders.

"What on earth are you people doing here?" she demanded.

"Now, honey, don't be rude. They came to help with the delivery."

"The midwife is coming."

"No, we sent her away," Thistle said. "You're in much better hands with us."

"Aiden," Dahlia said in a heightened tone.

"Everything is going to be okay, honey, better than okay. Our baby is special."

Dahlia waddled back upstairs. She reached the bathroom door as the sound of footsteps followed her. She locked the door and moved whatever she could find in front of it.

"Honey, please try to understand. We can have another baby. The angels told me," Aiden called out from behind the door.

Why is Aiden doing this? What did those people do to him? He knows how hard we worked to keep this baby after we lost the others, Dalia thought. She had begged him not to spend time with them. He ignored her and took the poisoned apple they'd offered.

She could feel the anger bubbling up inside her. Hot tears streamed down her face. Another cramping pain shot up her body. *Stay calm, breathe, don't speed up the labor.* She clasped her cross and prayed to God that she could hold off delivering as long as possible.

God must have been on a break.

She was acutely aware of every inch of her body as she cried out in pain. The contractions were getting closer now. She would have to get ready to deliver despite everything inside of her, desperately wishing for more time.

Dahlia turned on the water and filled up the tub as she carefully submerged herself. Her contractions were mere minutes apart now, the pain unbearable. She could hear her husband and the Gibsons outside like ghouls waiting to pounce on the door. She couldn't hold back any longer, as the baby was crowning. A long moment later, a beautiful baby girl was in her arms.

Dahlia reached for the blanket to dry her off after she wiped away the blood and mucus. The baby wasn't crying. "Come on, little Hyacinth. Breathe. Just breathe," Dahlia said while patting her back gently. A mighty and powerful scream came out of her tiny lungs. Dahlia cried out in joy and exhaustion, forgetting for just a moment the evils beyond the door. She quickly grabbed the pair of scissors to cut the umbilical cord and slowly climbed out of the tub. Water dripped all over the floor, making it slippery.

Aiden had broken down the door with a crazed expression. "Give us the baby, honey."

Over my dead body. Something took over her as she stared at the man she once knew. The man she once loved. She was a force to be reckoned with. Drenched with a crying baby in her arms, staggering and wobbling, but upright and alert.

Dahlia clasped Hyacinth and swung her body to the side. Aiden rushed toward her and slipped on the water on the floor, heading face-first into the windowpane. He missed Dahlia by an inch. His head smashed into the edge of the wall with a crack, breaking off a piece of the wall as he fell. She turned to face Jonah and Thistle.

"Get the hell out of my house!" Dahlia yelled. Jonah took a step toward her. She put Hyacinth gently in the sink behind her as he got closer and grabbed her arm, bending it backward as she yelled in pain. She used all her strength and kicked as hard as she could, colliding with his crotch. Jonah doubled over. She moved quickly and shoved his head in the tub and held it there as long as she could.

She'd never killed anyone before. It was never even something that crossed her mind. Watching the bubbles was an excruciating experience. She hated the Gibsons for everything they believed, this stupid cult, this idea that her baby was some conduit for heavenly riches, and what they did to Aiden's mind. Still, she felt sick.

When he stopped moving, she saw Thistle sneaking behind her. She chased her to the stairs as Hyacinth screamed from the sink. This was going to end one way or the other, but only one of them was making it out alive. Dahlia rushed at Thistle, thrusting her arms out. Moving back and forth at the edge of the stairs. Dahlia used her body as a battering ram and swung Thistle's foot from underneath her, causing her to tumble down the stairs with a thud.

Dahlia waited for Thistle to move. She stared at the pool of blood trickling on the floor. The crimson red color that would surely stain. It glistened as the sunlight poured into the room.

Hyacinth continued to cry until Dahlia stumbled back into the bathroom and picked her up, cradling her in her arms. She moved back out to the hallway and slumped to the floor with fatigue, closing her eyes as she patted her daughter on the back, bringing her up to her face.

"You're safe now, my little flower," Dahlia said, clutching her baby. She lay herself and the baby on the floor. Aiden's lifeless body haunted her from the bathroom. She shifted her body away from him as tears flowed down her face.

1995

Hooded figures clad in walnut-colored robes sat in a concentric circle around the parlor in the Dubarry mansion. At the center of the circle, the head of an older man popped up during their prayer.

Father Jove wore his head shaved with a salt and pepper goatee. There was a dullness behind his eyes that left the person meeting his gaze hollow and cold. The way he spoke projected an air of authority and arrogance.

Large black tarps covered the once beautiful, picturesque bay windows, eliminating all traces of the outside world from creeping in. Purposefully placed candles were the only source of light allowed now. Father Jove bowed his head and raised his arms.

He knew his family regarded him as a god. They were all under his leadership, under his control, under his watchful eyes.

"Soon, my family, soon we will leave these mortal shells and ascend. The solstice is nearing."

"Father Jove, we are ready. Through your capable hands, we can do all. Please give us your latest visions. Tell us what the angels said," a barely twenty-year-old boy asked.

Father Jove became a way for the members to escape from their old lives, their traumas, their disappointments, even themselves. Rising from the center of the room, he walked over to the fireplace. Father Jove clasped his hands behind him, meeting everyone's eyes. He knew the time was coming for them to ascend. He also knew there was only so much time before the nonbelievers found him and his group.

"The archangels Michael and Gabriel visited me during our morning prayer," he said. "They were pleased with us and our progress, but we need to show even more devotion for the ritual to work. Through me they communicate, through me your love should flow to them."

Everything clicked into place. He had the family, the power, and soon he would have the coveted baby.

Father Jove beckoned a young pregnant woman to rise from her spot in the circle. "As you all know, Rhoda came to us once she found out she was pregnant and offered herself and the child as a sacrifice to bring forth the opening of the gates of heaven. Her child will be born on the solstice, the same night the foretold Demeter comet will pass Earth. Those two events will coincide, and we can be rid of these mortal bodies once and forever. Once Rhoda and the child have returned to the archangels, it will be our turn."

Father Jove spun Rhoda around before kissing her forehead. "In two weeks' time, we shall be ready."

Rhoda returned to her spot on the floor. "It's my honor to be the sacrifice, Father Jove. I'll never feel pain again," she said.

Father Jove eyed another woman in the back of the parlor. "Sandra, it's time for my breakfast."

Father Jove demanded specific feeding times. Anyone who dared to eat before he did faced punishment expeditiously.

Sandra, a petite brunette, walked into the kitchen and returned with a tray of pancakes and a glass of orange juice. "Rye pancakes with ginger and juice, Father Jove," she said, handing him the tray.

There was something about the pancakes that had a peculiar taste, not entirely unpleasant, but it made him a little queasy.

"A new recipe?" he asked her.

He would castigate Sandra if these pancakes caused him any pain. He would not tolerate any disobedience. Nor would he tolerate anyone seeing him as less than perfect.

"Something I picked up from a bakery some years ago."

When the solstice finally came, Rhoda lay in the center of the room. The rest of the flock gathered around her, sitting on the floor.

"In one hour, the clock will strike 4:45, and the comet will pass. At that time, we will all make our way to heaven." Father Jove reached for a long knife and held it to Rhoda's stomach. "Is everybody ready?"

"Yes, Father Jove," everyone said in unison.

"Then let's begin." He sterilized the knife and began making an incision into Rhoda. She refused to scream in pain and instead started chanting. The flock joined her, repeating the same words. Father Jove carefully took his time to slice below her belly button to perform her cesarean. He finally pulled the child out of her mother and wrapped the baby in a cloth.

"Drink now!" The members picked up the paper cups they scattered nearby and drank them, tossing their heads back. Loud knocks on the door made everyone look around. Father Jove picked the knife back up and held it over the child. Before he could bring it down, a gunshot rang out, echoing down the halls. Bodies hit the ground left and right as more police barged into the room. A young officer picked up the infant and rushed back outside. Father Jove lay on the floor in front of Rhoda's body, a bullet hole between his eyes.

The once great messiah, reduced to nothing more than a headline in tomorrow's newspaper. As officers peeled off the window coverings to let in more light, they revealed just how gruesome the parlor was. Fresh blood trickled over the floorboards, pooling in front of the staircase where an even older blood stain was.

Once the scene was clear, several more officers went inside. The officer holding the baby handed her over to the EMTs.

"What's the status, Rookie?" the Sergeant asked.

"The child seems okay. They are taking her to the hospital now," said the young, uniformed officer, her light auburn hair pulled in a tight bun.

"The mother?"

"Dead."

"What about the father of the child?"

"He was the one who reported his wife missing. He's on his way to the hospital."

Two more officers came out of the house with lots of rye plants. "Found these in the kitchen, sarge." One officer held up the plants. "I think they were eating them."

"So what?" the Sergeant asked, sweeping his open hand to the side.

"So, they're covered with fungus." The officer pointed to the dark purple and black buds. "See? It shouldn't be that color."

"What kind of fungus is that?" the sergeant asked.

"It looks like ergot. Uh. Sir," the young officer said. "Ergot has caused wild hallucinations and convulsions. If these people were consuming any type of rye, they would have ingested the fungus, and it looks like these plants have been here for decades."

"What did you say your name was again, Rookie?" the sergeant asked.

"Hyacinth, Sir. Hyacinth Jones."

Rust

By Jonathan Maberry

-1-

I was seventeen when I died.

I'm going to be seventeen forever.

That's how it works.

I was murdered on the way home from the junior prom.

That new boy. The pale, dark-haired one who transferred in mid-semester. He killed me.

Fed on me.

Drained me.

Left me dead in a ditch.

-2-

When I woke up, it was still dark. Still night. Still *evening*, I found out.

I'd left the prom early and hitched that ride. It was about nine when he pulled off the road.

"What's up?" I asked, looking around at a lot of nothing outside the window. Part of me was bracing for him to make a move on me. I'm cute. Guys like me. They hit on me all the time. And the prom dress showed a lot of skin. No way this guy could know I was hoping someone *else* would notice.

Sarah.

She's why I went to the prom alone. Torrey Pines High was lit up like Christmas. Everyone was happy, nervous, excited, high on the moment. Sarah was there with another guy from school. The one we all thought was gay. We figured he was going as her beard.

Until I was alone with Sarah for two minutes in the girls' bathroom. She was doing her hair, and I knew there might not be another chance. We'd grown up together, lived next to each other. Played together. Talked endlessly and texted all the time. We'd get our periods on the same day nearly every month. We even made out once when we were thirteen. Nothing came of it, but the moment stuck in my head like it was burned there. She had the softest lips. My dreams that night were insane. So hot. It was the first time I'd ever had a real sex dream.

There have been a lot of them since.

Always with Sarah Clark.

Sarah and Rust. That's what they call me. Olivia Rustam. Half Irish, half Indian. Indian face and skin, dark red hair. Rust-colored. You get it.

Sarah looked like a San Diego surfer girl. Curves, blond curls, and the bluest eyes anywhere up and down the Pacific.

In the bathroom, we stood there like a couple of Disney princesses. Low-cut dresses that were probably too high on the thighs. Silk and lace and all the trimmings. Wrapped like gifts.

I told her how I felt and waited for her face to show relief. I ached to hear her say that she had been wanting to come out to me, too. It was going to be beautiful. A real moment. I kept staring at her, waiting for her to smile that thousand-watt smile. The one that made the SoCal sun look dark by comparison.

"Jesus fucking *Christ*," she cried and backed away. Literally stepped back from me like I had the plague.

"What . . . ?" I asked, still pretty sure she was just surprised. Only that. I sure as hell was.

"You think I'm queer?" she said, eyes wide, cheeks flushing red. "You think I'm a lesbian? Jesus, what's wrong with you?"

I felt like the floor was tilting under me. I felt like there wasn't enough air in the room. "But I . . . we . . ."

"We *nothing*," she snapped. "God, Rust, you do this *now*? At the prom? While I'm here with someone I really like? Someone I maybe love?"

"Bobby Durmond . . . ?"

"Of *course* Bobby. What are you . . . stupid? It's always been Bobby. It'll always *be* Bobby. How do you not know that? God, I thought you, of all people, understood. But instead, you come on with this lezzie bullshit. What the fuck?"

She said more, but I couldn't hear it over the roaring, screaming in my head. She pushed past me and went back to the dance.

Not sure how long I was in there. Five minutes? A year?

When I came out, there was a Bad Bunny song on, and everyone was dancing. Everyone except Sarah, Bobby, and, like, ten other girls. All of them stared at me. I saw them lean close to speak to one another, their eyes on me as I walked ten thousand miles across the dance floor. Out the doors. Across the lobby. Through the main doors. Out into the chill of an April night, with a wind off the ocean and the palm trees bending away from me in embarrassment.

I was so messed up. Confused. Lost. I felt ugly and stupid and wrong.

There were kids in the parking lot, but they were in their worlds, not mine. Not then and never again in mine. I pulled my cell out of my bag and started to call Dad for a ride home. But I stalled right there. He would ask questions. So would Mom. And what could I tell them? I hadn't come out to anyone else. Only Sarah. Mom and Dad would freak the fuck out. No question about that. I was their little girl. Their princess. They probably had plans already for when I got engaged and married and started pumping out kids.

This would kill them.

It nearly killed Sarah.

It killed me.

-3-

I started to walk.

At first, I didn't have a plan. I let the wind push me the wrong way on Del Mar Heights Road. Then I realized that I'd turned onto Carmel Valley Road. Kind of heading home, but not quite. Just heading away from the school. Trying to outwalk what I was feeling. Trying to outrun the memory of Sarah's reaction. Walking for miles, not wanting to *be* anywhere. Stumping along in heels. I could have taken them off, but I felt that I earned the punishment I got from those shoes.

I put my head down and kept going.

When the black SUV pulled up, I moved to the far side of the shoulder. But then the window rolled down, and I saw a face I recognized. Not someone I knew all that well, but well enough. Colin something-or-other. Good-looking, pale, nice hair, eyes the color of fog. Kind of a mix between book nerd and Goth. If I were straight, he'd be a maybe.

"Hey," he said. "Saw you leave. You looked pretty upset. Your date dump you?"

I debated not answering, but finally said, "I came alone."

His eyebrows went up. "Really. *You* didn't have a date? How's that even possible?"

"Shit happens," I said.

"Yeah." He laughed. "It does."

The moment stretched.

"Hop in, Rust. That's what they call you, right?"

I nodded.

"Come on, I'll drive you home."

"You're not an axe murderer, are you?"

He laughed. "I work at Jimbo's. I stack fruit."

That made me smile. A little. There was nothing about Colin that looked shady or spooky or dangerous. Bit of a loner in school, though he had some friends. Mostly the choir and the school show crew. I thought he might be gay. Still don't know if he is. After what happened with Sarah, I lost all faith in my gaydar.

So, I got in.

His car smelled of cinnamon. No idea why, and I never found out.

"Got cold all of a sudden. Need the heat up?" he asked because I was hugging myself and shivering.

"No thanks." My shivers had nothing to do with the weather.

We drove.

Then he pulled onto a dark patch between the lights on that road. Lots of black night sky, not a lot of lights.

"What are you doing?" I asked.

And he showed me.

I saw his eyes change from gray to red.

I saw, by the light of a sickle moon, how big his teeth suddenly got.

I fought. I screamed.

None of that mattered.

And I woke up in a drainage ditch at a construction site by the side of the road.

My clothes were dirty, but still on me. He never even tried to cop a feel. But he got what he wanted, and he took it all.

Every last drop.

-4-

For a while, I lay there and tried to cry.

More about Sarah and how stupid I felt. That was deflection, though. I didn't really know what Colin had done to me. What I remembered couldn't be the truth. There are no real vampires. I didn't even let the V word have its say in my head.

It was *what*, though?

Wasn't rape, like I said.

My purse was on the ground next to me. When I could move, I checked it. Wallet, keys, and cell phone were all there. Even the nice necklace Mom loaned me for the prom was still around my throat.

The stars above were little white points that offered no help in figuring it out. The swaying palms kept their opinions to themselves.

Then I touched my throat.

The bite.

The holes.

The dried blood.

That's when I started screaming. But it came out hoarse and dry. A croak, really. Kept trying, though. Wanted to scream. *Needed* to. In pain and outrage and sheer freaking terror. I wanted to yell at God. Not that I believed in Him. My folks are the church nuts. But right then, I was ready to believe in God or Buddha or anyone who would take the call.

All I heard were frogs and crickets.

And my own dry, tearless sobs.

-5-

It took a long time to get up.

Part of me just wanted to lie there and die. To not be me anymore. To not *be*. Not sure which scared me most—thinking about the fact that Sarah lived next door and that I'd have to see her there or in school on Monday. Or trying to explain any of this to my folks. Or the fact that I had been attacked. Each one of those things had a complete set of emotional baggage attached to it. I could open a trauma luggage store.

Yeah. I joke. It helps. Especially since screaming was for shit. And I couldn't cry because there wasn't enough moisture left in me.

Once I was on my feet, the night did all sorts of cartwheels around me. Made me so nauseous that I threw up. Mostly in the mud, but enough of it got onto my dress. Four-hundred-dollar dress covered in blood, mud, and my own puke. Classy.

When there was nothing else left in my stomach, I felt the panic trying to come back and really kick my ass. It tried. I think I even wanted to let it because it would scramble my mind and maybe that would—I don't know—make it less real?

That panic followed me like a rabid dog all the way home.

A few cars slowed as they passed, but what they saw probably looked like trouble, and then they hit the gas and shot by.

By the time I reached my house, all I could think about was the cold. Not the weather, but me. My skin was like ice, but worse than that was the cold inside.

"I'm not dead," I said aloud, still standing in the yard. "I'm not, I'm not, I'm not."

That's when it occurred to me that I had to deliberately inhale in order to speak. Like breathing wasn't normal and automatic anymore. Like I didn't have to breathe.

Like I was the kind of thing that didn't need to breathe.

"No . . ." I said.

That denial was as false as me saying I wasn't dead. The V word kept trying to claw its way into my brain.

Took a while to get my shit together and even longer to figure out what to say. The lights were on in the living room, and there was a blue flicker from the TV. Dad watching something G-rated because that's his speed. Mom sitting next to him, playing some game on her phone. *Candy Crush* or something a million years old like that.

When I had a half-ass plan, I climbed the porch steps, unlocked it, and went inside.

They freaked. But they bought the story. I told them that I

slipped and fell into a mud puddle and nicked my neck on a stick. Then lied and said someone from school drove me home.

They gasped and yelled questions, and then Mom started crying. They wanted to take me to urgent care, but I insisted that the cuts on my neck weren't bad. Dad fetched the first aid kit, and they tag-teamed with alcohol swabs, antiseptic cream, and Band-Aids.

Eventually, they told me to go and get some sleep.

"Sorry you ruined your dress, sweetie," said Dad. That's how he put it. Not sorry I fell, and that ruined my dress. Sorry *you* ruined it.

Mom said, "Take a nice hot shower, honey. That'll make everything better. I'll make you some broth — you're white as a sheet."

More like a ghost, but whatever.

I went upstairs, took off the dress, and kicked it into a corner. Then showered for about a year.

I was still under the spray when I heard Mom come up the stairs. Think about that. The shower was on high, and my head was right below the spray, and the stairs are at the far end of the second-floor hall. There's no way I should have been able to hear her. No way at all. So, how could I hear every single step? The house is pretty new, and nothing creaks out loud. It's not old enough for that, but I could hear the carpet compress with each step. I heard the tiniest creaks from every footfall. I could hear the way the fabric of her bathrobe whisked against her legs. I heard everything. Her breath. The tiny rattle of the mug of soup on the tray.

And the smells . . . Her perfume and what was left of that day's deodorant. Her hairspray. The bone broth in the mug. All of it.

She came in, told me I still looked pale. She'd used waterproof bandages and checked to make sure they were good. Then she told me to drink all of the broth, drink the chamomile tea. Have the crackers. And then go to bed.

"Straight to bed, too," she insisted. "No texting or TV. You need sleep." Then she kissed me, gave me a long hug, and left.

When I was alone, I sat on the edge of the bed and stared at the door. When Mom had hugged me, I smelled something else. I couldn't legit know it was what it was. But it was.

I smelled her blood. A sharp smell like hot copper wires.

It smelled so good.

God help me, it smelled so good.

-6-

I didn't sleep at all.

Instead, I locked my door and sat on the floor with my back to it. I needed her to not be able to come in. Her or Dad.

Not with all that hot blood.

My stomach growled and snarled.

Somewhere around three in the morning, when the whole world seemed to be quiet, I had a few minutes where I tried to give Colin a pass for what he did. Yeah, that sounds sick, but the hungrier I got and the more I could smell yummy blood, the more I understood the need.

Fuck, did I just call blood yummy? Shit. That's wrong on every level.

Except that I knew it would *be* yummy. It would be so delicious.

I wanted to drink until I was bloated and fat and then drink some more. I wanted to rub it all over my face. I wanted . . .

And that's the problem. I wanted.

-7-

I didn't start getting sleepy until just before dawn.

Then I had a panic attack thinking about sunshine making me burst into flames and then crumble into dust. By the time I got up off the floor, there was a beam of light slanting through the blinds. Pale but there.

"Shit," I said and walked over to it, stopping just outside of the beam. Then, with my hand shaking like crazy, I passed it quickly through the sunlight.

Nothing.

Getting braver and more curious, I held my hand inside the beam.

Nothing. So, that myth is for shit.

Not that this was a superhero origin story bullshit, but it did make me want to know what else was true or false. So I squatted down and grabbed the two ends of a heavy oak bureau. Packed with my clothes, it was about a hundred and fifty pounds.

Couldn't lift it even a little. Couldn't bend metal. None of that.

"Maybe I'm not . . . *that*," I said, still not using the word.

Mom knocked, and I told her I was feeling out of it and wanted to sleep in. She thought it was a great idea. I locked my door, closed the blinds, and climbed into bed.

No dreams. Nothing. It was like my head just shut off. When I woke, the sun was already going down. For a really sweet moment, I thought it was all a bad dream.

Bad? Oh, yes.

A dream?

No. Not even a nightmare. No matter how bad they ever get, you wake up from those. This was something else.

It was a horror story.

And now?

Now I'm the monster of my own story.

-8-

Mom and Dad were both still at work. She was an assistant manager at REI; he handled car leases for a Ford place in Clairemont Mesa.

When I checked my cell, there were a zillion text messages. I answered the ones from Mom first and told her that I'd slept all day and felt good. I lied and said I made myself some mac & cheese. Even went downstairs, emptied a box of it into the garbage, and placed the container on top of the trash so she'd see it.

The other texts were a mix. A bunch from friends who wondered why I left the prom. A couple from girls who wanted me to know on the DL that they were cool with me being gay. Sounded nice, but some of them were standing with Sarah and smiling at me. Those texts were crap. Fake empathy.

Fuck them.

Back in my room, I checked the other texts. There were two that nearly knocked me down. One was from Sarah:

> Sorry I freaked.

> We should probably talk.

I couldn't decide how to react to that. What did it mean? Was she really sorry? Was she being as phony as the other girls? Did one of the girls kick her ass over it? There were at least two lesbians in our grade. Ginny Murphy and Cathy Howell. They had always been out. There were probably others, too. And at least nine gay guys. Just not in our crowd. What had been my crowd.

Then I saw the other message.

> I didn't mean to hurt you.

> I'm sorry.

> I hope you're okay.

I sat and stared at the screen.
It was from Colin.

I was home alone. I may have screamed.

I did go all emo cliché and cried in the shower. The falling water made it feel like I had tears.

Did I text him back?

Yes.

Not at first. Of course not. No way. Guy was a psycho vampire prick. He *killed* me. So, yeah . . . no.

Then I did.

> Why did you do this to me?

He wrote back.

> When I get that hungry, I can't stop myself.

To which I responded,

> That's bullshit.

> You liar.

> You asshole.

> I'm going to kill you.

There was a long pause, then a series of rapid-fire messages.

> I wish you could.

> I really do.

> I've been trying to die for 67 years.

> I can't die.

> Neither can you.

> I'm sorry.

I wrote a lot of *Fuck Yous!* No emojis or anything. I'm dead, but I'm not crazy. Lots of exclamation marks though.

And sat there like some angsty tween waiting for him to reply.

He never did. Not then or ever again. I never found out what happened to him. God, how I hated him. God, how I wish I could ask him a million questions. When I tried again later, it came up as *Account not found*. I checked his Facebook, Instagram, TikTok, Snapchat, X, and Threads. All of his accounts were closed. Gone. Erased.

I sat there and thought about Colin.

Then Sarah came into my head and crowded that to one side.

Sarah.

God, she's everything. Smart. Kind. Gorgeous. Funny.

Also . . . a total bitch for what she did in the bathroom. A double-bitch for that coven of witches she was giggling with. I re-read her text.

> Sorry I freaked.

> We should probably talk.

Yeah. Guess we should.

But did I even dare? I looked like shit. White as a ghost. Pun intended, I guess. Skinny because I had no blood in me. Pasty weird. And dry as dust. My eyes were dull, like I was getting glaucoma. When I looked at myself in the mirror, what I saw looked like I'd been found in some old Egyptian tomb. The only thing about my appearance that hadn't changed was my hair. Still rust-colored.

It was getting late. Mom and Dad would be home in an hour.

Then Mom would make dinner, and I would have to be at the table. The thought of cooked food made me want to hurl. I'd been vegan for two years, but I wanted something red and bloody and delicious and . . .

I don't remember leaving the house.

I really don't.

One minute, I was standing in my bedroom looking at my phone. The next, I was all the way over in the Del Mar Preserve. My jeans were scuffed with grass and mud stains on the knees. Yet I don't remember dressing. I'd just gotten out of the shower and had been sitting in my underwear on my bed. Then I was wearing jeans, a sweatshirt, and sneakers, and was in the woods.

With blood on my hands.

And my mouth.

But I felt so much better. Stronger. Less dried out. More like me.

Until I looked down and understood why.

There were two rabbits on the ground at my feet. Torn apart. Ripped apart. And completely drained of blood. I could almost hear Colin say it.

When I get that hungry I can't stop myself.

Oh God.

Please, God. No . . .

-10-

My cell was in my pocket. I had to use fresh grass to wipe the blood off my hands and mouth. Then I turned it on and looked at the texts again.

There was a new one. From Sarah.

> I'm home alone if you want to come over and talk.

> I really think we should.

-11-

She was home alone.

Her house is on a corner where they're building a church. Catholic, I think. The Church of St. Michael.

I'd never really given the name a lot of thought, though I knew who Saint Michael was. My dad idolized him and had paintings and little resin statues of him with his sword raised to kill a dragon.

Saint Michael, who protects against evil.

As I walked toward Sarah's house, I stopped to watch the workmen pouring tons of concrete into what would become the foundation. Trying to get part of the job done before five o'clock. I could hear bubbles popping inside the gray glop.

Sarah was waiting for me on the porch. She wore a big Pine Deep Scarecrows football hoodie over black tights and looked like the most beautiful thing in the history of the world. I hated her as much as I loved her.

I came to the foot of the stairs and waited for her to start this. Whatever this was going to be. Not sure what I expected. One of those 'I just don't think about you that way' speeches, no doubt. Or some fake 'I love you no matter who you are.' Meaning *what* I was. Like I was an alien or a...

A monster.

She said, "I'm sorry."

I stared at her, not trusting myself to speak.

"I'm really sorry, Rust," she said. Leaning on it. And, I think, meaning it.

I cleared my throat and remembered to take a breath. "Me too."

She came down the stairs at a run and jerked to a stop right in front of me. Standing close. Way too close. I could smell her soap, her shampoo, her perfume. That Billie Eilish *Eau de Parfum* crap her sister gave her for Christmas. I could even smell a grain of cat litter on the bottom of her shoe, and Diet Coke on her breath.

But . . . God, she smelled delicious.

"When I realized you left, I got so upset," she said.

I just looked at her. At her eyes. At those lips. At the pulse beating in her throat. Her blood screamed at me. Wanting me. Needing me to taste it.

"I felt like shit for what I did."

"Yeah, well," I said. I actually wanted to say more, to be articulate, to start rebuilding the bridge between us. Wanted to, but her blood kept screaming.

"I didn't know you were gay," she said.

"I'm a lesbian," I said. "I've always been one."

"No, you haven't," she said, then stopped and seemed to cock her head and listen to the echo of her own words. "I mean . . ."

"I know what you mean."

We stood there looking at one another like Old West gunslingers. It was beyond weird.

"And you thought I was gay . . . or a lesbian . . . or . . ."

"Queer. Yes. I thought you and I were the same." It sounded so strange to say it. And mean it. I felt older than seventeen somehow. In both good and bad ways, now that it was out there on the wind.

"Because we kissed . . . ?" She looked surprised and almost amused. A quarter of a smile. "We were just kids messing around. Being silly. Pretend kissing."

"You were pretending," I said.

That filled her eyes with tears. I looked away because the screaming of her blood was getting to be too much to bear. It was hard to hear her over it. Hard to hear my own thoughts.

"Look, Rust," she said, "I love you and all. I always will. It's just that I don't think about you that . . ."

But I was walking away by then.

Then I was running.

-12-

I ran around behind St. Michael's and hid between a pair of dumpsters.

From there, I could see Sarah standing on her front walk. I saw her hitting keys on her phone and, like an idiot, I waited for my phone to vibrate. To tell me she was calling. Or texting. Or caring. Anything.

But my phone was as dead as a rock in my pocket.

The construction guys were working overtime. They must have gotten their last load of concrete late. I watched them pour it and smooth it just so I could focus on something other than Sarah's blood. Or the memory of Mom's.

This was my truth now. The hunger.

If I'd stayed five more minutes with Sarah, I think I would have killed her. And don't think I didn't consider it. To drain her sweet blood and then have her rise as my . . .

My what?

This wasn't an Anne Rice novel. She wasn't going to wake up queer just because she was a vampire.

There. I said the V word.

No, my brain was trying to scam me. It wanted me to think that Sarah would turn gay because I loved her and because I made her immortal. What do they call that? The Dark Gift. Oh please.

I thought about what Colin had said about not being able to help himself, and now I really understood it. The hunger was huge. It was bottomless. It was bigger than the moon. Bigger than life. I was able to run away instead of biting her, but what would happen if I got as starved around her as I did in my room? Would I have another blackout and wake up with her blood on my mouth?

Yes.

The answer was bright as a fire in my head.

I was a monster, and monsters kill. I was a *vampire,* and vampires kill whoever's closest. Mom. Dad. Sarah. Everyone.

Being gay had nothing to do with it. Funny thing is, I could actually imagine past the hurt and embarrassment of last night and just now. There would be college, and I'd go somewhere far away. Someplace where one defined me by the color of my skin or the truth of my sexuality. Somewhere with people who didn't think being gay was a choice. I might never come home.

Yeah.

It didn't matter now, though, did it? I knew I wasn't going to college. I couldn't. To be around strangers and *their* blood? To be able to hide my crimes? To live like Colin. As a monster. As someone who only apologized for what he did. I wonder if he ever really tried to stop himself.

Even though Sarah broke my heart, I knew she was living her truth. And that sucked, but on some level I loved her all the more for it. Even though she fucked up how she reacted, she was who she was.

I was who I was.

And I was *what* I was.

None of it was a choice. But there still was a choice open to me.

I squatted there until the workmen left. They put warning tape around the huge squares of wet concrete. I'd watched them pour that foundation. It was deep.

So deep.

I bet it was so deep and so heavy that I wouldn't be able to hear Sarah's blood screaming. Or Mom's. Or anyone's.

I got up and walked to the edge of it. Would they even look? If the top was all messed up, would they dig it all up and look? It would have set over night. Would they bother, or just think it was vandalism?

Would the screaming really stop?

I looked over at Sarah's house. She was inside now, and her bedroom light was on. I saw her silhouette for a moment. Just a moment.

And then I was falling.

Falling.

Falling.

And it was so quiet.

Down there, the only one who screamed was me.

But only for a while.

I knew I couldn't die. But . . . maybe I would dream.

Anything can happen in dreams. Even something as weird and unlikely and unreachable as love.

In my darkness . . . I dreamed.

ACKNOWLEDGEMENTS

This charity anthology was a testament to the fellowship of horror authors in coming together to support others in need.

A huge thank you to the San Diego and SoCal authors who contributed stories for this cause. We are especially appreciative to local publisher No Bad Books Press for taking on the project, Lexy Tanen for copyediting, Christy Aldridge of Grim Poppy Design for the stunning cover art, and Scott and AB Sigler for working with us and coordinating the audio version of this book.

Independent bookstores are an integral component to any community. This is especially true for writers. Those stores, their owners, and the booksellers are champions of literature. No matter the genre, they save space for writers to find their audience, and for readers to find their next great escape. We'd like to give a big shoutout to our local bookstores that act as hubs for the San Diego literary scene, particularly Mysterious Galaxy Bookstore, Artifact Books, and Verbatim. (Note: You can order books from them and have them shipped anywhere in the country! Support them!)

Speaking of the literary community, we want to acknowledge the wealth of talent that exists in San Diego. Every contributor to this collection has grown in their craft as the result of advice or workshops received from someone in this writing community. We are especially grateful to Jonathan Maberry and Henry Herz for hosting the Writers Coffeehouse at Mysterious Galaxy every month, where writers of all levels come together for comradery and support. We thank you, and guest hosts, Peter Clines and Scott Sigler, for creating a safe space for writers to learn more about their craft and the publishing business.

A massive thank you to the horror writing community who donated stories to this anthology—many of whom are members of the Horror Writers Association San Diego. You are all incredible ambassadors of the genre, and we are grateful for your support. Extra special thanks to Indigo Halverson for creating lovely graphics and social media content to help promote the book and to Sarah Faxon for co-chairing the chapter.

Thank you to everyone who assisted, and continues to assist, in the wildfire relief efforts. From First Responders to neighbors, you showed the world what it means to come together in a time of need, and you inspired many to do the same. While the wildfires have faded from the public eye, it will take years to restore the damage done, and we hope that this collection aids those efforts.

AUTHORS OF DREAD COAST

David Agranoff is a novelist, screenwriter and Horror and Science Fiction critic. He is the Splatterpunk and Wonderland book award-nominated author of 13 books including the WWII Vampire novel - *The Last Night to Kill Nazis* from Clash Books and *Punk Rock Ghost Story* from Deadite Press. For the last five years, David has co-hosted the Dickheads podcast, a deep-dive into the work of Philip K. Dick reviewing his novels in publication order as well as the history of Science Fiction. He also hosts a personal podcast Postcards from a Dying World. His non-fiction essays have appeared on Amazing Stories (he is a regular columnist), Tor.com, NeoText, and Cemetery Dance. His most recent novel is the science fiction novel *Great America in Dead World*, which you can buy now! He can be found playing pick-up basketball around San Diego.

Brian Asman is a writer, actor, and director from San Diego, CA. He's the author of the forthcoming *Man, F*ck This House (and Other Disasters)* as well as *Good Dogs, Our Black Hearts Beat as One, I'm Not Even Supposed to Be Here Today, Neo Arcana, Nunchuck City, Jailbroke,* and *Return of the Living Elves.* He's recently published short stories in *American Cannibal, The Dark Waves of Winter,* DreadPop, Pulp Modern, Kelp, and comics in Tales of Horrorgasm.

A film he co-wrote and produced, *A Haunting in Ravenwood,* is available now on VOD. His short "Reel Trouble" won Best Short Film at Gen Con 2022 and Best Horror Short at the Indie Gathering.

Brian holds an MFA from UCR-Palm Desert. He's represented by Dunham Literary, Inc. Max Booth III is his hype man.

Find him on social media (@thebrianasman) or his website www.brianasmanbooks.com.

From geeky zombie apocalypses to laugh-out-loud joke books, **Kevin David Anderson** is a versatile writer living in sunny Southern California. He's the mind behind the geeky cult classics *Night of the Living Trekkies* and *Night of the ZomBees,* as well as the collections *Night Sounds: From Podcast to Print* and *Midnight Men: The Supernatural Adventures of Earl and Dale.* His short fiction has appeared in over fifty anthologies, thirty magazines, and notable podcasts like Pseudopod, Horror Hill, and The NoSleep Podcast. Anderson's latest work includes *TNTD in Roswell,* part of the Try Not To Die choose-your-own-adventure series. Under the pen names Giggles A. Lott and Nee Slapper, he also writes genre-themed joke books such as *Star Wars: The Jokes Awaken* and *Jurassic Jokes: A Joke Book 65 Million Years in the Making.*

Peter Clines is the toy-collecting, movie-loving, New York Times bestselling author of numerous novels. Some of which you may have read.

He grew up in the Stephen King fallout zone of Maine and—inspired by comic books, *Star Wars,* and Saturday morning cartoons—began writing horrible X-Men and Boba Fett stories at an early age. He got his first rejection letter at age eleven from then-Marvel Comics editor-in-chief Jim Shooter, and made his first sale to a local newspaper at age seventeen.

His writing includes *God's Junk Drawer*, *The Broken Room*, *Paradox Bound*, several books set in the Threshold universe, the *Ex-Heroes* series, a pair of short story collections, a classical mash-up novel, some unproduced screenplays, and countless articles about the film and television industry.

He currently lives and writes somewhere in southern California. If you have any idea exactly where, he would really appreciate some hints.

Jon Cohn is a horror novelist and professional board game designer. His works include 2024 Indie Book Brawl Quarter-Finalist *Slashtag*, and the much less popular, but award winning novel *The Island Mother*. He gets his best ideas from a tarot reader who lives in Hawaii.

As a designer, Jon is very excited to finally be able to merge horror books and games together by bringing *Ghostland* to life as a board game, coming to Kickstarter. He's also designed games like *Thanksgiving*, co-designed with Eli Roth, *Basket Case*, and *Taboo Horror*.

Order autographed books and get updates for new games and upcoming novels at www.joncohnauthor.com. Sign up for the newsletter for free short stories and games, and follow at @joncohnauthor on Facebook, Instagram and TikTok.

Jon lives in San Diego with his supernaturally patient wife Delaney, and their adorable dog, Miss Cordelia Chase.

Ronald Coleman has a PhD from The Scripps Research Institute in La Jolla, California. Although he was born and raised in Los Angeles County, he has lived and worked in San Diego County for over 20 years.

By day, he is the principal scientist of a small biotech company. In the evenings, he likes to hang out in the north county with his amazing wife and their two adorable dogs. He also likes to write horror stories of all lengths, from drabbles to novels.

Dennis K. Crosby is the award-winning author of the Kassidy Simmons novels, *Death's Legacy*, *Death's Debt*, and *Death's Despair*. Since 2020, he has published three urban fantasy novels and fourteen short stories in various anthologies and most recently, *Weird Tales* magazine.

Dennis holds a Master of Science Degree in Forensic Psychology and a Master of Fine Arts Degree in Creative Writing. With experience in retail sales, private investigation, and social service, Dennis uses his knowledge and experience to craft compelling characters experiencing real world challenges, often against the backdrop of magical, supernatural, and mythological phenomena. He's been the subject of several interviews and podcasts, has been a guest speaker and workshop facilitator for writer's groups and multiple conferences, and he's been a panelist and moderator at WonderCon, Comic-Con International, and Stoker Con 2024 in San Diego, where he also served as Co-Chair.

Dennis grew up in Oak Park, IL, and currently makes his home in San Diego, CA.

Luke Dumas is the *USA Today* bestselling author of *Nothing Tastes as Good*, *The Paleontologist*, and *A History of Fear*. He won the 2024 ITW Thriller Award for Best Paperback Original, and his work has been optioned for film and TV. He received his master's degree in creative writing from the University of Edinburgh and has worked in nonprofit philanthropy for more than a decade. Luke was born and raised in San Diego, California, where he lives with his husband and dogs.

S. Faxon is an award-winning author of dark fantasy, horror, and paranormal thriller short stories and long fiction. Sarah is an English Language Arts high school teacher, the co-chair of the San Diego chapter of the Horror Writers Association, and is enrolled in the University of San Diego, pursuing her PhD in Education for Social Justice.

KC Grifant is an award-winning author who writes speculative stories in the horror, fantasy, sci-fi and weird west genres. She authored the award-winning supernatural western *Monster Gunslinger* series and *Shrouded Horror: Tales of the Uncanny*. She is editor of *Women of the Weird West,* and co-editor of *Dread Coast: SoCal Horror Tales* and *Of Terrors and Tombstones*. She is the author of hundreds of nonfiction science articles and dozens of fictional stories published in podcasts, magazines and Stoker-nominated anthologies. She also is co-creator of *Monster Gunslingers: The Game.*

She teaches genre and short story workshops and has been a moderator, panelist or speaker at dozens of conferences and events. She is co-founder and co-chair of the Horror Writers Association San Diego Chapter and a Science Fiction & Fantasy Writers Association mentor. Aside from constructing imaginary worlds, she works as an award-winning science communicator in her day job and tries to keep up with two small wildlings. Learn more at www.KCGrifant.com.

Indigo Halverson started her writing journey with editorials for her high school newspaper winning Outstanding Editorial from the American Scholastic Press Association, Scholastic Newspaper Awards in 2013. She was a staff writer for a comedy sketch group in 2015. In addition to becoming editor-in-chief of her undergrad college newspaper in 2017, she also graduated with her BA in Photography from Whittier College and achieved her MS in Advertising in 2019 from Syracuse University. She returned to her childhood pastime of fiction writing in 2025 with her first short story, *The Demons on Bunker Hill* featured in *Dread Coast Socal Horror Tales*. She has a lifelong obsession with all things horror. When not writing, she spends her time drinking coffee, watching movies with her husband, and cuddling her three cats, Reaper, Mogwai, and Goblin.

Theresa Halvorsen has never met a profanity she hasn't enjoyed and is an author, publisher, editor, and YouTuber. She's overly-caffeinated, and at times, wine-soaked. The author of multiple cross-genre works, including *Warehouse Dreams, Lost Aboard* and *River City Widows,* Theresa wonders what sleep is. She's the owner of No Bad Books Press and one of the hosts of the popular YouTube channel, the Semi-Sages of the Pages. In whatever free time is left, (ha!) Theresa enjoys board games, concerts, geeky conventions, and reading. Her life goal is to give "Oh-My-Gosh-This-Book-Is-So-Good!" happiness to her readers. She lives in Temecula with her husband, her adult children, their partners (she has no idea who actually lives in her house and who's just visiting) and many pets. Find her on all the social medias, but double check that spelling of her last name–it's tricky.

Henry Herz has written for *Daily Science Fiction, Weird Tales, Pseudopod, Metastellar,* Titan Books, *Highlights for Children, Ladybug Magazine,* and anthologies from Penguin-Random House, Albert Whitman, Blackstone Publishing, Third Flatiron, Brigids Gate Press, Air and Nothingness Press, Baen Books, elsewhere. He's edited ten anthologies and written fourteen picture books. www.henryherz.com

Elle Jauffret is a French-born American author, former criminal attorney for the California Attorney General's Office, and an Agatha Award nominee. Her debut novel, *Threads of Deception,* received praise from *New York Times* bestselling author Jonathan Maberry who described it as "a powerful, complex, and compelling mystery," and *USA Today* bestselling author Hank Phillippi Ryan who called her "a smart and fresh new voice."

An active member of Sisters in Crime, Mystery Writers of America, and International Thriller Writers. Elle writes across genres, always within the mystery and suspense realm. In addition to her Suddenly French Mystery series, Elle writes horror short stories that delve into the darker side of suspense. She is a frequent panelist and speaker at writers' conferences and book festivals/conventions.

Elle is an avid consumer of mystery and adventure stories in all forms, especially escape rooms. She lives in Southern California with her family, along the coast of San Diego County, which serves as the backdrop for her Suddenly French Mystery series.

To know more about Elle, check https://ellejauffret.com/ or follow her on social media @ellejauffret.

J.A. Jensen is a member of the Horror Writers Association and the Mystery Writers of America. His work has appeared in anthologies such as *California Screamin'*, *Sherlock Holmes and the Occult Detectives* Vol II, and *The Decameron Project*. He is represented by the Cherry Weiner Literary Agency. You can find out more about him at www.jajensenbooks.com

TJ Kang's love of ghosts and ghoulies started at a young age, watching *Dark Shadows* with her mom and reading every ghost story she could get her hands on. She is a member of the San Diego Chapter of the Horror Writers' Association and has written one novel, *Guardian*. She is working on a second novel, which she promises will be ready to keep you up at night soon. Her short stories reflect the psychological impact of ordinary people encountering the uncanny, whether in the form of supernatural creatures or the ghosts of their own past decisions. By day, TJ Kang is a behavioral health professional specializing in substance use treatment and recovery in San Diego, where she lives with her husband of 35 years, two malicious cats, and one nervous dog.

Lisa Diane Kastner is the Founder of Running Wild, LLC, a content creation, distribution, and licensing company. A writer and editor for more than twenty years, she has identified talent like Jamie Ford's Hotel on the Corner of Bitter and Sweet, Suzanne Samples' Frontal Matter: Glue Gone Wild, Shay Galloway's The Valley of Sage and Juniper, and many other authors whose works have been named groundbreaking in their respective genres. Lisa began

Running Wild with the belief that we can change the world through story.

Jonathan Maberry is a *NY Times* bestselling author, 5-time Bram Stoker Award-winner, 4-time Scribe Award winner, Inkpot Award winner, and comic book writer. His vampire apocalypse book series, *V-Wars*, was a Netflix original series starring Ian Somerhalder (*Lost, Vampire Diaries*). His Joe Ledger thriller novels are in development for TV by Chad Stahelski, director of the John Wick movies; and his YA zombie series, *Rot & Ruin* is being developed for film by Alcon Entertainment. Jonathan writes in multiple genres, including horror, sci-fi, epic fantasy, mystery, and thriller. His comic book work includes *Black Panther,* and many elements from his story were included in the hit movie, *Black Panther: Wakanda Forever.* His first novel, *Ghost Road Blues* was named one of the 25 Best Horror Novels of the New Millennium; and his recent book, *Necrotek*, was named the #1 sci-fi novel of 2024 by DiscoverSF. His other works include the *Kagen The Damned* trilogy, *Glimpse, Ink, The Wolf Man, X-Files: Devil's Advocate, Dead of Night,* and many others. And his comics include *Captain America, The Punisher, Wolverine, Godzilla Vs. Cthulhu, Marvel Zombies Return, Road Of The Dead, Pandemica,* and more. He is the president of the International Association of Media Tie-in Writers Association, and is editor of the world's oldest horror magazine, *Weird Tales*. He was a featured expert on the History Channel's *Zombies: A Living History* and *True Monsters.* He founded and hosts the Writers Coffeehouse networking events. Jonathan lives in San Diego, California with his wife, Sara Jo. www.jonathanmaberry.com

Greg Mollin is a fiction writer and the owner/bookseller at Artifact Books, an independent bookstore in Encinitas, CA. His stories have appeared in print and digital publications including *Weird Tales, Starlite Pulp Review, Crime Factory* magazine, Thrillers, *Killers 'n' Chillers, Gothic Blue Book: Haunted Edition* (edited by Cynthia

Pelayo), and *Dark Moon Digest*. He is a member of the Horror Writers Association, the International Thriller Writers Association, the American Booksellers Association, and the California Independent Booksellers Association. More info at: www.gregmollin.com www.artifactrarebooks.com

C. D. Oakes grew up in a small village in the Mojave Desert, where he spent a great deal of time in the public library devouring all manner of fiction, but particularly enjoying horror and gritty storytelling. After graduating high school, he joined the U.S. Army, becoming an Explosive Ordnance Disposal (EOD) technician. Following a long career in unexploded ordnance (UXO) remediation, C. D. Oakes shifted gears, moving to Carlsbad, California. He now works in adult literacy in his community. C. D. Oakes is an active member of the Horror Writers Association, and sharpened his writing skills in the HWA's mentor program, as well as the Mountain View MFA program in southern New Hampshire, and writes short stories that tend to fall under the umbrella of speculative fiction.

#1 *New York Times* best-selling author **Scott Sigler** is the creator of twenty novels, seven novellas, and dozens of short stories. He is an inaugural inductee into the Podcasting Hall of Fame.

Scott began his career by narrating his unabridged audiobooks and serializing them in weekly installments. He continues to release free episodes every Sunday. Launched in March of 2005, "Scott Sigler Slices" is the world's longest-running fiction podcast.

His rabid fans fervently anticipate their weekly story fix, so much so that they dubbed themselves "Sigler Junkies" and have downloaded over 55 million episodes. Subscribe to the free podcast at scottsigler.com/subscribe.

Scott is a co-founder of Empty Set Entertainment, which publishes his Galactic Football League series. A Michigan native, he lives in San Diego, CA with his wife and their wee little Døgs of Døøm.

Born and raised in California, **Benjamin Spada** has had a lifelong passion for storytelling. His award-winning Black Spear series of military thrillers includes *FNG*, *The Warmaker*, and the upcoming *Project: Darkheart*. A dedicated taco aficionado and self-described "Professor of Batmanology," he has made a career in the United States Marine Corps. He has been a martial arts instructor and a section leader in the Wounded Warrior Battalion for our nation's wounded, ill, and injured. Also, he has served overseas to help train our foreign military allies in defense against chemical, biological, and nuclear weapons. Despite these grim assignments, he has carried on with equal amounts of sarcasm and stoicism.

When out of uniform, Benjamin is an avid sci-fi and horror movie fan, tattoo collector, comic enthusiast, and two-time holder of the platinum trophy in *The Elder Scrolls V: Skyrim*. Benjamin lives with his wife and their four daughters, in Oceanside, California.

Chad Stroup is the creator of the novels *Secrets of the Weird* and *Sexy Leper*, as well as the short story collection *Teeth Where They Shouldn't Be*. When not writing, he is also the vocalist for the bands *Icepield* and *Resting on Pretty* (the latter of which they perform as their fierce drag alter ego Jenn X). No, he doesn't sleep much.

Rose Winters is a copy editor and musician by trade, Rose has worked as a journalist and has been published in magazines, anthologies, on Reedsy (where one of her stories was shortlisted), and on her own blog at rosewinters.com. Rose is also a published songwriter and has performed across the globe. Her full-length game novel, Planet Sindor, has been published on IFFLY.co

Made in the USA
Las Vegas, NV
28 September 2025

28828062R00215